The Puppeteer

The Puppeteer

A Mauro Bruno
Detective Series Thriller

Alan Refkin

THE PUPPETEER
A MAURO BRUNO DETECTIVE SERIES THRILLER

iUniverse books may be ordered through booksellers or by contacting:

iUniverse
1663 Liberty Drive
Bloomington, IN 47403
www.iuniverse.com
844-349-9409

ISBN: 978-1-6632-7060-3 (sc)
ISBN: 978-1-6632-7061-0 (e)

Library of Congress Control Number: 2025901374

Print information available on the last page.

iUniverse rev. date: 01/24/2025

PREVIOUS BOOKS BY ALAN REFKIN

Fiction

Matt Moretti and Han Li Series
The Archivist
The Abductions
The Payback
The Forgotten
The Cabal
The Chase
The Archangel

Mauro Bruno Detective Series
The Patriarch
The Scion
The Artifact
The Mistress
The Collector

Gunter Wayan Series
The Organization
The Frame
The Arrangement
The Defector

Nonfiction

The Wild Wild East: Lessons for Success in Business in Contemporary Capitalist China
By Alan Refkin and Daniel Borgia, PhD

Doing the China Tango: How to Dance around Common Pitfalls in Chinese Business Relationships
By Alan Refkin and Scott Cray

Conducting Business in the Land of the Dragon: What Every Businessperson Needs To Know About China
By Alan Refkin and Scott Cray

Piercing the Great Wall of Corporate China: How to Perform Forensic Due Diligence on Chinese Companies
By Alan Refkin and David Dodge

To my wife, Kerry
and
Zhang Jingjie - Maria

Chapter One

It was 1:00 am when five men arrived at the Catania Airport in Sicily to board the aircraft that was presented to airport authorities as a medevac flight. Despite the fact that both of its runways were closed from midnight to 4:00 am, for an unreasonable amount of money and the explanation that they were going to pick up a patient in Rome for treatment on the island, the logic of which baffled aviation officials given the extensive medical facilities available in Rome, an exception was made and the tower was staffed and the runway lights activated.

As the pilot and copilot completed their preflight check the five men, three of whom wore white lab coats, boarded the aircraft and the stairway was retracted. The Bombardier Global 8000 aircraft taxied to runway two-six, where the pilot smoothly pushed the throttles forward—rapidly accelerating the eighty-two million dollar plane until it effortlessly lifted skyward fifty-eight hundred feet later.

As the aircraft climbed to its cruising altitude, one of the men opened the insulated food bag he brought onboard and handed out individual containers of pasta alla norma, a classic Sicilian dish of pasta and tomato sauce that was covered with slices of fried eggplant and served with grated ricotta salata cheese and basil. Originating in Catania, it was named after the opera "Norma" by Vincenzo Bellini, who was a native of that city.

The aircraft landed at Rome's Ciampino Airport, which was nine miles from the center of the city, at 2:50 am. As with Catania, although the airport was closed and wouldn't reopen until 8:00 am., the fact that they were a medevac flight and were willing to pay for a tower controller and any additional staff the airport could add to increase their fee meant they were allowed to land and depart during their closure period.

When the plane came to a stop in front of the private air terminal, the pilot extended the stairway and the group's leader, Gennaro Caruso, who was holding a manila envelope, stepped onto the tarmac. He was followed by the three white-coated men, each carrying an identical canvas bag, and the group's sniper, who was carrying a plastic rifle case. The five men silently made their way to the black Mercedes G63 SUV, which they were told would be parked in the lot beside the private terminal and, as Caruso got into the driver's seat and pulled down the visor, catching the car keys before they landed in his lap, the others stowed their gear in the rear cargo compartment. Because he was familiar with Rome, he didn't need the vehicle's GPS to find their destination, and the five were soon underway.

The black extended-length Range Rover entered the Campo Verano Cemetery at 5:35 am, just as the sun rose. Constructed in the early nineteenth century, the garden-like two-hundred-and-five-acre cemetery, which was essentially flat except for several hills, the most prominent of which was not far from the entrance, was in the heart of Rome and six miles from Vatican City. Once inside, the Range Rover veered right, robustly passing scores of majestic tombs and mausoleums as it wove its way to the top of the prominent hill, a thousand yards as the crow flew from the entrance. After it stopped, one of the occupant's two tactical gear-clad bodyguards got out of the bulletproof vehicle, surveilled the immediate area, and after determining it was safe, gave a thumb up to the driver, who was also the second bodyguard, although he couldn't be seen through the vehicle's darkened windows. Seconds later, the driver stepped out of the car and opened the door behind him, helping a sixty-four-year-old, expensively-dressed woman carrying a bouquet of long-stemmed red roses, to exit.

Pia Lamberti was five feet six inches tall with black hair and brown eyes. She carried herself with an aristocratic stature, meaning how she looked and acted exuded respect, intellect, and privilege. All were accurate descriptions of Italy's intelligence czar, a position that gave her control of every intelligence function within the government. Surprisingly, her position, established by the previous president, didn't appear on any organizational chart because Italy's head of state had classified the position. Therefore, knowledge of it was provided only on a need-to-know basis. Answerable solely to the office of the president and empowered to act in their name, very few ministers, high-level government employees, senior law enforcement officers, and a select number of foreign officials knew of Pia Lamberti's role in the government and the immense influence she possessed.

Nicknamed the witch by most of those with whom she interacted because she was unforgiving and exploited a person's frailties, she was the widow of the ex-president of Italy and the former lover of the woman whose grave she was visiting. Beginning her career with the Department of Information Security, which oversaw both foreign and domestic intelligence activities, and without outside influence, she worked her way to becoming second in command of that department. However, upon seeing that the lack of coordination between these intelligence functions resulted in intelligence failures and delayed responses to situations of urgency because each organization jealously guarded its turf to retain their bureaucracy and budget, she approached her husband, who was then president, and convinced him to create the off-the-books position of intelligence czar—a position she was asked to retain when his predecessor, President Enrico Orsini, knowing of her extraordinary and unpublished accomplishments, decided to continue the ghost function.

The reason for making the office of intelligence czar a state secret was that it shrouded whoever was in that position from scrutiny by the nine-hundred-and-forty-five members of the legislature, which consisted of the Chamber of Deputies and the Senate of the Republic. It also allowed her to bypass being second-guessed by the President of the Council of Ministers, the Interministerial Committee, and the Department of Information Security—all of which had some involvement with the nation's intelligence functions. "If my position of intelligence czar was known," she told her late husband, "I'd spend my days answering questions, most of those asking questions trying to find a way to politically embarrass you rather than protecting the country. I'll leave the unenviable burden of working with these bureaucrats to the agency directors below me."

One of her areas of focus was recruiting and directing intelligence assets, one of whom was Carolina Biagi, an undercover operative and her former lover, who was murdered on June 15th while on assignment. On that date, just as she'd done for the past three years, she visited her grave.

Getting out of her vehicle, Lamberti walked to the black granite tombstone on which the image of a cameo ring was carved, replicating the one she'd given Carolina Biagi, the top lifting to reveal Lamberti's photo as a reminder of their secret relationship. The ring, placed in a stainless steel box, was buried with her lover.

As Lamberti placed the flowers in front of the tombstone and stood in silence while looking at the grave, Franco Zunino, her driver/bodyguard, positioned himself a respectful distance away and looked intently at the surrounding area for anything that might pose a threat. He was six feet two inches tall with black hair and had an athletic build with broad shoulders and a narrow waist. Her other bodyguard, Silvio Villa, was standing beside the vehicle using gyro-assisted 14x binoculars to surveil the area, the optics within making objects appear as if they were fourteen times closer. The gyro was necessary for surveilling locations far away, providing input to image stability sensors that detected even minute vertical or horizontal movements or shakes, afterward sending the mathematics of these changes to a microcomputer, which adjusted the prisms within the binoculars to provide a stable image. This stability enabled Villa to look closely at the numerous monuments and statuaries behind which an assailant could hide and pose a threat. Standing six feet two inches tall, he was three hundred pounds of sculpted muscle, with his thick neck and large biceps constantly threatening to tear the fabric of the shirts that he wore under his jacket.

As Lamberti spoke to her lover in a low voice that only she could hear, Villa saw a momentary glint of low-intensity light at the top of one of the two towers flanking the three-arched entranceway to the cemetery but was unable to detect its source despite moving around to look at the tower from different angles. With his military training kicking in, he knew that metal had a strong reflectivity, while that of glass was weak. Subsequently, he had no doubt that the rising sun had exposed a set of binoculars or a rifle scope pointed in their direction rather than a piece of metal that caught the sun.

Knowing they needed to get Lamberti into the vehicle as quickly as possible, he planned to alert Zunino and closely precede them to the Range Rover, blocking the person's shot at Lamberti. However, before he could speak into his wireless mic and tell Zunino what he'd seen, he was struck in the chest by a .338 Lapua round which imparted enough inertial energy to throw his body several feet backward onto the ground, the lack of sound indicating the bullet came from a silenced weapon. A second and a half later, with Zunino looking for threats in the opposite direction of Villa and not seeing what happened to his partner, he was struck in the back by another .338 Lapua round.

Once Lamberti's bodyguards were neutralized, a black Mercedes G63 SUV screeched to a stop in front of the Range Rover.

ALAN REFKIN

Immediately after that the three lab-coated men, wearing sunglasses and black masks to cover their faces, got out of the vehicle and ran toward Lamberti, who seeing Villa and Zunino lying on the ground pulled a Glock 26 from beneath her dress and quickly put a 9mm round into the foreheads of two of her would-be attackers. She was about to extend the same courtesy to the third but, as she adjusted her aim, that assailant pressed the trigger on a stun gun and sent two darts through the intelligence czar's dress, the jolt of electricity overwhelming her central nervous system and causing her to drop to the ground with severe and uncontrollable contractions. Seeing their target was now under control, the sniper returned his rifle to the carrying case and started down the tower's stairway, not wanting Caruso to wait for him and delay their escape.

As Lamberti lay on the ground, the surviving lab-coated assailant returned to the Mercedes and retrieved one of the canvas bags, all three having identical contents. Knowing that the effects of a stun gun only last a few minutes and that the incapacitation time varied by person, he removed a sterile bag of saline, tied a tourniquet at the top of Lamberti's right arm, and started an IV, afterward taking a syringe preloaded with a specific amount of Propofol and injecting it into the line. The anesthetic, a short-acting drug commonly used during colonoscopies and other light surgical procedures, put Lamberti to sleep. Once she was unconscious, he removed from the canvas bag a cannula that was connected to an oxygen tank, turned on the flow, and inserted the twin-pronged plastic tubing into her nostrils. As this was happening, Caruso placed the manila envelope on Biagi's tomb before helping to carry the intelligence czar to the vehicle where, after reclining the driver-side back seat until it was nearly flat, he strapped Lamberti in it.

As Caruso returned to the driver's seat and waited for the lab-coated assailant to come around and open the rear passenger-side door to sit beside his patient, he was startled by the sounds of two near-simultaneous gunshots that broke the morning silence. Turning to his right, he saw through the passenger window that the

6 |

lab-coated assistant was lying on his back with his eyes open, bleeding from both his throat and right temple. Zunino and Villa, who'd been wearing bulletproof vests under their tactical gear and were only rendered unconscious by the heavy rounds fired by the sniper, were now standing, pissed off, and looking for targets of opportunity. With only one bad guy visible, the two expert marksmen focused on the lab-coated assailant, the pair not thinking twice about sending him to get fitted for a harp. Afterward, they went after Caruso, firing a series of rounds in rapid succession into the front windshield, all impacting in a tight grouping that should have struck his face between the forehead and nose. However, because the vehicle was armored, their rounds only cracked the Mercedes' bulletproof glass. As the SUV took off, the pair's subsequent shots at the fleeing vehicle's rear tires fared no better because, even though each sent multiple rounds into them, the self-sealing adhesive closed the holes and gave Caruso approximately an hour before they deflated. Subsequently, the two bodyguards watched in frustration as the armored vehicle sped off the hilltop with Lamberti, the person they were charged with protecting, in the rear seat.

Noticing the manila envelope atop the grave, Zunino picked it up and read the one-paragraph note inside. Afterward, following a protocol he hoped would never need to used, he removed the cellphone from his pocket and called Dante Acardi, chairman of the Agenzia Informazioni e Sicurezza Interna or AISI, the country's domestic intelligence service, alerting him to the kidnapping and the contents of the note. Acardi, who had his protocols, one of which were the procedures employed following the kidnapping of a senior government official, began with item one on that memory checklist and called President Orsini, repeating his conversation with Zunino, afterward being told to drop whatever he was doing and come to his office.

The AISI chairman arrived at the Quirinal Palace, the official residence and workplace for the President of the Italian Republic, at 7:00 am. Acardi was five feet eight inches tall, of medium build, sixty-six years of age, and had short gray hair that was parted to the right. President Orsini, who was sitting at his office desk, was also sixty-six years of age, of average weight, five feet eleven inches tall, and had gray hair that was longer than Acardi's and combed straight back. He had what Italians called a Roman nose, meaning it had a prominent bridge that made it look curved or slightly bent. Others called it an aquiline nose, derived from the Latin word aquilinus, meaning eagle-like, alluding to the curved beak of an eagle.

"Tell me again about the ransom note," Orsini began.

"It demands ten million dollars in gold for Lamberti's return and makes clear that any publicity regarding the kidnapping or government investigation to try and find our intelligence czar will result in her death. It also states that instructions on where and when to deliver the gold will come in seventy-two hours."

"Do you have the ransom note?"

"Forensics is examining it and the manila envelope in which it was delivered to see if there are fingerprints, a DNA sample, or anything else useful in an investigation."

"And no group or individual has taken credit for the kidnapping?"

"I don't believe that's going to happen," Acardi answered. "Ask yourself why the kidnappers took the wife of the former president when they could have abducted the wife of a hedge fund manager or the CEO of a major corporation, who don't have Lamberti's security and who could probably withdraw the ten million dollar ransom from their checking account. In today's world of billionaires, this is a relatively small amount of funds. The money, their choice of target, and my thirty years in the Polizia di Stato before I retired and took this job leads me to believe the ransom note is bogus. They're red herrings meant to mislead us."

"Keep going."

"By my calculations, ten million dollars in gold weighs almost three hundred pounds and would be difficult for kidnappers to transport and hide. Diamonds or other precious stones make more sense. Either these kidnappers are inexperienced and haven't thought this through, or they're disingenuous in their demands. I think it's the latter."

"Why?"

"Lamberti's abduction was demonstrably well-researched and executed, and beyond the scope of amateurs. Subduing her with a stun gun and sedating her rather than resorting to physical restraints shows another level of refinement. Also, they had a sniper overlooking the gravesite and a bulletproof escape vehicle. This sophistication and cost to mount such an operation tells me the ransom note is bogus, and they want to keep us at a standstill for three days."

"What happens in three days?"

"They'll have had time to initially interrogate Lamberti and sell that knowledge, afterward handing her over to an unfriendly nation-state who will continue the interrogation at a location we'll probably never find. What she knows is worth substantially more than the ransom they demanded. No matter the scenario, she'll die once her usefulness is over."

"Unfortunately, I agree," Orsini stated. "Did you put out a BOLO on the Mercedes?"

"As it turns out, that wasn't necessary. Local police found it torched a mile from the cemetery," he told the president. "I had the vehicle put on a flatbed and taken to one of our crime labs to see if they could find a VIN number or other clue. But, if the kidnappers are as professional as they've so far demonstrated, we'll find it's been stolen and, because it was gutted by fire, there won't be a fingerprint, hair, or fiber sample."

"What about the three corpses?" The president asked.

"I called the coroner on the way here. Each is listed in their system as Mario Rossi, the equivalent of John Doe in the United States. He'll autopsy the bodies and run the fingerprints through the national database. If any are identified, he won't change the

Mario Rossi status. Instead, he'll give that information to me," Acardi stated.

"They might be our strongest chance to find out who's behind this and rescue Lamberti because people in their profession generally have a criminal record. I also want to find out how they knew Lamberti went to the Campo Verano Cemetery at dawn every June 15th," Orsini said.

"They could only have gotten this information from someone who knew of her position with the government and was intimate with her habits. That's a tiny group."

"Which places us in a conundrum," the president stated. "Pia Lamberti is vital to our national security and integral to the European intelligence community. She knows not only our most intimate secrets but those of our allies, including the names of foreign and double agents, NATO defense plans for the European continent, the dispersal of nuclear weapons throughout Europe, and so on. We can't let anyone extract that information from her."

"What are you implying?"

"I'm not implying anything. I'm saying that if we can't rescue Pia Lamberti, we need to kill her."

Acardi took a deep breath before he responded, clearing away the emotion he felt at possibly having to order the death of a friend. "It's your call, sir. However, not to get ahead of ourselves, we first have to find her, which may take time given that we have nothing to go on but a ransom demand that we believe is disingenuous."

"Time is something we don't have because the longer it takes to find her, the more information they'll extract," Orsini stated.

"Lamberti will be a very hard nut to crack."

"Eventually, everyone throws in their cards. However, I agree that breaking her will take longer than they expect. Regardless, we can't let them get a brain dump of what she knows. If our allies find out she's been abducted, they'll cease sharing their intelligence with my government until her fate is known, NATO will change their contingency plans for Europe, foreign operatives will be recalled, safe house locations changed, and other aspects of our intelligence functions altered. Her loss will also make it difficult for other nations to trust us with sensitive information in the future."

"I know," Acardi conceded.

"Then, how do we launch a meaningful search for Lamberti and keep it off the grid?"

"I asked myself the same question."

"Did you come up with an answer?"

"We use Mauro Bruno and his partners," he said, referring to BD&D Investigations, the letters representing the first letter of the surnames of the firm's partners—Mauro Bruno, Elia Donati, and Lisette Donais.

"I should have thought of that," Orsini conceded, familiar with the firm who'd saved his life when Antonio Conti, a terrorist whose real name was Ammar Nadeem, tried to blow up the Quirinal Palace and kill him and several heads of state, one of whom was the president of the United States. The investigative firm not only prevented their assassinations, but also informed U.S. intelligence of the dirty bomb that Nadeem's group had smuggled into the United States and planted near the White House. Additionally, Lamberti confided to Orsini of several assignments she'd given the firm where, if they'd failed, the consequences would have made global headlines.

"I'll call Bruno and get them started," Acardi stated.

"Brief them in person and bring them to Rome so they can get started on the investigation. Take Lamberti's aircraft and tell Bruno it's theirs for as long as needed because I don't want them delayed by relying on commercial transportation."

With their conversation over, Acardi left for Ciampino Airport, where Lamberti's aircraft was hangared. On the way, he notified the government's flight operations office that President Orsini had temporarily reassigned Lamberti's aircraft to the AISI, and he needed two pilots to immediately preflight the plane and file a flight plan for Milan's Linate Airport, which was six and a half miles from downtown.

The two pilots, who had the misfortune of being on call that day, arrived at Ciampino twenty minutes after being informed. Once the flight plan was filed and their preflight complete, the Gulfstream G700, an upgrade given to Lamberti when her G550 was reassigned to another government agency following a report that it needed an overhaul and would be in the hangar for a month, started its engines and was roaring down the runway five minutes after Acardi stepped onboard.

BD&D's office was a twenty-eight hundred square feet, four-bedroom apartment on the second floor of a white five-story historic building in Milan's Corso Di Porta Romana neighborhood, a few steps from the Duomo. Their business cards also showed a Paris address, which looked impressive because it made the firm appear to be an international investigative agency. However, had someone typed either address into Google Earth, they would have seen that both locations were residential apartment buildings, the office in Paris being Donais' former domicile. At one time, the three partners agreed to cancel the lease because it was an unnecessary expense, but after seeing the sadness on Donais' face because it'd been her home for some time and was a connection to the city that she loved, Bruno and Donati contacted the landlord and said she was maintaining the residence, afterward telling her what they'd done, their partner grateful for their sensitivity and thoughtfulness.

Their Milan headquarters didn't have individual offices for the partners. Instead, each worked at a long rectangular conference table in the living room. Prior to forming their investigative agency, Bruno and Donati were former chief inspectors with the Polizia di Stato, while Donais was a private investigator for a law firm in Paris; the three becoming a team after adverse circumstances forced them to work together to solve a case. It was 9:50 am when they heard a knock on the door. The trio had been up for the past hour having a cup of espresso while waiting for their croissants from the Cremeria Buonarrati to arrive, the pasticceria famous since 1920 for its crumbly and fragrant pastry. However, when Bruno answered the door, instead of seeing the pastry shop's delivery person, he saw Acardi holding the bag of warm croissants.

"Buongiorno," Acardi said as he walked past him and entered the apartment.

"How did you end up with our morning pastry? Come to think of it, why are you in Milan?" he asked.

Mauro Bruno was fifty-three years old, five feet eleven inches tall with a waistline that reflected he was carrying an extra ten pounds of baggage. He had salt and pepper hair that was combed straight back, a neatly trimmed black mustache with flecks of gray, and piercing brown eyes. Not comfortable with wearing casual clothing, he habitually wore a dark blue suit, white shirt, and light blue tie. Finding it impossible to sleep late, Bruno routinely rose at 5:30 am.

"To answer your first question, the delivery person and I arrived at the door simultaneously. Not wanting to spoil the surprise, I showed him my badge and tipped him ten euros, after which he handed me the bag. Before I answer your second question, I could use an espresso and one of these," Acardi said, handing the bag of croissants to Donati, who went into the kitchen to make the espresso. Bruno's partner was forty-one, six feet tall, a trim one hundred eighty pounds, had black hair, and was also impeccably dressed. Today, he wore a tan suit, pink-striped shirt, and navy tie.

Donais came forward and hugged Acardi. The stunning five-foot-four-inch blonde, a doppelganger for Jennifer Aniston, had a voice that was sensual without being flirty. Like most French women, she liked fashion and tended toward trendy attire that flattered her shapely body. She wore tight-fitting jeans, a white knit top, which some women might criticize as a size too small, but most men would applaud as being the perfect choice, and black Steve Madden Ecentrcq sneakers.

"In answer to your second, Pia Lamberti is in trouble," Acardi said, taking his espresso and a small plate containing the croissant from Donati's hands.

"In my experience, Pia Lamberti creates bad days for others, not vice-versa, because she has the resources of virtually the entire government at her disposal and has never been shy about using their assets against an adversary," Bruno stated, directing Acardi to a chair at the head of the conference table and taking the seat to his left while Donati and Donais sat to his right.

"She's been kidnapped."

"That's impossible," Donais impulsively exclaimed before realizing it must be true or Acardi wouldn't be there.

The domestic intelligence chief went on to explain what he knew about the actual kidnapping, which wasn't much, the impounding of the burnt SUV, and that three of the kidnappers were at the morgue with their fingerprints and faces being run through the national database.

"Why would the kidnappers use a bulletproof G63 for the kidnapping?" Donati asked once Acardi finished. "That's a very expensive vehicle and a head-turner for anyone it passes. Therefore, it's not something you'd want to use in a kidnapping. On top of that, there can't be many of them that have been sold or leased, and very few that would have been bulletproofed, meaning it should be easy to compile a list of those who own them." Donati, who came from a very wealthy family, drove a BMW and was familiar with expensive vehicles. "Off the lot, a G63 costs a couple of bills," he continued, meaning $200,000. "Bulletproofing adds another bill and a half."

"If the kidnappers are as calculating as they've demonstrated, they stole the Mercedes," Acardi replied, "burning it afterward to get rid of the forensic evidence."

"That makes sense," Donati admitted. "And it was a smart move for the kidnappers to steal a bulletproof vehicle because if they hadn't, Villa and Zunino would have killed the driver and rescued Lamberti."

"Whoever orchestrated this kidnapping spent a lot of money to grab her, indicating they have deep pockets. This abduction isn't about a ransom. It's about having seventy-two hours to extract what's inside her head," Bruno said.

"After which they'll kill her," Donais stated.

"That's what the president and I believe," Acardi stated. "However, she won't be easy to interrogate, and it'll take some time for the kidnappers to get useful information from her."

"And you want us to find her before then," Bruno clarified.

"That's your primary objective. But if you can't effectuate her rescue, you're to kill her because, either by torture or through the use of drugs, whoever has Pia Lamberti will eventually learn everything she knows. We can't let that happen. Does anyone have a problem with that caveat to this assignment?" Acardi asked as he looked around the table.

Reluctantly, the three verbally accepted that condition.

"Does the Campo Verano Cemetery have surveillance cameras?" Bruno asked, getting back to the investigation.

"I asked the administrator that very question on the flight here. He told me they do, and that one camera captured the kidnapping, and those at the front of the cemetery caught the Mercedes entering and leaving. However, its license plate was removed."

"What about seeing the faces of those in the car? The resolution of surveillance cameras is usually excellent."

"I'm told that although the cemetery cameras photographed the driver and one other person in the SUV, just as with the perps in the morgue, they wore sunglasses and a mask to hide their faces. Therefore, we have no ideas as to their identity."

"If the car was stolen, as we believe, we have nothing to go on that will help us learn their identities," Donais added.

"Even so, I'd like to take a look at the background of the Mercedes owner and speak with them," Bruno interjected. "A car like that doesn't get stolen without a police report being filed. If, however, the owner hasn't noticed he has a missing vehicle, for whatever reason, maybe we'll get lucky and one of the VIN strips survived the fire. Either way, we'll want to speak with him."

"Can this administrator be trusted to keep quiet, or will what he saw on the video end up in the tabloids?" Donais asked.

"He's ex-military and says that he knows how to keep a secret. He also said he'd ensure he was the only one at the cemetery who knew about this incident and could access the recordings for these cameras," Acardi stated.

"Do you believe him?"

"I believe the word of anyone who's ex-military over that of a government bureaucrat. Setting that aside, I don't think he wants the publicity or to jeopardize the government subsidy that Campo Verano receives to maintain the military section of the cemetery and its common areas."

"Because we can't issue a BOLO for Lamberti," Bruno said, referring to the police abbreviation for *be on the lookout*, "or everyone would know she's missing, thereby causing a great deal of concern and uncertainty within our intelligence community and that of foreign governments with whom we share information, we won't have the wide net that law enforcement would cast over the country to search for her."

"I want the kidnappers to believe we'll deliver the gold in seventy-two hours and that our government wants to keep this quiet. Therefore, your investigation needs to be below everyone's radar. Given the circumstances, the lack of leads, and the short amount of time you have to find Lamberti, that will be difficult. Nevertheless, to maintain that level of secrecy, I'll be your sole contact, feeding you whatever intel I have and getting you what's needed to get the job done," Acardi stated.

"That works for us, Dante. You can start by giving us a list of those who knew that Lamberti visited the Campo Verano Cemetery each year on June 15th," Bruno said.

Acardi removed a small black notebook from his jacket pocket and noted the request.

"We'll also need tickets on the next flight to Rome so we can go to the cemetery, visit the gravesite, speak to the administrator, see the video of the kidnapping, inspect the burnt Mercedes, view the bodies of the dead kidnappers, and investigate whatever lead we come up with" Bruno continued, giving him the laundry list of actions that required his support.

After Acardi added those requests to his notebook, he addressed their transportation request. "President Orsini doesn't want you to waste time waiting for commercial flights. Therefore, he's giving your team sole use of Lamberti's aircraft. It's waiting at the Linate Airport to take us to Rome."

"When do we leave?" Donati asked.

"How long will it take all of you to pack your bags?"

"Five minutes," he replied, his partners agreeing with that estimate.

"In that case, we'll be in Rome within the hour."

Chapter Two

Bruno and his partners arrived at the Campo Verano Cemetery at noon, while Acardi returned to his office to compile a list of those he believed knew of Lamberti's annual graveside visit. Expecting their arrival, the administrative official in charge of the cemetery escorted the trio to an office where a video of the kidnapping was ready for viewing, afterward explaining how to start, stop, and zoom in and out. He then left the room and closed the door behind him.

The video began with Lamberti's arrival and gravesite visit, progressing to her bodyguards being shot and the Mercedes screeching to a stop in front of the Range Rover, after which the three white lab-coated assailants got out and rushed toward Lamberti. Bruno paused the video.

"We're fortunate this camera had a wide-angle lens," Bruno said, zooming out so that the entire hilltop was visible. "Because we don't see the sniper who shot Zunino and Villa, they must have been some distance away in an overwatch position that was high enough to make those shots," he continued, overwatch being the military term for a vantage point where one can observe the terrain far ahead.

"And, since there's no other hill nearby, the only places high enough to make those shots are the towers on either side of the entry arches that we saw when we entered the cemetery," Donais stated, with Bruno and Donati agreeing.

"That explains why the person in the lab coat was armed only with a stun gun," Donati added. "He expected the sniper to kill Lamberti's security detail and anyone else who posed a threat, so he could tase what they believed was a defenseless older woman."

"Likewise, the sniper must have thought they'd dispatched Zunino and Villa. Otherwise, they would have gone for a headshot once they were immobile on the ground. Instead, believing they were dead, they must have left the tower and waited for the driver of the Mercedes to pick them up on the way out of the cemetery," Bruno stated.

"That begs the question of whether the sniper picked up the shell casings. When you're kidnapping a high profile figure, you don't want to hold up the exfil," Donati added, using the military term for exfiltration or extraction from a hostile environment. "The sniper would have wanted to be at the base of the tower waiting for the escape vehicle, which explains why he didn't see Zunino and Villa get up."

"Acardi told us they wore hard armor vests. If they hadn't, because those rounds had enough impact energy to knock out someone from that long a distance, it would have burst half the organs in their body," Bruno stated, hard armor referring to bulletproof vests that were constructed from rigid materials made to defeat high-velocity rifle rounds, such as those fired by the sniper. In contrast, soft armor vests were composed of multiple layers of Kevlar and were designed to defeat bullets from small arms.

Bruno unpaused the video but stopped it again after Lamberti killed two of her attackers before being tased by the third.

"No one expected her to carry a gun nor be that good a marksperson," Donati said.

"There's a lot we'll never know about her," Bruno conceded. "What we do know is that she's as tough as they get," he said before restarting the video and pausing it after the third lab-coated assailant inserted the IV into her arm and injected something from a syringe into the line, which the trio believed was an incapacitating drug.

"That was a very smooth insert into her vein," Donais commented. "It was as good or better than most labs that draw blood, which shows they probably had medical training. But why the lab coats? They're not in a medical facility. Tactical gear would have been more appropriate for an abduction."

"That's true, from our point of view," Bruno agreed. "But from what we've seen, whoever planned this takes nothing for granted. They may have thought their sniper, looking at the top of a hill through a scope a thousand yards away, or however far the towers are, could more quickly discern his people if they wore white. Also, as Lisette said, given the medical skill of the person inserting the IV line, we should consider that those in lab coats may have been wearing their daily work attire."

"That makes sense," Donati conceded, with Donais nodding in agreement.

Bruno let the video continue, ending with the SUV leaving the gravesite while being shot at by Villa and Zunino. A few seconds later, a second video appeared on the screen. Taken by cameras high above the entrance to the cemetery, it showed the Mercedes entering Campo Verano, while a third video captured its departure. Although the driver could be seen through the windshield, their face was hidden beneath a mask and sunglasses. The same was true for the person beside them, who the trio assumed was the sniper.

"Let's look at the towers before going to the gravesite to see if the sniper left spent brass or any other clue," Bruno said, Donati and Donais agreeing that was the logical place to start since the towers were nearby.

Leaving the administrative office, they got into their rental vehicle, a white GMC Yukon, and with Donati driving, went to the towers. From the ground, the cameras that photographed the kidnapper's vehicle entering and leaving the cemetery were visible, facing opposite directions atop a tall steel pole on the roof of the tower to the right of the entrance archway. They decided to explore it first.

The thick, heavily painted wooden entry door looked as if it'd been there since the cemetery opened and, judging from the size of the hinges, probably weighed north of two hundred pounds. Because of its age, it had an antique mortise lock, meaning one which had a pocket cut into the edge of the door into which the lock would be fitted, and a black ornate Eastlake-style back plate made of cast iron, which was popular around the 1920s. Finding the door unlocked, they pushed it aside and climbed the three-story cast iron staircase to the small rectangular roof, where they could see the hilltop on which Carolina Biagi was buried.

"This is the perfect vantage point for a sniper. There are no obstructions between here and the gravesite, and the cameras don't have a field of vision that includes the top of either tower, making the shooter invisible," Donati remarked.

"Adding to our bad news, the shooter picked up their brass. They knew what they were doing," Donais stated.

"That's also apparent from the shots they made," Bruno said. "The rounds from their rifle must have been very heavy to have the impact power necessary, despite its energy dissipating with distance, to strike Zunino and Villa's vests and still have the inertial force to render them unconscious. Since a heavy round drops significantly with distance, the expertise required to make that shot is normally only found in someone with military sniper training. This isn't a skill a civilian attains at a gun range."

"Military or not, they knew what they were doing," Donati replied as he focused on the top of a tall tree in the distance that had a long piece of red string waving from a branch. He pointed it out to Bruno and Donais.

"That's an improvised windsock," Bruno said, having worked cases that involved a sniper. "If the string is limp, there's no wind at the top of the tree. If it flutters, the sniper can estimate the wind's velocity and direction. They'll be another string close to the grave, which the shooter could view with their scope, giving them the wind conditions at the top of the hill. Let's take a look," he said, leading the way down the stairway and to the vehicle, the trio forgoing their inspection of the second tower.

The gravesite was less than five minutes away. Donati parked the GMC Yukon in the same spot where the Mercedes had stopped, which was easy to find because of the black tire marks. Walking to the grave, they saw the bouquet of long-stemmed red roses still lying in front of the tombstone. Ten yards behind it was a magnificent Italian stone pine tree with a broad canopy resembling an umbrella. Fluttering from the top was a red string.

"It'd be nice to have that string," Bruno said. "Maybe we can find where it was purchased."

"Let me get it," Donais volunteered, knowing she was better dressed for climbing the tree because she was wearing jeans, in deference to her partner's suits. She was also seven years younger than Donati and had nineteen years on Bruno, which didn't hurt. After Donati handed her a small Ziplock bag, he stooped down, boosted her atop his shoulders, and stood until she was high enough to grab onto a lower branch of the stone pine. Climbing to the top, Donais photographed the string with her cellphone camera before untying and putting it in the plastic bag. Once she was safely on the ground, the trio spread out and searched the gravesite and surrounding area for clues.

"I see two 9mm shell casings," Donati said, pointing to them nestled in the grass beside the grave. "This must be where Lamberti stood when she killed two of her abductors."

"I'm looking at six other casings," Bruno added. "Pick up the brass with the tip of your pen," he told Donati as he removed a pen from his pocket and began lifting them from the grass and putting the brass in one of the plastic bags he, just as Donati, kept in their suit pocket as a matter of habit. "Maybe we'll get lucky and get a print."

After picking up the brass, they returned to their vehicle where Bruno called Acardi, getting the address of the crime lab where the Mercedes was taken, and asking him to direct the staff to provide whatever information and assistance they requested. He also asked him to check if a G63 had been stolen anywhere in Europe within the last six months.

"Why look at the vehicle?" Acardi asked. "I'm told it's a distorted mass of metal and that all forensic evidence has been incinerated. What are you hoping to find?"

"Years ago, I thought the same. However, a lab tech once told me that a luxury vehicle like a Mercedes has its vehicle identification number on metal tags in as many as six locations, one of which is the engine block, which might have protected it from the fire. If we retrieve the VIN, we'll have the owner."

Acardi liked what Bruno said and promised that the lab manager would give them his undivided cooperation.

When they arrived at the facility, they were escorted to the manager's office, a nondescript room with well-used mid-50s furniture, and greeted by a slender, middle-aged man with gray hair.

"I've been at this facility for twenty-three years," the man began, "and this is the first time the chairman of the AISI has ever called me. He made it clear that I should provide whatever you requested and then forget that you were here and everything that was said. Therefore, what do you want to discuss before I develop amnesia?" He asked, getting a chuckle from the trio because of the paradox of that statement.

Bruno thanked him for his cooperation and said they'd like to see the charred remains of the G63 and have his staff get the VIN number from one of its tags.

"If it's there, we'll get you the number," the manager said, escorting them to where the Mercedes was kept, along the way asking a tech who was dressed in grime-impregnated overalls to accompany them.

Upon looking at the vehicle, the trio's belief that they could retrieve the VIN number came into serious doubt after seeing the twisted and charred remains that the tech, using a nearby forklift, had hoisted off the ground to begin his examination. Thirty minutes later, things didn't get any better when he stepped away from the charred mess and, covered with residue from the fire, reported that the metal tags had been removed prior to the fire.

"They were removed and not destroyed?" Bruno questioned.

"No doubt this was a scorching fire, although I don't believe it was intense enough to melt away every trace of the metal VIN tags. Some remnants would have survived," the tech said. "Therefore, the only explanation is that they were removed before the fire."

After he finished giving Bruno the bad news, Acardi called and didn't make his day any better.

"You'd think that a car costing $200,000 plus would be at the top of any car thieves' list," Acardi began without preface. "However, worldwide, I've discovered that dubious honor belongs to the Mercedes C-class, followed by the BMW 3 series, the Infiniti G, and the Mercedes E-class."

Bruno was about to tell him to forget the history lesson and get to the reason for his call when Acardi got to the point.

"Only one G63 theft has been reported in the past four months. Interestingly, that was this morning when a security company on the Via Salaria, which isn't far from the cemetery, reported it missing from their warehouse."

"That's not a good advertisement for a security firm. Why steal a bulletproof vehicle? For that matter, why even have one?"

"The company's CEO says their clients like this type of car because it's a status symbol among the corporate elites and Hollywood types. It massages their egos," Acardi stated.

"Can we get a list of those who've had their egos massaged?"

"He's pulling the data as we speak, but it's not going to be helpful because the company's website advertises this particular bulletproof car and shows a photo of it. That means, beyond the company's clients and those they've told, anyone who's accessed their website would know about it," Acardi said.

"Cars of this caliber are almost impossible to hot wire. Therefore, they must have had the keys."

"They did, breaking into the safe where they were kept during non-business hours."

"That tells me that someone knew where they were stored, most likely a current or past employee," Bruno said.

"Finding them will take more time than we have."

"I have another idea."

"What's that?"

"I'll tell you after I see a friend," Bruno replied.

"Who?"

"Ernesto Labriola."

"Didn't you almost get him killed the last time you were together? In fact, didn't he block your number on his phone?"

"He threatened to do that, but I don't think he pulled the trigger."

"Nevertheless, I don't think he considers you a friend."

"Friend may not be the correct descriptive," Bruno admitted.

"You should probably use begrudging acquaintance instead."

"We'll soon find out," Bruno said, ending the call.

The trio left the crime lab for the morgue, Bruno deciding not to call Labriola to say that he was on his way. He hoped that his questionable friend, who was Rome's ranking coroner, would have already learned the identities of the lab-coated assailants from the fingerprint and facial recognition searches he ran on them. Armed with this information, Bruno thought that he and his partners could find the person who employed these three, believing this individual was also behind the theft of the Mercedes and Lamberti's abduction.

The investigators entered the parking lot at the rear of the coroner's office twenty minutes after leaving the crime lab, taking the sidewalk that surrounded the rectangular structure to the reception area on the opposite side of the building. Five minutes after giving their names to the desk clerk, Ernesto Labriola walked into the lobby. He was five feet nine inches tall, had gray hair, a muscular physique, and a thick neck, all of which made him appear younger than his sixty-four years. He didn't seem thrilled to see Bruno.

"Three bodies with bullet holes come to my morgue, and now you're here. This sounds like a replay of your last visit," the coroner said. "Who's trying to kill you, and by extension will soon want to murder me?"

Labriola had worked at this facility for thirty-six years and had known Acardi for a quarter-century. Four years ago, when the trio came to view Carolina Biagi's remains, they got embroiled in a fierce gun battle when Mafia gunmen tried to retrieve her body prior to it being autopsied. Labriola and the trio survived only because of the rescue team that Acardi sent. This was the first time the four had seen each other since then.

"No one is trying to kill us or you," Bruno reassured him. "We're only here to gather information for our investigation."

"Isn't that what you told me last time? The only difference is that I now have several bodies lying on steel tables instead of one. You three attract trouble with the same certainty that bees are attracted to wildflowers," Labriola responded. "I'd like to at least survive until retirement."

"You're retiring?"

"That's what I just said."

"When?"

"As soon as the person stepping into my shoes feels he's ready, which I expect will be in the next week or so."

"Is this retirement voluntary or mandatory?" Bruno asked, knowing that Labriola lived for his work and didn't have any hobbies, at least none that he knew about.

"The mandatory retirement age for this position is sixty-five."

"I wish you the best, Ernesto," Bruno said, a sentiment echoed by Donati and Donais.

"Getting back to business, can you tell me why the deceased are wearing lab coats? I assume that means they have a medical background," Labriola said.

"We believe they do, but that's unconfirmed."

"Did you kill them?"

Bruno shook his head. "Lamberti killed two and Villa and Zunino the other. Despite their efforts, she was abducted."

Knowing Lamberti's classified position within the government, Labriola looked at Bruno with disbelief. "And you're hoping these bodies will give you a clue as to who's behind the kidnapping," he stated.

"That's my thought. Did you run the three through the national database?"

"I did and know the identity of each," he said.

"Who are they?"

Instead of answering, Labriola told the trio to follow him. When they reached the coroner's office, he removed three folders from his desk and handed them to Bruno. "They're from Agrigento, Sicily. Given where they live and their involvement in Lamberti's kidnapping, one might assume they're Mafia."

"They're not?" Donati asked.

"Who knows? On one side of the scale, they were associated with those who abducted Lamberti. On the other hand, they have no priors which, as you know, is unusual for someone of their age in this line of work. All three also work as physician's assistants, which might explain the lab coats they were wearing," Labriola volunteered.

"That would also explain why they're good at starting IVs," Donati added, directing his comment to his partners, the remark confusing Labriola.

"I can't visualize them as being associated with the Mafia," Donais said. "To me a Mafioso is rough-edged. They take part in loansharking, drug smuggling, kidnapping, and a laundry list of other illegal activities. Medical workers who punch a clock don't seem to fit that mold, although the circumstances show I'm obviously wrong."

"In my experience, most Mafiosos are rough-edged and can't pass the background checks increasingly required by many companies, including those in the medical profession," Labriola agreed. "For that reason, the mob is transitioning and putting a substantial effort into recruiting professionals who don't have a criminal record from legitimate companies and organizations that may be of future value."

"Why a physician's assistant?" Donais asked.

"Because they can produce a certificate or finding of a negative result on a drug or alcohol test. The lack of these in one's system makes it possible to get an employment position that would be unavailable if the results came back positive. Additionally, following a major accident, a negative finding for drugs or alcohol lessens the possibility of landing in jail, incurring civil liabilities, or getting one's driver's license revoked."

"It also enables the mob to perpetrate a very profitable fraud," Bruno said, he and Donati having arrested, while with the Polizia di Stato, those who've taken part in this type of deception.

"What type of fraud?" Donais asked.

"Let's say a husband with a wife and kids is diagnosed with a life-ending malady which can't be cured. If the Mafia discovers their situation, they'll approach the husband about applying for a life insurance policy from an agent who's in their pocket, naming the wife as beneficiary. When the insurance company sends one of their nurses to examine the husband, because they rarely send a doctor to take the person's blood pressure, temperature, and other non-invasive measurements, the husband will say he's feeling fine. Afterward, the nurse will either draw blood or send the husband to get a lab test from a facility that the insurance company has approved. However, the Mafia has infiltrated many of the major lab companies with technicians who can switch the vial of the person who is terminal with that from someone who has no health problems. Instead of the results indicating the person's blood chemistry shows they're dying, the blood tests demonstrate they're healthy. Once this happens, the Mafia has the dying person take out a loan from a financial institution connected to the organized crime entity, amounting to around eighty percent of the insurance policy, but no money passes hands. When the person dies, his wife pays off the non-existent loan from the insurance proceeds, ending up with the remainder. This is just one example. There are other ways medical professionals assist organized crime," Bruno stated.

"Why doesn't the insurance company refuse to pay?" Donais asked. "They have to know the lab test was incorrect."

"The wife and her attorney will say it's not the insured's fault that the lab got it wrong, and they did everything the insurance company requested. To avoid liability, the lab will also say that it's not their fault because their analysis is done by an automated process, which makes it impossible to generate a false test result. In fact, they can prove their results are 99.99 percent accurate because if a malady is detected, the blood sample is rerun. Therefore, the insurance company has only conjectures to dispute their findings. Without proof of wrongdoing, they're cutting the check because their legal counsel will tell them the last thing they want is to put a grieving widow, with her children sitting behind her in court, in front of a jury who could make an example of the insurance company's insensitivity and greed with a huge judgment."

"How much of Sicily does the Agrigento Mafia govern?" Donais asked.

"There are ninety-four Mafia families in Sicily," Bruno answered, having learned quite a bit about the Mafia from his father, who was a prosecutor in Milan. "Representatives from the largest Mafia families in Italy comprise the Commission—their decision-making body charged with governing the interests of the families comprising the Mafia. Every family operates territorially, with the

Commission ensuring each focuses their activities exclusively in the area they've been given and doesn't try to profit from another family's territory. No family has a historical right to their area. The Commission assigns the privilege of running a criminal enterprise within a geographic boundary and can take it away if circumstances warrant. Therefore, if the Agrigento clan were operating in Rome, Dante Sciarra would need to get the approval of the Commission before conducting the kidnapping."

"Dante Sciarra?" Donais asked.

"The head of the family governing Agrigento," Donati added, also familiar with this Mafioso.

"Without approval, the Commission would sanction his family. That could mean anything from losing his territory to the death of the family members involved," Bruno added.

"Assuming Sciarra received permission, the Commission knew in advance about Lamberti's abduction and tacitly approved it," Donati said.

Bruno agreed with that statement. "Getting back to the corpses. Who else knows their identities?" He asked the coroner, holding up the folders that Labriola had given him.

"Including you three, only me and Acardi. I kept their autopsy reports off the morgue's computer system. Should I be worried because last time, how do I put it, you were less than perfect about telling me about the risk?" Labriola asked. "Sciarra is an especially nasty piece of work who kills without compunction anyone he even suspects could have an adversarial effect on his empire."

"If he or someone, it'll be the three of us and not you," Bruno assured him.

"I only ask because last time you told me something close to that, I almost ended up on one of my tables," the coroner replied.

"The circumstances aren't remotely the same," Bruno stated.

Labriola shook his head in response, unconvinced by this assurance. "Let me show you the bodies," he said, escorting the trio through the maze of corridors where they'd previously protected him during a raging gun battle. Eventually, they entered the viewing room. The three bodies were on steel tables, each covered to the neck by a white sheet.

Bruno handed each partner a folder, the trio taking their time reading through the results of the autopsies. The reports showed each thug died of a gunshot wound, which wasn't surprising given the trio saw their demises on video. What did surprise them was that their stomach contents showed their last meal was pasta alla norma, a regional dish common in Sicily and uncommon in Rome and its environs. That meant they either had the meal as a late dinner or early breakfast because it took two to four hours for the stomach contents to move into the small intestine.

"Based on their stomach contents, they flew from Sicily to Rome early this morning, which is only an hour flight, and went straight to the cemetery," Bruno stated. "That's interesting because I can tell you from experience that both Ciampino and Fiumicino are closed in the early morning, even for private aircraft."

"They could have eaten at a Sicilian restaurant in Rome and had leftovers before going to the cemetery," Donais volunteered.

"I love this dish," Labriola said, interjecting himself into the conversation. "However, I found that most Sicilian restaurants here leave it off the menu because it takes so long to make, and if there isn't a significant daily demand for it, meaning they can prepare the sauce and caramelized eggplant early, the restaurant owner would rather focus on easier and more profitable Sicilian dishes. At least that's what one of the servers told me when I tried ordering it off menu."

"If the kidnappers work for Dante Sciarra, as we suspect, he must have orchestrated the abduction for personal reasons; otherwise, why would someone hire a Sicilian mobster to carry out a kidnapping in Rome when there's more than enough local talent?" Donais questioned.

"Whether Sciarra was hired or did this on his own, either way he'd be infringing on another Mafia family's territory and would need to get the Commission's permission for the abduction," Donati added.

"Sciarra's involvement is based on the premise that the three physician assistants from Agrigento are closet members of the Mafia," Donais reminded them. "But that's a thin thread. We'll need more than their city of residence to tie them to him."

"Their body art puts that assumption to rest," Bruno said, looking for the first time at the autopsy photos, which were behind the report.

"They're Mafia, alright," Donati confirmed, the former police officers familiar with Mafia ink.

Donais and Labriola studied the photos, the coroner then asked Donati to explain, as he couldn't understand how the body art he was looking at tied them to the Mafia.

"The word omerta refers to their code of silence, which means you will never betray your peers or reveal family secrets," Donati began. "The black hand represents extortion and protection, while the praying hands symbolize devotion and loyalty to that code. The Italian horn or cornicello signifies good luck. The rose on each could have several meanings. It's not only a symbol of the sacrifice required to keep the family's secrets but also a reminder of the rewards that come from loyalty and devotion. The dagger represents strength and power, the flame symbolizes passion and intensity, and the snake is associated with knowledge and wisdom. These are common throughout the Mafia, regardless of family."

"What about the faces?" Donais asked.

"They're not just any faces. This one is Maurizio Di Gati," Donati said, pointing to it. "The other is Giuseppe Falsone. Both are former bosses of the Agrigento Mafia. If you were in the Polizia di Stato, these faces would be burned into your memory because they had been on Italy's most wanted list for a long time."

"It's obvious that no one from another family is going to have a tattoo of a former Agrigento boss," Donais said. "This ties them to Sciarra."

"Circling back to what we discussed earlier, let's check if an aircraft landed and departed from a Rome airport when it was supposed to be closed," Bruno said.

"Ciampino is the closest airport to Rome," Labriola stated, again inserting himself into the investigation.

"And Catania is the closest to Agrigento," Donati added.

"We'll start by going to Ciampino," Bruno said. "Because airports have good video surveillance, let's see if their security cameras recorded who boarded a plane for a flight to Catania."

"Calling airport security would be faster," Labriola volunteered.

"If Sciarra has someone at the airport on his payroll, calling ahead will give them time to erase or misplace the surveillance video," Bruno replied.

"That makes sense," Labriola said. "Can I tag along?"

"Doesn't the city's coroner need to be here? It's not like there's a scarcity of arriving bodies."

"The person taking over my position is in the building. I'll tell him the future ex-coroner is gone for the day. He'll be thrilled to be in charge. Besides, no one who comes here complains if they have to wait for an autopsy," the coroner said as he removed his lab coat.

Chapter Three

How did the kidnapper's plane take off or land if the airports were closed?" Donais asked. This question arose after Donati mentioned the anomaly while driving the group to Ciampino, with Labriola sitting next to him and Donais and Bruno in the back.

"Pilots are aware that both Ciampino and Catania airports are closed from late night to early morning because this information is noted on flight charts," Donati explained, having once held a private pilot license but let it lapse because he didn't have the time or inclination to keep it current. "This means the control tower must have been staffed since they are responsible for operating the runway lights. At uncontrolled airports—those without a control tower—or at smaller airports where the tower is closed at night, pilots can transmit on a specific frequency to turn on the runway lights. However, that capability doesn't exist at larger airports like Ciampino, Catania, and others with nighttime restrictions. It's possible to pay to have the tower staffed outside normal operating hours. It's costly, but my father's company has done so at Malpensa, which is closed between ten at night and seven in the morning," Donati continued, his father an executive at the Milan office of Kering, the Paris-based luxury group that owns prestigious brands such as Gucci, Balenciaga, Bottega Veneta, and Saint Laurent.

"Why would Milan's Malpensa or Rome's Fiumicino and

Ciampino airports ever close?" Donais asked. "They serve large metropolitan areas."

"The issue is noise. The surrounding communities don't want aircraft flying over them in the middle of the night. Airports will let one-offs fly in for a steep price, and area residents seem to put up with singular traffic during off-hours, but not regular commercial traffic. The good news is that the towers and approach controls, both here and in Sicily, will have a record of these flights, including the aircraft's tail number. Once we provide that information to Acardi, he can identify the owner or the person who rented the aircraft," Donati explained.

"We already know that person is Sciarra," Labriola interjected.

"Which we're assuming is Sciarra," Bruno corrected. "The ownership or rental information may or may not confirm that."

As Bruno spoke, they entered Ciampino airport. They attempted to park in front of the building that housed the control tower, flashing their private investigator licenses and coroner's badge to security, only to be turned away because they weren't associated with the airport or law enforcement. Consequently, they pulled into the parking garage and made their way back to the building. Along the way, Bruno called Acardi to ask him to clear the way with airport security to allow them into the tower.

"You should have made that call before we pulled into the garage," Labriola reminded him.

"Yeah, I know," Bruno admitted. "Can you tell me again why you wanted to come?"

"Because coroners have intuitive investigative skills, and based on my experience with the three of you, that's something you're seriously lacking. So, I'm here to help."

"Wonderful," Bruno replied as they approached the same security guard who had previously sent them away. Since then, he had been contacted by his boss and instructed to allow the four of them inside and provide any assistance they requested. As a result, when he saw them again, he pressed his RFID card to the reader, opened the door, and waved them into the building.

Upon entering the tower, they spoke with the supervisor on duty who, after typing a series of commands on his computer, reported that a Bombardier Global 8000 aircraft left Catania at 1:20 am and arrived at Ciampino at 2:50 am, the Sicilian airport charging the owner $10,000 for the early departure, while Ciampino charged triple that amount for lighting the runway and staffing the tower."

"When did it depart from Ciampino?" Bruno asked.

The supervisor told him.

"Do you have the tail number of that aircraft?"

After typing another series of commands on his keyboard, the supervisor wrote the number on a Post-it Note and handed it to him.

"Thank you. One more thing before we leave you to your work. Can we review the airport's camera recordings from earlier today?"

"Access to those feeds is restricted to security personnel. Their office is located on the bottom floor and to the right as you exit the elevator. I'll inform them of your arrival and that you have authorization to access all aspects of the airport's operations, which should save your boss from making another call," the supervisor said.

Bruno thanked him for his time and thoughtfulness, not mentioning that Acardi had already spoken to security, which was how they gained access to the building.

After the four entered the elevator that would take them to the bottom floor, Bruno called Acardi to provide him with the aircraft's tail number.

The airport security office occupied the entire floor, and judging by the numerous camera monitors in the room, it seemed that no part of the airport was free from visual surveillance. The four introduced themselves to the shift supervisor, who indicated that she had been expecting them. Afterward, Bruno inquired whether they could view the surveillance video of the Bombardier 8000 that had landed and departed earlier that morning.

"Do you know the landing time?"

"2:50 am," Bruno answered.

The shift supervisor began typing on her keyboard, bringing up feeds from eight surveillance cameras on her desktop. The split-screen images displayed the Bombardier landing and taxiing to the private air terminal. Afterward, they observed five people disembarking—the three white-coated men each had a canvas bag, the fourth person carried a long plastic case, and the fifth held an envelope, which they suspected contained the ransom note. The video was clear enough to show their faces as they hurried to the parking area beside the private terminal and entered a Mercedes.

"Can you pull up the feed from the private terminal's surveillance camera for later that morning when the plane departed?" Bruno asked, providing her with the takeoff time he had received from the tower supervisor but subtracting fifteen minutes to capture what went on earlier.

In just a few seconds, she pulled up the requested video. It showed two men arriving at the terminal in a white Ford Transit van. The driver exited the vehicle and opened the rear doors to assist his companion in carrying a person on a stretcher, with an IV bag resting on their chest, from the van to the Bombardier aircraft. To their disappointment, the individual on the stretcher was covered with a blanket up to their neck, wearing an oxygen mask over their face, and a bouffant cap on their head. No matter how much the supervisor adjusted the camera angle and zoomed in, there was no way to identify the person on the stretcher, though the four of them all suspected it was Lamberti.

"Can you send a copy of these videos to the chairman of the AISI?" Bruno asked, providing her with Acardi's email address.

Once she confirmed they'd be sent, the four left to return to their car. As they walked, Bruno updated Acardi, who reciprocated by sharing what he'd discovered about the ownership of the aircraft.

"The Bombardier is owned by a shell company incorporated in Vanuatu, which is in turn owned by another shell company based in the Cayman Islands. This second company is controlled by a noncitizen trust that uses intermediaries to accept legal and tax documents," Acardi began. "The offshore jurisdictions where these shell companies are established are notorious tax havens that refuse to cooperate with other countries in revealing the beneficial owners. Their reluctance to provide information, combined with the anticipated legal obstacles that the attorneys for the trusts and their intermediaries will present, makes it unlikely that we will ever identify the person who purchased that aircraft."

"Is there any other good news?" Bruno asked. When Acardi said he had none, he said he'd call if they learned anything else, afterward telling the others what was said.

"There must be another way to uncover who's behind this," Donati said.

"Maybe there is. What if our basic assumptions are incorrect?" Bruno suggested.

"Incorrect?"

"We're assuming that the Mafia was hired to kidnap Lamberti for a third party because she holds a vast amount of sensitive intelligence that affects not only Italy but also our allies. That someone wants the information in her head. However, what if the kidnappers aren't interested in that at all, but rather in what she's currently working on?"

"That's an interesting possibility," Donais conceded. "But how would anyone know what she was working on? Lamberti wasn't trusting and didn't confide in anyone, giving them only the minimum information necessary to get the job done. The only exception might be her boss, President Orsini. Perhaps he knows if she was working on something that could have led to her abduction."

"We can ask," Bruno replied. "But from experience, we know she usually kept him in the dark to maintain plausible deniability if there was an investigation into an incident involving her. However, there is someone else who might know."

"Other than the president?"

Bruno nodded. "Yes."

"Who?"

"Franco Zunino."

"Why would confide anything sensitive to her bodyguard?" Donati interjected.

"She trusts him and Villa, and his knowledge would be indirect, not direct," Bruno explained.

"What does that mean?" Donais asked.

"Think back. Zunino was there when Lamberti interrogated the Rivas and uncovered their treachery," Bruno replied.

Bruno, Donati, and Donais were involved with exposing the couple, one of whom was an assassin, while the other worked closely with the Mafia. This person was responsible for numerous deaths as he rose to increasingly prominent positions within the government. Among those victims was Carolina Biagi.

"Zunino and Villa, at Lamberti's direction, took the Rivas to their final resting place which, from what I was told, wasn't a cemetery," Bruno continued.

"That's true," Donati admitted.

"He was also present when Lamberti visited Indro, convincing him on Lamberti's behalf to hack into various computer systems," Bruno added, referring to Indro Montanari, a tech geek who he caught during a robbery. This incident led to Montanari being sent to prison, although Bruno later secured his early release after assisting the then chief inspector in bypassing the sophisticated electronic security at the residence of Federigo Rizzo, whose family had been stealing treasures and money from the Papacy for generations.

"I could go on, but there's a good chance Zunino might know something," Bruno continued.

"We might as well. At this point, all we have is that Lamberti has been taken to Sicily by Sciarra's men," Donati agreed.

"We have nothing to lose by talking to him, and we can drop the doctor off along the way," Donais said.

"Not a chance," Labriola responded. "This is just getting interesting."

Lamberti's estate was the largest in the Parioli area of Rome, an enclave of mansions on magnificent tree-lined streets just north of the Villa Borghese gardens. The 1930s-era residences were magnets for the affluent who wanted to live in the city yet be far enough away from business and commercial areas to have some measure of privacy. The estate occupied one side of a short residential feeder street, with a fifteen-foot-high wall enclosing the five-acre property. A similarly tall wrought-iron gate opened to a gravel driveway that led to the mansion.

Donati stopped the Yukon beside the call box post, pressed the button, and requested to see Zunino. As he spoke, he noticed the camera on the gate post swivel, indicating it was adjusting for a better view of the driver. The gates opened moments later, and Donati drove up the driveway, passing the mansion before parking in the visitor area, which he'd done numerous times in the past. As the four exited the vehicle, they saw Zunino approaching.

"This is unusual," Bruno said to Donati and Donais as the bodyguard approached. His partners also noticed that he wasn't holding a device to wand them, which was standard procedure for all visitors when Lamberti was in residence.

"Come inside and we'll talk," Zunino said when he got within ten feet, waving his right hand for them to follow.

As they walked toward the residence, the trio noticed the absence of a guard with an automatic weapon standing outside the front door. Zunino led them to the first-floor kitchen, asking them to sit at the counter and offering to make them espressos. All accepted.

"I take it that Acardi wants you and your partners investigating the kidnapping," he said while looking at Bruno, who confirmed his guess was correct.

"That's a step in the right direction. You three are better than any of the bureaucrats he has on staff. Who's he?" Zunino asked, pointing to Labriola.

"Ernesto Labriola is assisting us with the investigation," Bruno reluctantly replied, not wanting to reveal to Zunino that he was involved because he was stepping down as the city's coroner and found their investigation more interesting than standing over cadavers.

"How can I help?" The bodyguard asked.

"We reviewed the security footage from the cemetery incident, but we'd like your perspective," Bruno explained.

Zunino recounted what had happened, handing out espressos as he spoke.

"That matches what we were told and what we observed," Bruno said. "We believe the ransom demand is a ruse to buy time. We also suspect they plan to kill Lamberti after extracting information from her. She's too big of a liability to keep alive. If she is released, she'll pursue everyone responsible with all the resources at her disposal."

"Which means finding her quickly is imperative," Zunino stated.

"Since you were always in close proximity to her, we'd like to know what she was working on prior to the kidnapping. We believe it has a direct bearing on why she was abducted."

"The Signora never discussed her business with outsiders or the staff. That said, because I was always in the room when she worked and spoke on the phone, it was impossible not to overhear at least some of her discussions."

"Do you remember her last conversation before she was kidnapped?" Labriola asked, drawing disapproving looks from the trio, who were clearly unhappy that he had inserted himself into the discussion.

"It was with the French Minister of Foreign Affairs. She was planning to travel to Paris to see him, but the meeting was canceled and postponed for a month."

"Do you know why?" Labriola continued, unfazed by the piercing stares from the trio, who didn't want to interrupt Zunino's recollection of what occurred for fear that breaking his concentration might affect his recall of the conversation.

"Please understand that I usually stand by the entry door to her office to place myself between the Signora and a potential attackers. While I never try to listen to her conversations, she speaks in a firm voice that carries a long distance, making it hard not to overhear what's being discussed," he said defensively.

"Understood," Labriola replied.

"After speaking with the minister, she expressed her frustration about the postponement of their meeting, stating that the French needed to embrace the twenty-first century and centralize their intelligence data. I interpreted this as meaning the delay was so the minister could gather more information from one or more intelligence databases."

That's a reasonable assumption," Labriola remarked. "Did she say anything else? It'll be helpful if you could recall her exact words," he added.

The trio exchanged glances, their expressions showing they were impressed with the coroner's line of questioning.

"Our intelligence on the puppeteer's activities will become outdated in thirty days," Zunino said after a moment of reflection. "Those were her exact words."

"The puppeteer?" Labriola asked, wanting to ensure he had heard correctly.

"The Signora often used a codename for someone whose identity she wanted to keep secret; at least, that's what I assumed."

"Is there any way we can access one of her computers to

identify the person she associated with that codename?" Bruno asked, interjecting himself into the questioning.

"As you know, the Signora has two computers equipped with highly advanced encryption and decryption technology."

"I'm aware of that," Bruno replied. "She informed me that the device where she stores sensitive information isn't connected to the internet. That's the computer I want to access."

"It's air-gapped," Zunino clarified. "This means it has no physical or wireless connections to any network, making it virtually unhackable."

"Assuming that I'm sitting in front of it, how do I gain access?"

"You can't. This computer has a second highly sophisticated encryption and decryption program, and only she has the access keys. That makes her the only person who can read those files."

"That's the computer we need to access. As I understand it, the contents of the device connected to the internet were immediately deleted after being read, or transferred to a flash drive and then stored on the air-gapped computer."

"Your understanding is correct."

"I take it you don't know where she keeps the access keys?" Bruno asked, throwing up a Hail Mary.

Zunino shook his head. "She kept that information to herself."

"The puppeteer," Labriola repeated.

"That's what she said."

"Do you know if this person is French, Italian, or of another nationality? Are they male or female?" Donati asked.

"I have no idea," Zunino admitted. "I don't eavesdrop on her discussions. I'm here to protect her, so even though I'm in her office every day, I only catch snippets of her conversations."

After the trio asked a few more questions, the four returned to their car. On the way, Bruno updated Acardi.

"She was going to Paris to meet the French Minister of Foreign Affairs?" Acardi said.

"That's what Zunino told us," Bruno confirmed.

"Then you'd better come to my office. If there's a possibility that your investigation will take you to foreign soil, you'll need to meet my counterpart in the AISE. He has assets outside the country and a database that may be useful for your investigation."

"That could be very helpful," Bruno agreed. "We'll be there in less than fifteen minutes. By the way, we might have added a new member to our team."

"Who?"

"Labriola."

"The city's coroner? Why?"

"Because we can't seem to get rid of him."

The joint headquarters for the AISI and AISE were at Palazzo Dante 25, which was 3.2 miles from Lamberti's mansion. The quadrangular five-story building, with a large central atrium, was constructed in the early twentieth century, housing several government agencies until it was redesignated in 2012 as the unitary headquarters for Italian intelligence.

Donati stopped the GMC Yukon beside the guardhouse and in front of a row of bollards that blocked the road leading to the building. Each cylindrical steel post weighed twelve hundred pounds, extended thirty inches into the ground, and could stop a fifteen-thousand-pound vehicle traveling fifty mph. He told the uniformed security person they were there to see Dante Acardi and handed her four IDs. The guard checked the names against the computerized access list on her iPad and, after asking Donati to roll down the rear window to match the individuals in the vehicle with the photos on their IDs, gave a thumbs up to her partner who had been watching them through the guardhouse's bulletproof glass window. Moments later, the bollards lowered.

"A space has been reserved for you in the VIP parking section. Do you know where that is?" She asked Donati.

The investigator replied that he had only been to the visitor parking area.

"Instead of turning right when you enter the garage, continue straight ahead to the barrier arm. Someone will be there to guide you to the correct parking space and escort you inside."

Even though the investigators had visited Acardi's office several times, they were unaware of the VIP parking spaces, although its existence should have been obvious given the visitors' area was an unkind distance from the entrance. Now that Donati knew, instead of following the large signs that led him in a descending spiral past employee parking to an area four levels below the building, he continued straight until he reached the barrier arm, which had been raised. Twenty yards further, a uniformed security officer instructed him to park in the space to his left. The officer then escorted the four into the lobby, where they saw Acardi waiting with their visitors' badges.

"Before you meet my counterpart," Acardi began, pulling Bruno aside, "I need you to explain in more detail—beyond just that we can't seem to get rid of him—why Rome's coroner is now acting as an investigator."

"He's up to speed on what we know," Bruno replied, going on to explain that Labriola had been present when he and his partners discussed the kidnapping and the significance of the tattoos on the three corpses, which seemed to implicate Sciarra as the person behind the abduction. "He was also there when we spoke with Zunino."

"You're giving me acid reflux. So far, all I'm hearing is that Labriola is a good listener."

"When we spoke with Zunino, he asked surprisingly insightful questions, which led to the discovery that Lamberti assigned a codename to the person she and the French minister were discussing.

"You told me about the codename when you left the mansion, but you didn't mention that Labriola played a role in uncovering this information. I know you, Mauro. You're keeping him around for a reason. Why?"

"If you think about it, a coroner is essentially an investigator. They uncover facts through the autopsy process, toxicology reports, and forensic evidence to determine how a person died. These conclusions must withstand rigorous scrutiny in court, where even the smallest error could result in a guilty individual being set free. Labriola has been around law enforcement long enough to know the questions we typically ask, and he can contribute a few of his own. Plus, he has a folksy demeanor that makes people trust him."

"A folksy coroner."

"He's good, Dante. And, given the urgency with which we need to find Lamberti, we can use all the help we can get."

Labriola grinned upon hearing Bruno's comments, the team also having quietly approached Bruno and Acardi to listen to their conversation.

"We've worked together in the past," Donais volunteered.

"I don't think that dodging bullets qualifies as working together. Nevertheless, if you want him on board, I won't stand in the way. If anyone asks, he's a consultant whose insights have proven helpful in the past."

"A consulting coroner," Bruno said.

"Don't go there," Acardi responded as they entered the elevator, went to the top floor, and entered the conference room next to Acardi's office, where he sat in the chair at the head of a long rectangular table with a middle-aged man on to his left and a man and woman of similar age to his right.

He introduced the man to his left as Maurizio Baudo, his administrative assistant, and to his immediate right as Renzo D'Angelo, the Chairman of the Agenzia Informazioni e Sicurezza Esterna (AISE), Italy's foreign intelligence service responsible for protecting national security, primarily through the use of foreign agents. The woman beside him was his administrative assistant, Bianca Ferrara.

Acardi began the meeting by introducing the trio, stating

that his agency had previously utilized the services of BD&D Investigations.

"Your reputation precedes you," D'Angelo remarked, having heard of their past exploits. "However, I'm not familiar with the fourth member of your team."

"Allow me to introduce Ernesto Labriola," Acardi interjected before anyone else could speak. "He's a consultant for BD&D Investigations with a niche expertise that we can explore further when we have more time," he added, effectively cutting off any questions about Labriola's presence.

D'Angelo nodded in agreement.

"Let's start by reviewing what the investigators have uncovered so far," he said, turning it over to Bruno, who began by discussing the tattoos and stomach contents of the three kidnappers.

"And this led to your conclusion the deceased were members of the Agrigento Mafia, which has been ruled for decades by Dante Sciarra?" D'Angelo asked.

"That's correct," Bruno confirmed.

"He would have needed the Commission's permission for this kidnapping since it took place in Rome. There are serious consequences if a family operates in another's territory."

"That aligns with our conclusion," Bruno agreed. "However, we don't believe that Pia Lamberti's abduction was intended for Sciarra's benefit. If it were, the Commission wouldn't have granted their permission. Allowing it would be a direct affront to the family overseeing Rome, indirectly signaling to other families that they believed Sciarra had more capable soldiers than his Roman counterpart. Regardless, whoever engaged Sciarra would have paid a substantial sum to secure the Commission's approval and that of the family overseeing Rome for his soldiers to operate, even briefly, on their turf."

"That makes sense," D'Angelo conceded.

"We also know that the aircraft used in the abduction is very expensive and owned by a trust through a series of shell corporations," Acardi added. "Given that the Mafia is generally averse to showing such opulence—since doing so attracts unwanted attention from the government—we concluded that the entity that hired Sciarra also owns this plane."

"Define very expensive," D'Angelo said.

"Google lists a factory-delivered Bombardier Global 8000 at around eighty-two million dollars. This price can increase significantly based on aircraft performance enhancements, such as adding extended range capabilities and customizing the interior," Acardi stated. "Documents we have accessed show that the plane which landed at the Ciampino and Catania airports was purchased from the company's manufacturing plant in Saint-Laurent, Quebec, Canada. The buyer was an offshore shell company, making it difficult to determine the individual owner. As of thirty minutes ago, the plane is in a hangar at Catania Airport."

"Your working theory is that Dante Sciarra is holding Pia Lamberti somewhere in the Agrigento province of Sicily," D'Angelo remarked.

"Yes," Bruno responded.

"As I remember, that's a vast area with many towns and villages."

"It's a twelve-hundred-square-mile region with forty-two communes," Acardi added.

"However, while she could be anywhere within the province, we believe that Sciarra will want to keep her close. Therefore, we're starting our investigation in the city of Agrigento," Bruno stated.

"That makes sense, but you should consider that she might be held in a nearby town, where outsiders—specifically you and your team—will stand out."

"Point taken."

"I don't need to remind everyone that it's crucial to keep this situation under wraps," Acardi admonished. "If news of this kidnapping leaks, it will alarm the intelligence agencies of our allies, as Lamberti knew many of their deepest secrets, including the identities of numerous covert agents. It would take a significant amount of time for these agencies to trust us with their secrets again. That would be a catastrophe for our intelligence apparatus. Moreover, it won't be long before her abductors start their interrogation, if they haven't already. We need to act quickly to locate Lamberti and rectify this situation."

"What's your definition of rectify?"

"If she can't be rescued, the investigators have been instructed to kill her."

"Will they do it?" D'Angelo asked.

"Ask them," Acardi replied, with all eyes now on Bruno.

"Only if we determine that her rescue is impossible," he said. "However, that determination may be posthumous."

"Meaning you four gave it your all but fell short, requiring the use of four body bags to return home," D'Angelo stated, understanding what he meant.

Bruno nodded.

"You have my full support. I should add that none of Lamberti's abductors or those who assist them, if they are apprehended, will ever see the inside of a courtroom. No one wants to answer questions in court as to what Lamberti does or has done for this government. We're not part of the Ministry of Justice. Therefore, feel free to put a bullet into them without consequence, rendition sites are expensive," the AISE chairman said as he stood and, with his assistant, left the conference room.

During the discussion, Maurizio Baudo listened attentively and refrained from participating in the dialogue, as he was not there to offer advice. Instead, Acardi had brought him to the meeting to ensure they were on the same page with what needed to be done to support the investigative team.

"Since we'll be starting in Agrigento, do you have any suggestions on the best way to find Sciarra?" Bruno asked.

"You won't have to worry. Your usual bull in a China shop approach will catch his attention."

"We'll be subtle in our search."

"Subtlety is not in your nature. As I mentioned earlier, he will find you. Ernesto," Acardi said, shifting his focus to Labriola. "Unlike my investigators, you possess a great deal of common sense. It would be wise for you to stay in Rome, enjoy a well-deserved break from a lifetime of public service, and embrace retirement. Associating with these three will put your health and longevity at significant risk, especially since they will be facing a hardened Mafioso and his men."

"I was terrified during the gun battle in my morgue, expecting to die at any moment Because of that near-death experience, I wasn't happy to see these three only hours after the arrival of several bodies who'd been killed by gunfire because, as you pointed out, they seem to attract trouble."

"But you changed your mind."

"I've changed my perspective. I'm unsure which is worse: aging gracefully in retirement until I'm put in a pine box or working for the greater good in another capacity. Being involved in this investigation has provided me with a new outlook. I'm not suicidal, but if I'm going to die, I want it to be for a reason other than old age, where all I have to look forward to each day are three meals, meaningless conversations with other seniors, and being utterly bored.

The truth is, I don't know how to relax because I've worked my entire adult life. I believe I can make a substantial contribution to this investigation and assist in finding Pia Lamberti. I might make a critical observation or offer an alternative perspective that hasn't been considered. So, despite my fear of bullets and the possibility of ending up on one of my tables due to my involvement in this case, I'd like to stay."

The trio, taken aback by what Labriola had said, didn't object.

"Sciarra is a killer. Once he realizes you four are after Lamberti, he'll come at you with everything he has. Worse, you'll be in his territory where, if you get into trouble, no one will lift a finger to help for fear of offending this mobster. You're not as young as you once were and can't move as quickly as this trio. In other words, in a confrontation, you're the most likely to end up dead," Acardi stated.

"I understand, but I don't want to be found dead while watching TV with a bowl of pasta in front of me. I want to contribute my inquisitive and observational skills to their efforts and help find Pia Lamberti. I want some excitement in my life before I go."

"I can promise these three will give you all the gusto you can handle. Will your successor assume your responsibilities?"

"He'll be happy to take charge."

"Can you use a weapon?" Acardi asked after pulling Labriola aside.

"I've fired guns and rifles when I've gone hunting with others, but that's usually only every four or five years. I never hit what I aimed at because I've had no formal weapons training; I go on these hunts mainly to get some exercise rather than to actually shoot something."

"My advice is not to stand behind the investigators if you're firing a weapon. We need them. Do they know about your shooting skills?"

"No."

"Good. This may not be the best time to tell them. But heaven knows these three could use someone as smart as you on their team. With your help, they'll have a better chance of finding Lamberti," Acardi stated.

"We appreciate your confidence in us," Bruno said, the sarcasm evident in his voice, having heard only the last part of their conversation while walking toward them.

Acardi ignored the jab. "Before I knew Labriola was joining you, and considering what you're about to face, I asked someone else if they would accompany you. They agreed," he said as he took out his cellphone from his jacket pocket and requested the person on the other end to come to the conference room.

Bruno started to object, feeling that adding a fifth person would only slow them down. However, he stopped mid-sentence when a familiar face entered the room.

"Hunkler," Donais said with a smile.

"With his agreement and the Pope's blessing, I've asked Colonel Hunkler to join you," Acardi said, as the trio enthusiastically welcomed the man who had saved their lives in Abu Dhabi and Rome.

Colonel Andrin Hunkler stood at an athletic six feet two inches tall, with a ramrod-straight posture, salt-and-pepper crewcut hair, and piercing brown eyes. A former member of the Italian military, he served with NATO's International Security Assistance Force (ISAF) in Afghanistan before becoming the Commandant of the Vatican's Swiss Guard, which protects the pope and discreetly conducts investigations on his behalf.

"The director believes you won't be safe unless I accompany you," Hunkler said as he joined the group.

"Unfortunately, our previous associations reinforce that belief," Donati replied, prompting a smile from his partners.

"Where do we stand?" the colonel asked.

"We believe that Lamberti was kidnapped and taken to Agrigento, Sicily, or a nearby town or village by those working for Dante Sciarra, the Mafia chieftain of that province," Bruno began. He went on to explain the reasoning behind this assumption and their belief that the ransom note was an attempt to buy time. "We need to rescue her or, failing that, kill Lamberti before she's tortured or drugged by her abductors to reveal what she knows," he concluded, believing the colonel wanted a concise explanation devoid of hyperbole.

"Due to the three deceased men he left behind, Sciarra will think we ran their fingerprints and faces through national databases, identified them, and subsequently connected them to him. However, I doubt he would believe or even consider that their body art could connect him to the abduction," Hunkler stated.

Everyone agreed.

"Also, consider that the extensive resources used in the kidnapping of Lamberti indicate it was well-funded. Since kidnappers usually commit abductions to acquire wealth, this expensive operation involving perps from Agrigento seems to further confirm Sciarra's involvement, as the Mafia likely faces few financial constraints."

"That's a valid point," Labriola said, as the others also agreed with Hunkler's statement.

"If I were in his position, and believing what he assumes we know, I would expect a rescue attempt before the seventy-two-hour ransom deadline. Since he anticipates that agents employed by the Italian government will try to rescue Lamberti, our arrival in Catania, or anywhere else in Sicily, won't go unnoticed," Hunkler continued.

"Because we're arriving by private aircraft, we could easily pass for wealthy tourists visiting Taormina, which is less than an hour away," Donais stated. "And since we won't be using our real names on the passenger manifest, how will Sciarra know that a team of investigators is on board the aircraft?"

"Director Acardi informed me that we will have access to Lamberti's plane, which presumably has government registration."

Acardi nodded his assumption as correct.

"Someone in Sciarra's position has had decades to build a network of contacts, especially at transport hubs. He'll deduce that those arriving on a government plane—regardless of whether the aircraft can be directly linked to Lamberti—are not tourists; they're there to investigate her kidnapping. If he possesses the informant network I expect, he will pursue us with everything he has, choosing the time and place to strike. In his province, there will be a multitude of locations he can select for us to die quietly and be buried someplace where we'll never be found. Therefore, Director, where will the Quick Reaction Force (QRF) be stationed if we need to extract quickly? The speed of their arrival could mean the difference between life and death," Hunkler said as he turned to face Acardi.

Acardi cleared his throat. "There is no QRF. For obvious reasons, no one but this group and the president will know that Lamberti has been kidnapped. Consequently, you'll be on your own from the moment you arrive in Sicily," Acardi clarified.

"In other words, we're entering an environment where locals and law enforcement won't assist us for fear of being killed by this mobster. And since we'll be in his territory as soon as we land, our survival depends on avoiding his men long enough to locate and retrieve Lamberti, whose whereabouts could be anywhere in the province. We think."

"That's the mission. I should add it's not too late for anyone to back out. Once you land in Catania, you're committed," Acardi replied.

"And we're returning Lamberti to Rome on her aircraft, not a government plane sent to retrieve us?" Bruno asked.

"That's correct. No one outside our group must know she has been kidnapped. Sending a government aircraft would compromise that secrecy. I cannot allow that to happen because, as I mentioned, not informing our allies about her abduction would be considered a serious breach of trust."

"Most Italian military units don't see as much action as you three," Colonel Hunkler remarked, earning a smirk from Bruno and nods of agreement from Donati and Donais. "I'll only make one promise," he added, locking eyes with Acardi. "No matter what Sciarra throws our way, if Lamberti is in Sicily, we're not leaving without her."

Labriola's expression during the discussion resembled that of a deer in headlights; he seemed surprised by the unemotional tone of the conversation and what he perceived as Hunkler's casual attitude toward the dangers they faced.

"While you're in Sicily, I'll be in Paris meeting with the French Minister of Foreign Affairs to discuss his conversation with

Lamberti and what he knows about the person she codenamed 'the puppeteer,'" Acardi said. "This means we'll be conducting parallel investigations and exchanging information to ensure we're all on the same page."

"Being Parisian and familiar with how our culture reacts to foreigners conducting investigations in our country, I can unequivocally say that you will need a French equivalent of Hunkler to serve as your intermediary," Donais stated. "Otherwise, you are wasting your time. While the French minister knows Lamberti and they have developed a degree of trust—or he wouldn't be discussing an exchange of information—he does not have a relationship with you. In my country, trust is earned and not simply granted based on one's position. Until that trust is established, the minister will press for information about what Lamberti may have shared with you regarding her work. In return, he will provide you with only a small portion of what he discussed with her to keep you engaged while making you believe he has revealed too much. He will also likely make an insincere promise to pass along any new information he learns and ask the same of you."

"I agree, which is why I'm going to ask a French government official with an impeccable reputation to help me."

"Edgard Bence," Donais said, quickly deducing the person Acardi wanted.

"It is," he confirmed.

Everyone except Labriola was familiar with the former border surveillance officer and shift supervisor at the Côte d'Azur Airport in Nice, France, a position he held before helping the trio and Hunkler retrieve French masterpieces that the Nazis had stolen during World War II. The discovery and return of these artworks, previously thought to be destroyed or lost, led to his promotion to major and his appointment as the head of the Mission for Research and Restitution of Spoliated Cultural Property, which was responsible for repatriating artwork looted during the war.

"Bence and I are having dinner, but I didn't mention it was more than a casual meeting between friends because I was concerned our call might be monitored," Acardi said. "That brings up another issue. To keep our conversations confidential, we'll use these." He went to the credenza, took out five cellphones and chargers from a large leather satchel he had previously brought into the room, and handed them out. "Press the green button to encrypt the conversation and the red button to speak openly to anyone who doesn't have the decryption chip specific to this series of phones, which are strictly controlled. If you accidentally press the green button, all the other side will hear is noise. Besides the six of us, only Bence will have a compatible device."

"Weapons?" Hunkler asked.

"You'll collect those from the armory in the basement. Get whatever else you need from the tactical equipment room. Don't worry about discarding your weapons; they've had their factory serial numbers removed, making them untraceable. Lamberti's aircraft also contains a wide variety of weaponry hidden in the ceiling and side panels. The pilot can show you how to access them. You'll also need these," he said, handing out five envelopes. Inside each was a stack of euros. Lastly, he took a credit card from his pocket and handed it to Bruno, who was surprised to see his name on the card.

"We have a stack of nameless debit cards and the equipment to stamp whatever name we need on them," Acardi explained. "Afterward, we activate the card with the credit agency. Use it at your discretion, including getting additional cash. Since it's a government card, it's coded to bypass daily ATM limits. The PIN is four zeros. Please be prudent, as the money comes out of my meager budget," Acardi said as he stood to escort them to the armory.

"I never asked Labriola if he could fire a weapon," Bruno said as they left the room, with the coroner following behind and out of earshot.

"We spoke about that," Acardi said.

"And?" Bruno prompted.

"He has fired a weapon in the past, but he's not on the same level as the rest of your team. Hunkler may want to give him a few tips."

"That bad?"

"Not if you're Sciarra's men."

Chapter Four

Pia Lamberti remained sedated until she reached her final destination, where a drug was injected into her IV line to bring her back to consciousness. Upon awakening, she looked around and noticed the steel cot in the otherwise empty room, where her four limbs were secured to each corner with leather straps. To her left stood two men. One was in his mid-twenties, with the physique of a bodybuilder. He wore khaki slacks and a white short-sleeve shirt that looked as though it might tear under the strain of his bulging biceps. To his left was Dante Sciarra. The sixty-four-year-old Sicilian Mafioso, whose haggard, rail-thin figure suggested he was suffering from hunger, was five feet eleven inches tall with thinning gray hair, intense brown eyes, and a joyless facial expression that made it seem as if he was perpetually stressed.

Suffering from hyperthyroidism, which caused an overproduction of thyroid hormone and accelerated his metabolism, he struggled to gain weight and appeared anorexic, the affliction also causing him to experience occasional hand tremors. While various treatments, such as radioactive iodine and surgical procedures, could help his illness, he refused them, fearing that someone might try to poison or kill him during the treatment—a reasonable assumption given his profession and one he confessed he'd do to a rival if their roles were reversed. Therefore, he long ago accepted his medical malady and resulting physical appearance.

"I'm happy to see you're unharmed," the Mafioso said.

"Dante Sciarra," Lamberti replied.

"I'm flattered that you know me."

"I make it a habit to memorize the faces of all the degenerates in your profession."

"I'll attribute your American-like rudeness to the drugs," the Mafioso responded in a calm voice, devoid of emotion.

"I've moved past that confusion," Lamberti continued unabated. "I'm surprised by your lack of understanding regarding the impossible situation you created for yourself by kidnapping me."

"An impossible situation? Only one of us can claim that. Look around. You're my captive, and once I get what I want, this room is where you'll die. That's an impossible situation."

"You're ignoring the consequences of my abduction. When the government realizes you're behind this, they will pressure the Commission to hand you over, interfering with the organization's daily criminal endeavors and severely impacting their revenue streams until they comply. What do you think will happen after that? Let me answer that for you. They'll gladly sacrifice you to protect themselves and the other families. That's the predicament you're in."

"It might have been, although we've weathered government reprisals in the past with little impact since they never last long, had the Commission not sanctioned your kidnapping," Sciarra said, surprising Lamberti.

"Getting permission for this must have been difficult because abducting or killing a government official—especially the wife of an ex-president—would trigger an immense wave of public condemnation. This would force the president to take harsh action against your organization. Moreover, even if the repercussions were short-lived, the financial consequences would still be significant. The Commission would know this. Therefore, the payment to persuade the other families must have been substantial."

"The monetary compensation was substantial," Sciarra

admitted. "Since you seem fully awake now, perhaps this is a good time to begin our conversation," the Mafioso suggested as he stepped closer.

"What would you like to discuss?"

"What you and the French Minister of Foreign Affairs know about the person you've codenamed the 'Puppeteer,' whom I refer to in my inner circle as 'Opus' for the sake of anonymity. I'll also need the names of those with whom you've shared this information."

"I'm not a very forthcoming person."

"I've heard that. I will also require the locations of the paper and electronic files that you or anyone with even a tangential knowledge of his activities have compiled, so I can obtain and destroy this information."

"If that's what you were hired to do, then your client has paid an enormous sum for nothing because you won't get even a sliver of information from me."

"We'll see about that."

"How did you know I'd be at the cemetery this morning?"

"Let me begin by saying that you weren't my initial target. Your kidnapping became my focus when I learned about the annual visit to your lover's grave. If I hadn't discovered that, I would have targeted the French Foreign Minister instead. It would have been much easier to abduct him on his way to the office than to breach your estate."

"Why is that?"

"Unlike him, you don't have a set schedule for when you leave for the office. In fact, you rarely leave your mansion, which poses a considerable risk as the information I received indicates that you have substantial security, most of whom are ex-military, and likely a safe room. This setup would make any attack time-consuming and allow responding law enforcement to surround and apprehend my men."

"And once you learned of my annual visit?"

"The decision to choose you instead of the minister was clear.

I was informed that you preferred to keep a low profile and wanted to arrive and leave before the cemetery staff began their workday. Consequently, you came with minimal security. However, I was not aware that you would be armed and that you were quite an expert marksperson."

"If you discovered my annual visit and the details of my security, and are aware of the minister's schedule, then you must have an informant in both governments."

"That is a logical assumption, and as it turns out, it is indeed true."

"Who is your client?"

"Ultimately, it is the person you've codenamed the 'Puppeteer.'"

Lamberti looked at him with a questioning expression, curious about why he used the word *ultimately*. "That's a codename that very few people know. Who told you about it?"

"Are you asking who my informant is? I'll leave that question unanswered, but I am curious as to why you chose that particular name."

"It's more of a descriptor than a name. What little we know suggests that he orchestrates and directs others to achieve specific objectives while remaining unseen. Like a puppeteer, he manipulates from the shadows."

"You used the pronoun *him* once and *he* twice. How can you be certain that this puppeteer is a man?"

"Because you said earlier that I had given him a codename."

Sciarra smiled and shook his head. "The careless mistakes of an old man."

"He must have an enormous amount of confidence in your abilities. Otherwise, why would he pay what is arguably a fortune to the Commission and hire a Sicilian mobster from the Agrigento province for a kidnapping in Rome? It would have been easier and cheaper to engage a group of professionals from that city instead."

"It came down to trusting my ability to successfully abduct and interrogate you."

"Since his faith in you seems to be significant—which is something usually earned—I'm guessing you had a preexisting relationship," Lamberti pointed out.

"He was my classmate."

"Classmate?"

"His family lived in Siculiana, a small fishing village twelve miles away. Because the nearest middle school was in Agrigento, he came here, and we became friends, remaining so for over half a century."

"Is he a fellow Mafioso?"

"That wasn't his calling. While I took over the family business, succeeding my father as the head of the family and taking his seat on the Commission, he moved to Rome in pursuit of great wealth and became exceedingly rich."

"What's his name?"

Sciarra shook his head, implying that her question would go unanswered. "Given our positions and the reason you're here, I'm the one who asks the questions."

"Why does it matter if you're going to kill me?"

"Because I'll take pleasure in knowing that the great Pia Lamberti will die without having all her questions answered or learning the identities of everyone involved in her kidnapping and murder, especially the person she coined the puppeteer. Moving on and returning to your particular circumstance, tell me what you know about him and where you and the minister keep these files."

"That will never happen," Lamberti retorted confidently, making it clear she wouldn't cooperate.

"Then you'll be tortured until I get my answers. No one can withstand pain indefinitely. It's also important to think about the consequences that follow. When I have what I want and you're of no further use, your body will be thrown into a hole in a remote patch of earth where you'll never be found, or tied to a heavy chain and shoved into the water miles from shore. In both situations, you'll be alive until you suffocate or drown. You're an intelligent woman. What's the point of a prolonged and painful death when it's inevitable that you'll eventually reveal the information to me?"

When she didn't respond, Sciarra knelt beside the cot, leaned over Lamberti, and looked her in the eyes. "I have an offer," he whispered. "In return for shortening the time it takes to get what I need, I'll make your death painless by injecting you with a drug that will gently put you into an eternal sleep. Afterward, you have my word that I'll have you embalmed and your coffin brought to the Campo Verano Cemetery with a notarized note from you requesting to be buried in the space you purchased beside your lover's grave and not in the crypt with your late husband. You and Carolina will be together forever. Isn't that better than fish tearing away your flesh in the ocean or worms feasting on your remains? Don't you think Carolina would have pleaded with you to stay by her side forever?"

"Being my best operative, and in many ways tougher than me, she would have emphatically told me to decline your offer because, if my prolonged death gives others the time needed to uncover the puppeteer's identity and put an end to their illegal activities, then that's the price my position requires me to pay."

"You will regret that decision," Sciarra said as he stood and nodded to the guard, who removed a stun gun from a holder in the small of his back and, stepping forward, fired two high-voltage electrodes into her torso.

Sciarra's classmate was sitting in the living room of his twelve-thousand-square-foot residence at the top of Rome's tallest building when his cellphone chimed. He put down the twelve-hundred-dollar Gurkha Black Dragon cigar in his hand and answered on the third ring, afterward listening as Maurizio Baudo gave a detailed summary of the meeting he had attended in the AISI conference room and mentioning the addition of Labriola and Bence to the investigative team.

"Why the city's coroner?"

"Acardi included him at the request of the investigators because they found he asked astute questions."

"Including him suggests they need extra help and are grasping at straws to obtain it. What do you know about BD&D Investigations and Colonel Hunkler?" The classmate asked.

Baudo shared information about the trio's background that he discovered on their website, and Lamberti's connection to the investigative agency and their notable successes, such as discovering and preventing a terror attack on the Quirinal Palace, which saved the lives of the president and the heads of state he was hosting.

"Impressive. What can you tell me about Colonel Hunkler?"

"He was a former officer in the Italian army who'd taken part in previous BD&D investigations."

"Ex-military. He's the muscle protecting the others. Is there anything else?"

"The investigators informed Acardi that Dante Sciarra had kidnapped Lamberti. Since he is the head of the Mafia in the Agrigento province, it's presumed he took her there. They're traveling to Sicily to rescue her."

"You could have mentioned that earlier," the classmate exclaimed, his tone harsh and clearly expressing his displeasure that Baudo hadn't prioritized this information.

"I'm still gathering data to determine what they know and what is conjecture," he replied.

"I want information in real-time, not when you think it's appropriate."

"Understood."

"How could they reach this conclusion in just a few hours?"

Baudo explained that it was a combination of the distinctive tattoos on the bodies of Sciarra's men, along with discovering the owners of a very expensive jet had paid hefty fees to takeoff from Catania, land in Rome, and return. "The investigators are heading to Catania and then driving to Agrigento to search for her. Meanwhile, Acardi is meeting with France's Minister of Foreign Affairs to find out what he and Lamberti were discussing, as the minister was the last person to speak with her before the kidnapping."

"Are the investigators taking a commercial or private plane from Rome to Catania?"

"Acardi has provided them with the use of Lamberti's plane while he takes one of the agency's aircraft to Paris," Baudo added.

"Give me the tail numbers of their aircraft. I'll get their arrival times and handle both situations."

After the call ended, Baudo reached out to the Civil Aviation Authority to obtain the requested flight plans and tail numbers. Since the request came from the office of the AISI chairman, he received the information within ten minutes. He then passed it on to his classmate, who subsequently called Sciarra to inform him of the investigative team's estimated arrival time at the VIP terminal in Catania, where private jets disembark their passengers.

"We cannot allow them to ask questions in your backyard, not only because it could alert others to what has happened, but also because, according to Baudo, this group of investigators has an impressive track record of solving difficult crimes. Therefore, kill them as quickly as possible and make it appear to be an accident," the classmate stated. "Do you have any ideas since they'll soon be in Sicily?"

"The road from Catania to Agrigento has treacherous stretches with frequent hairpin turns as it winds through the hills and mountain villages outside this city. Cars have been known to go over the edge and tumble to the valley below. The fact that the drivers are from Rome and unfamiliar with the driving conditions in the area adds to the believability of the accident," Sciarra replied.

"It's critical there be no witnesses. Since the investigators are from Rome and Milan, we don't want the national police to investigate their deaths. We need to keep this matter local," the classmate stated.

"The car accident won't involve the use of weapons."

"Since Lamberti is believed to be in Agrigento, you need to

interrogate her quickly to find out what she knows and dispose of the body before the government decides they can no longer keep her disappearance a secret and begins using all available resources to search for her."

"On that, we agree. The benzodiazepine will take effect in about fifteen minutes, after which I'll start the interrogation," Sciarra replied, referring to the drug clinically known as Versed. Used by the CIA to influence a prisoner's state of mind during questioning, it made the interrogatee more compliant and less able to lie when answering questions, with the beneficial side effect of the recipient having no memory of their interrogation.

"On another subject, I need a sniper in Paris on short notice. There will be two contracts," the classmate stated.

"I may have someone, but before they commit, they'll want to know targets, as well as when and where the hits will occur," Sciarra said, familiar with the details required for a contract killing.

"The targets are two government officials: one French and one Italian."

"Who?" Sciarra asked, already certain of the answer.

"The French Minister of Foreign Affairs and Dante Acardi."

"Sweet Mother of God, Corrado," he exclaimed, addressing his classmate by his first name. "You must realize the DGSE will fiercely investigate the minister's death," he said, referring to the Directorate-General for External Security, France's version of the CIA, "and the AISE will be working alongside them looking into Acardi's killing. Our assassin isn't invisible, and when police look at every security camera within a mile or more of the murders, afterward running those feeds through both government's facial recognition programs, they'll find him. This also means I will be implicated, as he'll give me up to make a deal."

"We won't let that happen."

Sciarra grasped what his classmate was inferring. "You want me to kill him following the assassinations?"

"This is the only way to protect us. I know I've put you in a difficult position and what you're undertaking is a huge risk, but I don't have a choice. Offer the assassin $1,000,000 for each hit. I can't imagine anyone refusing that amount."

"The assassination of a French minister will create an anger that won't easily fade. The French people will demand someone's head."

"Which we'll give them. As I said, I have no choice. I got careless, and Lamberti caught my mistake and told the minister. Subsequently, they began looking in an entirely new direction and gathering incontrovertible data that will expose us," the classmate stated.

"I understand the minister and Lamberti, but why kill Acardi?" Sciarra asked. "Are we taking an unnecessary risk?"

"Not if we assume that the Minister of Foreign Affairs tells him what he and Lamberti knew. That makes him as dangerous as her. Besides, he's in intelligence, which the public understands comes with an inherent risk of physical harm. He won't be considered an innocent like the French minister."

Sciarra agreed.

"Additionally, ensure the destruction of the information collected by the minister and Lamberti. This is crucial."

"I understand the situation. I'll arrange for the hits, but I have to believe that erasing information residing in the government databases of countries as sophisticated as France and Italy will be extremely difficult."

"Not if Lamberti tells you where the data is located and how to access it," the classmate replied. "I know I'm asking a lot from you, but don't forget about the money and power that will come from our success. Once this is over, you'll be worth more than the combined wealth of every family on the commission."

Unbeknownst to his classmate, Sciarra took a deep breath to calm his anxiety before delving into specifics. "You said short notice. When do you need the sniper?"

"Today, when Acardi goes to the minister's office at 37 Quai d'Orsay. I'll update you once I find out the time."

Sciarra wrote the address on the notepad in front of him.

"My informant says this minister is a stickler for following protocol and will greet Acardi outside the ministry building and escort him to his office, just as he does with all arriving foreign dignitaries, weather permitting. Therefore, they'll need to be killed during this greeting while they're in close proximity to one another."

"I'll inform him," Sciarra said.

"How will you get rid of the sniper?"

"I'll handle it the same way I have in the past when I don't want witnesses. One of my men will accompany him, ostensively to provide the offshore account where their money is held following verification of the assassinations. Once Acardi and the minister are killed, he'll eliminate our loose end. When the police find the sniper's body alongside his rifle, they won't try too hard to find his killer."

After speaking with his classmate, the Sicilian mobster called two of his men to his office and explained what needed to be done, emphasizing they needed to create a believable accident that killed the investigative team, and providing them with their estimated arrival time in Catania. Sciarra then handed one of them photos of the five that were taken off the internet. "An associate at the airport will let me know the make, model, and color of the vehicle they're driving, as well as the time they leave the rental agency. I can't emphasize enough that their deaths must appear to be an accident. Therefore, there will be no bullet or knife wounds, or anything else that would suggest a killing," he warned the men before sending them on their way.

The two soldiers left Sciarra's compound in their black H2 Hummer, driving ten miles from the mobster's house and parking at a scenic overlook alongside the roadway, where they waited for Sciarra to give them a description of the vehicle carrying the investigators along with their departure time from the car rental agency. The two had chosen a dangerous stretch of highway near Favara, a small town not far from Agrigento, which would be a likely site for a fatal accident. What they had planned would result in the death of the investigators, while making it look like a driver who was unfamiliar with the roadway made a critical driving error that resulted in five casualties.

Chapter Five

Acardi's plane landed at Orly Airport one hour and twenty-three minutes after takeoff, which was a half hour faster than commercial flights, as government aircraft received priority for takeoffs and landings. Once on the ground, the pilot was directed to a section of the tarmac reserved for VIP aircraft, where a limousine awaited to take the AISI chairman to the Ministry of Foreign Affairs, a drive that typically took about forty minutes at that time of day.

As the limousine approached the Seine River, Acardi called Bruno to let him know he was almost there and would call again after the meeting to share what he had learned. Meanwhile, the investigators, who had already landed in Catania, were en route to Agrigento when they received Acardi's call. Bruno placed his phone on speaker so that everyone in the vehicle could hear their conversation.

"I've been meaning to ask how you plan to convince the minister to share what he and Lamberti were working on and show you his files. Given his important position, he might recommend you speak with her instead. This assumes he doesn't inquire why you're seeing him without Lamberti calling to arrange the meeting, which would be a diplomatic way of asking if she knows you're there," Labriola said.

"That assumption hasn't escaped my attention."

"What's your response?"

"Unless anyone has a better suggestion, I was going to say that Lamberti is in a sensitive debrief with a defector for the next day or two, and possibly longer, and is unavailable to speak with him. However, because of the importance of what they were discussing, she asked me to get a preview of what he was going to bring to her attention so she could integrate his data into hers, ensuring they were aligned and saving time in their future meeting."

"I like it. Although on the thin side, it's a plausible explanation," Donais said.

"A question. How did you get the meeting with the minister?" Donati asked. "You have nothing to do with foreign policy."

"President Orsini asked our Minister of Foreign Affairs to set it up. The French ministry, although curious as to why a domestic intelligence chief wanted to see their foreign minister and not my counterpart, granted the request as a courtesy and, I suspect, because they were curious about what I had to say. I'll find out soon enough," Acardi stated upon seeing the ministry building in the distance, after which the call ended.

The Ministry of Foreign Affairs was on the Quai d'Orsay, which was on the Rive Gauche or the left bank of the Seine River, opposite the Place de la Concorde. A quay, sometimes called a wharf, is a structure built parallel to a waterway's bank. In the 7th arrondissement, one of twenty districts that administratively partition Paris, the ministry is one of several French national institutions and tourist attractions, such as the Eiffel Tower and the Musée d'Orsay, that permeate the arrondissement. It's also been an upper-crust residential area since the seventeenth century, with the average home going for around eighteen hundred dollars a square foot.

The ministry's three-story headquarters was built between 1844 and 1855, with a brief interruption during the French Revolution of 1848. Its design was oriented to face the river, providing a magnificent view from its reception rooms. To preserve both the building's lines and the views from within, the architects positioned the entrances on the sides of the rectangular structure. The west entry was designated the main entrance, which is to the right when viewing the building from the river.

"It's a magnificent structure, but I don't see a parking entrance," Acardi stated when they approached.

The driver explained there was underground parking at the west end of the building, which was designed to be unnoticeable from the road. "We're going to the east gate, which serves as the VIP entrance," he added. "Because we French are big on ceremony and our national pride demands more grandeur than directing a dignitary to an elevator in a parking garage, the minister will meet you at the east entrance and escort you inside, at least that's what I was told."

"I would prefer our meeting to be low-key. Is there any chance you could take me to the underground parking area to avoid the grandeur?" Acardi suggested.

"Not if I want to keep my job."

"Then it's ceremony and grandeur," Acardi said as the limousine approached the east entrance. After the car stopped beside the gatehouse, a guard walked a bomb-sniffing dog around the vehicle while the driver handed over his ID and Acardi's passport to another guard. The guard compared their names to the entry log before phoning someone—most likely to notify the minister's office of Acardi's arrival. A minute later, he returned their IDs, presumably allowing time for the minister to reach the entrance of the building, before opening the gates.

The limo entered a rectangular gravel courtyard, slowing to a stop perpendicular to the colonnaded portico—a covered walkway which led to the entrance. Acardi, not anticipating that the driver would come around to open his door, exited the vehicle and briskly strode toward the minister—who hadn't yet made it to the gravel courtyard, expecting the driver to wait beside the door and only open it once he arrived, as protocol dictated. Instead, he found himself standing beside one of the large columns when Acardi, unaware of this diplomatic procedure, approached him. As they shook hands, the minister's security detail, which had planned to spread out as their protectee approached Acardi, instead remain clustered around the two men until the minister turned and led the AISI chairman into the building.

Acardi's breach of protocol saved his and the minister's life, the sniper unable to get a clear shot at either because they were sheltered beneath the columned portico and surrounded by security, rather than standing in the open courtyard.

"Sfiga," Gennaro Caruso exclaimed as he looked through his Vortex Optics spotting scope, the curse word a crass way of saying bad luck. In a prone position beside the sniper atop the tallest structure in the area, a ten-story building three-quarters of a mile away, he'd hoped to see the sniper kill the minister and Acardi, after which he'd put a bullet in his head. Bada bing bada boom, as members of his clan might say—slang that indicated something easily accomplished. However, when their plan went off the rails, they both stared at one another with a look that asked *what now?*

The thick-chested mobster from the Agrigento family was forty years old, standing five feet nine inches tall, with black hair and an olive complexion. His face was deeply pockmarked due to a combination of chickenpox and severe acne during his teenage years. As Sciarra's capodecina, often simply called a "capo," he served as the family's second-in-command and was a made member of the clan.

"Any ideas on how we get another chance to kill them?" Caruso asked, both men agreeing to converse in English because neither spoke the other's language as well.

"If he arrived in a government limo, he'll be leaving the same way, probably from this entrance."

"Probably?"

"Because they already had their photo opportunity, departing from the underground parking area would be easier and faster. However, the optics of diplomatic courtesy may be better served if he left from this gate."

"You seem familiar with the building."

"Comments on the ministry's meet and greets are online. I reviewed them before accepting the job," the sniper replied.

"Let me update my boss," Caruso said, going to the far corner of the roof and calling him while the sniper continued to observe the ministry through his scope.

After relaying the situation to Sciarra, the capo asked what he should do if Acardi left from the underground garage.

The response was immediate. "You'll kill him at the restaurant tonight. I have another way to take care of the minister."

"What about the sniper?"

"Nothing's changed."

Three and a half hours later, Caruso's cellphone vibrated. As before, he went to the far corner of the roof so the sniper couldn't hear him.

"My classmate's contact in the French government informed him Acardi has left the ministry and has been taken to the Le Basile Hotel in central Paris, not far from the Place Vendôme. He'll have dinner tonight at Chez Monsieur with another French official, Edgard Bence," Sciarra continued. "I'll text you the details. Ensure Acardi doesn't make it back to his hotel."

"What about the French official?"

"Focus on Acardi. If Bence gets in the way, kill him. Otherwise, he gets a pass."

"Understood. That brings us back to the minister."

"I may someone who will take the contract. He's very good at getting the job done, but his methods often result in considerable collateral damage, which is why I didn't initially consider engaging his services."

"Collateral damage will stoke the anger of the French government even more," Caruso warned.

"Given what I was told, I haven't another option. Clean up there while I contact this person. Afterward, I'll text you their address. Once he fulfills the contract, make sure there are no loose ends in Paris before you return home."

"Understood," Caruso responded. Putting his cellphone in his pocket and removing his silenced handgun from the small of his back, he put two in the head of the sniper who was still looking through his scope when he died—bada bing bada boom.

When the Gulfstream G700 landed at the Catania-Fontanarossa airport, a middle-aged woman greeted the five at the bottom of the plane's stairway. The owner of the fixed-base operator, or FBO, the entity having the contractual right to provide aeronautical services such as fueling, the hangar or tie-down of an aircraft, catering, and anything else that the crew or passengers of a private plane needed, asked how long they'd be in Catania.

"I don't know," Bruno answered.

"You can either keep the aircraft in the tie-down area," she said, pointing to a section of tarmac where several private jets were parked, "or we can tow it to the hangar where my office is located," she added, gesturing by nodding toward it.

Since having such a high-profile aircraft in the open might raise questions about its ownership and why it was in Catania, Bruno told her they'd keep it in the hangar. "We'll also need accommodations for the pilots," he said.

"There's a hotel less than a mile from the airport. I'll make the arrangements and add the cost to your bill. All that's required is a deposit," she continued.

Bruno handed her the government credit card. Going to her SUV, which was parked thirty yards from the plane, she returned with a five-thousand-dollar authorization receipt that she had processed using a mobile device. Bruno's hand shook slightly as he signed it, even though it was the government's money, not accustomed to the expense of operating a jet aircraft.

"This is an authorization and not an actual charge," the woman explained as she handed him the back copy of the receipt. "If the pilot requests fuel, you decide to keep the aircraft in the hangar for a shorter or longer time than expected, or if the plane needs maintenance, we'll adjust the authorization accordingly," she added matter-of-factly as she returned the credit card.

"I'm curious. What's the cost to maintain and operate this aircraft?"

"Isn't this your plane?"

Bruno shook his head. "We're just using it."

"I had a feeling you weren't the owner after seeing the look on your face when I handed you the authorization."

Bruno smiled.

"The price for the skinny version of this plane, meaning before changes are made to the interior and upgrades to the equipment and increasing its nonstop range, is around $75,000,000, which makes the charter rate approximately thirteen thousand dollars an hour. Whether you fly it for thirty or five hundred hours, the fixed costs are the same. I'd estimate that to be around a million dollars annually."

"Fixed costs?"

"Things like pilot salaries, insurance, annual inspections, hangar fees, and so forth."

"But not fuel?"

"That's an operating expense, the definition of which is everything it costs you to operate and maintain the plane. If this aircraft is in the air for two hundred hours a year, the operating expense should be around two million dollars. Of course, those estimates don't include the cost to fix a big-ticket item, such as a mechanical, hydraulic, or electrical issue. This aircraft will be the second most expensive plane in my hangar."

"Second only to the Bombardier Global 8000," Bruno said.

"How'd you know."

"Word gets around," Bruno deflected. "We'll need to rent a car."

"The rental agencies are on the ground floor of the arrival terminal, just outside the sliding doors for passport control and customs. I'll drive you there," she said.

The pilots said they'd take care of the aircraft and for Bruno to call and tell them when he wanted to leave Catania. After retrieving their bags, the team went to the FBO's car.

Knowing that going up against the Mafia meant they were likely to get into a gunfight, the men selected Glock 17 handguns from the armory, choosing to carry them in shoulder holsters under their jackets and putting two spare ammunition magazines in their pockets. In contrast, Donais selected a Glock 19 handgun, the lighter weapon having a slightly shorter barrel and grip than her partner's Glocks, carrying it and three magazines of ammunition in her shoulder bag.

After putting their carry-on bags in the back of the FBO's vehicle, except for Labriola, who didn't have time to pack, they were driven to the arrival terminal where they went to the shortest rental car line, which was Sixt. Ten minutes later they signed for a four-door Volkswagen Touran, the largest vehicle that was available. Hunkler volunteered to drive and, after entering Agrigento as their destination into the vehicle's navigation system, saw the town was one hundred and one miles away, and it would take an hour and fifty-four minutes to get there. They left the airport with Donati in the front passenger seat and Bruno, Donais, and Labriola in the back.

"Did anyone notice someone who was paying undue attention to us?" Bruno asked once they were underway.

"There was an airport security vehicle that parked near our aircraft and followed us to the arrival terminal," Donais said, with everyone besides Labriola saying they noticed the same thing.

"There was a porter at the rear of the terminal who watched as we rented this car and followed us outside with his cellphone pressed against his ear, all the while pushing an empty cart," Hunkler added, something everyone except Labriola noticed.

"With so much activity going on around us, how do you see these things?" The coroner asked.

"Years of experience and the scars we've accumulated from

failing to observe that we're being followed," Donati answered, drawing agreement from the others.

"More people are tracking us, but they're out of sight," Bruno stated.

"Who?" Labriola asked.

"I suspect someone working in the tower or another airport employee with access to arriving aircraft tail numbers. They'll report our plane's arrival and we'll automatically become persons of interest because, if I'm right, photographs were taken and our identities were learned."

"Sciarra knows we're here?" Labriola asked, turning around to look out the back window. "No one is behind us."

"There's no need. He knows we're on our way to Agrigento. That's where we can expect the fun to start."

"Fun?"

"People shooting at us," Hunkler clarified, drawing a laugh from everyone except Labriola.

The bombmaker lived and worked in Gennevilliers, a suburb of Paris six miles northwest of the city. Caruso drove there in a rented vehicle, finding that the address texted to him was a tiny two-story aluminum-sided building fifty feet to the side. It had been painted gray long ago but absorbed enough pollution over the years from the industrial area surrounding it to become nearly black. The steel entry door had a buzzer beside it.

"I've been expecting you," the bombmaker, an elderly person who appeared to be in his late sixties or early seventies, said as he motioned the capo to enter.

The interior appeared to be a light industrial workshop, Caruso not seeing anything that could be construed as an explosive device within view. Against the rear wall, with florescent lights directly overhead, was a line of manufacturing equipment consisting of a belt and disc sander, drill press, vertical milling machine, and other small pieces of equipment that he couldn't identify. To the right were workbenches with numerous handheld meters spread atop them. Had the capo been an expert in electrical circuitry instead of killing people, he would have identified these devices as a Criterion dielectric strength tester and voltmeter, used to test electrical cables, their components, and electrical motors; a Wheatstone bridge to measure unknown electrical resistance; a potentiometer for measuring electrical potential; a capacitance meter; an EMF meter to measure electric and magnetic fields; and other precision devices necessary for the manufacture of a sophisticated explosive device. Taking up three-quarters of the wall to the left was a series of metal cabinets which, if he could see inside, contained rolls of various gauged wire, a variety of circuit boards, and numerous electrical components and remote detonators. The last quarter of the wall had small sheets of aluminum resting against it, in front of which were various-sized metal and plastic containers.

"I was told you have an urgent request for my services but wasn't given the target," the bombmaker said.

The capo told him who his boss wanted to kill, but the revelation didn't seem to cause any concern. "Is a car bomb out of the question?" He continued.

"I've been told his security is tight. Therefore, I don't expect we can get near his vehicle."

"Do you have an RPG?"

"I have a rocket-propelled grenade upstairs. It's a good choice against a non-hardened target because it leaves the barrel at three hundred eighty-three feet per second, and the cone-shaped charge ensures that the energy from the explosion is focused outward. This gives it immense penetrating power," the bombmaker explained.

Caruso, who wanted a simple yes or no, considered this superfluous information since he already knew the lethality of an RPG, which is why he asked.

"However," the bombmaker continued, "although it will destroy an armored passenger vehicle, despite what you see on TV it doesn't always kill the occupant. That depends on where the RPG strikes the car and the type of armor protecting it. Some civilian armor is as good, if not better than that used in the military."

"What do you suggest?"

"Does the minister come down the same street every time he goes to his office?"

"I've been told he lives in a highly secured dwelling on a one-way street. Therefore, the answer should be yes."

"How long is the street?"

"Why do you ask?"

"It affects the placement of the bombs. If his vehicle can turn onto a feeder street a short distance from his residence, we need to place them before the turn. However, the closer we put them to where he lives, the easier they'll be for his security detail to detect."

"Bombs?"

"We'll need one on either side of the street to be certain his vehicle is demolished and he's killed."

Caruso withdrew the cellphone from his pocket and, going to Google Earth, typed the address he'd been given and brought the image of the minister's residence onto the screen.

"It's a typical tree-lined Parisian street with cars along both sides because parking is scarce in this city, as many homes don't have garages because the price of land is astronomical," the bombmaker said. "This street looks approximately ten feet wider than most residential roadways in Paris. However, two bombs will still work. I'll just make them a little larger. That'll mean significant collateral damage."

"How much damage are we talking about?"

The bombmaker explained.

"If we're talking this much damage, how will we detonate the bombs and survive?"

"We use this?" The old man said, opening a large plastic case.

"I can't operate that device."

"But I can."

Chapter Six

The route the navigation computer selected from Catania to Agrigento, which was the shortest in terms of mileage, was a series of meandering roads that passed centuries-old villages and hilltop towns as it weaved southward toward the Mediterranean Sea. These narrow thoroughfares, which had been dirt paths used by locals for millennia to move livestock or transport goods, only transitioned in the mid-twentieth century to asphalt to accommodate the increase in vehicular traffic. However, while the smoothness of the ride got better, the government wasn't willing to spend the funds necessary to straighten or widen the paths, which sometimes narrowed so severely through rocky passes and hairpin turns that there were only inches between vehicles going in opposite directions. Therefore, Hunkler was micro-focused on his driving when Donais asked him a question that had been on her mind for some time.

"Andrin," she began, addressing him by his first name. "I have a question."

"What?" He replied, slightly irritated at having to divert his attention from driving.

"Why isn't a handsome person like you married?" She asked, bringing about WTF looks from Labriola, Donati, and Bruno.

"This road isn't exactly user-friendly, and it's not getting any better," Labriola cautioned before Hunkler could respond. "Now may not be the best time to take his deposition."

"You're handsome, have an important job, and most importantly, act in a way that shows you're a good person who makes those with you feel safe," she continued, undeterred by Labriola's comment and the stares from her partners. "What's your story?"

Donais, who figured his response could be anything from telling her that he needed to focus on what was in front of them rather than his personal life, to saying what she'd asked was none of her business, to simply ignoring the question, instead engaged her in conversation.

"I was married, but my wife found she couldn't cope with military life. She didn't like government housing, the restrictiveness of living on base, and had other issues with being a military spouse. As a result, she didn't want to have children and subject them to what she perceived were the hardships of military life. When I was transferred to Afghanistan to lead Italy's NATO International Security Assistance Force (ISAF), which is considered a remote assignment, meaning spouses aren't allowed to come, that was the proverbial straw that broke the camel's back, and she asked for a divorce. Coincidentally, before she told me, I'd decided to resign my commission when I returned to Italy, feeling I couldn't make her happy unless I left the service. However, when I told her I would leave the military and become a civilian again, she said it didn't matter because we'd already grown too far apart."

"I'm sorry," Donais said.

"Don't feel bad for either of us. She married a doctor and has three children, a boy and two girls. I'm happy for her. I went on to become Commandant of the Swiss Guards, protecting the pope and infusing a young generation of guards with my military knowledge while aging gracefully in one of the most sought-after positions in the Vatican."

"Aging gracefully is a misnomer. If I'm not mistaken, aren't you in your early forties?" Bruno asked.

"Forty-one," Hunkler replied. "If I were still in the military, they'd call me nonnetto," he said, which translated to grandpa. "For all I know, those under my command may be using that term behind my back."

"I'm curious," Donati said. "How could the Vatican hire you if you're divorced? Also, I thought the requirement to be a member of the Swiss Guard was that you had to be a Swiss citizen who'd completed military training in Switzerland and still had an attachment to that country. Yet, you were an officer in the Italian army."

"I was born in Geneva. Therefore, I'm a Swiss citizen. On graduating college, I entered the military, where service of at least two hundred forty-five days is compulsory for males who serve in the army. I met my future ex wife, an Italian citizen living in Rome, when on leave. We fell in love, and I resigned my commission with the Swiss military at the rank of lieutenant colonel after serving for twelve years. I moved to Rome, where we married and became dual citizens."

"Your wife didn't express a problem with you being in the Swiss military?" Donais asked.

"Not at the time. But it didn't matter because I moved to Italy so we could be together and she wouldn't have to abandon her friends by moving to Geneva."

"That's when you entered the Italian military," Donati said.

"Because operating in a military environment was my only skill, I applied to become an officer in the Italian army. I was thirty-two then, which is generally considered too old for someone to enter the military. However, I was accepted because of a shortage of experienced infantry officers. When I left the army following my divorce and returned to see my parents in Geneva, the hand of God, fate, or whatever you want to call it intervened. I attended Sunday church service with my parents the first week I was back. Afterward, my father happened to see the cardinal, who was his childhood friend. They spoke, and after hearing about my military experience in the Swiss and Italian armies, he told me that the commandant would be retiring in six months and that he'd try and arrange a meeting with the pope to see if I would be a suitable replacement."

"There was no previous announcement of your predecessor's retirement?" Donati asked.

"No. Switzerland's two cardinals were the only ones the pope informed because they were tasked with putting together a list of candidates they believed would be acceptable for that position."

"And obviously the meeting with the pope went well. But you're divorced," Donati continued. "Didn't that disqualify you from the position?"

"But I didn't remarry. That made a difference with the pope because I kept my side of the marriage vows, and the divorce became a non-issue. Let me turn the tables. You're still single. Have you ever been married?" Hunkler asked Donati while focusing on the road before them.

"No, and I don't have a reason other than I haven't found the right person."

"I'm sure being single is an unpopular subject around your parents," Donais said.

"They, of course, want grandchildren."

"Did you ever come close to getting married?" She persisted.

"I came close once, but we eventually concluded that, although we loved one another, it wasn't the deep and abiding type that would last to our final breath. Therefore, we were better suited to being friends."

"You have time," Bruno interjected.

Donais told him that remark was the pot calling the kettle black since he was a widower and she hadn't seen him date anyone.

"I'm with Elia. I haven't found the right person."

As they continued their conversations, time seemed to fly by, and they were soon ascending the Monte Caltafaraci hill, which had the highest elevation in the area, passing the turnoff for Favara, which was five miles from Agrigento. The road had narrowed, with a vertical face of weather-worn rock to the left and, as there were no guardrails, a steep drop-off into the valley to the right. Therefore, there was little room to maneuver whenever another vehicle going in the opposite direction passed them, Hunkler hoping they stayed in their lane because he wasn't always able to see oncoming traffic on the twisting road.

A quarter mile past the turnoff, Hunkler looked in his rearview mirror and noticed a large vehicle speeding toward them from the rear, insanely using the oncoming traffic lane to pass. As it got closer, he saw it was a black H2 Hummer, which wasn't the narrowest of vehicles, with darkened windows. Therefore, he slowed down and edged the Volkswagen to the right as far as he dared to give the monstrous car more space on the narrow road, especially since there was a hairpin turn ahead. Incredibly, however, the Hummer slowed as it got beside their vehicle. To avoid a collision in the narrow turn ahead, in which he was sure the Touran would get the worse end of it and be bumped over the edge and down the one thousand feet gray stone embankment to the valley below, Hunkler yelled for everyone to ensure their seat belts and shoulder harnesses were tight, after which he slammed on the brakes to let the nutcase beside him pass. However, as he hit the brakes, so did the other vehicle, which angled to the right as it did. The mismatch was immediately apparent when the eight thousand five hundred pound Hummer impacted the four thousand eight hundred pound Touran, pushing it over the steep embankment. As the Volkswagen tumbled, it struck the numerous outcroppings of rocks that protruded from the hill, the sound of dented and crushed steel echoing loudly until the vehicle slammed onto the valley floor.

The bombmaker worked until four in the morning to construct the two bombs. Because sunrise was at 5:50 am, they had less than two hours to place the explosives before people in the neighborhood started waking up and, in the daylight, saw what they were doing and called the police.

"The C-4 in these explosive devices," the bombmaker said, pointing to his creations, "was stolen from the Quartier La Horie, a French Army base near Strasbourg. The steel balls and electronic components were taken over time from other targets of opportunity, meaning when the French police analyze the bomb residue and fragments, they'll encounter an investigative dead-end when trying to discover the purchaser of these materials. This anonymity, coupled with the marriage of the right amount of explosive and fragmentation components and the mathematics to design and construct these devices, which must be perfect to get the desired result or all you'd have is a large explosion producing an uncertain amount of damage over an indeterminate area, is why I'm so expensive," he proudly proclaimed, clearly happy with what he'd created.

With time running short, Caruso ignored the comments. He knew the basics of bombmaking, although he didn't have the artistry of the narcissist in front of him. He'd created roadside bombs using Combination 4, which nearly everyone referred to as C-4, and understood it would only explode after a rapid chemical reaction that was triggered by a shockwave from a detonator or blasting cap. The impact of a bullet or being engulfed by fire wouldn't detonate the stable material, which was malleable enough to be cut into smaller pieces without exploding. However, that's where Caruso's knowledge of C-4 ended.

In contrast, the bombmaker understood that once the C-4 ignited, the resulting gases released by the explosion expanded at twenty-six thousand five hundred feet per second, a distance equivalent to five miles. At this speed, they created a low-pressure area, sucking most of the gas into it and bringing about a partial vacuum which created an inward energy wave. Subsequently, unlike the movies where someone outruns the explosion coming behind them, the aftermath of a detonation is near-instantaneous, with no one having time to think about it because the aftermath occurs before that thought process begins. One second everything is normal, and the next there's total devastation and you're plucking a harp.

"Do you have a hand truck so I can take these devices to my car? They look heavy," Caruso asked.

"They are. Each contains two hundred and fifty pounds of C-4 and steel balls," the bombmaker stated.

"I can lift that weight, but a hand truck would make moving them to my vehicle faster and easier."

He pointed to a tight space between two benches where the hand truck was stored. "There's one more thing that needs to be done before we leave," he told Caruso.

"What's that?"

"I require payment. Your boss has the banking information."

"Once the job is done."

"I was contracted to design and construct two explosive devices for a specific purpose, which I've accomplished. I'm only agreeing to place and remotely detonate my devices out of respect for him because I don't believe you possess the skills to accomplish those tasks."

Caruso understood he was in a difficult position because the bombmaker was right. "One moment," he said, calling Sciarra, who after hearing the contractor needed to be paid before he'd position and detonate the devices, said he'd wire the money. The irritation in the Mafioso's voice showed that he knew the immense amount of money he'd send was akin to putting it in a shredder since the bombmaker was going to die following the assassination, and he'd be unable to get the offshore bank to return it. Nevertheless, within a minute of Caruso's call, Sciarra typed the necessary information into a computer program and sent the money.

When their call ended, Caruso told the bombmaker to check his offshore account and, upon seeing the money was deposited, had an attitude adjustment. Getting the hand truck, he helped the capo lift the bombs off the bench and transport them to Caruso's vehicle, placing one in the trunk and the other in the back seat so they wouldn't bang against themselves and damage the electronic components.

They arrived on the street where the minister lived at 4:50 am, an hour before daylight, Caruso driving two-thirds of the way down it, far enough so they wouldn't be seen by those guarding the residence, before the bombmaker told him to stop. Since there were no open parking spaces on either side, he stopped the car in the middle of the street and removed the bombs.

The bombmaker's plan was to create two simultaneous explosions, one on either side of the minister's two-car convoy. The devices were supersized Claymore mines. The difference between these and the military version was that the latter had a convex case that was eight and a half inches long, five inches high, and one and a half inches wide. In comparison, the bombmaker's was thirty-six inches long, twenty-one inches high, and six inches wide. Each version was supported by two pairs of scissor legs.

The destructiveness of the military's Claymore was due to a matrix of seven hundred one-eighth-inch steel balls set in an epoxy resin matrix in front of a layer of C-4 explosive. When detonated, the fragmented matrix was forced out of the device in a sixty-degree fan-shaped pattern at almost four thousand feet per second. The bombmaker's version worked the same except, because of the additional quantity of C-4 and the number of steel balls, it was ten times more lethal.

Since the cars parked on both sides of the residential street were so close to each other, the bombmaker couldn't set the devices against the curb, where they'd be virtually impossible to see from the road, because the vehicles beside it would disrupt the fragmentation pattern of the bombs thereby shielding the target. That meant they needed to be exposed and in front of the narrow space where the front of one car nearly touched the rear of the other, allowing the device to discharge without being blocked by the surrounding vehicles. Although they'd be visible in daylight, they'd be difficult to see from a distance and, by the time the minister's convoy was beside them and someone noticed the devices, it'd be too late.

After placing the bombs, they left the street on which the minister lived, Caruso following the bombmaker's direction to an open field five blocks away and parking the car. Showtime was in approximately two hours when the minister, who Sciarra was told was a creature of habit, departed his residence for the office. Caruso pushed the driver's seat in his vehicle back, spread out his legs, and began to relax.

"I know you said more C-4 was required because of the width of the street," he said, turning slightly to face the bombmaker, who had similarly pushed the passenger seat back. "And you also mentioned the mathematics needed to design and construct these weapons. Now that you've been paid, did you say that to impress me because, in my experience, the only math I require when killing someone with an explosive device is to count the money is all there when I'm paid. Therefore, between us, forgetting street size, car armor, and other concerns, did you just make the bombs this large to be sure the minister died in the explosion?"

"Do you mean: did I guess how much explosive material was needed and throw in a figurative ton of steel balls to be sure I penetrated the car's armor?"

"That's exactly what I mean?"

"First, I don't guess. That means my designs never have too much or too little explosive. Predictability is essential, necessitating that the destructive force be based on sophisticated mathematical calculations."

"As I said, math doesn't enter into my construction of a bomb. The bigger the boom, the more certain I am that someone's dead."

"For everyday targets, that logic holds most of the time. However, this hit requires sophistication. Last night, I put the situational numbers into the Friedlander waveform equation, which describes the pressure of the blast wave as a function of time. I also used the Kingery-Bulmash Blast Perimeter Calculator, which gives the shock wave velocity, its time of arrival, the duration of the positive pressure phase, the incident and reflected impulses, and other design parameters you wouldn't understand. From those, I calculated the amount of C-4 to use and the number of steel balls required to penetrate two armored vehicles across a thirty-four-foot wide space, the standard width of a residential bi-directional or one-way street in France, that had been narrowed by cars on both sides, with the average width of a vehicle being six feet. Because the target is inside a moving vehicle, a focused explosion was necessary, the mathematics leading me to the Claymore design. A big boom, as you put it, from one device may not work because the explosion could cause a three-axis rotation of the car, thereby creating uncertainty as to the pattern of the steel ball impacts."

"Which is a fancy way of saying that the vehicle may flip or turn enough to protect the minister from being killed by the steel balls."

"Correct. Twin big booms have other complicating factors, which can also result in uncertain lethality."

The expression on Caruso's face showed the bombmaker's knowledge exceeded his expectations.

"However, the mathematics I employed in my design concluded that the bombs we planted have a ninety-nine percent lethality. With the street being thirty-four feet wide, and the width of the minister's car being six feet, as well as the vehicles parked along the curbs, that means the street is actually twenty-two feet wide and that each side of the two-car convoy will be approximately eight feet from a device. No matter how the vehicle turns or rotates in the explosion the steel ball pattern will impact as designed."

"What does all that mean?" Caruso asked, confused by all the numbers.

"In terms that you and Signore Sciarra would understand, the minister is a dead man walking."

At 7:20 am, the bombmaker opened the two backpacks he'd brought with him and removed the drone from one and the flight controller from the other. French law limited the altitude at which consumer drones could fly to four hundred and ninety-two feet, which was one hundred fifty meters, a height he could give a flip about because he intended his drone to hover at one thousand feet, an altitude high enough to ensure it'd be out of sight to those in the convoy.

After prepping the aerial vehicle, he removed a burner phone from his pocket and conferenced the phone numbers of the modified cellphones he'd placed in the devices. He then launched the drone, guiding it to the minister's residence using its video feed. When it came time to set off the explosions, the transmission would come from his burner phone—the radio signal energizing a relay connected to the blasting cap that detonated the C-4 in each device.

"Both bombs have just been activated and they're connected to this phone," the bombmaker told Caruso, handing him the cellphone. "Since I'll be flying the drone, you'll detonate the devices. When I tell you, press the asterisk and the green transmit key."

Caruso said he understood.

At 7:35 am, with the drone overhead, the residence gates opened, and two identical vehicles with heavily tinted windows left the minister's residence. Because there was no way to know which one was transporting their target, the bombmaker compensated for this uncertainty by designing devices that ensured both vehicles would be destroyed with enough force to kill the occupants within.

As the two cars approached the devices, the bombmaker began giving instructions. "Get ready to press the asterisk and transmit keys, counting down from three," he said, "two, one, hit the keys!"

Caruso did.

Immediately afterward, both men heard the twin explosions. That should have been the end of it. However, in concert with these sounds, they saw red and yellow vortexes of fire rise in the distance, followed by secondary explosions that were too numerous and close to one another to count. Looking at the video from the drone, instead of seeing the shredded remnants of two cars, they saw a six-foot-deep and twelve-foot-wide crater emitting fire and smoke, the devastation much larger than Caruso expected.

Zooming out to get a better view of the area, they saw that most of the homes on both sides of the street were ablaze and that many of the vehicles parked along the curbs were on fire, Caruso failing to understand why the collateral damage was significantly more extensive than the bombmaker warned.

The bombmaker, in contrast to Caruso's belief that he'd miscalculated the size of the explosion, knew what happened. Before designing and placing a bomb in the open, he habitually obtained the routing of utilities in the area, which included gas, electricity, and water, accessing this data online because it was a matter of public record. However, this report was unavailable for the minister's neighborhood, believing that it was because of security concerns. In the rare instances when this occurred, he'd call a government official in the permitting department who wasn't averse to getting paid for accessing his computer terminal and providing the utility's routing. However, the time constraints imposed on him prevented obtaining this information from his contact, a French civil service employee working the statutory thirty-five hours a week. Because of their seniority, his official was entitled to take Friday or Monday off to enjoy a long weekend. Today was Friday, the day his contact perpetually took as his day off. Subsequently, with no way to get this information, he had to assume that the routing of utilities in the minister's neighborhood was the same as most residential streets. It wasn't.

Code required a one thousand feet safety gap between a gas line and other utilities. Because gas pipelines were rarely dug up, the practice was to bury them on the backside of a neighborhood and run the other utilities under the street, where periodic upgrades and maintenance wouldn't tear up a resident's yard. However, unbeknownst to him, the high-pressure gas line in this upper-end community was an exception to the rule because, as an older area, gas was introduced to the neighborhood after the placement of other utility lines, reversing what was now the norm. Therefore, the explosions ignited the high-pressure gas line, continuing into the secondary feeder lines to the lower-pressure pipelines that entered the residences. The result was the destruction or setting ablaze of forty-four mansions, including that of the minister.

"This is what happens when I'm pushed to do something in a hurry and don't have time to do my research," the bombmaker angrily stated, indirectly blaming what happened on Sciarra.

"The assassination of the minister and the destruction of this monied neighborhood will launch a massive investigation. Because of your reputation, it won't be long before an informant talks to police and you become their prime suspect."

"I know. That's why I'm returning with you to Sicily. I need your boss to ensure I'm left alone by authorities. Is that possible?"

"It is," Caruso said, putting two into the bombmaker's head.

Chapter Seven

❧✦❧

"Should we drive down and see if they're dead?" The driver of the black Hummer asked the person who'd been sitting beside him.

As both men looked at the wreckage, which had tumbled down the gray stone embankment to the valley floor, the last revolution putting it upside down with the crushed roof protruding into the vehicle's interior, neither believed anyone could have survived the crash.

"No one's moving, and we need to leave before another car comes by and sees us parked on the side of the road. Our vehicle isn't inconspicuous and, with the scrapes and dents we got shoving the Volkswagen over the edge," his partner said as he looked at the side of the Hummer, "that'll be hard to explain if we're reported to the police."

"We own the police," the driver countered.

"Not everyone, and they're mostly in the larger cities and towns that are more useful to the boss's enterprises. Even so, it'll cost him a favor, money, or both to make it go away. He won't be happy. He doesn't like publicity."

"What do we say if he asks us to confirm that the five investigators died?" The driver asked as they got back into the Hummer.

"The truth. We made it look like the driver was careless and went off the road near Favara, their car rolling down the hill until it landed upside down on valley floor. Given what we saw of the wreckage, no one could have survived."

Agreeing that being seen alongside the wreck would invite questions about their involvement in the accident, they returned to Agrigento. However, had they stayed five minutes longer, they would have seen Hunkler, who after unbuckling his seatbelt, fell onto the ceiling of the vehicle and slowly extended his left arm out the shattered side window, pulling himself onto the hard-packed ground. Unsteadily getting to his feet, he wasn't mentally playing with a full deck because of the simultaneous impacts of the side and front airbags, which deployed within twenty nanoseconds and struck him at around two hundred mph. Looking into the vehicle, he saw the others were strapped into their seats and not moving, casting uncertainty as to whether they were unconscious or dead.

He began with Bruno. After putting his fingers to his carotid and verifying he was alive, he unfastened his seatbelt with his left hand while holding onto him with his right arm so he wouldn't come crashing onto the roof. After pulling him through the broken side window, he laid him on the ground. He then went back and got Labriola and Donais, taking her shoulder bag with him because he knew her weapon was inside. By this time, Bruno was sitting up. Although he, Labriola, and Donais were bruised, Bruno sporting a black eye, none of the three were seriously injured.

Donati wasn't as lucky. When Hunkler went to pull him from the vehicle, he saw that the investigator's shoulder looked out of place.

"Do you need some help?" Bruno asked, seeing Donati's injury and the colonel getting ready to release his seatbelt.

Hunkler said he did, and after putting his arms around Donati's torso, Bruno released his partner's seatbelt, the colonel gently lowering and pulling him from the vehicle. As they began to lay him flat on the ground, Labriola arrived and said to put him in a sitting position, anticipating what would come. As they did, Donati threw up.

"You've dislocated your shoulder," the doctor said as he knelt beside Donati. "Try not to move it, or the pain and swelling will worsen."

Donati didn't respond, giving Labriola a blank stare instead.

"Do you hurt anywhere else?" The coroner asked.

The blank stare remained.

The doctor moved his fingers forty-five degrees on either side of Donati's eyes, observing that the investigator didn't follow his movements.

"He has a concussion," Labriola stated. "Without further tests, I won't know if there's additional trauma."

"We need to get him to a hospital," Hunkler said.

"How?" Donais asked. "We're in the middle of nowhere with nothing in sight."

"Not quite," Bruno said, looking at the black exhaust smoke in the distance accompanied by a rhythmic thumping sound.

The urban center of Favara, which wasn't much larger than a half dozen Costco's, was surrounded by small farms, the closest to the highway being a forty-acre walnut grove owned by Maria Bianco. Because of the intense and repetitive slamming of metal against rock as the Volkswagen somersaulted down the hill, the forty-five-year-old widow heard the crash and ran to her small red Fiat, whose muffler had long ago relinquished its job, and drove toward the sound of the impacts. Bianco, whose husband died three years ago, was slender, five feet four inches tall, and had an olive complexion and salt and pepper hair cut fashionably short.

"Is everyone alright?" She asked after getting out of her car.

"Most of us," Bruno answered, "but our friend has what appears to be a dislocated shoulder and a concussion. There could be other injuries. Is there a doctor nearby?"

"There's one in Favara, but the hospital is in Agrigento. It'll call an ambulance. I should only take ten minutes to get here," she said, removing the phone from the side pocket of her jeans.

"It would be better if we saw the town doctor. Those who pushed us off the road believe we're dead, or they'd be down here to finish the job," Bruno countered as he gently put his hand on her phone. When he did, Bianco saw the shoulder holster containing the handgun. Accustomed to living in an area saturated with Mafia, where being too nosey or asking questions could get one killed, she didn't comment on what she saw and kept her expression neutral.

"I'm a doctor," Labriola volunteered, re-directing her attention. "Perhaps you can take us to a physician."

As he spoke, she saw he was also carrying a handgun in his shoulder holster. Looking at the others more closely, she noticed Hunkler and Donati also had bulges under their jackets. Bruno, who saw her staring at their weapons, decided he needed to explain why they were armed if he was to gain her trust.

"Don't be afraid. Even though we're carrying weapons, we're not Mafia," he told her, addressing the issue head-on.

"Are you police?"

"We're investigators sent by the government to Agrigento to find someone who was kidnapped by the Mafia in Rome and brought to this province. Somehow, the kidnappers found and tried to kill us. The driver of the black Hummer that pushed us off the road probably tried to make it appear that our driver, who isn't from this area, was careless and went off the edge."

"It's happened. What's a Hummer?"

Bruno described the vehicle.

"Most of the towns and villages in Agrigento province are farming communities, the residents driving broken pieces of rust like mine," she said, pointing to her car. "The vehicle you described is well known in the area and belongs to Dante Sciarra, although he doesn't personally drive it," she said.

"He's the Mafia boss for this province," Bruno stated.

"Si. His family extorts money by wetting their beaks, as they say, in every business within the province. I grow walnuts, but I must sell my crop to him even though he pays far less than I could earn on the open market. In Sicily, they call this the black hand, which is another term for extortion. Those who aren't farmers pay their tribute weekly in cash. If they aren't able or refuse, they're beaten as an example to others. If a person continues to resist, their property is destroyed and they're killed. Again, as an example."

"That must be a terrible burden to live with."

"No one has a choice. If Sciarra is trying to kill you, it's because you're a threat to him. That earns you my respect and cooperation. You said you were here searching for a woman who was kidnapped from Rome. She must be important for the government to send the five of you to find her. What's her name?"

Bruno thought for a second, unsure if he wanted to share that information. However, after receiving nods from Hunkler, Donais, and Labriola, who understood they needed her trust if they were going to survive and find Lamberti, Bruno told her it was Pia Lamberti.

"The wife of the late president?" Bianco asked, surprised by what he'd said.

"Yes, and we could use your help to find her."

Prior to arriving in Sicily, they believed they could rely on their investigative skills to find Lamberti and return to Rome on her aircraft or, if the shit hit the fan, call Acardi, who'd send military or police assets to help with the extraction. No one wanted to contemplate the alternative to rescuing her, which was killing Italy's intelligence czar. Although they expected Sciarra to have an effective intelligence network, that they were nearly killed soon after they arrived in Sicily made the investigators, except for Donati, who was still out of it, realize they'd underestimated his ground game. Therefore, having someone like Bianco helping them was a necessity because, without a car or someplace to hide, they couldn't avoid Sciarra long enough to find out where Lamberti was being held and conduct a rescue.

Bianco didn't immediately respond to Bruno's request for help, which disturbed the investigator, although he didn't say anything for fear of alienating her. However, those fears were laid to rest moments later.

"Put your friend in the back of the Fiat, and we'll take him to a doctor I've known from childhood. He'll help, no questions asked," she told Labriola. "The rest of you will have to wait here until I return because there's not enough room in my car."

"Following on what you said earlier, if Sciarra finds out that you and the doctor helped us, you'll be killed as an example to others," Bruno cautioned.

"But if you succeed, the government will arrest him and everyone else who was involved in the kidnapping or that's trying to kill you. Isn't that correct?"

"No one's going to court. We're going to resolve this matter outside the legal system if you understand what I mean."

"Even better."

"That won't be the end of it. If Sciarra dies, I'd expect the Mafia leadership to appoint someone else to fill that vacuum unless there's a family member who would take over."

"His wife and children are dead," she said, not having the time to explain what happened to them. "Nevertheless, replacing him will take a while. Maybe Favara can set an example for the rest of Sicily that it's possible to remove this burden from our lives and not share the bounty of our hard work with the leeches of society. I'm hoping that given the importance of the person you're rescuing, they or someone in your government helps to take this weight off our backs," Bianco said.

Bruno wanted to tell her that the woman Sciarra kidnapped was an unforgiving person who didn't believe in half measures and that, if she survived this ordeal, Sciarra and everyone associated with what he'd done had better get their affairs in order because she would be their worst nightmare, having carte blanche to use the military and law enforcement to take whatever action she directed. Instead, he told her that Lamberti would help balance the scales of justice.

After killing the bombmaker, Caruso called Sciarra and told him about the massive explosions so that he wouldn't be blindsided by the devastation on the news, explaining the bombmaker didn't know the location of the high-pressure gas line running through the minister's neighborhood before placing the devices.

"I trust he won't be able to tell anyone about that mistake."

The capo said the bombmaker and sniper had the same retirement plan.

"And nothing ties you to what happened?"

"Nothing. There's no serial number on my weapon, and I wiped it and the bullets in the chamber and magazine clean of prints before leaving it beside the bombmaker's body," Caruso stated.

"My classmate will be angry with the destruction of a neighborhood of influential people, which will magnify the public outrage over the minister's assassination and intensify the investigation. That urgency could lead to uncovering what's in the minister's files before we destroy them. Therefore, nothing has changed regarding Acardi's fate. It's still imperative that you kill him before he returns to Italy and tells others what he and the minister have discussed."

"I received your text about the time of his reservation at Chez Monsieur and confirmation that he's still staying at the Le Basile Hotel in central Paris, not far from the Place Vendôme," Caruso confirmed.

"I don't care if you kill him at the restaurant or hotel. He needs to die before morning."

"Don't worry. The only way that Acardi is returning to Rome is in a casket."

"Call me when it's over."

Donati was driven to a residence built at the turn of the century, whose warped wood exterior had transitioned from white to charcoal over the years. Bianco parked her vehicle behind the house, she and Labriola helping the injured investigator to the back door where Bianco pressed the buzzer.

Matteo Albani opened the door. The doctor was in his late seventies and five feet ten inches tall with an olive complexion and thinning gray hair parted to the left. He wore wire-rimmed glasses that were popular in the 1960s, which over the years had become bent and sat slightly crooked on his nose, angling to the left. Upon seeing Donati's shoulder, he waved them into the house, noticing as they entered that the investigator's eyes didn't perceive the motion of his hand and that he had a thousand-yard stare. After directing them to the study, which also served as his examination room, he helped lay the injured investigator on the exam table, after which he and Bianco spoke for several minutes before she approached Labriola.

"I'm going back to get the others. Doctor Albani has my cellphone number if you need to contact me," she said.

Once she left, Labriola introduced himself, telling the doctor that, although he accompanied the investigators he was with as an advisor, he was a coroner by profession, although soon to be retired.

"Besides being doctors, we have that in common because I'm also the town coroner. The morgue is at the rear of my residence," he said, pointing to the door to his right.

Labriola looked around, seeing that Albani's living space consisted of a small kitchen, a compact living/dining room, a bedroom, and the examination room they were in.

"Judging from the size of this building and what I see within, the morgue appears to be small. The people of Favara must have a long lifespan."

"That depends on a person's profession and the intervention of others," the doctor said, Labriola interpreting that to mean that one's lifespan was longer if they weren't a member of the Mafia, had dealings with them, or pissed Sciarra off.

"Why does a coroner, who's also an advisor, feel the need to carry a handgun?" Albani asked, pointing to the weapon in Labriola's shoulder holster.

"To fit in with the investigators. It's more for show. Confidentially, I never could shoot worth a damn."

"Can you explain what's happening? Maria told me some of it, saying you and the others were here to rescue the wife of the late president, who Sciarra had kidnapped. That, in itself, is unbelievable, especially since there's been no public announcement."

"And there won't be."

"She also said Sciarra knows you're in his province and is trying to kill you. This is a lot of intrigue for me to process without understanding the cause. What else can you tell me to fill in the blanks?"

As Donati was lying on the table and oblivious to his surroundings, Labriola went into detail, believing the more the doctor knew the better he'd understand why they needed his and Maria's help. As the two spoke, they rapidly bonded.

"Thank you for the explanation. Now, it appears we have a patient. Let's see if two coroners can reduce a shoulder," Albani said, referring to putting it back in place. The pair began by removing Donati's jacket and shirt.

While Labriola steadied Donati to prevent him from sitting up and interfering with the reduction, Albani pulled the arm downward and outward to realign the joint, causing their patient to scream in pain as he popped the ball back into its socket.

"That went well," Labriola told Albani.

"Do you think so?" Donati asked, seemingly back to reality. "That hurt like hell. Where am I?"

"In Favara, about five miles from Agrigento," Albani answered. "This is my house and, depending on one's medical condition, either a doctor's office or the morgue, as I'm also the town's coroner."

"Where are the others?" Donati asked, looking at Labriola.

"They're being brought here by Maria Bianco, the person who found us. She has a farm near our crash site," Labriola explained.

"The last thing I remember before being in this room was the Hummer pushing us off the road. How long ago was that?"

"Perhaps an hour," Labriola answered. "Let me tell you what's happened following the crash," he continued, finishing his explanation as Bianco and the others entered the house, Maria introducing the investigators to Albani.

"How is your patient?" Bruno asked the doctor.

"We popped the ball back into its socket. Although there doesn't seem to be any permanent impairment, he should take it easy with his right arm for a couple of weeks."

Donati was ready to tell the doctor what he could do with that suggestion, but was prevented when Bruno began speaking.

"Maria expects Sciarra to send his men to check the wreck and verify that we died in the crash. I agree, as that makes sense."

"And when they don't find any bodies, Sciarra will launch an intensive search for us," Labriola stated.

"They'll search every dwelling in Favara, beginning with Maria's because it's the closest to the crash, and ask what she heard or saw. Given the proximity of her farm to the wreckage, saying she didn't hear or see anything isn't going to work," Bruno said.

"What's the alternative?" Hunkler asked.

"Maria has an idea, which she told me on the way here," Bruno answered. "I think it'll work."

"I saw you two carrying on a conversation in the front," Hunkler, who sat in the back of the Fiat with Donais, commented.

"Which involves?" Donati asked, inserting himself into the conversation.

"For starters, taking off your clothes," Maria said, causing him to wonder if he still had a concussion.

Sciarra's compound was a walled thirty-acre enclosure that surrounded a three-story white stucco home at the top of the highest hill in Agrigento, giving the Mafioso a magnificent and unobstructed view of the Valley of the Temples and the remarkably preserved two and a half millennia old Greek structures spread across it. However, as he stood on his patio and looked at the valley, he wasn't taking in its intoxicating view. Instead, he was sucking down a glass of limoncello and trying to calm himself because Lamberti's interrogation had gone badly. While the drug she was administered made every other person he'd interrogated accurately answer whatever question he asked without hesitation, it had the opposite effect upon her. Not only did she refuse to answer some questions, but on the others she provided deceptive information, something he only discovered moments ago.

He attributed this uniqueness to her force of will, which overrode the drug's previously predictable effect. Consequently, he was forced to take the interrogation up a notch and give her a more potent compound, which he had previously decided against because it sometimes had the extremely adverse side effect of killing the person to whom it was administered. Even if all went well, it was so toxic to the body that the person being interrogated could only answer questions for around an hour before they lapsed into a coma-like state, taking between three and four days to regain consciousness. The reason for this unpredictability was that there was no universal safe dosage because each person metabolized the drug differently. Given this disparity and the serious consequences for his classmate that would ensue if she died, he briefly considered torture. However, he believed if drugs didn't work on this strong-willed woman, torture would be a walk in the park, allowing her to convincingly lead him down a rabbit hole by providing false information. That was a time-consuming risk he couldn't afford to take. Therefore, with little choice, he decided to roll the dice and give her the more potent compound.

Because it took two hours for the drug to take effect, he went to the kitchen where the two from the Hummer were waiting, expecting to hear that the five investigators were dead.

"We forced their car off the road and into the valley as directed," the driver stated when asked how it went. "It'll look like an accident."

"They're dead," the other person proclaimed.

"Did you see the bodies?" Sciarra asked.

"We didn't drive into the valley to inspect the wreck, fearing we'd be seen and someone might believe that because our car was damaged, we knocked them over the side, leaving doubt that it was a driving accident," the partner said, expecting Sciarra to complement them for staging the incident as he directed.

"So, you didn't see any bodies?"

"The car was lying on its top, and we saw no movement inside. No one could have survived that crash," the driver stated.

"But, you never saw a body?" Sciarra persisted.

"No," both men replied in unison.

They saw Sciarra's expression rapidly change from one of satisfaction at doing what he ordered to being pissed. They were familiar with that look, knowing it resulted in one of two outcomes: killing those with whom he was dissatisfied or telling them to get out of his sight and not to come back until they'd fixed the problem. The soldier in the back, who kept an eye on Sciarra when Caruso was away, had his hand on the butt of his gun, ready to put a bullet in them if he received a nod. As it turned out, this was their lucky day, as Sciarra looked at him and shook his head.

"Go back to Favara, find the wreck, and don't come back until you verify there are five bodies inside. If someone survived, kill them and anyone they may have spoken with," the Mafioso said, dismissing the pair with an imperious wave of his hand.

As the five investigators were getting undressed, Donais using the doctor's bedroom, Bianco went into the morgue and returned with five sets of green medical scrubs and disposable booties, giving one set to Donais and handing the rest to Albani.

"Put these on and use the booties in place of the shoes," the doctor said, handing out the scrubs. Once you're done, bring your clothing into the morgue. It's through that door, he said, pointing to it.

"What's this about?" Bruno asked.

"Maria will explain in morgue," he said.

When the five entered, they saw Maria removing a body from one of the dozen coolers along the wall. However, instead of placing it on a gurney, the morgue only having two along with one autopsy table, she lowered it to the floor as Albani rushed to help.

"I don't believe we have much time, so here's the plan," Bianco began. "When Sciarra's men check the wreckage, they're going to find five burnt bodies wearing the incinerated remnants of your clothing and carrying your IDs. Believing you're dead, Sciarra won't search for you. Each of you will dress a body, and when we're done, we'll put them in my vehicle."

"Won't five corpses be missed?" Labriola asked Albani.

"It's unlikely."

"Transients?" Hunkler asked.

"This close to Agrigento, Favara and the surrounding towns are dumping grounds for those Sciarra kills because, I've heard, he doesn't want the deaths recorded in his city as the violence might draw too much attention from the government, as if his presence doesn't already do that. When a murder victim is brought to my morgue, it's generally missing all forms of identification. Therefore, I send the fingerprints of the deceased to Rome to try and identify the body, which is usually successful. Sometimes, the deceased have families, and if they want, they can pay to transport the remains to a final resting place. However, when we can't find a living relative, or they don't want to pay for transport and burial because of the way the deceased has chosen to live their life, or can't afford it, the town leaves the disposal of the body to me. In that instance, they're brought to a potter's field on the outskirts of town, where unclaimed, unknown, or impoverished people are buried. These five are in that group and won't be missed, each having suffered a violent death, presumably at the hands of the Mafia."

With that explanation, the investigators got busy. They dressed the bodies in their clothing, afterward placing their wallets in the pockets of the deceased, everyone keeping their cash and Bruno withholding the ID card Acardi gave him. Since there was no female in the coolers, Albani chose someone of similar size to Donais, the consensus being that no one would look that closely at the charred remains of the victims.

After placing the bodies in the trunk and rear of the vehicle, Bianco drove to the wreckage with Bruno, where they positioned them inside. Having grabbed two of the twenty gas containers that Albani kept in the shed next to the generator, which he used when the town lost power—a not infrequent occurrence, they doused the bodies and vehicle, then set it on fire. Once the car was engulfed in flames, Maria drove Bruno back to the morgue before returning to her farm to wait for the arrival of Sciarra's thugs.

As the Hummer approached the crash, the driver and his partner saw smoke coming from the vehicle's interior.

"No one survived this crash," the driver stated as he parked the car and, with his partner, approached the demolished Touran.

Getting down on all fours, they looked inside the charred interior and saw five bodies. Even though the driver took a cellphone video to show their boss, he knew Sciarra was a nitpicker who thrived on detail and would have a problem with the five faces being unrecognizable. Therefore, they frisked each victim, finding their wallets and, in the process, getting covered with black flaky soot. Although the plastic credit cards and driver's licenses had primarily melted, there was enough to identify the victims as the investigators. After photographing what remained, they put these remnants back in the wallets and returned them to the victims.

"Look at these tire tracks," the driver said, pointing them out as they returned to the Hummer. The slight indentations were barely visible on the hard-packed dirt and would have gone unnoticed had the driver not parked two feet from them.

"These are from a small-wheelbase vehicle. I don't know how long they've been here because there hasn't been rain in our area for a month," the partner volunteered.

Walking around the wreck, they found similar tracks further to the right.

"The same vehicle," the driver confirmed. "The question is: were they here before or after the crash?"

"I'm thinking it was after," his partner said. "There's nothing around us except for this wreck."

"I can't see any footprints on the ground, but this dirt is so hard that even we don't weigh enough to warrant a print. The car might belong to the person living there," the driver said as he pointed to Bianco's farm.

"They're close enough to hear the crash or have seen the fire," the partner agreed.

"Then why didn't they call the police? If they did, the bodies would have been taken to the morgue, the wreck taped-off, and there'd be other tire tracks in the area."

"Let's ask."

"And if they saw something?" The driver asked.

"Seeing the wreck and the bodies isn't bad because this was supposed to look like an accident. However, seeing how the crash came about is a different matter."

As the Hummer entered the farmhouse's driveway, they saw a small wheel-based Fiat and parked behind it. Walking to the front door, they looked in the direction of the hillside highway, noticing that although the road wasn't visible from the house, wisps of smoke from the still-smoldering car were. The driver knocked on door, with Bianco appearing moments later.

Asking questions is necessary if you want to get information from someone. However, they needed to be asked in a way that didn't create suspicion about why you want them or the other party might not cooperate. The pair, who looked like Mafioso thugs from the way they dressed, spoke, and their less than colloquial demeanor reinforced Bianco's belief that was their occupation when she opened her door. Without introducing themselves, which by itself was suspicious, they said they noticed smoke coming from the valley as they were driving to Agrigento and, pulling to the side of the road, saw an overturned vehicle on the ground and went to check for survivors.

"You must have seen the crash," the driver said, stating the question that would determine the woman's fate.

"I didn't. I heard it rolling down the hill and hitting the ground. Afterward, I drove there to check for survivors."

"What did you see?" The driver asked.

"The same as you, a car with bodies inside. If the crash didn't kill them, the fire did. Why did you come to my farm asking so many questions?"

"Sorry about the questions; I'm a naturally curious person. We came here to see if anyone survived and to offer to take them to the hospital in Agrigento, believing it would be faster than waiting for an ambulance."

"If you saw the wreckage, you know no one could have survived," she said, understanding their explanation for being there made little sense but that she was speaking with Sciarra's soldiers, not Nobel Prize winners.

"Did you report the crash to the police?"

Uneasy with the direction of the conversation and believing that one more casualty wouldn't bother Sciarra, she decided to take out an insurance policy. "I was just about to do that," Bianco, replied.

Because she was holding her cellphone and had the Favara police's FaceTime number on it, as did most residents, she touched it and began speaking to the officer before the driver or his partner could react.

"These two gentlemen want to report a crash with multiple fatalities," she began, the two men staring at her phone as if it was a weapon. "I didn't catch your names," she said, putting the pair in the impossible position of either giving false names to the officer, which wouldn't work because they had criminal records and the officer was probably recording their FaceTime call and would run them through the national database, or giving their real names and avoiding further suspicion. They chose the latter, hoping the officer was either on Sciarra's payroll, which he wasn't, or that their candor would keep them from being suspects in the crash, which it didn't.

"I'll send a squad car to the scene," the officer said. "The police will need you three to make a statement and go through it with you afterward."

"We're happy to cooperate. Perhaps later today," the driver replied as he and his partner left the house and started toward their vehicle, only to have Bianco accompany them while still on FaceTime with the officer. When she got to the Hummer, she and the officer noticed the long scrape marks along the side.

"It looks like you had an accident," the officer commented.

"Tourists," the driver said before rapidly getting into the vehicle with his partner and driving off without further explanation.

Two officers arrived at the crash site ten minutes later. After taking Bianco's statement, they summoned Doctor Albani, who was also the medical examiner in addition to being the town's doctor and coroner.

Once Albani got there, looked at the bodies, and took his photos, he released the site to the officers, who placed the five into body bags and put them in the morgue's van. Later that day, the bodies were taken to an Agrigento mortuary, which was under contract for the town of Favara, and cremated for a second time.

Sciarra had just returned to his residence following his second session with Lamberti. Having the same degree of success as the first, he was in an even fowler mood than after his last interrogation when the driver and his partner returned from Favara.

"Are they dead?" The Mafioso tersely asked.

"They are," the driver replied, showing him the videos they'd taken of the bodies and the contents of their wallets. That part went well, the Mafia chieftain seeming to calm down. What followed, however, didn't go as well.

"You didn't tell me there was a fire following the crash," Sciarra stated.

"There must have been a small fire inside the car that we didn't see, and it spread once we left," the driver remarked.

"Possibly."

"We couldn't stay and look at the wreck for long because we didn't want anyone to see us," the partner added.

"Looking at this video, I see the bodies are on the ceiling of the car, and their seatbelts are dangling overhead. How could they have the strength to release themselves and yet not crawl out a broken window to avoid the fire?"

"The fire must have consumed them before they could," the driver offered.

"Not if it was a small fire that spread."

The driver nervously shuffled his feet while his partner ran his fingers through his hair.

Sciarra continued with the video, noticing the tire tracks and nearby farm. He asked the driver about them.

"We thought the only person who could have seen or heard the crash lived at the farm. When we went there, we saw a car in the driveway with the same small wheelbase as the tire tracks at the wreck, which told us she was there. We asked if she saw the crash and if there were any survivors," the driver proudly stated, wanting to impress Sciarra with his thoroughness.

"You asked if there were survivors when you knew there were five charred bodies?"

The Nobel laureates said they did.

"I'm sure that didn't cause her to become suspicious."

"Did she see the crash?"

"No," the driver answered.

"What happened next?"

The driver hesitated before answering. "She made a FaceTime call to the police and reported the accident, telling them we were at the wreckage."

"And the police saw your faces?"

"Only for a short time," he answered, hoping that made a difference.

"And they have your names?"

"We thought about giving them a false name but decided that since our faces are in the national police database, lying would make us suspects, especially since they want statements and to go over our answers afterward," the driver said.

"We could kill her," his partner volunteered.

"To what end?" The police saw your faces, will soon have your names, and know you were with her. You'll become the prime suspect in her murder. If you were on FaceTime, did the camera take in the damage to your vehicle?"

The driver cleared his throat and said they did.

"That's unfortunate," Sciarra said.

"What should we do?" The driver asked.

"There's nothing you can do," Sciarra answered as he nodded to the person at the back of the room who put the pair in the mob's accelerated retirement program and, ironically, dumped their bodies in Favara.

Chapter Eight

Edgard Bence arrived at Chez Monsieur looking dapper in a suit and tie. The bistro, his favorite in Paris, was on the Right Bank between the Place de la Madeleine and the Place de la Concorde. It was a popular spot among locals because of its ambiance, delicious food at reasonable prices, and friendly staff that made everyone feel like family. Additionally, having the meeting here was convenient, being a short walk from the AISI chairman's hotel.

Acardi requested that they dine at the restaurant when it opened at 7:00 pm, an hour and a half earlier than most French diners and one to two hours earlier than the average Italian dinner. Bence believed the early dining was due to the chairman's preference for a quieter atmosphere, allowing them to converse more freely without many other patrons around.

When Bence arrived, he spotted the AISI chairman at a corner table. Acardi stood to greet him, and the two briefly embraced before Bence took the seat across from him that faced the front of the bistro. As soon as they were seated, the server approached, and Bence ordered a bottle of 2022 Domaine Vacheron Guigne Chevres Sancerre. He chose it because he was familiar with the family producing this spectacular wine for nine generations not far from the village of Sancerre, a medieval hilltop town about one hundred twenty-five miles south of Paris.

"I was stunned to learn that your foreign minister was

assassinated this morning," Acardi began. "My condolences. I met with him yesterday."

"About what?" He asked, curious if what they were about to discuss related to the minister's death.

"To ask for his help."

"It must have been extremely important for you to fly to Paris instead of speaking over the phone. Clearly, the minister agreed with your assessment of the urgency to clear his calendar."

"One reason I requested the meeting was that he and Pia Lamberti were working on a project so confidential that discussions about it were limited to the two of them. They were scheduled to get together in Paris this week, but the minister postponed the meeting at the last minute, claiming he needed to gather more information," Acardi stated.

"If only the minister and Lamberti were aware of their joint project, whatever that was, why did you come to Paris to meet with him? Why not ask Lamberti? You work for her."

Acardi was about to answer when the server arrived with their wine and, after Bence tasted and approved it, she poured each a glass. "Would you like an appetizer?" The server asked.

"Nous commanderons un peu plus tard," Bence said, indicating they'd order a little later. Once she was out of earshot, Acardi answered the question.

"I couldn't ask because Pia Lamberti was kidnapped early yesterday morning," he said, stunning Bence. He then told him everything he knew about the abduction, including the belief that the kidnappers were members of the Sicilian Mafia from Agrigento province and that a team comprising Bruno and his partners, Hunkler, and Labriola were there searching for her.

"I know everyone except for Labriola."

"He's a medical professional," Acardi replied, avoiding explaining why Rome's coroner was part of the team.

Bence was just about to express his agreement that it was suspicious how Lamberti's kidnapping and the minister's death occurred within a day of each other, especially since both events seemed connected to their investigation. However, before he could share his thoughts, Acardi asked a question.

"Have you ever heard of someone your government refers to as the 'puppeteer' or someone going by that moniker?"

Bence shook his head.

"Lamberti used that codename to refer to the individual she and the minister were discussing."

"The puppeteer being the person on whom the minister was gathering information."

"I would assume so."

"Which makes them the prime suspect for orchestrating the assassination and kidnapping."

"That's my belief. Look, Edgard, we both have substantial experience dealing with the Mafia—yours with the Corsicans and mine with those on the mainland and in Sicily. We know that a Mafioso chieftain won't kidnap someone of Lamberti's stature unless they are certain of a huge payday. The investigative pressure and increased scrutiny that would follow such an act are significant. They behave like cockroaches, attempting to stay in the shadows and below law enforcement's radar while profiting from illegal activities in the areas the Commission allows them to control. They won't risk disrupting their profitable enterprises unless a substantial benefit is involved.

Moreover, for a kidnapping to take place in another family's territory, the head of the Agrigento clan, Dante Sciarra, would need permission from the Commission and the Mafia family that oversees Rome. This would only happen if someone offered both factions an enormous sum of money. Thus, whoever wanted Lamberti kidnapped must have deep pockets and an established relationship with organized crime," Acardi stated.

Bence concurred with him. "The minister was killed to prevent him from revealing what he knew about this puppeteer to Lamberti. She was kidnapped to discover what information they had. I also believe that abducting her was easier than taking the minister. If the situation were reversed, she would have been killed. Ultimately, both will need to be silenced to keep what they uncovered a secret."

"I should mention that if Bruno and his team can't effectuate a rescue, their orders are to kill Lamberti to prevent her captors from reaping an intelligence bonanza that would not only irrevocably harm my government but others as well."

"Unfortunately, that makes sense. You realize that what happened to her couldn't have occurred without the kidnappers knowing her schedule in advance, understanding the extent and placement of her security, and being aware of her routine at the cemetery," Bence stated.

"That's clear. And, for security reasons, she made it a practice that no one outside Italy knew her domestic schedule."

"This means you have a domestic traitor or mole who had Lamberti's schedule, was familiar with her security arrangements when she left her home, and knew she held the position of your country's intelligence czar. Not many people are going to check all three boxes. I only learned about her position because she was involved with Bruno and his team, and by extension with me, in our recovery of the Mona Lisa and other priceless works of art. Since you have no idea who the traitor might be, I strongly recommend keeping any information that's uncovered about this kidnapping to you and Bruno's team."

"That's good advice."

"I want you to know that during my meeting with the minister, I requested that he temporarily reassign you to work with my government to uncover the puppeteer's identity. Given what happened to Lamberti, he verbally approved my request. However, I'm unsure if he had the chance to finalize your reassignment before his death."

"He did, and it took me by surprise," Bence said, pulling out a folded piece of paper from his inside jacket pocket. "These orders state that, for the foreseeable future, I'm assigned to a joint

French-Italian task force under your leadership and should consider you, or your designated representative, as my interim commander. Why do you want me?"

"I needed someone I trusted to interface between the French government and Bruno's team," Acardi confided. "Do you think your orders were rescinded because of the minister's death?"

"I haven't been notified, but I'm certain they will be once my boss finds out. The French typically prefer not to work under the direction of another country unless the benefits of such collaboration outweigh the public relations challenges of explaining why we need the assistance of a foreign government."

"When do you expect they'll discover your reassignment and recall you?"

"That's anyone's guess. However, believing it was no coincidence that I received my reassignment to your task force and you invited me to dinner the same day, I submitted a basket leave request for my thirty days of annual vacation in case we need flexibility with my schedule. This way, even if I'm recalled from the task force, you have a month of my time."

"By 'basket leave' you mean you've filled out the paperwork and can activate it with a call to administration?" Acardi clarified, making sure they were on the same page.

"Yes."

"That's good thinking. Are you eager to return to the field?"

"My job is important, but I'm not a bureaucrat. The countless meetings and discussions have taken a toll."

"You haven't been in your job for very long."

"Notwithstanding, I've reached my tipping point. This week, I applied for a position with the GIGN," he stated, referring to the Groupe d'intervention de la Gendarmerie nationale, an elite police tactical squad that conducts hostage rescue, counterterrorism, and surveillance.

"How old are you?"

"Thirty-three. I know you think that's too old for this group of fast-chargers, and you're right if I were applying to be a member of one of the assault teams. However, the opening is in their intelligence unit."

"They'll be fortunate to have you, just as we are. However, I want you to know this assignment will be as dangerous as anything you've undertaken. If this puppeteer orchestrated assassinating a minister and kidnapping someone as important as Pia Lamberti, nothing is off the table for them, and they'll kill you or anyone else on the task force without hesitation."

"You don't have to tempt me any further. I'm in. Tell me how I can dovetail into your investigation."

Acardi took a ghost-chipped cellphone out of his pocket and handed it to him, explaining how it worked. "The first step in finding this person is to get the files, documents, and data the minister has gathered on them. Even if those don't reveal their identity, they may provide a clue that leads us closer to who they are."

"That will be a challenge," Bence said. "For the past year, my government has been progressing toward going paperless. This means that current files are kept in electronic format, and older files, if deemed to have no historical value, are scanned into the system and then destroyed."

"By 'challenge,' do you mean 'access'?"

"The government database consists of thousands of partitions, organized by ministry, agency, function, security classification, and more. Each partition contains electronic filing cabinets. Therefore, the minister's files will be in his personal file cabinet within the section designated for the Ministry of Foreign Affairs."

"That certainly makes record searches more efficient. I assume there are strict safeguards to prevent one department from accessing another's records?"

"The system is designed to prevent unauthorized access between departments. If I need to review a file or data from another agency, I submit a request for access. If approved, they send the necessary information to an area that allows for its transfer to my side of the partition or permits its viewing for a specific period without the ability to copy or transfer it. The system is tight."

"That's clear. However, I might have another way to obtain the minister's data," Acardi said, being intentionally vague.

"Does that involve Montanari?" Bence asked.

"Are you familiar with Indro?"

"Only by reputation. Without his exceptional hacking skills, we would never have located nor retrieved the priceless art stolen by the Nazis from museums and private collectors. How did you find him?"

"Bruno arrested Montanari while he was committing a high-tech crime, which led to his incarceration. He was also responsible for getting his sentence commuted and helping him begin his career in security consulting by securing the Vatican as a client after vouching for him to the pope."

"It sounds like they have a close relationship."

"It's complicated," Acardi explained. "The condition for Montanari's commutation was that he help Bruno bypass a sophisticated alarm system—the very crime for which he was convicted—allowing Bruno to expose a dangerous individual. Since then, Bruno and Lamberti have asked Montanari to use his exceptional hacking skills for similar illegal activities, which could risk his return to prison if the government denies its involvement. As a result, they share a love-hate relationship. We'll need to see how the winds of cooperation are blowing before we know if he'll work with us."

"Unless we have someone with his skills, we won't be able to access the minister's files. Perhaps you and I could talk to him."

"I believe we're too close to Bruno to convince him if he doesn't want to become involved, the government having already exceeded its quota for favors with him. However, there is someone who might convince him to cooperate."

"Is he a friend?"

"Not exactly."

Caruso entered the bistro five minutes after Bence and made his way to the bar, located to the left of the entrance. He chose a chair close to the door, ordered a bottle of Bordeaux, and asked for the check as soon as the server brought the wine, so he could leave quickly without waiting for the bill. Afterward, he sipped it slowly while watching Bence and Acardi during their hour-and-a-half dinner. Knowing that Bence arrived by taxi, Caruso believed he'd take the same mode of transport when he left, the queue for which was across the street, thereby allowing him to follow and kill the unaccompanied Acardi as he walked to his hotel.

Subsequently, as the Mafioso anticipated, after they said their goodbyes, Bence jogged across the street to take the fourth position in the taxi queue while Acardi walked casually toward the Le Basile Hotel. He strolled along the sidewalk parallel to a row of townhouses, which began about fifty yards from the bistro. Although streetlights were positioned every ninety-eight feet along the road to his right, they emitted a weak glow, per the residents' wishes, who preferred not to have anything bright shining into their homes at night. With the surrounding area quiet and the locals either out for dinner or settled in for the evening, Caruso found this to be the perfect environment for what he was about to do.

He planned to kill Acardi by slitting his throat and pushing his body into the deep shrubbery along the sidewalk. If all went well, no one would discover it until he was on his flight to Catania. Experience had taught him not to rush the kill. Wearing shoes with non-slip rubber soles, which were quieter than those made of smooth or hard materials, he could hardly hear his footsteps as he kept pace with Acardi.

A little more than a minute later, he saw the perfect kill zone and substantially increased his pace. Pulling a switchblade from his pocket and opening it, he confidently strode toward his victim and horizontally positioned the blade so that he could reach in front of Acardi and, in one motion, pull it hard across his neck and sever both carotid arteries. However, as he planted his right foot to give him the leverage he needed to make the deep slice, three shots shattered the night's calm. The bullets impacted Caruso in an area no larger than a quarter, striking in the upper left quadrant of the back and throwing him forward into Acardi, sending both men crashing to the sidewalk. Looking up, Bruno saw Bence standing over him with a weapon in his right hand, extending his left to help lift him off the sidewalk.

"Let's get out of here," Bence said as he pulled Acardi to his feet and returned the handgun to his shoulder holster.

"We should call the police. Your actions saved my life; you're a hero."

"For our sakes, this has to be an unsolved crime. If we report this, some bureaucrat will check their computer, see our names, and revoke my temporary reassignment and basket vacation. Additionally, because you're a visiting diplomat, I would have to answer questions from various government committees and investigators, all of which I would rather avoid. Let's skip those pleasures and leave before anyone sees us," he said.

Acardi agreed, and they quickly walked to the hotel and headed to his room.

"How did you know that someone was trying to kill me?" Acardi asked as he opened his liquor cabinet, uncorked a bottle of red wine, and poured two glasses.

"A police officer's instinct. When I saw him enter the bistro within minutes of me and sit in the bar chair that was closest to the entrance, a spot most people avoided unless all the other seats are taken because of the noise and the congestion of people entering and leaving the establishment passing within inches of those chairs, I believed that to be an odd choice. My suspicion that he had ulterior motives for being at the restaurant grew stronger when I observed that he'd consumed less than a glass of wine from his bottle and didn't order food."

"I'm a police officer, and I didn't notice any of that or pay attention to him during our discussion," Acardi stated.

"If you were in the field instead of an office, I'm positive you would have seen these inconsistencies," Bence stated, cutting him some slack.

"Perhaps I should get my ass out of my chair more often. Did anything else heighten your suspicion?"

"He was focused on us to the exclusion of everything else, which struck me as odd because just thirty minutes before we left, there was an undeniably beautiful woman sitting at the bar several seats to his right. Despite her efforts to make eye contact with him multiple times, he completely ignored her. In France, women typically take great care to look as attractive as possible when they go out; they want to be enticing and noticed by men. However, any doubt I had that he was surveilling us vanished when I saw him follow you toward your hotel. That's when I decided to trail him. When he removed his blade and made a move toward you, I shot the perp."

"From what I briefly saw, that was a small cluster of bullets, especially for nighttime shots. You're quite the skilled marksman."

Bence removed the gun from his pocket and showed him the laser sight. "Not if you put the red dot on your target," he remarked. "Are you returning to Rome in the morning?" He asked, changing the subject.

"Not after today. I'll remain in Paris to investigate why Lamberti and the minister considered the puppeteer a threat to our countries and work to uncover their identity."

"Where will you start?"

"At this point, I need computer data, and I only have one option."

"Montanari," Bence said, receiving a nod in response. "Will he take your call? I've heard he sometimes avoids them."

"I think Bruno's calls are the only ones he avoids. However, to be sure, I'm going to send him an invitation to help us," he said.

"Delivered by the person who's not exactly a friend?"

"Precisely," Acardi replied, removing the cellphone from his pocket to call Zunino.

Indro Montanari was a technology savant and a convicted felon who earned an extremely profitable living as one of the world's premier hackers and thieves. His extraordinary talents enabled him to enter the most sophisticated vaults and secure areas, disappearing with their contents without leaving a clue, and hack nation-state-level computer systems believed to be invulnerable to such efforts. Because of these talents, Bruno sometimes referred to him as "the Savant," a title his partners and others also adopted.

One day, his career as a felon ended when, while disabling a particularly complicated circuit, his farsightedness caught up with him as he touched the wrong connection and set off a silent alarm. That was the day he not only discovered that he should have been wearing reading glasses but also when he met his arresting officer, Mauro Bruno.

Two years into his five-year sentence, he was surprised to receive a call from him asking how to bypass a sophisticated alarm system in a private residence—the very crime that had landed him in prison. Bruno's request was driven by his belief that the owner of the residence that he'd broken into and entered without a warrant was hiding art and artifacts stolen from the Vatican. Finding a high-security room within the person's study, Bruno believed the stolen works were inside. However, because this individual was extremely wealthy and a highly respected member of society, he knew that he'd never obtain a search warrant without concrete evidence of a crime, which he lacked because he was acting solely on gut instinct. Therefore, he turned to Montanari, believing he was the only person capable of bypassing the sophisticated security system.

They struck a deal: in exchange for helping him gain access to the secure area, the hacker would have his sentence commuted to time served. The Savant agreed, and with his help, Bruno got the evidence he needed. Keeping his word, three years were lopped off Montanari's sentence, and the need for parole was eliminated. Afterward, Bruno went a step further by setting the Savant up in business by securing the Vatican as the first client for his startup company, New Life Consulting, Montanari using his expertise to protect the Holy See's computer and electronic security systems against internal and external breaches. As his business thrived, the Savant continued to assist Bruno and later Lamberti, although he often tried—unsuccessfully—to refuse their requests to use his illicit skills.

The thirty-eight-year-old savant stood five feet six inches tall, had short black hair, and weighed one hundred thirty pounds, which is anorexic by Italian standards. He was working on a particularly complicated program for one of his clients when there was a knock at the door. Not expecting any visitors and assuming someone had the wrong address, he ignored it. However, he found it difficult to refocus on his program because the knocking continued.

"Indro, it's Zunino. Open up," the bodyguard said, solving the mystery of who was at the door.

Having met him several times, the Savant knew he worked for someone he and others called the witch. Unlike Bruno, who tried to persuade Montanari that the bad guys would cause injury or death or create a significant injustice if he didn't help, Lamberti used a different motivational technique by threatening to put him in jail until he changed his attitude. Since Zunino only took orders from her, he opened the door.

"I have someone who wants to speak with you," the bodyguard said flatly without preface or the hint of a smile, dialing a number before handing over the ghost-chipped phone.

The Savant, who had expected to speak with Lamberti, was surprised to hear Acardi's voice instead. After apologizing for the late-evening interruption and saying that he was on speakerphone with Bence, with whom Montanari was familiar, the chairman got straight to the point. He informed him that Lamberti and the French Minister of Foreign Affairs were assembling data on someone she codenamed the puppeteer when she was kidnapped and he was killed. Montanari was already aware of the latter, as it had been the headline across every media platform. "We need to identify this person. However, the data necessary to expose them resides in the French government's database, which I'll need your expertise to hack," Acardi stated.

"The French will put me in jail if they discover that I'm the source of the hack, and you'll let them because the Italian government doesn't want to be accused of such a blatant violation of international law."

"That would be the situation," Acardi agreed.

"Putting aside my possible incarceration, this hack will be extremely difficult if not impossible. While I've previously breached the French system, the data I obtained was on a server at the Louvre. Accessing a ministry-level server is infinitely more difficult, and given the sophistication of their firewalls, tripwires, and passive triggers to detect people like me, it could be impossible. However, for the sake of argument, let's say that I get into the ministry's database. There will be terabytes of files to sort through. If 'puppeteer' was Lamberti's codename for this person, the late minister may have used a different designation altogether; he could have had his own codename. Because we're talking terabytes, do you see the challenges in finding the information you need?"

"Why can't you export all the minister's files, or at least those dated within the last six months?"

"Systems used by nation states have strict controls for exporting data outside the system. Those will be as stringent as entering the system."

"I understand the magnitude of what I'm asking, but you are the most creative person I know. You've consistently found ways to accomplish the impossible by thinking outside the box," Acardi said. "I'm asking you to do that once more."

"Although it's not part of the Ministry of Foreign Affairs, what if I could get you into my agency's database?" Bence asked.

"That would be a game changer."

"Write this down," Bence instructed, providing him with his remote log in procedures, username, and password.

"All my actions will be attributed to you when I log in. When I leave your section of the database and hack into the Ministry of Foreign Affairs server, if I'm detected, the government will either believe it was you or that you collaborated with a hacker," Montanari explained.

"Which, as you said, only applies if you're caught."

"Yes."

"Then, let's hope you're as good as everyone believes and that we uncover who is behind the kidnapping and assassination without discovery or, if detected, you get this information before I'm arrested," Bence replied.

After the call ended, the Savant attempted to return the phone to Zunino, only to be told that it was now his to keep. "I'll get another one," he said. "Keep what was said to yourself. I would take it personally if you told anyone of this discussion."

Chapter Nine

Sciarra was about to prove true the ancient superstition that bad things happen in threes. At the top of his list of troubles was Lamberti, whose stubbornness in refusing to meet his demands was hindering a lucrative financial arrangement. Next was the blunder made by his soldiers, who were given a prejudicial early retirement because they lacked common sense. The third blow that was about to accelerate his already bad day into an even steeper decline came from a call he received from his counterpart in the Parisian branch of the Corsican Mafia, the largest criminal organization in France. The two men were business acquaintances rather than friends; the profits from their joint smuggling operations involving goods and people between France and Italy were the only ties binding them, and then only for the period of the transaction. The Corsican wasted no time in telling him that Caruso's body was discovered in a bed of plants by someone walking their dog.

That revelation shocked Sciarra, leaving him momentarily speechless. When he finally responded, he asked for details and inquired about the location of the body.

The Corsican informed him that Caruso was murdered in a residential area near the Le Basile Hotel. Sciarra knew Acardi was staying there because he'd told Caruso.

"How was he killed?"

"Three small caliber bullets to the back."

"Was he robbed?"

"No. This was a killing and not a robbery. Now, it's my turn to ask questions. What was your capo doing in Paris without so much as a courtesy call to me that he was in the city?"

"I'm not sure. I have nothing going on in Paris. If I did, I would need authorization from the Commission to operate there before seeking your permission."

"Why do I believe you cut a few corners and sent your capo into my backyard without that authorization?"

"What makes you say that?"

"Four significant and unexplained events occurred during his time here. The first involved the killing of a sniper, whose name I provided to you years ago, on the roof of a building that had a clear line of sight to the Ministry of Foreign Affairs offices. The second event involved killing this minister with two roadside bombs after the sniper was unable to fulfill his contract. Following that, the bombmaker was also killed, with his body discovered five blocks away. As far as I remember, I also introduced him to you. Why did you kill the minister?"

"I didn't, and you and I aren't the only ones who hire these professionals. I have enough problems with Sicilian politicians without looking for trouble off the island," Sciarra countered. "What's the fourth unexplained event?"

"Caruso's death. I've spent enough time with him to know he wasn't the tourist type. His idea of relaxation would have been going to a gun range. Therefore, I can only conclude that he was in Paris to arrange for the minister's assassination and then kill those involved. If I find that's true," the Corsican continued before Sciarra could respond, "I will take it personally, and there will be significant repercussions."

"An unnecessary threat. I didn't send him to Paris; he went there of his own volition because I assume he liked the city and wanted a change of atmosphere from Italy."

"I'm not naive, and neither are you. Tell your men to find

another vacation spot," the Corsican stated, not believing what the Mafioso told him. "If I see one of your men in my city, I'll return them to you in a box," he stated before ending the call.

Sciarra struggled to understand how Caruso, who had proven over the years that he was exceptional at tailing and killing people, could have failed in what basketball players called a layup. He also had difficulty believing that Acardi possessed a weapon because if a foreign government official had one, it would imply that their government considered France unsafe, which would be an insult to the country. However, since Baudo said that Acardi's security team remained in Rome to avoid calling attention to his meeting with the minister—something that would raise questions from Italy's Minister of Foreign Affairs about why domestic intelligence was meeting with his ministry's counterpart—he wondered what went wrong because the director didn't have a bodyguard. And, if Acardi wasn't responsible for killing his capo, who was?

He still needed to eliminate Acardi, but time was running short. According to Baudo, the director was returning to Rome in the morning, after which he'd be significantly more difficult to target because of the security assigned to him. Therefore, someone needed to go to Paris to kill him. Bringing in another Parisian contractor wasn't an option since the Corsican seemed to know every assassin in the city. Once he found out, he'd tell the Commission that one of their families was operating outside the country, after which they'd come down hard on him.

Knowing the Corsican would keep Acardi under surveillance to follow through on his threat to kill any of his men who'd operated on his turf, he had to send someone who had no possibility of being known by him or his men. This person also couldn't look like a thug; otherwise, their presence near Acardi would arouse suspicion. He needed an outsider who no one would suspect of being a killer. After several minutes of contemplation, only one person came to mind. Going to his safe, he retrieved an address book he hadn't used for several years and found the person's cell number. He needed to call in a favor.

Antone Mattei was the Renaissance man of lowlifes, breaking just about every law in the French government's penal code. His offenses ranged from smuggling, car theft, burglary, witness tampering, extortion, assault, loan sharking, arson, and murder for hire. One might think that someone with this pedigree would have a cell named after him at a government penitentiary. However, because he worked for Sciarra, witnesses were too afraid to testify against him, and prosecutors avoided charging him for crimes, fearing for their safety and that of their families.

Sciarra nicknamed Mattei "the Pantellerian" during the three and a half decades he worked for him as a soldier. Eventually, age took its toll and he retired to Pantelleria, an island fifty-five miles southwest of Sicily and thirty-five miles east of the Tunisian coast. Generations of Mattei's family had lived on the island before his parents moved to Agrigento in search of better economic opportunities, as the chance for prosperity on the small island was limited.

His father became involved in Sciarra's organization and took the vow of Omertà, or code of silence while working as a soldier. Tragically, his parents were killed in a car explosion—a retaliation by the police for the assassination of two officers by Sciarra's men. These officers had provided the government, which was investigating the Mafia, with insights into the illegal enterprises owned by Sciarra. In Sicily, there was a unique understanding of accountability and a belief in ensuing balancing counteractions, a principle that has permeated the island for centuries.

When Mattei retired to the tiny island of seventy-three hundred residents, he bought a small vineyard that produced Moscato wine, intending to spend the rest of his life in tranquility. However, three years later, a call from Sciarra changed that sedateness when the Mafioso said he needed a favor and explained what that entailed.

Refusing wasn't an option because, in their world, one never officially left the family; retirement was merely seen as sitting on the bench and being a backup player until needed. Therefore, he didn't ask why his former boss wanted him because one didn't question the head of a family, nor ask what he'd receive in return, although Sciarra volunteered that the mortgage on his modest home and the debt he incurred to acquire the vineyard would be erased once he completed the favor. With no choice but to comply, Mattei responded that he'd be happy to perform the service without payment, which Sciarra flatly turned down, Mattei's offer and Sciarra's response predictable by tradition.

"I need this service completed by the end of today because my source tells me Acardi will return to Rome in the morning. That cannot happen. Is your passport up to date?"

Mattei replied that it wouldn't expire for five years. However, he explained he couldn't reach Paris in time to be effective because the island's airport only had flights to Italian cities and not to international destinations. As a result, he would need to take a connecting flight, meaning he'd get to Paris later that day. "I'll also need explosives and weapons, which I decide to use will depend on the opportunity that presents itself."

"I expected these issues. A plane is waiting at Pantelleria Airport. If you leave your home now, you'll be at the Orly Airport in two and a half hours. Upon your arrival, the pilot will provide you with the location of a car in the parking garage. The keys and an envelope of cash will be above the visor, and a variety of weapons and explosives will be in the trunk. After you kill Acardi, return the car to the airport and put the keys above the visor. The aircraft that brought you will take you back home."

"Understood. What's his schedule?"

"My source says his calendar is free, and he's at the Le Basile Hotel."

"I won't let you down. He's as good as dead."

"I know."

The Bombardier Global 8000 was waiting at Pantelleria Airport with its boarding ramp extended when Mattei arrived, landing in the City of Light three hours later. The flight experienced a thirty-minute delay due to heavy air traffic in the Paris area, where air traffic control prioritized commercial aircraft, leaving private planes to bring up the rear. During the flight, the pilot was given the make, model, and location of Mattei's vehicle at Orly, which he passed to him.

It was early afternoon when the Pantellerian arrived at the Le Basile Hotel. During the flight, he had devised a plan to kill the director, which required Acardi to be in his room. To determine if he was there, he went to the house phone in the hotel lobby and asked to be connected to his room, feeling relieved when he answered on the third ring. Mattei, speaking in English—the business language of hotel employees when addressing guests from other countries—identified himself as being with room service, explaining that the hotel was sending a complimentary bottle of white wine as a thank-you for staying there.

"What makes me so special?" Acardi asked.

"It's a courtesy we extend to all our guests," Mattei replied, anticipating that question because he would have asked the same thing if someone called and offered a complimentary bottle of wine.

"Your accent sounds Italian."

"My parents immigrated from Turin to Paris when the company my father worked for transferred him here," Mattei replied in Italian, again anticipating Acardi's question because his accent was pronounced and something he couldn't change.

"You can send the bottle to the room," the director said.

"Please confirm your room number," Mattei said.

Acardi wondered why he didn't already know the number if he was going to deliver a bottle of wine. However, because he felt he'd already interrogated the man enough, and the confirmation was probably hotel protocol and out of the server's control, he let it slide and gave him the number.

"It'll be there within thirty minutes," Mattei replied.

"What was that about?" Bence asked, having only heard Acardi's side of the conversation.

"The hotel apparently provides arriving guests with a complimentary bottle of white wine. Room service called to ask if they could deliver it to our room."

"What about the accent?"

"The server mentioned that he and his parents moved to Paris from Turin when his father's company relocated them."

"We French have long said that Turin is the most French city in Italy. It's only thirty miles from our border, and many French companies establish subsidiaries there because of its logistical advantages. If you've been to Turin, you might have noticed that walking down many of its streets feels reminiscent of strolling in Paris, thanks to the architectural similarity."

"I've been there, and you're right. If I moved to France, my accent would also change," Acardi admitted.

After calling Acardi, the Pantellerian picked up the house phone and ordered a bottle of white wine from room service, using the director's name. The next part of his plan was the trickiest. He needed to wait for the room service staff member to exit the elevator on Acardi's floor, incapacitate or kill them, and then put on their service jacket to deliver the wine.

The server stepped off the elevator and onto the second floor fifteen minutes after the call, pushing a cart holding a bottle of wine in a bucket of ice, two glasses, and a container of Fiji water. As he approached, Mattei pulled a Taser from under his jacket and stunned the young server. After removing the server's jacket and putting it on, the Pantellerian dragged him to the emergency exit stairway next to the elevator, pushed him into the concrete passage between floors, and closed the door behind him.

He told Acardi that he'd receive a white wine and not a red because he needed the alcoholic beverage delivered in a bucket of ice. This would allow him to place the plastic explosive and detonator at the bottom of the container, covering it with the bottle of wine and redistributing the ice around the bottle to ensure the C-4 remained hidden when looking into the bucket.

Mattei knocked on Acardi's door, which was at the end of the second-floor hallway before it turned ninety degrees to the left and paralleled the front of the hotel. After being let in, he wheeled the cart to the center of the room. Bence, who had been staring at him from the couch, went to the cart, took the bottle from the bucket, and scrutinized it closely. "This is a nice wine," he remarked to Acardi, noting that it was a 2019 Louis Latour Meursault from the Burgundy region of France.

Acardi handed Mattei a twenty-euro note, after which the Pantellerian left.

"We need to keep this cold until we order something to go with it," Bence said, returning the wine to the bucket and pushing it down as far as it would go, feeling something was preventing it from reaching the bottom. Putting his hand into the bucket, he pulled out the gray plastic explosive with a detonator sticking out of it, knowing that all someone had to do was push a button to have it detonate and blow him and Acardi into oblivion.

Acardi, who saw what Bence was holding and was familiar with explosive devices, asked if he needed help.

"We're not going to be able to disarm this device," Bence replied, holding it in one hand and pointing to a wire running from the detonator to the explosive with the other.

Acardi understood.

The temptation for most would be to pull out the detonator, knowing the plastic explosive couldn't go boom without it or a blasting cap. But Bence and Acardi also knew that detonators can be booby-trapped, so removing them can trigger the explosion. They believed the only explanation for the wire running from the detonator had to be that it was connected to a blasting cap embedded in the plastic explosive. Therefore, removing the detonator would trigger the blasting cap and ignite the device.

Believing they had only seconds before someone ignited the detonator, they contemplated throwing it out the window. However, two obstacles stood in their way; the first was that the windows were sealed shut to maintain the room's temperature and reduce the hotel's utility costs by preventing temperature spikes. Second, even if Bence could break one and toss the bomb outside, there might be innocent bystanders below. Convinced they had only one option and with no time to discuss it, Bence removed the gun from his shoulder holster and grabbed Acardi.

As Mattei left the room, he took the remote detonation device from his pocket. He intended to wait until he got onto the stairwell before setting off the explosion, wanting to avoid the heat and concussive force of the blast that would disintegrate Acardi's hotel room and release the energy from the explosion down the narrow hall which, if he were in it, would make him a casualty of his bomb. Therefore, once he was in the concrete passageway between floors, and believing he was protected from the force of the blast, he pressed the detonation button. However, because the energy from an explosion travels at thousands of miles per hour, his errors in judgment and execution remained unknown to him as he was killed the instant he pressed the button.

Two major screwups cost the Pantellerian his life. First, the rectangular brick of C-4 given to him was eleven inches long, an inch and a half high, two inches deep, and weighed one and a quarter pounds. As a plastic explosive delivered an air blast that was thirty-one percent greater and fifteen percent faster than an equal weight of TNT, only a small amount was required to obliterate Acardi's room. Therefore, error number one was having a brain fart and using the entire block of C-4 rather than cutting off a small portion, which was all that would have been necessary to kill Acardi and Bence. In retrospect, the error was attributable to

Mattei being more familiar with TNT, an explosive he'd used for decades, rather than plastic explosives which, although he'd been shown how to insert the booby trap because that was standard for Sciarra's bombs, he'd only handled C-4 three times in the past, the person with him always determining the proper amount to use.

Screwup number two was believing the stairwell would be safe because it was a concrete enclosed area to the side of the hallway, the open space down which he knew the concussive force would go once it blew out the walls and door to Acardi's room. That would have been true had he calculated the proper amount of C-4 required to get the job done. But his unfamiliarity with plastic explosives, in addition to underestimating their destructiveness, also didn't take into account its blast radius. The three times he used C-4, the younger soldiers, who first calculated the blast range necessary before determining how much C-4 they'd need to cut from the brick, the calculations giving the kill and injury radiuses, were meticulous in their math to avoid precisely what happened to him. Mattei didn't bother to learn what they were doing because he didn't understand math all that well. Therefore, the Pantellerian had no idea that the block of C-4 he detonated had a horizontal kill radius of three hundred and thirty-eight feet, eight times further than the stairwell, and that the concussive force and the fire and debris it dragged along with it would instantaneously envelop what he believed was a protective enclosure, exploding his internal organs and searing his lungs.

"Is everyone in Paris trying to kill you?" Bence asked as he and Acardi lay half-buried in a field of shattered glass and debris after Bence shot out the side window of their room and, grabbing Acardi, leaped through it. Landing in an alley beside the hotel, they looked up and saw the row of rooms, above and below theirs on that side of the hotel, were destroyed. They would later discover that the same number of rooms at the front of the building had also been demolished. As a result, the twenty-seven-room hotel had to be closed until its structural integrity could be verified and workers let in to either dismantle it or clear away the debris and begin the multi-year reconstruction process. The only good news was that, because it was early in the day by Parisian standards, the guests in the rooms that were demolished were either outside the hotel or in the bar when the explosion occurred, making Mattei the only casualty.

As Bence and Acardi extricated themselves from the rubble and dusted themselves off, first responders arrived on the scene.

"How many people knew you were at this hotel?" Bence asked as he brushed debris from his hair.

"One."

"I believe you've found your mole."

"It looks that way. Let's get out of here. It would be better for us to go off the grid and let everyone assume the worst," Acardi said as he climbed over the debris and started down the alley that led them away from the street in front of the hotel.

"What are you thinking?" Bence asked.

"We need to give Montanari the time to get us what we need and not allow whoever is trying to kill me another shot at the brass ring."

"Return to Italy. I'll stay, and you can call and tell me what he discovers."

"Not until Montanari gets back to us. Besides, it's reasonable to assume the person we're searching for may not be in Italy but rather in Paris or elsewhere in France. Otherwise, the minister wouldn't have been involved. Besides, we have a better chance of seeing this through by working together."

"I don't disagree. Do you have your cellphone, or was it blown up in our hotel room?" Bence asked.

Acardi pulled it from his jacket pocket and showed it to Bence.

"Does it have a GPS chip?"

"No."

"Good, neither does mine," Bence said, tapping his pocket to show that his phone was there. "Let's go to my apartment and clean up."

"When the police don't find my body, they'll assume I either survived or wasn't in the room when the explosion happened. After determining I didn't have dinner at Le Basile, they'll look at nearby restaurants, including Chez Monsieur, where the reservation was in my name. After that, they'll examine the security footage from cameras around the restaurant and see you and I leaving together. You'll be easy to identify because your face will be in the government's database. Afterward, they'll call or come to your apartment to question you," Acardi stated.

"You're right; that would be standard police procedure. Do you have any ideas?"

"Are you good at picking locks?"

"I'm embarrassed to say that it's an illicit skill in which I excel."

"Then I have the perfect place for us to stay."

Sciarra learned of the destruction of the Le Basile Hotel when one of his men showed him a video that was viral on social media. The narrator said there was one confirmed casualty. However, he emphasized there could be more as authorities were trying to account for guests who were outside the hotel at the time of the blast, or not in their rooms and in another part of the hotel who fled outside following the explosion. Because Mattei never returned to the aircraft, and he didn't receive their agreed-upon phone call following the hit, Sciarra assumed the casualty mentioned was the Pantellerian and that he was a victim of his bomb.

The Mafioso knew the AISI director's room was on the floor where the narrator said the explosion occurred, and was one of those that was reportedly destroyed. Because of this and the extent of the damage he saw in the video, Sciarra was optimistic that Acardi was dead, an assumption he would soon regret.

Chapter Ten

Two hours before daylight the morning after the re-cremation of the four bodies from the morgue in the demolished Volkswagen Touran, Bruno and his team were in the kitchen, anxious to finally get their investigation underway and planning how they should start. In the process, they'd awoken Albani, who joined them, making everyone an espresso as he listened.

The first decision was to split up so they could get more accomplished. Donais volunteered to spend time with Bianco, who'd let the team use her vehicle, believing she could provide helpful insights into Sciarra and how his organization operated. Having bonded with Albani, Labriola said he'd stay and have a similar conversation with his counterpart. That left Bruno, Donati, and Hunkler to find and observe Sciarra's compound. Once their plans were set, Bruno asked Albani if he knew where Sciarra lived.

"Everyone in the province knows because he isn't trying to keep it a secret, building a massive house surrounded by a ten-foot high wall on the highest hill in Agrigento.

"Can you give me directions on how to get there?"

"It's not difficult. Just return to the main road," Albani replied.

"That's the one we were pushed off?" Bruno asked, wanting to get on the same page.

"That's it. Take the Agrigento on-ramp and drive for five miles until you see the turnoff for Mount Cammarata. Take that offramp and continue straight, ignoring the side streets which lead to other residences and neighborhoods. The road will get steep quickly as it ascends to the top of the hill. Four or five hundred yards ahead, you'll see a large *No Trespassing* sign. Fifty yards beyond that are a set of gates. That's the entry to Sciarra's compound, the gravel road on the other side leading to his house."

"Got it," Bruno said.

"A word of caution. A large vehicle with Sciarra's soldiers is always parked in front of the entry gates. The rumor, which I believe to be true because it's logical, is that his men inspect every vehicle for car bombs before they're permitted inside the compound and frisk whoever's within for weapons. The curious, who have driven to these gates wanting a glimpse of what was on the other side, reported seeing numerous surveillance cameras on the perimeter wall, with armed men stationed every one to two hundred feet along it."

"That's good to know."

"I'm not telling you this because I'm a tour guide; I'm saying this as a warning," Albani said firmly. "In every case, those who ignored the *No Trespassing sign* and proceeded to the gates were dragged from their vehicles. Both they and their cars were searched, and afterward, they were roughed up for ignoring the sign to serve as a warning to others."

"We aren't going to approach the gates or get within view of the cameras because we can't let Sciarra know we're alive. We're planning to observe the compound from a distance," Bruno replied.

"The best place to do that is from the adjacent hill. It's not as high as Sciarra's, but you can look inside his compound without pulling up to the gates. Take these," Albani said, pulling a pair of binoculars from a drawer and handing them to Bruno. "You should know that Sciarra's men are aware that someone can watch the compound from that hill. They also have binoculars. If they spot you, his soldiers will come to chase you away or kill you. I've heard it's gone both ways. So, get there while it's still dark, park your vehicle in the surrounding woods, and stay out of the open."

After dropping off Donais at 6:00 am, Bianco already having had breakfast and an hour into her chores, they followed Albani's directions and, after parking their car behind heavy vegetation on the adjacent hill, found a nearby spot in the dense undergrowth that provided an unobstructed view of Sciarra's compound. Nothing happened for the next thirty minutes until, at the first glint of sunlight, the white SUV that was parked in front of the gates moved, after which they swung open, allowing a black Hummer with a driver and accompanying soldier who Sciarra selected to replace the two involuntarily selected for early retirement, to roar past. "Do we stay here or follow the vehicle?" Hunkler asked Bruno and Donati.

"That's the vehicle that pushed us off the road. I need to have a word with them," Hunkler stated.

"We all need to speak to whoever's inside that car. They're our best chance to find out if she's being held in the compound or somewhere else, and the extent of the security that Sciarra has around her," Bruno replied. "Let's go."

After climbing into their vehicle, which was only ten steps away, Hunkler put the Fiat in gear and raced, as much as the rusted relic was capable, down the hill figuring they had a good chance of seeing the Hummer and following it since the only highway of any significance was the one they'd taken to Agrigento.

As the Fiat neared the bottom of the hill, they saw the Hummer in front of them as it raced down the road and veered onto the northwest on-ramp, indicating it was heading toward the coast.

"Let's give them some space," Bruno said as Hunkler closed on the car. I don't want them to get into another shoving contest."

"You and me both," Hunkler replied, with Donati agreeing.

The Hummer entered the highway, eventually taking the E931 expressway to the Villa della Liberta off-ramp leading to the fourteenth-century town of Siculiana. A mile later, they followed the vehicle as it turned onto the Via Calvario, which led to the center of the tiny commune. Due to the Hummer's size, which dwarfed the compact and subcompact cars that were common in the area, it wasn't hard to follow the massive vehicle and Hunkler was able to keep a significant distance between them. Several minutes after passing through the center of town, the Hummer stopped beside a three-story, twenty-two hundred square feet residence with peeling light yellow paint, which was in the middle of sixteen similar-looking residences in comparable states of disrepair.

Hunkler drove past the residence and made a U-turn, parking the two-decade-old Fiat on the opposite side of the street. Looking out of their vehicle, they noticed an older man, whom they believed to be Sciarra, accompanied by two younger men, leave the Hummer and enter the residence without knocking.

"Security doesn't appear to be strong if the front door is left unlocked," Hunkler said to Bruno.

"Everyone in this tiny fishing community knows that Sciarra owns or uses this residence, and no one is going to enter without an invitation," Bruno said.

Hunkler and Donati acknowledged that he was right.

"It looks like we may have found where he's hiding Lamberti, which also means we can expect one or more of his men to be guarding her."

"What's the plan?" Donati inquired.

"We wait until Sciarra leaves to rescue her. If she isn't there, we'll question whoever's inside to see what they know."

"That sounds reasonable. I suppose there's nothing to do now but wait," Hunkler said, contorting his six-foot-two frame to find a comfortable position, but failing.

Franco Zunino did not have an official job title because Lamberti believed such titles were meaningless. She had a small team of carefully selected professionals, expecting each to understand their responsibilities and those of their colleagues. Everyone, including herself, was employed off the books. This meant their names did not appear in any government database or organizational chart, with their salaries part of the nation's black budget and therefore not subject to public scrutiny.

Zunino and Villa were formerly first captains with the 9th Paratroopers Assault Regiment, which was part of the Army's Special Forces Command. They enlisted in the military the same month and underwent the officer training program in the same class, graduating at the top with Zunino scoring a hair above Villa. Since graduating officers picked their first duty assignment based on class rank, both selected the elite 9th Paratroopers, hoping to be deployed to combat zones in Afghanistan, Iraq, or another hot spot where Italy's military was part of a coalition force. Each got what they wished, distinguishing themselves in Operation Enduring Freedom in Afghanistan, Operation Ancient Babylon in Iraq, and covert actions with allies operating in those countries. However, after more than a decade of being in the field, both were summoned by the regiment commander and informed they were being promoted, which meant they were headed for an undisclosed desk job.

They understood this was the typical progression within the regiment; as soldiers aged, they tended to be slower, less adept, and took longer to recover from the rigors of fieldwork compared to the younger recruits. While those who'd previously been in their position were satisfied to sit behind a desk with a bump in rank, draw the increased pay, avoid the hassle of constant training and occasional deployments, and popping Advil daily to ease the muscle pain, Zunino and Villa wanted none of it. Instead, they sought a position that significantly impacted national security and gave them more satisfaction than pushing paper. However, they didn't know where that job existed when they put in their resignation papers, but were determined to find it.

Because members of the 9th Paratroopers were constantly

solicited to quit their low-paying military jobs and join one of the numerous security firms that actively sought to recruit them because of the regiment's high standards for selection and strong reputation in the field, Zunino and Villa knew they had a means of employment any time they wanted. However, they were uncertain if working for a security firm would give them the *protect the flag* satisfaction they needed to make a career of it or whether they'd be switching one desk job for another. As a result, both resisted the attractive offers from these companies, which pursued them with the intensity of sharks smelling blood in the water upon learning of their impending separation from the military. Instead, they looked for a better option.

Surprisingly, that came from the base personnel officer processing the paperwork that would once again make them civilians. He suggested they apply to the Department of Information Security, which oversaw the AISI and AISE, saying he received a notice that they were looking for security information officers or SIOs. After researching the DIS and learning what they could about the two intelligence agencies that comprised it, they examined the scope of work of an SIO. Liking what they saw, they decided to apply.

The hiring process was brief. After completing and submitting their employment forms to human resources, and following a review of their military records, Zunino and Villa were hired the next day to fill the SIO positions. They excelled in their jobs and quickly gained recognition for the thoroughness of their inspections of military installations and their records, looking for foreign agent infiltration of the installations and security deficiencies that could lead to a terrorist attack or intelligence failure.

Years later, they caught Lamberti's attention when she read several of their reports and learned from others that they were the best SIOs in the DIS, their inspections of several military installations sometimes revealing significant security deficiencies, including foreign infiltration that had existed for years and had gone unnoticed by previous SIOs who had inaccurately rated the bases as satisfactory. Afterward, two things happened: Lamberti dismissed the SIOs who failed to find these deficiencies and she summoned Zunino and Villa to her residence, both having no idea why the wife of the late president, and a former senior official in the Department of Information Security, wanted to see them.

Before the two men arrived at the estate, she reviewed their military records and SIO evaluations, finding both had a history of exemplary performance and the requisite experience and skills for which she'd been searching—wanting someone in her employ who could occasionally silence threats to the state and conduct covert operations without involving other government assets. Therefore, it wasn't long into their meeting when she explained her secretive position within the government and said that she wanted them to quit their jobs and join her team, the sudden request drawing looks of disbelief from both men.

"What would that involve?" Zunino inquired.

"You'd have multiple responsibilities. For those aware of my government position, your role would be to ensure the security of my person and the estate and act as my bodyguards and drivers."

Both men looked at her with an expression that indicated they'd take a hard pass on the offer.

"However," she continued, "unknown to all but my team and the president, I also intend to leverage your military and DIS skills to investigate security threats, either highlighted in intelligence reports or brought to my attention, and to occasionally conduct covert operations on my behalf to neutralize those who pose an imminent danger to this government."

"Neutralize?" Villa asked, seeking clarification.

"Kill."

"We're only interested in that last part. You don't need us for anything else," Zunino said, receiving a nod of agreement from Villa. "From what we've seen, security at your estate is tight. Our vehicle was expertly inspected for explosives, and we were competently wanded and searched before we entered your residence. Although we haven't seen much of the estate, your cameras appear to have overlapping video surveillance fields, which denotes a high level of sophistication in their placement."

"While the sophistication of my security procedures is important, they're tools. My protection ultimately comes down to competency, and you're both at the level I require to remain safe in an increasingly hostile world. Let me be clear: acting as my bodyguards is not a trivial responsibility. While only a small number of people are currently aware of my position as intelligence czar, if our country's enemies learn of it, there's a significant risk that one or more will try and kidnap and interrogate, or even kill me for what I know or the actions I'm taking against them. Therefore, I am entrusting you both with my life because, sooner or later, I will be attacked. Whether tomorrow or five years from now, I need to know that my team, and especially my bodyguards, will have the expertise to have my back."

"How many people are on this team?" Villa asked.

"Twenty-two as of today, excluding the two of you."

"What tools would we have to perform our jobs?" Villa inquired.

"Anything you request will be in your hands within a day. Nothing is off limits and you have no budget."

"We're in," Zunino said, with Villa also agreeing.

Later that day, both men were discretely removed from the employment roster at the DIS and covertly transferred to Lamberti's team and included in the black budget.

Because Baudo made reservations for Acardi at the Le Basile Hotel and kept that information to himself, President Orsini and D'Angelo only learned about Acardi's possible demise when Baudo called the AISE director, who then contacted the president. Zunino and Villa found out soon afterward when Orsini's executive assistant, Patrizia Palmieri, phoned them.

Zunino, who had just returned from Montanari's home, was shocked to hear about Acardi. Knowing that only an insider would have knowledge of Lamberti's annual cemetery visit and where the AISI director was staying, he and Villa began compiling a list of suspects. D'Angelo and his assistant, Bianca Ferrara, Acardi's assistant, and Patrizia Palmieri topped it, the four having been aware of Lamberti's unofficial position of intelligence czar and had been in their positions long enough that it encompassed at least one of her gravesite visits. Moreover, all four could have known about Acardi's schedule.

"What are your thoughts?" Villa asked, tapping his finger on the paper on which he'd written the names.

"This list is only accurate if there isn't an outlier," Zunino answered.

"By outlier, you mean an exception?"

"Exactly. The Signora may have told an outlier about these visits. However, I don't know how we'd begin to learn their identity as the Signora kept her business dealings private. Therefore, setting the possibility of an outlier aside, I think we can start by eliminating D'Angelo," Zunino said.

"Because he's also a repository of an enormous amount of intelligence data, all of which the Signora would have known. Therefore, whoever is behind this kidnapping wants something beyond this commonality. Whatever that is also has to be unrelated to the AISI and Acardi. Otherwise, being the easier target, they would have kidnapped and not tried to kill him," Villa said, following Zunino's reasoning.

"That's what I was thinking."

"Also, if D'Angelo was involved, why contract with the Mafia to kidnap and then keep the Signora in the country rather than at a foreign rendition site in which she'd be anonymous and could never be rescued?" Villa said. "However, the devil's advocate might say that he did this knowing an internal investigation would draw the same conclusion. The flip side of that argument is that he knows

President Orsini's would have a strong resolve to search for her, and that he'd commit the country's entire resources to find out who kidnapped the Signora. D'Angelo would also know that the Mafia was his weak link and that, when confronted, would give him up in a heartbeat to save their skin."

"Leading us to conclude the Signora was kidnapped for information unknown to the AISI and AISE. Therefore, if D'Angelo didn't know about this information, he couldn't have been involved in her kidnapping. Just to be sure, let's check his credit card and banking statements." As Lamberti had access to virtually the entire government database, and Zunino and Villa had pulled financial records during past investigations for her, it took less than a minute to obtain D'Angelo's records, which showed no financial irregularities or unexpected deposits. "He's clean," Zunino said.

Villa took his pen and drew a line through his name on their list. "What about Orsini, D'Angelo, and Acardi's assistants?"

"As we've seen from our dealings with them, unlike us, they know what's going on. They're deeply involved in interacting with others to accomplish their boss's agenda. They also make their travel and hotel arrangements," Zunino said. "Like us, they have ears and pick up things they may not be entitled to know. Therefore, they'd have knowledge of the Signora's cemetery visits, Acardi's trip to Paris, and where he was staying."

"Let's see what we have on them."

Accessing government and Interpol databases, Zunino started with Orsini's executive assistant, Patrizia Palmieri, examining her background and financial information.

"She's fifty-four years old, an only child, and is married with two children and three grandchildren. She was also the president's assistant for ten years before he became president," Zunino began. "Her husband is an aeronautical engineer working at Airbus Italia's office on the Via Dei Luxardo. They live in a small apartment near the Quirinal Place, where she works. Neither of them has a criminal record, and a review of their bank and credit card statements shows that they are not in financial distress. He occasionally flies to Toulouse-Blagnac Airport, which is near Airbus' headquarters," Zunino continued reading. He noted that the remaining information was just as unremarkable as what he had already covered.

"That summary almost put me to sleep," Villa commented— which was his way of indicating the couple was clear. "This leaves Bianca Ferrara and Maurizio Baudo. What information do we have on them?"

"Bianca Ferrara," Zunino began, reading from a summary compiled by the system about D'Angelo's assistant. "She is a sixty-two-year-old widow who lost her husband to pancreatic cancer two years ago. Born in Rome, she graduated from Sapienza University with a degree in political science and currently lives in an apartment in Trastevere, the neighborhood where she was raised."

Zunino and Villa were familiar with Trastevere, the expanse between the River Tiber and Janiculum Hill, which had a reputation for being one of the more romantic areas of the city because of its cobbled streets, medieval churches, small restaurants, artisan shops, and overflowing bougainvillea.

"She also doesn't have a criminal record or any suspicious banking or credit card transactions. Her savings account holds a modest amount of money, and she doesn't seem to be experiencing any financial distress."

"Children? Brothers and sisters?" Villa asked.

"No children, and just like Palmieri, she's an only child."

"Another sleeper," Villa stated.

"Moving on, there's Maurizio Baudo. He is forty-three years old, divorced eight years ago, has no children, and lives in an apartment within walking distance of his office at AISI headquarters on Piazza Dante. He has no criminal record and shows no signs of financial difficulties, as his credit rating is excellent. He became Acardi's executive assistant four years ago. Before that, he worked at Calvario, a traditional limited liability company headquartered in Rome, which has offices in the Eurosky Tower," Zunino said.

"Who owns that company and what's their business?"

Zunino did a computer search. "It's an advisory company with Corrado Bernardi listed as the sole shareholder."

"He must be good at what he does to be in the Eurosky Tower. What kind of advice does Calvario offer?"

Zunino dug deeper. "It's registered with the government as a financial, debt, commodity, and mining advisory firm licensed to conduct mergers and acquisitions."

"That registration covers a wide array of services. Does a mining-oriented company headquartered in Rome seem unusual?"

"It does to me."

"What type of mining?" Villa asked.

"It's not specified in their government filings."

"Does the company have a website?"

Zunino initiated another search, eventually responding that he couldn't find one.

"I've rarely encountered a company without a website. I wonder what Baudo's salary was at that firm?" Villa asked.

"Let's check his tax return," Zunino replied, taking five minutes to access the database of the Agenzia Delle Entrate, Italy's equivalent of the IRS. "His annual salary was ninety-eight thousand dollars," he eventually said.

"And his government salary?"

"Seventy-eight thousand dollars a year."

"That's a twenty thousand dollar a year cut in pay. Why would he leave? Was he fired?"

Zunino checked another government database. "His government job application doesn't indicate that he was fired. In fact, quite the opposite is true, as he listed Bernardi as a reference. HR called and spoke with him, receiving an excellent recommendation."

"What are you thinking?" Villa asked, noticing the questioning look on his face.

"I'm trying to put together what Signora Lamberti's kidnapping has in common with an attempt to murder Acardi, the Sicilian Mafia, the French Minister of the Foreign Affairs, and potentially a mining advisory company and Maurizio Baudo."

"Do you think he was involved in the kidnapping?"

"I'm not sure," Zunino admitted, "but so far, he's the only one on our list that raises a concern."

"How are we going to find out more about him because we have all we're going to get from our database?"

"I might know someone who can help, although I doubt he'll be happy to see me again. Does the Signora have any cannoli left in the refrigerator?" Zunino asked, prompting a puzzled look from Villa.

Since he wasn't fluent in French, Montanari brought a laptop from the other room and placed it next to his desktop computer screen, afterward loading a French-Italian translation program that enabled him to understand the menu items on Bence's server. Locating the Ministry of Foreign Affairs database was straightforward, the menu choices making it easy to navigate there. So far, he had a free ride, bypassing the government's initial layer of firewalls by entering the system as a user. However, since Bence didn't have access to the ministry's database, he needed to employ skills he'd used in his previous profession.

The Savant was skilled at breaching sophisticated firewalls, despite government systems being protected by robust security measures designed by reputable cybersecurity firms and skilled in-house IT professionals to protect their databases from people like him. In the early stages of his cybercriminal career, he concentrated on anticipating these complex obstacles, which some believed made their systems impervious to hacking. However, none succeeded in keeping him out. Montanari attributed his success, in part, to his engineering knowledge and meticulous planning, which included gathering extensive technical information about these highly advanced systems.

It was widely known among hackers that there were three

prominent European computer engineering firms whose prowess and intricately designed firewalls led to their being selected to protect most government databases in the European Union and most large corporate systems on the continent. Their selection was not the result of aggressive marketing or competitive pricing; instead, it was based on their proven performance. Each had an office in Rome and Paris.

Referred to as the *Big Three*, these firms incorporated numerous sophisticated electronic tripwires into their designs to expose any attempt at unauthorized access. If a breach were detected, the host system would automatically lock down, isolating the area of unauthorized access to prevent further entry while simultaneously alerting security and IT professionals. Many thieves tried to bypass these tripwires, and although some succeeded at getting past a few, none succeeded in overcoming them all. Therefore, if he had any chance at breaching the ministry's firewalls, he'd need to obtain the engineering drawings from the Big Three firm that designed the ministry's protection system. The challenge was that he didn't know which was responsible for the design, as this information wasn't a matter of public record. Consequently, if he had any chance of getting into the ministry's files, he first needed to hack the computer systems at all three security firms, whose very existence depended on that being an impossibility.

Montanari recognized that brute force hacking methods, the most common way to access a well-protected system, would be ineffective against a nation-state's computer network because, unlike other targets, a country has unlimited resources to contract for defenses against such intrusions and continually update its systems. As a result, he decided to try an approach he had been considering for years but had not used because he was technically out of the hacking business, although Bruno and Lamberti occasionally sucked him back into that void.

The typical user accessed their system by striking a keyboard that, due to its plastic construction, unavoidably produced noise and generated sound waves when the keys were struck. From a blogger's comments, he knew that larger keys such as Shift, Enter, and Space produced distinct sounds compared to the others, and the timing between key strikes correlated to what keys were pressed. Therefore, whether a user typed words or an alphanumeric character code in the login and password fields, there was a wealth of online data available, especially since there were limited combinations of consonants and vowels, to reconstruct the sequence of keystrokes or identify the words typed. As a result, he believed he could develop an algorithm that combined these elements to recreate the sequence of keystrokes necessary to access even the most sophisticated computer systems.

By including this published data into the framework of an existing program, writing the algorithm took less time than the Savant anticipated. Afterward, he continued to refine it until the program plateaued at ninety-five percent accuracy in identifying what someone was typing on their keyboard. Because he didn't know which one of the Big Three had designed the ministry's system, he needed to gain access to each firm, and once inside find a way to unobtrusively get close enough to one of their keyboards to capture its sounds as someone entered their login and password.

Realizing that gaining this information required having access to their workplace, and that applying for employment was uncertain due to his criminal record—even though he would otherwise be viewed as an extremely desirable candidate—he came up with a way that he believed would allow him to penetrate these firms with relative ease. With the help of Zunino, who had access to the Italian government's database, he searched for external vendors that had contracts with these firms. As he suspected, each company outsourced its housekeeping functions, with the government database listing the names and addresses of these contractors since they were included as business deductions in the firms' tax filings. Therefore, instead of trying to gain access by applying for a job directly with these companies, he instead applied to the housekeeping contractor each used to get inside.

Generally, working in a housekeeping service as unskilled labor is not a career choice but rather a necessity for many individuals. People often choose this path because they lack other employment options, need a second job to supplement their income, or want to avoid expensive daycare costs by allowing one spouse to stay home with the family while the other works. These factors, along with many others typical in an industry that employs unskilled labor, contribute to a high turnover rate. Subsequently, when Montanari applied for employment with each of the service companies used by the engineering firms, he was immediately accepted with the stipulation that he needed to pass a drug test; his criminal record having no bearing on his application. The Savant took his lab tests early the next day and was told within hours that he could begin working the following day.

Because he'd done his share of custodial work while in prison, Montanari required no on-the-job training. Therefore, when the crew arrived at the Big Three firm, he asked the supervisor for permission to clean the top floor, knowing that's where the executive offices were located and that corporate leadership would have the highest level of computer access. No one on the crew opposed this request, as the top floor offices needed vacuuming, while the lower floors primarily had uncarpeted spaces. Additionally, the upper floor offices had much more furniture to dust and polish, whereas the lower floors consisted mostly of cubicles with small offices that contained minimal furnishings. Subsequently, he was able to tape digital recorders under the executives' desks or in other discreet locations that were close enough to capture the sound of typing.

It took longer than expected to obtain the login and password required to access the security company's system. The delay was due to the user either pausing too long before pressing the keys or striking them too hard or too softly, which made it difficult for the program to accurately compile the login information. Eventually, one manager logged in and struck them in a consistent manner, giving Montanari's program what it needed to obtain the login and password sequences to enter their network. However, these efforts were to no avail because when he entered the system he discovered that this firm didn't engineer the ministry's system. Consequently, he quit and repeated his custodial chores at the next contract vendor, only to discover the second firm also didn't have the drawings. This left him wondering if the engineering was done outside Europe and not by the Big Three. However, the third firm proved his initial assumption was correct, obtaining the security architecture for the Ministry of Foreign Affairs' firewalls and tripwires, and other security enhancements he hadn't anticipated.

When he obtained the engineering plans for the system, he found what he was looking for: a backdoor intentionally designed into the system architecture to bypass the standard authentication and encryption processes, allowing the firm to troubleshoot and resolve issues when conventional access methods failed. By exploiting this little-known vulnerability, which is generally unknown to the client and heavily protected by the designer from external access, the Savant was able to circumvent the ministry's firewall and gain access to the categorized data menu within the system.

Once inside, he was looking for anything that mentioned the word *puppeteer*. Given the terabytes of data in the minister's extensive electronic filing cabinet, even a cursory glance would take a considerable amount of time—the longer he remained in the database the greater the possibility that he'd be discovered. As he navigated through the menu, hoping he'd find a selection titled *The Puppeteer*, he struck gold when he found such a label. This meant he didn't have to download and transfer the entire filing cabinet via an internet connection, which posed its own set of challenges. However, there were still two major drawbacks to obtaining the file. First, the attachments within this folder were enormous. Second, designers had installed Endpoint Detection and Response

(EDR) software that prevented the downloading or transferring of files outside the electronic file cabinet. This installation didn't appear within the engineering firm's design, either because it was a new addition and the plans weren't updated or the EDR had been intentionally left off as a failsafe against unauthorized transfers. As a result, he needed to devise a way to trick the system into believing he was transferring the files within the cabinet when, in reality, they were being sent to his computer.

The first step in achieving this goal was to disable the EDR without triggering an internal alarm that would cause the system to shut down and lock out everyone except the IT manager, who alone had the code to reactivate it. According to written procedures, once it was shut down, the system could not be brought back online until the IT manager investigated the situation and implemented fixes to prevent a recurrence.

Montanari began by opening the task manager to examine the active processes running on the system, knowing that if he analyzed them correctly, he'd find the location of the EDR sensor. This examination required a high level of expertise, as the EDR didn't appear in the system's menu. As a result, he had to meticulously review hundreds of system functions in order to locate the sensor software. Once he successfully disabled the EDR, he proceeded to install malware that facilitated the covert transfer of the puppeteer file and its attachments to his offshore data vault.

It took twenty minutes for the data to transfer. Afterward, the Savant deleted his malware and altered the ministry's server logs to hide his access before disconnecting from the government system. He then focused on the data, which, as expected, was entirely in French. After processing it through a translation program and converting it to Italian, he transferred the file and its attachments to an account he had set up at a local data vault, intending to provide Zunino with the login information. However, that call became unnecessary when he heard a knock at the door. Upon opening it, he saw Zunino standing there with a small cardboard box. Montanari knew from experience what was inside because Lamberti had previously brought him cannoli in a similar box. Without saying a word, the Savant took it from his hands and extracted one of the tasty desserts as he walked to his desk, leaving Zunino standing in the doorway.

"This is amazing," the Savant mumbled with his mouth full. "Where does she get these?" He asked, aware that Lamberti was also addicted to the creamy pastry.

"She has them flown in from Pasticceria Cappello in Palermo," Zunino replied as he stepped inside and closed the door behind him.

Montanari knew that cannoli originated near Palermo, with some believing they were introduced to Sicily during the Arab rule of the island, and that Sicilian pastry shops produced the best cannoli in the world.

"I was about to call you," Montanari said between bites. "Here's the internet address, username, password, and the link where I transferred and stored the minister's file on the puppeteer," he said, writing the information on a slip of paper and handing it to him.

"There's something you need to know," Zunino said as he glanced at the paper before putting it in his pocket. The bodyguard then informed him about the explosion at the Paris hotel where Acardi was staying and said he had been unable to contact him.

Montanari, who was fond of Acardi, accepted the news stoically, even though he was struggling internally to hold it together. "If anyone could have survived, it would be him," the Savant said, explaining how the director lived through a similar explosion when a device detonated as he was entering his hotel room, the door shielding him from most of the blast.

"I remember," Zunino stated. "The silver lining is that because of this attempt on his life, we may have identified the mole. But I'll need your help to confirm it."

"Anything."

"You need to do several things. It might help to write these down."

Montanari opened an electronic notepad on his desktop.

"I need to find out what job functions Maurizio Baudo, Acardi's administrative assistant, held with his previous employer, Calvario S.r.l., whose CEO is Corrado Bernardi. Additionally, I want to understand why he left that job for a lower-paying position as a public servant and whether he has any current connections to Bernardi. I am particularly interested in any evidence linking Baudo or Bernardi to Dante Sciarra, the Mafia head of the Agrigento family, or to the late French Minister of Foreign Affairs. I believe there's a common thread connecting them, and I hope you can help me find it," Zunino stated.

"I'm a computer nerd, not an investigator," Montanari responded as he looked at the tasks he'd been given.

"Since the Signora is still missing, you're both," Zunino replied.

Chapter Eleven

Prior to moving to Milan to form BD&D Investigations, Donais lived in a small seven hundred and fifty square feet two-bedroom and two-bathroom apartment in Paris, which she kept out of sentimentality because she loved it and a Paris address looked good on their firm's business card. Knowing it was a sacrifice for her to work in Milan, which she and her partners agreed was a necessity for the team to operate as a cohesive unit, the investigative agency covered the rent and associated costs of maintaining their Parisian office, making it a no-brainer for her to keep the apartment.

Donais returned to Paris four or five times a year, primarily to re-immerse herself in the French culture and enjoy the local cuisine. Her partners occasionally visited when they wanted a break from Milan without traveling too far, as the flight time between the two cities was only one hour and twenty minutes. Acardi would sometimes join them, with the flight from Rome taking just thirty minutes longer.

When Acardi and Bence arrived at Donais' apartment, Bence had no difficulty picking the lock. Acardi, who hadn't bothered to look at his phone for some time because a lot was going on, finally did when they entered the apartment, seeing he had messages from President Orsini, Baudo, and several others asking him to call them and confirm that he was alright.

"I think people are uncertain as to whether I'm dead," Acardi said, showing Bence the messages.

"Let's hope it remains that way, at least until Montanari gets into the minister's database and uncovers something we can investigate. Are you hungry?"

"I'm famished," Acardi replied.

"Me too. It's probably not wise to leave the apartment to get a bite to eat. Our pictures may already be on TV as potential victims of the explosion, and if someone recognizes us and reports it to the media, we'll lose our advantage of being presumed dead. I'll order something from the small restaurant we passed down the street. I have enough cash to keep us fed for a while so we can stay off the grid by avoiding ATMs or using a credit card," Bence explained.

"That's a good idea. I have around four hundred euros," Acardi added.

Bence Googled the restaurant's name on his cellphone and inquired about what they could prepare and deliver quickly, adding that he would be paying cash and that he was a generous tipper. With those last two admonishments, they didn't have to wait long; they received two Croque Monsieur's—essentially glorified ham and cheese sandwiches—in less than thirty minutes. After finishing their meal, Acardi called Montanari.

"You're alive," Montanari exclaimed.

"Barely."

"What about Bence?"

"He's unharmed. It's important that you don't tell anyone you spoke with me. Whoever was behind that explosion knew where we were staying. We have a mole, and until we find them, everyone needs to assume we're dead."

"Zunino was here and expressed some thoughts on that," the Savant said, relaying what the bodyguard told him, with Acardi agreeing that Baudo was the leading candidate for being the mole. "Do you have an issue with me telling him that you and Bence are alive?"

"Not if you're working with them. Tell Zunino to keep this between himself and Villa. They're ex-military and know how to keep a secret."

"I got into the minister's files pertaining to the puppeteer and gave a digital copy to Zunino," Montanari added.

"Can you forward the data to me?" Acardi asked, unsurprised that the Savant had found a way to access the French database.

"I can, but while the files aren't large, the attachments are. Do you have access to a fast internet connection and a computer with a large hard drive?"

"Neither Bence nor I have computers. That means you'll have to review the data and attachments, summarizing what you believe is relevant."

"I'm not an investigator, so I have no way of knowing what information is relevant."

"Don't underestimate yourself. You're an excellent investigator. Over the years, I've watched you analyze situations and solve problems that confounded others, even though they weren't related to your techno world. You have a knack for identifying associations and disassociations in data, leading you to the solutions others overlook. While others may read the same information and find nothing, you have a unique ability to assemble seemingly unrelated data into a cohesive whole. What you possess is truly special. Indro, I know you can do this. Call me when you have something to share," Acardi said, concluding the call.

While Montanari was closely examining Baudo and his connections with Bernardi and Calvario, Zunino and Villa devised a plan to place video and audio devices in Baudo's office and monitor his cellphone conversations. Their strategy involved allowing him to discover one of the surveillance devices, leading to the belief that an intelligence agency suspected him of being a spy and triggering a call to the person to whom he was providing information.

Both understood they couldn't enter the intelligence agency's building unannounced nor pass through security with the surveillance gear. Therefore, to place their devices, which they obtained from Lamberti's extensive inventory of electronic surveillance equipment, they'd need the help of someone who could get them into the building with their gear. Most importantly, that person needed the ability to decrypt the call from Baudo's ghost-chipped phone. Without that, their efforts would be futile. The key question was: whom could they trust enough to reveal their plan?

After talking it through with Villa, Zunino reached out to Patrizia Palmieri, whom they believed was the least likely to be their informant because she went out of her way to inform them about the attack on Acardi. However, when Zunino called and asked her to come to the estate because they had something important to confide and not to tell anyone about the meeting, Palmieri turned them down flat.

"I work for the president. If you have something to say, come to my office," she said. Since she knew just about everything the president was told, she didn't bother to ask why Lamberti wasn't calling.

This surprised Zunino who, along with Villa, considered going to the Quirinal Palace to ask for her help. However, they realized that their presence there without Lamberti would raise questions about why she wasn't accompanying them. Therefore, not wanting to draw attention to their boss, they found themselves in a difficult situation. Aware that a foreign power could easily monitor their call—since it was sent unencrypted and could be intercepted by a satellite or other detection device—he also understood he had no choice but to provide Palmieri with a compelling reason to come to the estate.

"Villa and I believe we've identified the informant responsible for Signora Lamberti's kidnapping and we need your help, without anyone else becoming involved, to prove it."

"Don't say any more; I'm on my way," Palmieri replied.

With that statement, Zunino believed she knew about the

kidnapping since she didn't seem surprised nor question what he'd said.

Palmieri, the no-nonsense person who carried out the day-to-day directives from the president of Italy with the precision of a military non-commissioned officer, dropped everything and arrived at the estate thirty minutes later. The fifty-four-year-old grandmother was met outside the mansion by Zunino and escorted into the kitchen, he and Villa deciding to hold their meeting there and not use Lamberti's office out of respect for her.

"Expresso?" Zunino asked as they sat at the kitchen table, receiving a nod. The bodyguard held up two fingers to Villa, who was standing near the machine.

"Why did you call me and not President Orsini or Maurizio Baudo?" Palmieri began.

"Because we don't know where our investigation will lead, and if something goes wrong, we want to avoid politically damaging the president. Just as importantly, we trust you," Villa stated, explaining how they came to that decision. "Signora Lamberti told us on several occasions that you're the catalyst for implementing whatever the president requests, with everyone you speak to recognizing that you are acting on his behalf. Therefore, your involvement is not unlike receiving assistance directly from him."

"To be clear, I don't make decisions; I carry out his instructions and do my best to ensure he's not blindsided, which is why I'll tell him about our conversation."

"As we would expect."

"You said you've identified the informant responsible for Signora Lamberti's kidnapping. Who is it?"

"We suspect it's Maurizio Baudo," Zunino said as Villa handed Palmieri her espresso.

"Tell me what you have."

Zunino did.

"Acardi is alive? Everyone thinks he's dead," Palmieri said, surprised that the president hadn't been informed.

"He wants to keep it that way until we can confirm the informant's identity, as it makes his investigation easier if he isn't being pursued."

"How can it be easier if he can't get computer or intelligence data, which would be available if he were alive?"

"He has in-country help."

Palmieri had been around long enough to know not to ask where the support was coming from. "Being off the grid is understandable. Tell me how you plan to get the evidence necessary to prove that Baudo is the mole."

"By placing audio and video surveillance devices in his office. One will be carelessly installed so as to be discoverable," Zunino said, explaining why that was important. "We also want to know who he calls and what's said during those conversations. For that, we'll need the AISE to monitor incoming and outgoing calls on Baudo's ghost-chipped phone since they'll have the government's algorithm to decrypt them. This will allow us to identify with whom he's speaking and provide a transcript of what's said."

"President Orsini can direct Director D'Angelo to do that, assuming he supports your actions, which I believe he will. I can arrange for you to access Baudo's office since the president has a master disengage that applies to every cipher lock in every government facility. How were you planning to enter the intelligence headquarters building with your surveillance devices?"

"We were hoping you might assist us."

"Put the devices in a box and give it to me. As the president's executive assistant, I'm exempt from passing through security. They tried that once when I accompanied him and were told that the president's exemption from being scanned or searched also applied to me. As Baudo will be in his office when I arrive, I'll put the contents of the box on Acardi's desk. You can unlock his office using the master disengage. I will also obtain unrestricted building passes for both of you. These don't require you to specify whom you're visiting and will allow you to move around the building unaccompanied."

"Can you get Baudo out of the building while we bug his office?" Villa asked.

"I'll ask him to accompany me to give President Orsini a briefing on the Acardi situation. I'll make sure he's there long enough for you to place the devices. Is there anything else?"

After Zunino confirmed that was all and that he would retrieve the devices, Palmieri finished her espresso and asked Villa for another. By the time she consumed half of it, Zunino returned with a box containing the video and audio equipment and the tools needed for the installation. The pair then escorted her to her vehicle, with Zunino placing the box in the trunk of her car.

"Follow me to Piazza Dante 25," Palmieri instructed. "Once you receive your passes and clear security screening, look outside. You'll have a view of street that runs parallel to the front of the building. When you see my car pull onto the street, wait an extra ten minutes to ensure Baudo has also left. After that, proceed upstairs."

With everyone in agreement on what would happen, Villa got into Zunino's car and they followed Palmieri as she left the estate.

"This woman is all business. What do you think?" Villa asked.

"I expected to face more resistance or at least the imposition of strict restrictions regarding what we can and cannot do. If our actions are exposed, the president's political opponents will use that against him to remove him from office."

"She's smart and understands that we're the president's best chance of catching the mole and finding Lamberti," Villa replied.

"Maybe. I hope we haven't given the fox the key to the henhouse," Zunino said.

While Zunino and Villa were on their way to the intelligence building, Baudo was setting in motion a plan for escaping blame for Acardi's assassination. Because of the death and the extensive damage caused to the Le Basile Hotel, Baudo knew both the French and Italian governments would intensively investigate the incident. The investigation would first focus on who knew where Acardi was staying. Because he'd made the reservations and couldn't think of a single person he'd told other than the director, he'd become the prime suspect as to who leaked this information. Therefore, he needed to shift the blame.

He began by getting the burner phone from his safe, which he occasionally used to email Sciarra and Bernardi, receiving their replies in return. He then entered Acardi's office and placed it in the top drawer of his desk. Although he should have used his ghost-chipped phone for these communications, he chose to use a burner instead. This forced Sciarra and Bernardi to respond to it, providing him with an insurance policy in case the two powerful individuals decided to use him as a scapegoat. If he was going down, he wanted to ensure they would go down with him. He could always turn state's evidence, as he was the least significant player among the three.

Once everything was in place, he contacted Bianca Ferrara, his counterpart at the AISE. He asked her, in light of the recent events in Paris, if she could audit the contents of Acardi's office to determine what he had been working on. This was to ensure that nothing was overlooked when the position was handed over to his successor.

"Do you have confirmation that he's dead?" She asked.

"No, but the explosion occurred in his room. The police have accounted for everyone except him, and medical personnel have no record of taking him to a hospital. I don't mean to sound callous, but considering the size of the explosion, I doubt there would be anything left of Acardi. Hope is a beautiful thing, but if he were alive, he would have called or been admitted to a hospital."

Ferrara admitted that he was probably dead and then asked why he hadn't called someone in the AISI for assistance. Baudo, who had anticipated this question, explained that since Acardi was the director, it was better to have someone from the AISE conduct the audit. This way, no one could accuse the agency of concealing anything in the investigation that was sure to follow. Unsure if she believed him, she thought it sounded like a reasonable idea and agreed to help.

The audit went smoothly at first, Baudo looking through Acardi's credenza while Ferrara searched his desk and subsequently found the burner phone.

"What's this?" She asked, showing it to him.

"It looks like a burner phone."

"I know it's a burner phone," she said sharply, "but why would he have one when he already has a ghost-chipped device?"

"I've never seen this phone before," Baudo said. "He might have kept it for emergencies in case he needed to call someone off the grid."

"Again, that doesn't make sense. The phone he was issued can communicate with non-encrypted devices," she countered.

"Check to see if it's been used," Baudo suggested, setting the hook.

Ferrara set to work, scrolling through the emails for several minutes. Baudo could see her excitement growing until she finally handed it to him to take a look.

"Who would have thought he was behind Lamberti's kidnapping and the killing of the minister," Ferrara remarked.

Baudo pretended to be hurt and betrayed, claiming he had no idea his boss was involved in these crimes. "We need to bring this to President Orsini's attention as soon as possible," he said.

Ferrara said she agreed and would tell her boss what they discovered because, if Acardi were involved in the death of a French minister, as it appeared, their agency would take the lead on that aspect of the investigation. As they were speaking, Palmieri entered Orsini's access code and walked into the office carrying the box that Zunino gave her. Surprised to see Baudo and Ferrara inside, she demanded to know what they were doing.

"We could ask you the same question," Baudo replied.

"The president asked me to review his files to determine if there was anything critical that needed to be handed off," she explained to Baudo, gesturing toward the row of file cabinets with combination locks. "I was planning to call you, but it seems you and Ms. Ferrara had the same idea," she added. "Now, it's your turn to explain."

Baudo recounted the same story he had shared with Ferrara before transitioning to the burner phone that she found, along with the messages it contained. He mentioned they were just about to call her to request a meeting with the president to show him the phone's contents.

"Let me see the phone," Palmieri said. As she scrolled through the emails, disbelief spread across her face.

"Has anyone been in this office since the director left for Paris?" Palmieri asked.

"I don't think I like what you're implying," Baudo responded, feigning indignation.

"It's a reasonable question, and it's one the president will likely ask. I can call him so he can ask you directly if you prefer not to answer me."

Baudo had witnessed the consequences of disrespecting Palmieri or treating her as an unimportant pawn within Orsini's administration. He learned that the president was very protective of his executive assistant, and anyone who offended her would find themselves reassigned to a trivial role in the government before the day was over. As a result, he decided to tone down his behavior.

"As always, I respect your judgment," he backtracked. "We can check the entry logs, but to my knowledge, I'm the only person who has entered this office prior to Ferrara joining me to jointly audit its contents to ensure consistency for the incoming director."

Ferrara confirmed Baudo's account, saying that as she walked down the hall, she saw him enter the office just seconds before her.

"What's in the box?" Baudo asked, having overlooked it earlier in the excitement of the moment.

"Something for the president," Palmieri responded, taking any discussion of what was inside out of play. She then suggested that she and Baudo take the phone to the Quirinal to show it to the president while Ferrara briefed her director. That wasn't the plan she originally had for getting Baudo out of the building, but it'd work just as well. She suspected the phone was a plant, given Baudo's presence in Acardi's office, and hoped that what Zunino and Baudo were doing would refute what was on it. Otherwise, even the president couldn't save Acardi from what would follow. "We'll drive separately. I'll meet you in the lobby and authorize your pass," Palmieri added.

With that, Baudo and Ferrara left. After they were gone, Palmieri opened the box and placed its contents in the center of Acardi's desk. She then left the office, carrying the empty box under her arm.

Zunino and Villa were issued unrestricted building passes and had passed through security when the confrontation between Baudo and Palmieri took place. While sitting in the lobby, they gazed out the floor-to-ceiling windows toward the street, waiting for Palmieri's car to leave the building. Although it took longer than they expected, they finally spotted her departure. They then waited the extra ten minutes as instructed to ensure Baudo had also left before taking the elevator to Acardi's floor and heading to his office. The code provided by Palmieri allowed them entry and, once inside, they found their surveillance gear in the center of the desk.

"Let's get started," Zunino said, after which he and Villa put the surveillance gear in their jacket pockets and walked down the hall to Baudo's office.

The meeting between Baudo and President Orsini was short and took place after Palmieri briefed him about her meeting with Zunino and Villa, as well as what to expect from Baudo. As Acardi's executive assistant went through the incriminating documentation found on the burner phone, Orsini couldn't help but notice his smugness, as if relishing that the purported evidence he was presenting would put his boss in a cell for the remainder of his life.

The president had no definitive proof that Acardi was innocent of the alleged crimes, but he understood honor, character, and commitment—qualities he'd observed in his AISI chairman. The fact that Lamberti, a shrewd judge of character who wasn't easily fooled, trusted him only further cemented his belief that Acardi wasn't a mole and was being made the scapegoat to divert the investigation away from the true perpetrator of the kidnapping.

Once Baudo left, Palmieri returned to his office.

"How did that go?" She inquired.

"Let me answer your question with one of my own. How is it that someone who has been a law enforcement officer their entire life—someone who understands the mistakes that criminals make that lead to their capture—would use the same burner phone to send and receive the most incriminating communications and then leave it in their desk drawer? Anyone with a bit of common sense would have used multiple burner phones, destroying the previous ones to avoid exactly what just happened, or at the very least, they would have stored it in a wall safe."

"It's too convenient," Palmieri agreed.

"I'm not sure if Baudo is our mole, but I'm inclined to lean in that direction given that he preceded you into Acardi's office, which would have given him the opportunity to plant the device in his desk drawer."

"I believe Zunino and Villa are looking into his involvement," she replied. Orsini knew that, in addition to being bodyguards for his intelligence czar, they also conducted investigative work on her behalf. Palmieri then went on to explain their plan regarding Baudo.

"That could work. However, They'll need D'Angelo to decrypt his calls because the AISE has authority over the cipher algorithms used in all ghost-chipped devices. Since D'Angelo believes that

Acardi is a mole and views Baudo as a hero for exposing him, convincing the director to decrypt his communications will be a tall order."

"What other options do you have? You can't order D'Angelo to do the decryption. If that became known it would expose you to harsh criticism for concealing the kidnapping of the wife of the late president. Even if word didn't get out that she was your intelligence czar, which would make the situation exponentially worse, the existence of a government mole and the possibility that the head of one of your intelligence agencies may be responsible for the assassination of a French minister would be catastrophic for your administration," Palmieri said, accustomed to being a sounding board for Orsini and expected to give her opinion. "While D'Angelo is undeniably skilled at keeping secrets, if he feels that he'll take any part of the blame, he'll leak what you told him to do, taking away your plausible deniability and dragging you into this mess."

The president thought for a moment. "Perhaps there is a way. While the AISE has authority over cipher algorithms used in all ghost-chipped devices, they aren't the only organization utilizing these algorithms. If I know Baudo's cellphone number, I'll ask the Agenzia per la Cybersicurezza Nazionale (ACN) to use the decryption key for those series of devices and give me a transcript of incoming and outgoing texts and conversations associated with that cellphone number. I'll also tell them to provide the identity of whoever is texted or called under their mandate to protect national security in cyberspace, and to keep their actions confidential to ensure D'Angelo and the Minister of Justice remain unaware."

"How is that different than involving the AISE?"

"Because the ACN is in the business of cyber intercepts, this will be routine for them."

"You'll no longer have plausible deniability, and this situation could have the same ending: you'll be accused of covering for a friend or, even worse, attempting to pin the crime on Baudo."

"I know, but now that D'Angelo is aware of the phone and its contents, I don't have the luxury of putting this on the back burner because, before long, Baudo will leak the contents of the burner phone he found in the desk of the person who is overseeing domestic security. Complicating matters further is that Acardi is alive, making the fact that he hasn't called, which even I have to admit is unusual, appear as though he wants everyone to believe he died in the explosion so that he could disappear—making him appear guilty of whatever crimes Baudo wants to pin on him. Because of his disappearance, D'Angelo, who is a straight arrow, will also assume he's guilty. Given his role in investigating Italian interests abroad, he'll ask the Minister of Justice to indict Acardi, thereby allowing him to use Interpol's resources to find him. Baudo, who undoubtedly orchestrated this, has made Acardi the perfect scapegoat."

The President's phone rang as he finished speaking, and Palmieri answered it. "It's the Minister of Justice," she said.

The president and minister spoke at length about Acardi, with Orsini not revealing that the subject of their discussion was still alive. Once their conversation ended, the president took a deep breath while giving Palmieri a look of deep concern. "The minister informed me that the French, following a call with Interpol, believe that Acardi hid a bomb in his hotel room and that it prematurely detonated. Based on this assumption, they speculate—whether logically or illogically—that since he was the last person to meet with the minister before his death, he could have had a role in his assassination by inquiring when he left home for work, the route he took, and other useful bits of intelligence."

"That makes no sense," Palmieri volunteered.

"Unless you're in politics," the president replied. "Accusing Acardi shifts the pressure off the French government to find the real perpetrator. If he's dead, they can conveniently close the case as solved."

"But the real killer will never be found," Palmieri pointed out.

"They don't care. As I mentioned, this situation revolves around politics, where many believe that sacrificing justice is an acceptable cost for gaining power or advancing their agenda. Unfortunately, the French government's belief in Acardi's involvement indirectly implicates the Italian government, suggesting that we may have had a motive to want him dead for a reason they've yet to uncover. Make no mistake: the relationship between us and France is about to become very strained. It's crucial that Zunino and Villa provide me with exculpatory evidence for Acardi and proof of who is behind the minister's assassination."

Seconds later, the president's phone rang, and Palmieri answered it. "It's the president of France," she stated.

"This day just keeps getting better," Orsini said, taking the phone from her.

Bence learned that Acardi was believed to be responsible for the bombing at the Le Basile Hotel and was also a suspect in the killing of the Minister of Foreign Affairs when he checked his office emails on his cellphone. He also learned an arrest warrant had been issued in case Acardi survived the explosion, and that his photo had been circulated throughout France and distributed by Interpol to member countries.

"You're a wanted man, both here and in Italy," Bence said, reading one of the emails that had been sent to law enforcement agencies across France.

"With my face all over the media and sent to every police precinct, it's going to be difficult to investigate whatever Montanari provides us. It's better if everyone assumes I'm dead. Since no one has made the connection between us, you'll need to carry on the investigation by yourself."

"I'm sure President Orsini has ways to covertly get you out of the country and back to Italy. If not, I'll charter a boat and get you," Bence offered.

"Involving the president might lead to his removal from office by his political opponents. Besides, if I return to Italy, he won't be able to protect me indefinitely. Obtaining proof as to who's behind this is the only way to exonerate me. That means if Montanari can't help us identify this person, I'll end up spending the rest of my life in a French or Italian prison because I can't hide forever."

"There's a second possibility."

"What's that?" Acardi asked.

"If Bruno and his team can rescue Lamberti, and if she's as smart as you say, she may know who's behind this."

"That's a possibility," Acardi admitted.

"Any idea how he's doing?"

"None. However, keeping me in the dark during the investigation is the norm. I used to take offense; however, since his progression to accomplishing what he set out to do is non-linear, updates are often meaningless and only serve to heighten my anxiety."

"Explain non-linear."

"He and his team succeed by acting instinctively rather than with careful thought, creating a path of destruction that eliminates anyone or anything in their way until only they are left standing when the dust settles."

"I wish I was with them," Bence said.

Chapter Twelve

Bruno, Donati, and Hunkler waited in Bianco's car, watching the three-story residence in Siculiana where Sciarra had entered. Since it was still morning, the midday heat had not yet set in. However, the small Fiat was cramped for the three large men, and without air conditioning, they were already dripping with sweat and feeling dehydrated by the time Sciarra emerged two hours later. Preceded by the two soldiers who'd accompanied him inside they got inside the Hummer, which then made a U-turn and headed toward the main highway.

"I don't know how many of Sciarra's men will be in the residence, but judging from the lack of security in front and that the door was unlocked, I don't expect many," Bruno stated. "Assuming Lamberti is here, as we have no hard evidence that she is, we take down whoever is inside without firing our weapons unless we need to protect her or ourselves. A gunshot may result in one of the neighbors calling Sciarra or his soldiers. In his province, we are not going to come out on top in a gun battle or be able to outrun anyone chasing this Fiat. Once we have her, we return to Favara and get Labriola and Donais, then drive like a bat out of hell to our aircraft in Catania."

"About that. We need to reconsider the last part of our plan because driving at high speeds in this car is not feasible. As you may have noticed, the engine is on life support, something that you wouldn't notice unless you drove it on the highway. In Favara, we didn't go much beyond twenty miles per hour. In fact, I doubt it can make it to Catania," Hunkler stated.

"Is it really that bad?" Bruno asked, as he was not as familiar with vehicles as the colonel.

"The squealing noise coming from under the hood is likely due to a loose or worn belt. If that breaks, we will lose both the alternator and the water pump. The clicking sound, which I initially thought was caused by low oil before checking it in Favara, indicates a valvetrain issue, which explains why we're not getting optimal power. The knocking sound could be due to several factors: clogged lifters, misaligned combustion timing, carbon buildup on the cylinder walls, or back pressure from the exhaust. I could elaborate further, but you get the point. As I mentioned, if we drive locally, it might hold up for a while since there's less strain on the engine. However, I doubt it will last long enough for us to reach Catania."

"We'll ask Albani if we can drive his car or the coroner's van and give him a generous donation from Acardi for its use and retrieving it from the airport," Bruno said.

"Getting back to the present, doesn't the lack of security at this residence make you suspicious?" Donati inquired, putting the question out for discussion. "It's like a spider inviting the fly into its web."

"That's a good analogy, but I believe the unlocked door is about ego," Bruno replied. "Sciarra is making a statement about his omnipresence in his territory, saying he doesn't need a lock because he controls the province, and anyone who thinks otherwise won't survive. His estate, however, is different. He requires security to protect himself from assassins and those who might harbor grudges or covet his territory. I'm sure there's a long list of those who want to end his omnipotence. Regardless of the reasons behind the lack of security, since we believe Lamberti is in that house, we don't have a choice but to go inside and look for her."

"Great pep talk. Let's head into the spider's web," Hunkler said as he opened the car door and stepped out.

Bruno was the first to step inside. He slowly opened the front door and entered a small foyer with an open seating area behind it. Noticing no one was visible, the trio moved toward the staircase at the back, where they could hear two distinct voices coming from the floor above. With guns drawn, Hunkler took the lead, followed by Bruno and Donati.

Each of them, seasoned in their respective fields—Hunkler from his military service and Bruno and Donati from decades in law enforcement—knew the best way to ascend a staircase quietly was to crouch. They moved forward with their hands out to the sides at waist level for balance and crouched lower with each step to absorb the noise. They followed the general rule that the slower you move, the quieter you are. Keeping their weight on their back foot with each step allowed them to absorb the movement in their knees and ankles. Although this cautious approach took a couple of minutes, they were so silent that they couldn't even hear themselves as they ascended the stairs.

When they reached the top, they saw two men conversing in the kitchen, each facing away from them. As they entered the room, they stopped five feet behind the pair. Hunkler then cleared his throat. The startled pair turned in unison and saw three guns pointed at them, prompting them to raise their hands.

Without exchanging any words, Hunkler and Donati kept their weapons trained on the pair while Bruno frisked them, removing a handgun and a knife from each individual. "Find something to tie them up with while I search upstairs," Bruno said before heading back to the staircase.

Hunkler took off the men's belts and shirts, tying them up while Donati kept his gun trained on them.

Since each floor measured just over seven hundred square feet, searching the top floor didn't take long. Bruno returned a few minutes later and reported that it contained two small bedrooms.

Judging by the clothing scattered around and the unmade beds, it seemed to be where Sciarra's men were sleeping.

"Was there any sign that Lamberti had been here?" Donati asked.

"Not that I saw."

The prisoners, with their hands bound behind their backs and their legs secured, smiled upon hearing this comment. Their expressions did not go unnoticed.

"I was certain she was here," Bruno said.

"Why not ask them?" Donati suggested, eliciting another smile from the pair.

"I don't think this will lead us anywhere. They're already in enough trouble for not stopping us. They know Sciarra will kill them if they talk. The real question is: why would he come to Siculiana at this hour to meet with these two and stay with them for two hours? The fact that I saw suitcases in their rooms suggests that this isn't their home. Something is definitely happening, but it may not involve Lamberti."

"Whatever it involves, I'm not going back to the car without something to drink. I'm parched," Hunkler said, going to the refrigerator in hopes of finding bottled water. He did. However, in addition, he spotted three vials inside, two of which he didn't recognize. The third was benzodiazepine. While the truth serum piqued his interest, what truly caught his attention was the presence of bags of dextrose IV solution stored within.

"Take a look at this," Hunkler said, opening the refrigerator door all the way so that Bruno and Donati could see inside. "Dextrose IV solution and benzodiazepine."

"We need to take a harder look at this place. Gag them so they can't alert anyone," Bruno said. As Hunkler grabbed some kitchen towels, he and Donati took a closer look at what Hunkler had discovered.

Once the men were gagged, the trio went to the bottom floor, looking at seams in the wall and floor or anything else that might provide a clue to the location of a hidden room where they believed Lamberti was being kept. They found what they were looking for just ten minutes after they started when Bruno pressed on an almost invisible seam in the wall, causing a door to spring open revealing a descending stairway.

They slowly descended the unlit passageway with their guns drawn, opting not to turn on the light switch at the top of the stairs; doing so would make them even more of a target if any of Sciarra's men were below. The room at the bottom was lit, and as the trio entered, they quickly spread out to avoid making themselves easy targets.

Inside the room, they saw only one piece of furniture: a steel cot. On it lay an unconscious Pia Lamberti, her limbs secured to each corner with leather straps, and an IV was connected to her left arm. As they approached her, their concern grew upon seeing how frail she appeared. They hurried to unfasten her restraints.

"We have no chance of carrying her out of here in this condition without one of the neighbors seeing us," Donati said. "If she could walk, we'd have a shot at it."

"It's the hand we've been dealt," Bruno replied. He then turned to Donati and said, "Elia, go upstairs and grab the bags of dextrose. Meet us at the car."

As he left, Bruno had Hunkler gently lift her off the cot while he held the IV bag and draped a sheet over her. The colonel carried her up the stairs and to the car with Bruno in tow. Donati arrived as Hunkler put Lamberti in the backseat with Bruno. Afterward, Hunkler put the cancerous Fiat in gear and headed for Favara.

Sciarra learned of Lamberti's rescue from two nearby residents who'd debated for nearly forty-five minutes about whether to inform the Mafia don or let the incident go unnoticed. They were concerned that telling him what they had seen would imply they were curious neighbors, which could be hazardous to their health. On the other hand, not telling him could be just as dangerous if he expected the neighborhood to look out for his interests and learned they hadn't said anything. Ultimately, they concluded that concealing what they witnessed was riskier than their curiosity and informed him. They described seeing three men, one carrying a woman out of his residence while another held an IV bag, and that a third person joined them, with everyone departing in an old Fiat that headed toward the main highway.

Following the warnings from his neighbors, Sciarra tried unsuccessfully to phone the men guarding his captive, their lack of response confirming that Lamberti had been rescued. The neighbor's description of the car in which Lamberti left matched that of the woman in Favara whose farm was adjacent to the site of the crash that his now-deceased soldiers had visited. Putting it together, it was apparent that at least some, and possibly all, of the investigators had survived and were assisted by the woman and perhaps others in the town. It was also evident they were given the information and resources to rescue Lamberti. Angry that he'd been stabbed in the back by locals, he decided that when this was over, he would exact retribution for their disloyalty and leave the bodies of everyone even tangentially involved in the town square as a warning that being disloyal had consequences.

Sciarra believed that if the investigators were clever enough to find the residence and hidden room where Lamberti was being held and rescue her, they were intelligent enough to know their best chance for safety lay in reaching the Catania airport and leaving Sicily. However, what concerned him was that because they were receiving help from the Favara woman, she'd know the numerous backroads that branched through the countryside, which didn't appear on any map but had been known to the area's residents for generations. Some were only narrow strips of land barely a car wide, originally used in the era of horse and donkey transportation as riding and walking paths between towns and villages. If she'd given them directions on how to navigate the backroads to Catania, they would be difficult to track down.

180 |

To address this, he needed significant help from local residents to locate them. Controlling his urge to jump into his car and chase after their vehicle, he spent thirty minutes calling key members of his clan in the surrounding towns and villages and instructing them to look out for a red Fiat, capturing and holding those within until he arrived. Once the calls were completed, he and a dozen of his soldiers got into four vehicles and drove toward Catania.

When the trio arrived in Favara, they went straight to Albani's residence, where he and Labriola lifted Lamberti onto a gurney and brought her inside. Bianco and Donais, whom the doctor brought from the farm at their request, watched as the two doctors examined her.

"She's in a coma. Since I don't see any signs of injury or trauma, and there are puncture marks in her arm, it appears to be drug-induced," Albani said once their examination was complete.

"Do you have any idea when she might regain consciousness?" Donati asked.

"She may not survive because her vital signs are not good. Whatever they have administered has taken a toll on her body, leaving her hovering between life and death. The situation could go either way. The only thing we can do right now is continue the dextrose drip, which will keep her hydrated and provide her with essential nutrition, giving her a chance to survive."

"Call President Orsini and request that he send the military to extract Lamberti along with us," Labriola instructed Bruno. "Sciarra and his men are no match for them. The military can either helicopter everyone to Catania or provide an armed escort to convoy us to the airport. Either way, we get Lamberti the urgent care she desperately needs and we all make it out of here alive."

"That would normally be an actionable idea, and one I've considered," Bruno said. "However, it's not feasible for several reasons. We were ordered to keep Lamberti's kidnapping a secret. Mobilizing a rescue force can't be done discreetly, as landing even a single military helicopter with troops or arranging a vehicle escort to Catania would definitely attract attention from the locals and those at the airport. Someone will see us. Someone, even if it's the rescue force, will see her."

"Setting aside the optics, this isn't a movie. I've been part of a mobilization force, and in my experience, it usually takes hours, not minutes, to generate a response team," Hunkler pointed out.

"Sciarra will get to us before help arrives, having more than ample time to find us before then," Bruno stated. "We need to get Lamberti to Catania as soon as possible, not only because she may die without additional medical care, but Sciarra will by now have learned that she's missing and be after us with a vengeance. It doesn't take a genius to figure out that we're going to the Catania airport because that's where our aircraft is hangared, and it's our only way off the island. In my opinion, we reach the airport before him, or we'll die."

Albani conceded that Bruno was correct about Sciarra. "He isn't known for overthinking a situation. On the contrary, he's reactionary and impulsive, having a ready-fire-aim mentality."

"I have an idea that will buy you time to get her out of Sicily, but we must act quickly," Maria interjected, surprising everyone.

"Tell us what you have," Bruno said.

"My plan takes advantage of his impatience. Because you rescued the Signora using my car, and his soldiers have been to my farm and seen it, he'll follow it through the gates of hell if necessary, believing that all of you are inside. However, instead of you, I'll be driving, using the backroads that run northeast toward Catania to draw him and his men toward me while you escape."

"That's a death sentence. I don't want you involved," Bruno responded.

"I already am. As I said, Il Bastardo already knows that I'm involved with you. Even if someone in Siculiana didn't see you and Signora Lamberti getting into my car, those two morons in the Hummer took a video of it when they were at my farm. Sciarra had to see it, although I don't think he was happy with them because their bodies were dumped beside the coroner's van."

"If he killed his men for failing to do whatever, he won't think twice about killing you. Consider that when he stops your car, which we both know he will, your fate is sealed. I won't let you die to save us."

"The six of you will die if you try and get to Catania without my help. Afterward, Sciarra will come to Favara to deal with me and the doctor. The dice are already cast."

"Even if you act as a decoy, how do we escape?" Bruno asked.

"My cousin, Salvatore Costa, owns a small commercial vessel called the Sogno d'Oro, or Golden Dream, which he keeps at the Siculiana Marina. I'll call and ask him to take you to Malta, which is one hundred fifty miles from the marina. Your plane can meet you there and take you to Rome."

"Why can't we all get on that boat?" Hunkler asked.

"Il Bastardo isn't stupid. If he or any of his men don't spot my car soon, he'll assume you're leaving Sicily by boat—the only other way off the island. Because Siculiana is the closest marina, he'll start by looking there. In a few hours, it won't matter if he figures out you took a boat, because you'll be far from the coast and deep into the Mediterranean Sea, making it impossible for him to find you. Even if he suspects that Malta is your destination, he won't have the resources to track you in the vast area between the two islands."

"That's why the decoy is crucial; it diverts his attention from the possibility of us being on a boat," Donais reluctantly agreed.

"It's the only way. I figure I need to keep up the charade for at least an hour after you leave the marina. Given the speed of the Sogno d'Oro, you'll only be about twenty miles from shore. That distance may not be far enough because it's well known that Sciarra has cigarette boats along the coast, which he uses to run contraband. These boats can travel at three times or more the speed of my cousin's vessel, and if they have navigational radar—which I would assume they do, considering their operations—it will be easier to locate his boat the closer it is to shore, as the search area is more defined."

"Unfortunately, you make a strong argument," Bruno conceded. "Call your cousin and see if he's up for this."

Maria did, after the call confirming that he would take them to Malta.

"How do we get to the marina?"

"You'll take my coroner's van. The route is the same as when you went to Siculiana, but you'll get off at the marina exit instead of heading into town. It's an additional five minute drive," Albani explained. "There'll be enough space in the van for all of you, and you can lay the Signora in the back." He then handed Bruno the vehicle keys, who then passed them to Hunkler. "Since Maria isn't on the highway yet, you need to leave now in case Sciarra and his men come here looking for her."

Bruno agreed, and the doctors carefully slid Lamberti's gurney, with her bag of dextrose attached to its IV pole, into the back of the van. After Albani and Labriola secured it to the deck, Labriola gave Albani a tight hug, aware that this might be the last time he'd see him. Albani then stepped out of the van, leaving only Labriola, Hunkler, and Donati inside. Meanwhile, Donais stood beside Bruno, who was speaking with Hunkler through the open driver's window.

"Are you certain you want to stay?" The colonel asked as Bruno handed him his government credit card.

"I am."

"If you're captured by Sciarra, you'll be tortured for what you know and then killed. Consider this: no matter how strong our desire to help them is, what can you actually do? As Maria mentioned, the outcome is already determined—the die has already been cast."

"I'm unsure how I can help them, but I can't let her and the doctor suffer the consequences of our actions while we remain safe because of their sacrifices. I will do my best to keep them, and by extension me, alive until you return with what the Americans would call the cavalry."

"Your red line in the sand," Hunkler said.

"Something like that. One more thing: because it's crucial to keep your location secret, make sure to turn off your phones. This way, there's no possibility of anyone tracking you. Even if someone can't decrypt your conversation, they can still detect your transmission and determine your location with the right equipment. Nothing is more important than safely getting Lamberti to Italy."

"Understood. I'll be back. You can count on it," he promised.

Donais, who'd yet to get into the vehicle, followed Bruno as he walked away. "Are you sure you don't have another reason for staying?" She asked.

"Only what I said."

"I know it's been a while since you've dated or gone out with someone you care about. In fact, I don't recall either happening since I became your partner."

"Understanding what you're implying, you should know that I had the most wonderful wife anyone could ask for until she was taken from me. I'm not looking to replace her, so you don't need to worry about me. Now, please leave quickly—Sciarra could arrive at any moment."

"I'm going," she said, hearing Hunkler call for her to get inside the van. "So that you know, Maria didn't only discuss Sciarra with me while I was at her farm. She also asked about you in a way that made me think she's interested in getting to know you better. I told her what happened to your late wife, what you did to avenge her death, and what I know about Mauro Bruno as a person rather than just as an investigator. All I'm saying is that you should keep your eyes open and talk to her. The rest will either happen, or it won't." With that, and Hunkler yelling for her to get into the van, Donais climbed in and closed the door behind her, after which the vehicle sped away.

"Why are they leaving without you?" Maria asked, as she watched the van pull away.

Bruno told her.

"Thank you for caring about us," she said, tears welling in the corners of her eyes. "We'd better make ourselves seen, or your friends aren't going to get very far," she said as she opened the door of the red Fiat and got inside.

To make her plan believable, Bianco took the backroads toward Catania, the dirt thoroughfares weaving through the hills and leading her northeast toward Castrofilippo, a distance of seven miles. Along the way, she explained the town of thirty-one hundred was a stronghold of Sciarra loyalists, from which he routinely recruited his soldiers. Therefore, if Sciarra alerted for those in the area to watch for her car, as she expected, someone would likely report that they had seen her pass through.

"Why wouldn't they stop and bump our car off the road or set up a roadblock and hold us until he arrives if Sciarra wants us so badly?" Bruno asked.

"They won't attempt to force us off the road since we're in a moving vehicle. I suspect il Bastardo doesn't want us harmed or killed, at least for the moment. Besides, he'll want everyone, especially the Signora, to be alive and will have communicated that to his men. No one wants to take a chance stopping a moving vehicle for fear we'll be hurt, incurring Sciarra's wrath. As for the roadblocks, that remains uncertain. Implementing them requires manpower and organization, so they may not have put them up or placed them on other roads in the area."

"I know you said at least an hour, but how long is the optimal time that Sciarra needs to chase us?"

"Three hours."

"And after that?"

"By then, your friends will be too far offshore to locate. If we've managed to avoid capture, the plan shifts to lose whoever is following us and find a place to hide until your friends send help."

"What about the doctor?"

"He won't be easy to find," she answered, not going into detail.

Ten minutes later, they entered Castrofilippo. To increase their chances of being noticed, Maria stopped for pedestrians crossing the street, even though there was no crosswalk, as rural Sicily typically didn't have designated crossing areas. However, once they were in front of her car, she honked her horn at them, a gesture considered rude and typically associated with foreigners and people from large cities. She repeated this gesture several more times to ensure her car would draw attention. It seemed to work because, by the time they reached the other side of the small town, an old pickup truck was following them.

Upon arriving at the Siculiana Marina, Hunkler parked the van in an unobtrusive spot at the back of the parking lot, choosing this location to ensure it would be difficult to see unless someone was very close to it. Although there were numerous spaces nearer the docks and boat slips, he wanted to delay, as long as possible, the inevitable question about what a van with "coroner" stenciled on each side was doing at the marina.

Having seen the van enter the parking lot, a man walked to it just as Hunkler and Labriola slid Lamberti's gurney out the rear door. He was five feet eleven inches tall, with a slender yet muscular physique, a black stubble beard, and a tanned, weathered face that reflected the many hours he had spent on deck. As he got closer, he introduced himself as Maria's cousin, Salvatore Costa—Hunkler, Donati, and Donais also giving their names. Afterward, he pointed to his boat, saying they should get underway as soon as possible.

Once everyone was onboard, and Lamberti was safely below deck and her gurney secured so it wouldn't move with the rocking motion of the boat, he wasted no time casting off, telling them they could discuss what they needed to talk about while at sea. Later, Hunkler and Donais went topside to speak with Costa, while Labriola remained with his patient.

"I know we're going to Malta, but can you give us a little more detail?" Donais asked.

"I'm taking you to Marsa, a small town on the southeastern side of the island. It's the closest port to the country's only airport, where I was told your plane will be waiting," Costa explained as he steered the boat toward the breakwater.

"That sounds simple enough."

"Nothing is simple if Sciarra is chasing you. But I promised my cousin that I'd get you there, and I always keep my word."

"What type of cargo do you transport?" Hunkler inquired, trying to establish a rapport.

"The kind of cargo you wouldn't want to be caught transporting, or you'll spend a chunk of your life in prison. Contraband, to answer your question," he clarified. "I and others like me transport items that are too large to fit in Sciarra's cigarette boats," he added matter-of-factly.

"Does contraband include people?"

"It does for some, but not for me."

"When he discovers that the person he's pursuing isn't in your cousin's car, and then finds out your boat has left the marina, won't he be suspicious that she's on board?"

"I don't work exclusively for him. He prefers using his cigarette boats because hiring someone like me is expensive, the cost reflective of the jail time we'd incur if caught. That's why I haul legitimate cargo most of the time; it keeps us under the radar with authorities, who aren't suspect our activities, which include the occasional indiscretion."

Changing the subject, Hunkler asked when they would arrive in Malta.

"If the weather forecast holds, it should take about nine hours. Get some rest. The seas are expected to be calm, and there's plenty of food in the galley."

"Do you need anything?" Hunkler asked.

"Just luck," Costa replied as they passed the breakwater.

"Where are you now?" Sciarra asked.

The driver of the old pickup truck replied that they were on a backroad heading from Castrofilippo to Canicatti, which was six miles and change from them. "What do you want me to do?" He asked.

"Follow, but don't try and stop them," Sciarra instructed.

To the Mafioso's way of thinking, the news couldn't have been better. Canicatti was in his province, with nearly every public official directly or indirectly on his payroll. Strada Statale 122, known as the Agrigentina road, was the highway that would take them there, making it unnecessary to follow the investigators along the backroads. The fact that they were on this dirt path suggested that someone in Favara had given them this route to avoid detection on the main highway. When this was over, he planned to make an example of whoever did and the town.

"Step on it," Sciarra told the driver, who promptly pressed down on the accelerator, with the other three vehicles closely following behind.

"We're entering Canicatti. The truck following us has most likely informed il Bastardo of our position," Maria said. "They, or others, will try to stop us before long."

Bruno glanced at his watch. "We initially said we needed to hold out for an hour to give your cousin a chance to escape detection."

"We don't have that long," Maria replied, tapping her gas gauge to emphasize her point. "We have at most fifteen minutes before we run out of fuel. Any suggestions?"

Bruno was about to say he had none when a thought occurred to him. "Can you lose the pickup truck that's following us?" He asked.

"It looks older than my car," she replied, looking in the rearview mirror. "Maybe, if I don't blow the engine."

"If you lose it and we park the car where it'd be difficult to find, that will buy us the additional time—and possibly more."

"That makes sense. Let's give it a try," she said, making a quick U-turn and heading in the opposite direction and down a side street.

The pickup, caught by surprise, didn't have the wheelbase to make a tight turn in the narrow street and had to execute a three-point turn, grinding the gears as the driver shifted between drive and reverse and back again. By the time it had turned around and headed down the side street, the Fiat was out of sight.

For the next twenty minutes the pickup crisscrossed the area unsuccessfully looking for the car. Their search came to a halt when the driver received a call from Sciarra, who was entering the city and wanted to know the location of the Fiat. Reluctantly, the driver informed him that they'd lost sight of it, drawing a heated response from his boss.

As Maria zig-zagged through the town hoping to find a place to hide the car, she saw in the distance a dense field of prickly pear cacti. The thorny fruit had been part of the Sicilian landscape for centuries, as the island provided the perfect climate for them to thrive. Although there were numerous species of the cacti, the one that flourished around Canicatti was the opuntia ficus indica, which grew to a height of sixteen feet.

Without a moment's hesitation, Maria accelerated towards the field, driving down the dirt road that surrounded the grove and facilitated the transport of the harvested fruit. Radiating from this circular road were two-person-wide paths spaced at ten-foot intervals, allowing laborers to pick the fruit without getting injured by the cacti's sharp thorns. Turning off the perimeter road, she drove onto one of these paths before making a sharp left turn and severing the base of a cactus, the vehicle coming to a sudden stop upon impact with the cactus crashing down onto it.

"That was smart thinking, Maria. With that large plant covering us, it will be difficult for anyone to spot the car from a distance, giving my team the time they need to escape. Now we just need to figure out how to get out of this field without being seen."

"Since we were seen entering town but not leaving it, il Bastardo will scour every inch of Canicatti trying to find us. We'll have a better chance of escaping this grove and hiding in the town if we wait until nightfall. In the meantime, I need to call Doctor Albani and have him go to the marina to retrieve his van before it's seen and brought to Sciarra's attention. If that happens, our efforts will be meaningless since my cousin's boat is still close to shore."

"Give him a call."

"I can't."

"Why?"

"I don't have a phone. I broke it along with the SIM card when I decided to use my car as a decoy?"

"Why did you destroy your phone?"

"If il Bastardo got ahold of it, he'd have my contact list and could see those I recently spoke to, including my cousin."

"At least we have my satellite phone," Bruno said, holding it up for her to see.

"The screen is blank. Is it on?"

Bruno checked the phone and noticed a barely visible red battery symbol on the LED screen with one percent displayed below it. He remembered that the phone would automatically shut off when the battery life dropped to three percent. He told Maria.

"Did you bring your charger?"

Bruno shook his head. "It's at the doctor's house. We were in such a hurry to leave that I didn't think to take it or my bag."

Just then, they heard the sound of an approaching vehicle. "I think we should assume this is Sciarra or one of his men," Bruno said.

She nodded in agreement.

"We're an easy target in the car. Let's get out and hide in the field," Bruno suggested, as he put his shoulder to his door. However, because the vehicle was tightly wedged in the deconstructed cacti, it took considerable effort to open it wide enough to squeeze out. Maria, unable to open her own door, came to his side and followed him through the narrow opening. Both suffered puncture wounds and cuts to their exposed skin, along with numerous tears in their clothing from the sharp thorns as they painfully made their way from the car only seconds before they heard someone yelling that they'd found the vehicle.

It wasn't by chance that one of Sciarra's men discovered the Fiat. One of the Mafioso's informants, who'd been told to be on the lookout for such a vehicle, and who lived near the grove, spotted it. The information quickly reached Sciarra, who then directed his driver to head there, handing him the phone so the person on the other end could provide directions. However, when he arrived, one glance at the height of prickly pear plants told him that finding the vehicle and those inside would be anything but easy. It wasn't until one of his men discovered the trail of broken cacti and followed it that they located the Fiat's final resting place.

Il Bastardo's men were eager to impress their boss by being the first to catch the persons they were chasing, and fanned out to search for them. However, it wasn't long before they ran into trouble, Sciarra watching as they struggled to get through the prickly plants and winced in pain after going less than a foot.

He shouted for them to stop and return to their vehicles, knowing that only a stroke of luck would allow them to catch anyone as they had no idea which direction they'd gone and were advancing at a snail's pace through the dense field of thorny plants. He had a better plan to flush everyone out.

After asking one of his men to take off his shirt and hand it to him, which he did without hesitation, he pulled a lighter from his pocket, set the shirt on fire, and tossed it into the field. Since prickly pear plants are only watered every two to three weeks, the area was dry and fire spread quickly. The Mafioso then got into his car and drove to the front of the grove, which was slightly elevated, knowing that those within the car had two choices: leave the field and surrender or be burned alive.

Chapter Thirteen

When Baudo returned to his office, he felt satisfied that he had successfully made Acardi the scapegoat for not only his own illicit activities but also those of Sciarra. Now that the director, the French minister, and Lamberti were out of the way, nothing would hinder the venture that Bernardi was assembling which, when fully operational, would control a significant segment of the world economy. As he leaned back in his chair and envisioned the wealth and power that would flow to him from his benefactor, he noticed that one of the ceiling tiles at the back of his office was not perfectly aligned with its frame. Curious, he grabbed a chair and positioned it beneath the fiberglass tile. Leaning closer to inspect the protruding edge, he nearly fell off the chair when he spotted a tiny camera lens.

In a state of panic and eager to get a closer look, he hurried to the maintenance room down the hall. There, he found a ladder and a flashlight. After bringing them back to his office, he replaced his chair with the ladder and, removing the ceiling tile, peered into the space above, noticing the camera had a wire of the same diameter trailing from it. The wire and what appeared to be a transmitter, judging from the antenna protruding from it, were connected to a battery and secured to a small piece of wood.

Baudo realized that the camera would have been nearly invisible in the infinitesimal gap between the ceiling frame and the tile if the installer hadn't been careless and left the tile slightly ajar. He was fortunate to have noticed it. He also understood that no one could have accessed the building, let alone entered his office, without the highest level of clearance. Furthermore, a camera of this size could only originate from one of the intelligence agencies, suspecting it had to come from the AISE since he had insider knowledge of the AISI.

This led him to conclude that Orsini and Palmieri had staged a convincing act, making him believe he was still a trusted member of domestic intelligence by accepting his explanation and purported proof that Acardi was their mole. However, the presence of the camera told a different story. Since whoever was monitoring the video had already seen him discover the surveillance device, he retrieved a pair of scissors from his desk and cut the wire connecting the camera to the battery, thereby severing the video link.

After pulling himself together, Baudo called Bernardi and then Sciarra on his ghost-chipped phone. He could have sent them a text using a burner phone like he had done before, but it was difficult to carry on the type of conversation he wanted through text. Besides, he could better gauge their reactions by hearing their voices rather than reading a composed response. Therefore, he chose to use the encrypted phone to inform them about the surveillance camera placed in his office and his suspicions that the AISE had installed it under Orsini's direction.

Normally, Sciarra and Bernardi would be in agreement that he should receive the same accelerated retirement plan awarded to the two Mafia soldiers. However, because of the extraordinarily difficulty in getting someone through the interview processes and security clearances required for the position of an executive assistant to an intelligence agency director, they weren't ready to throw in the towel on Baudo until they were certain he'd been exposed. Consequently, they advised him that nothing had changed, but he should exercise more caution in the future and destroy the burner phone, relying instead on his ghost-chipped device, which could neither be hacked nor traced.

As Baudo spoke with Sciarra and Bernardi, Villa and Zunino listened to their conversations and watched the video being transmitted from a device hidden in a crease at the edge of his office, where the wooden floorboards met the molding. The wire, which had a micro-camera and miniature microphone at the end, received power from an electrical outlet less than a foot away. Although the audio and visual recordings conclusively proved that Acardi's executive assistant was the mole, they could not identify the individuals he had spoken with. To accomplish that, they would need Director D'Angelo's help. Even though Orsini could arrange that with a simple phone call, they preferred to keep the president publicly uninvolved since Acardi was being accused of murders that couldn't yet be linked to Baudo, and they wanted to avoid any suggestion that Orsini was orchestrating someone else to take the fall.

Zunino and Villa were aware that they were perceived as Lamberti's bodyguards, and if they called and asked Bianca Ferrara to request a meeting with her boss, they would be told that he was very busy, which was true. They would also be informed that they needed to present their agenda to her first to determine if she could be of assistance, which was political doublespeak for saying she wanted to evaluate their request before deciding if it was worth her boss's time.

To circumvent this process, they chose to avoid Ferrara altogether. They anticipated that once she learned they intended to inform her boss that Baudo was responsible for the crimes of which Acardi was accused, she would advise them to take those accusations to the police, as domestic investigations fell outside the AISE's scope of responsibility. And, if that wasn't enough to get them promptly escorted from her office, if they proceeded to explain that they had proof, including audio and video surveillance from Baudo's office, there was a strong possibility she would think they had illegally entered his office and planted a surveillance device, deserving that they'd be arrested rather than justification for granting the meeting. However, if they got this far without being arrested or sent packing, once she listened to the recording, and instead of accepting that it substantiated Baudo's guilt, she might instead conclude they had electronically altered his conversation to suit their purposes. Therefore, to avoid this potential predicament, they decided to bypass Ferrara and ask someone to arrange the meeting whom D'Angelo couldn't turn down.

Palmieri was Zunino and Villa's ideal choice to set the meeting because everyone knew she spoke for the president. Without her help, they could only ask Orsini to remove Baudo from his position, as their surveillance video was inadmissible in court because it was illegally obtained. However, they couldn't allow that to happen yet because he was their only means to find those responsible for the kidnapping. Therefore, with their backs to the wall, Zunino called Palmieri and requested a brief meeting, emphasizing they couldn't discuss what they wanted on an open line, but it was urgent that they meet. On the heels of Baudo's conversation with Orsini, and wanting to keep them away from the president because building security kept a log of everyone who came to his office, she agreed to meet in the cafeteria in thirty minutes. Zunino said they'd be there.

With Palmieri again providing them with unrestricted building passes and the information desk directing them to the cafeteria, they entered twenty-eight minutes after their call ended. They found her sitting at a corner table with three cups of espresso in front of her.

"You're intent on making me an accessory," Palmieri said with a note of humor as they approached.

"It's been difficult, but Villa and I believe we've finally found a way," Zunino replied, handing her his cellphone with wired earbuds attached.

Palmieri was expressionless as she looked at the video. "He's a sacco di feccia," she said, calling him a scumbag as she returned the cellphone to Zunino. "Put a bullet in him and do our country a favor."

"As much as we would like to do that, we need to find out what he knows first. To do that, we require your assistance," Villa said.

"You already know I can't involve President Orsini. That said, and given what I saw and heard, what do you want me to do?" She asked.

"Ask Director D'Angelo for a transcript of what was said on Baudo's ghost-chipped phone," Villa replied.

"Recording domestic communications, even if that conversation occurs on a government phone and uses an algorithm developed by his agency, exceeds the AISE charter and is prohibited by law. Besides, how can you be sure he possesses such recordings?"

"We don't," Zunino interjected. "However, we believe that on the pretext that many of the conversations on the encrypted phones are made by government officials to those outside the country or when they're on foreign soil, that he might want a record these discussions. After all, he is in the business of gathering foreign intelligence. If he does have such recordings, he'll be able to decrypt Baudo's conversations and identify the people he contacted."

"Like it or not, my involvement pulls the president into this," Palmieri replied.

"Baudo is leading D'Angelo and law enforcement in the wrong direction. That needs to change or he'll get away with this and Acardi, with no way to prove his innocence, will be in jail for the rest of his life. Even if he doesn't have transcripts of the conversations, we'll need the director's assistance to stop Baudo and to uncover who orchestrated the Signora's kidnapping," Zunino stated.

"Alright," Palmieri said, "let's get this done." Removing the cellphone from her jacket pocket, she called Bianca Ferrara to check if the director was available for an urgent meeting. Since both were executive assistants responsible for managing their bosses' schedules, and given that Palmieri worked for Orsini, Ferrara agreed to let them come to his office and assured Palmieri that she would ensure they were seen promptly.

"You have one shot at this," Palmieri said as both Zunino and Villa sipped their espressos. "I know D'Angelo. He has a fact-driven mentality. Give him details, not suppositions. Don't rush your words; be methodical and maintain eye contact when you speak," she advised, fully aware of his tendencies. "Remember, he directs our foreign spying efforts, which means he is naturally distrustful. Allow him to draw his own conclusions. If you try to lead the conversation without substantiated proof, he'll become suspicious and withdraw. Lastly, I'll arrange for different building passes that require you to be escorted and will take you to his office. He won't appreciate you having unrestricted access."

"Thank you. We would have fallen on our faces without your guidance," Zunino said, with Villa also thanking her.

AISE Director Renzo D'Angelo was not one who could easily be surprised. After years of witnessing the darker aspects of human nature, he had long ago lost his ability to laugh good naturedly or accept people at face value. Instead, he had developed a habit of analyzing those he conversed with to determine if they had ulterior motives, such as trying to change his opinion or extract information from him. His lack of trust in others' sincerity contributed to the perception that he was sanctimonious, with many believing that his tendency not to take what people said at face value indicated he considered his opinions superior to them.

"What's so important that you both feel compelled to interrupt my day?" D'Angelo asked as Ferrara guided them into his office after informing the director that they were added to his schedule at the request of the president's office.

While the director, who had limited social skills, might argue with Acardi or even Orsini, he rarely overruled any decisions made by Ferrara because she had built strong relationships with other executive assistants, which helped ensure the cooperation of those in various bureaus and agencies who, although they didn't particularly like the director, were willing to collaborate because the executive assistants would smooth the way and facilitated what needed to be done. As a result, even though he wanted to ask Zunino and Villa to leave so he could address several urgent matters, he didn't want to upset Ferrara. Consequently, sucking it up, his greeting was a little crusty.

"We thought you should take a look at this," Zunino said, following Palmieri's advice on how to approach D'Angelo, handing him his cellphone without the earbuds since they were in his office rather than in a public space.

The director played the video displaying, just as Palmieri, no emotion to what he'd seen. After watching, he remained silent for nearly a minute with his hands steepled in front of his mouth, which would indicate to whoever was good at interpreting such gestures that whatever he was thinking about, he was in control and confident about his conclusions.

""Who else knows about this?" D'Angelo asked, glancing in Villa's direction.

"Only Palmieri," came the reply.

"And that's why she called my assistant to set up this meeting," D'Angelo noted.

Villa confirmed his assumption.

"Why involve her?"

"We didn't think you'd agree to a meeting if we called your office, and we wanted to ensure that no one but you saw this video," Villa explained.

"You have good instincts," D'Angelo replied, validating Zunino's assumption that he'd be more interested in what he saw than how the pair obtained the surveillance video.

"Besides Baudo, do you have any other suspicions about who might be involved?"

"Only the codename that the Signora gave someone, whom we believe could be the person behind this," Zunino answered.

"And that is?"

"The puppeteer."

"Do you have any idea who that refers to?"

Zunino and Villa shook their heads.

"Do you have Baudo's cellphone number?"

They shook their heads again.

"That's not a problem," D'Angelo said as he accessed his computer and retrieved the number thirty seconds later. He then placed a call, informing the person on the other end that he needed a digital transcript of every conversation made on the phone number he was about to provide. After rattling off the numbers, he added, "Drop everything you're doing and send the data to my inbox as quickly as possible. How long will it take?" He paused for several seconds to listen to the response. "Make sure no one knows what you're doing or sees those conversations," he concluded before ending the call.

"Five minutes," D'Angelo stated.

"I expected it to take hours," Villa replied.

"It had better not. Every conversation is decrypted and stored in a digital file linked to the user's phone number. Because of this, and what you're about to see, there are two important things we need to get straight between us. You're intelligent enough to know that the AISE is prohibited from monitoring domestic communications. However, we do if the conversations are with someone outside the country, with a person or entity who we believe poses a threat to national security, or if someone is using an encrypted device with an algorithm developed by my agency. You could say that's a heavy dose of paranoia on my part. If this intelligence is useful to the AISE, I pass it to Acardi, who is smart enough to internally document that it came from a classified intelligence source. Therefore, knowing what I've explained, everything you see or hear remains only with you. Forever. The only exceptions are President Orsini and Pia Lamberti, assuming she's still alive."

Both men said they understood and have the same ground rules for developing amnesia in their current position.

"Second, is Dante Acardi alive?"

Zunino answered that he survived the blast and was still in Paris, intentionally not mentioning Bence, as he was uncertain whether Acardi wanted to disclose his involvement. He went on to explain that the bomb had been brought into Acardi's hotel room in a wine bucket, indicating that it was intended for him.

"Since Baudo was aware of his schedule and made arrangements for his accommodations, he could have shared this information with the bomber," D'Angelo remarked.

"That's what we believe," Villa responded.

"What about Lamberti and the investigative team that Acardi sent to Sicily? Any updates?"

"So far, we haven't heard anything," Zunino replied.

"Keep me updated, as I may be able to help. I'm curious why you didn't ask for my assistance earlier. I could have installed real-time surveillance devices in his office and decrypted those conversations on my desktop."

Zunino gave him an uncomfortable shrug while Villa didn't respond.

"Let me guess—you didn't know if I was the mole," D'Angelo replied. "You have good instincts. The first rule of intelligence is: don't trust anyone. You were right; this office would be the perfect cover for an undercover operative."

Just then, the director's computer chimed. Checking his inbox, he opened the folder that the techie sent and began reading, not offering to share what he was viewing. Several minutes later, he called the techie and requested digital transcripts for several other numbers.

"It's going to take time for me to digest this information. However, based on what I've seen, it appears that someone provided ghost-chipped phones to individuals outside the government. If we assume this was Baudo, it would explain why the AISI wasn't able to decrypt their domestic conversations, as they would know the devices had been provided by us."

"How?" Villa asked.

"Because we have an imbedded identifier within the algorithm, for which the AISI has the decryption key, identifying the device as ours."

"Considering what you've told us, why didn't one of your analysts or whoever examines intercepts, since the algorithm is yours, notify you of these conversations since they are in your system?" Zunino asked.

"Resources. No intelligence agency has the manpower or budget to manually read every intercepted communication. We only examine those that are flagged—specifically, those containing keywords, phrases, names of individuals, and other criteria specified by my staff for the intercept program. This allows us to focus on the communications that require the attention of an analyst. Further, the algorithms we use prioritize the order in which these intercepts are reviewed based on the importance assigned to those keywords and phrases. As a result, it may take some time to go through them, a fact you demonstrated by bringing to my attention what I just read. Regardless, now that I'm pulling all conversations involving Baudo and the numbers of the ghost-chipped phones with which he communicates, by the end of the day I'll have reviewed all these conversations."

"Then we'll leave you to it," Zunino stated as he stood up to leave, with Villa also rising from his seat.

"Call if you need my help," D'Angelo said, taking two cards from his drawer. That's my direct dial number. Forget about Baudo; leave him to me. Instead, find out the name of the person your boss codenamed the puppeteer."

Montanari discovered that the individual most frequently mentioned in the puppeteer file he downloaded from the Ministry of Foreign Affairs was Corrado Bernardi the founder and CEO of Calvario S.r.l. The information collected on him spanned his life from childhood to the present day, and included copies of his school records, known associations, bank statements, tax returns, and other data that would have been impossible to obtain without the help of a senior official within the Italian government, whom he assumed was Lamberti. The file also provided an insight into Calvario's ownership structure as well as its global business dealings, which were conducted on behalf of numerous offshore corporations, a list of which was included in the file.

What struck him as unusual was that, despite the thoroughness and depth of the documentation, the minister still felt it necessary to postpone his meeting with Lamberti. On the surface, it seemed that any additional input would only be redundant, as it was clear that both he and Lamberti viewed Bernardi as the puppeteer.

Furthermore, given what he'd read, he was puzzled about why the French were involved. Bernardi was an Italian citizen, residing and operating his business in Rome. Yet, Lamberti sensed that the involvement of the French Minister of Foreign Affairs held significance for reasons he had not yet uncovered. Clearly, he was overlooking something essential.

Taking Zunino's suggestion, he put himself in Bruno's shoes and wondered where, in this situation, he would begin his investigation. Having assisted Bruno and his partners with several of their cases over the years, he observed that the trio always started by examining the relationships among the key players involved. In this case, that meant focusing on the relationship between Sciarra and Bernardi, which had developed in middle school and persisted to the present day. Given that Sciarra was already identified as the prime suspect, he reasoned it was logical to assume that both he and Bernardi were involved in Lamberti's kidnapping.

However, there were inconsistencies. The extensive costs associated with such an operation suggested that whoever kidnapped Lamberti was not poor. This supported Zunino's assessment that the ransom note was merely a red herring meant to buy time. Additionally, the kidnapping required precise planning and patience—traits that are often the opposite of a typical Mafia operation, which usually lack subtlety and might instead involve a discussion on whether to use automatic weapons or handguns to avoid crossfire in a confined space, such as a cemetery. This supported the idea that Sciarra had help in planning the abduction.

Additionally, believing that the Mafia had no hesitation in murdering anyone who obstructed their plans, knew too much, or could endanger the organization or its operations, he found it inconsistent with that view that Sciarra kidnapped and didn't kill Lamberti if he truly considered her a threat. He was also intelligent enough to know that whether she was kidnapped or killed, either would provoke a significant show of force response from the government that was meant to demonstrate to potential copycats the dire consequences they could expect if they committed a similar offense. Unless what he did was sanctioned by the Commission, which was open to debate, there was little doubt in his mind that they'd order the death of one of their own to appease the government.

Considering these numerous inconsistencies, Montanari concluded that the kidnapping, although carried out by Sciarra, was orchestrated on behalf of a third party, and that individual needed to keep Lamberti alive to achieve their objective, although he had yet to determine what that was. He also concluded that Sciarra believed it would take time to uncover his involvement. Given this, along with the association between him and Bernardi, he suspected that the Calvario CEO was the third party involved. If so, what would he stand to gain? Information from the government database indicated that he was extremely wealthy, had never been suspected of committing a crime, and had no pending lawsuits, which added another layer of inconsistency to the situation.

Montanari decided to shift his focus from investigating Sciarra and Bernardi to examining Calvario's business dealings more closely. Regulatory findings indicated that Calvario was engaged in obtaining mining and production rights for rare earth elements (REE), often referred to as rare earth metals, with a particular emphasis on Africa. The documents also revealed that Calvario executed these leases on behalf of offshore corporations and managed their REE contracts. He suspected that using offshore corporations was done to limit their client's liability and conceal their identities and profits, which was not an uncommon practice in a highly competitive business environment.

Feeling disappointed after coming up with plausible theories and several names but lacking any evidence, he was left with nothing to show for his efforts except an empty box of cannoli and a depleted supply of Red Bull. He decided to go back and re-read the documents to see if there was something he'd missed. However, before then, to clear his mind, he concluded this was the perfect time to make his weekly batch of spaghetti sauce.

He began by putting half a dozen cans of crushed tomatoes in the large stainless steel pot that was a fixture on his stove, afterward adding tomato paste and water to thin it out. He followed with fresh basil leaves, red pepper flakes, and salt and pepper. Setting the stove's temperature on low, he used a wooden spoon to stir the mixture as it warmed. As he did this, he thought about the text that Bernardi sent to an addressee in France, surprised that was the only text he'd seen. Because it was in the puppeteer's file, it denoted that Lamberti was monitoring Bernardi's communications and was giving the minister this intelligence data for reasons yet unknown. What was curious about this text was that there was a notation from Lamberti that it was sent in the clear and not ciphered, implying there were communications between the two which were encrypted.

The text didn't seem like much, Bernardi indicating that they, whoever that word referred to, had achieved critical mass in their business venture after signing the latest contracts in Africa, and going on to say that he would continue his efforts to build on this momentum. The recipient of the message was identified only as

Opus, which didn't mean anything except to whoever sent and received the text, the term not appearing anywhere else in the minister's folder. Uncertain whether the addressee in France was a person, a group, a shell company, an offshore entity, or something else altogether, Montanari knew that only the telecommunications company possessed that information, which they wouldn't release without a court order. Therefore, falling back on his criminal skills, which seemed a common occurrence when Acardi or Lamberti were even tangentially involved, he decided to hack into these companies one by one until he uncovered the identity of Opus.

He began with Orange, the largest telecommunications and internet company in France. He didn't believe that accessing a list of their clients would be difficult given that cellular providers quietly gave the government a means to surreptitiously enter their systems, for no other reasons than they had the power to unilaterally regulate rates, veto potential mergers, and make laws that would have an impact on their earnings, all while misleading the public into thinking that the law required a warrant for the release of personal data, which it did. Subsequently, all the Savant needed to do to identify Opus was reenter Bence's government login and navigate through the menu of services to find the tab that led to the telecommunications provider's interconnect, which he correctly assumed would be restricted to department heads. This process took ten minutes, though it could have been much quicker had he been familiar with the layout of Bence's database. Once inside the Orange system, he entered the number associated with the text and immediately learned Opus' identity.

"You've got to be kidding me," the Savant exclaimed as he stared at the name and contact information. Not many things surprised a hacker, especially considering his experience—but this did. He called Zunino.

Following his and Villa's meeting with D'Angelo and the call from Montanari, Zunino called Acardi and summarized their discussion and AISE director's conclusion that he wasn't responsible for the killings or the explosion, believing that Baudo had set him up to take the fall. That was the good news. The bad news was that they couldn't prove Acardi's innocence. This meant until they could provide the French government with the names and evidence needed to convict those responsible for the killings and the destruction of a Parisian neighborhood of movers and shakers, allowing them to arrest and showcase them to restore confidence in law enforcement, Acardi needed to lay low to avoid being arrested as the placeholder to calm public opinion until the guilty parties were in custody.

"Have you heard anything from Bruno?" Acardi asked.

"Not a word. We tried reaching him and the other members of his team before calling you, but didn't receive a response. They may have turned off their phones to either conserve battery life or to avoid being tracked. I'd bet on the latter."

"Getting back to clearing me, do you have any idea how you can get the proof you need?"

"Montanari implied that you left that responsibility to him," Zunino stated.

"I suppose I did. He's one of the most resourceful people I've ever met. He'll find the answers we need."

"I think he's already on it," Zunino replied, after which he detailed his visit to the Savant and his discovery of a message addressed to the recipient that Bernardi referred to as Opus.

"Opus may very well be the person whom Lamberti codenamed the puppeteer."

"That could be true," Zunino conceded. "We may be able to determine that because he somehow managed to associate this individual's phone number with a name and location."

"Given the involvement of the French minister, I assume that person is in France."

"In Louveciennes," he replied, butchering the pronunciation.

ALAN REFKIN

Acardi repeated the butchered word, asking where it was located.

"Louveciennes," Bence said, overhearing Acardi's side of the conversation and correctly pronouncing the name of the town.

Acardi placed his phone on speaker and introduced Bence, who explained that the town was a western suburb located twenty minutes from the center of Paris.

"Did Montanari get an address?" Acardi inquired.

"The Château du Gabriel."

"A residence is considered an address when it's historic," Bence explained, noticing the confusion on Acardi's face. "It's similar to addressing a letter to the Élysée Palace or the White House."

"To whom did Bernardi send the message? Who is Opus?" Acardi asked Zunino.

"Qasim Fakhouri," Zunino answered. "I did a Google search and found that he's the Saudi Minister of Economy and Planning, often referred to as the MEP," he added, spelling out each letter. "This is a cabinet position within the government that's responsible for developing and implementing the country's long-term economic plans."

"Just when I thought this couldn't get any more complicated," Acardi remarked, "there's a high-ranking official in the Saudi government working in conjunction with the royal family."

"Why do you think that?"

"Without their consent, teaming up with the Sicilian Mafia to kidnap an official in Italy and kill another in France would get one's head lopped off."

"Getting their mole into the position of your executive assistant required time and patience. I'm curious as to why you were targeted instead of D'Angelo. You would think that having a source in foreign intelligence would be far more valuable to the Saudis," Zunino remarked.

"That's a good point, with which I agree."

"The answer might be as simple as them being unable to fill

that position. Being in your agency gave them the opportunity to establish rapport with the AISE," Bence added, joining the conversation.

"That's a fair assessment," Acardi replied. "Perhaps now would be a good time to accept D'Angelo's offer of assistance. He could take a close look at Qasim Fakhouri to see if there's a connection between him and Corrado Bernardi."

"That means the puppeteer could be either Bernardi or Fakhouri," Zunino stated.

"It may be that neither party alone that is driving this. Someone else might be manipulating them," Acardi replied.

"How do we find out?"

"We need to understand what motivated these strange allies to collaborate and what each gains from this association, as we've just scratched the surface of what this is all about."

"I'll call D'Angelo."

Chapter Fourteen

"This fire is intense and will reach us before long. The only bit of good news, which I admit is thin, is that the height of the plants makes us difficult to see," Bruno said.

"That is thin," Maria replied, glancing at the position of the sun as she tried to orient herself, which didn't go unnoticed by Bruno.

"I take it you're familiar with this town," he remarked.

"My late husband and his family were from here," she explained. "We got married in the church at the top of the hill. It's that way," she said, pointing to her right. "That's also where we held his funeral; he's buried in the family plot behind the church."

"How long ago was that?"

"Three years."

"I'm sorry."

"I refuse to give il Bastardo the satisfaction of having me join him. Going in that direction will take us to the road surrounding this field, which is opposite the way we entered. If we can cross the road without being seen and make our way through the town, we can hide in the church."

"How far away is it?"

"About a mile, possibly a little more."

"Let's do it. I'm getting a bit crispy," Bruno said, feeling the rapidly increasing heat from the raging fire, the remark bringing a smile to Maria's face.

Navigating their way between the thorny plants to reach the paths used during harvesting was a challenge. They not only faced scratches and punctures from the thorns but also struggled with the increasing level of smoke, which carried fine particles from the burning plants, making it difficult to breathe and elevating their heart rates. By the time they reached the perimeter road, Maria was gasping for air and barely able to stand.

"Do you have asthma?" Bruno asked.

Unable to respond verbally, she simply nodded.

Bruno cautiously poked his head out from between the thorny plants, noting that the road was only a couple of feet in front of him. Fifty yards to the left, barely visible through the smoke, he spotted Sciarra sitting inside his car and speaking on his cellphone. Three other vehicles were nearby, each filled with men who were also trying to escape the suffocating smoke and heat.

"Time to go," Bruno said. Because Maria was getting weaker by the minute and was having difficulty moving, he took off his tattered jacket and draped it over her to provide an additional layer of protection for her torso and arms. He then carefully guided her between the prickly plants, after which he hoisted her over his shoulder and dashed across the road, struggling for breathable air in the thick smoke, which made him feel lightheaded, nearly to the point of passing out.

After crossing the road and still carrying Maria, he veered down a narrow cobblestone street until the air around them became easier to breathe. He then entered the first alley he saw, searching for a place to hide and regain their strength. He found it when he noticed a dumpster and slipped into the narrow space behind it.

Gently lifting Maria off his shoulder, he grabbed a cardboard box from the dumpster, flattened it, and laid her down. As he did, her body began to spasm, and she stopped breathing.

"You've come too far to give up now," Bruno said as he started chest compressions. After thirty compressions, he paused to give two rescue breaths. He repeated this cycle three times, and on his third attempt, Maria started coughing and breathed on her own. A minute later, she was fully conscious.

"You gave me quite a scare."

"Where are we?"

"In an alley about a hundred yards from the perimeter road."

"You carried me here?"

Bruno confirmed he did, but he couldn't tell her exactly where they were.

"Help me up, and I'll tell you. We need to get to the church before Sciarra's men search this area," she said.

Bruno nodded and helped her to her feet, allowing her to lean on him as they moved around the alley until she regained her bearings.

"The church is that way," she pointed. "We'll take this alley and turn right on the first street."

"How far away is it?" He asked.

"Not too far, but there's still smoke in the air, and I can't breathe well enough to move very quickly. I'm sorry."

"We'll be fine," Bruno said as he gently placed her left arm over his shoulder and they started down the alley, both aware that the accuracy of his remark was uncertain.

Sciarra stood on the roof of one of his men's pickup trucks and surveyed the scene, seeing that the flames had engulfed the entire field. The fire attracted a large crowd, some seething with anger that the Mafioso had destroyed their livelihood. However, none were brave enough to express their feelings or confront Sciarra and his men, understanding that criticizing his actions could mean a death sentence. As a result, they watched in silence.

"They're dead," one of his soldiers said.

"No one is dead until I see a body. Until then, search the town for Lamberti, starting here and working toward the highway. Bring in my soldiers from the other towns and villages in the area to help, and continue through the night. No one sleeps until they're found."

Sciarra climbed down from the truck and was walking to his car when he received a call from one of his informants at the Catania airport telling him that the aircraft which had brought the investigators to Sicily had just taken off. According to their flight plan, Malta International Airport was listed as their destination, and there were no passengers on board.

"Malta," Sciarra repeated, now realizing that the investigators never intended to fly Lamberti out of Sicily. That left only one escape route. He checked his watch.

Given when Lamberti was spirited from his residence in Siculiana, and considering the current time of day, he didn't believe any boat he'd seen moored at the town's marina could have traveled more than sixty miles from the coast. His cigarette boats were each capable of speeds exceeding one hundred twenty-five mph, which was roughly six times faster than any vessel Lamberti might be on.

Sciarra didn't know much about boats, but he was smart. He understood that any non-law enforcement vessel attempting to stop another boat in international waters—or asking to board and search it—would appear suspicious and could be seen as the act of pirates. Such a request would likely be met with a hostile response. Additionally, since most vessels carried weapons, often including illegal military-grade arms, there was a significant chance that his men would end up in a gun battle if they tried to forcefully board another vessel. With only two men per boat, the odds were not in their favor.

The other consideration was that they may not even be boarding the correct vessel, as the waters surrounding Malta were vast, and Lamberti might not be on the one they stopped—if they could even stop it at all. Recognizing that he couldn't check every vessel they encountered, he decided to instruct his men to race at full speed to the waters outside the port of Marsa, which should put them ahead of any boat which could have left the Siculiana Marina with Lamberti, and wait there. He would provide them with the name of the specific vessel they needed to intercept and capture the female passenger on board, ensuring her safety while considering all others to be expendable.

He next conferenced his captains in Licata, Portopalo, and Pazzolo, where his cigarette boats were moored, and explained what needed to be done. After finishing his call, he told those in Canicatti to stay and search the town with the arriving soldiers while he went to Siculiana, cautioning them not to kill anyone they captured because he needed to interrogate them.

Once these orders were given, Sciarra hurried to the Siculiana Marina, Albani's van having left twenty minutes earlier. Upon entering the dockmaster's office, where daily management of the marina was handled, he inquired about which boats were currently at sea. Since everyone in the province knew Sciarra, withholding information wasn't an option. Therefore, the dockmaster provided him with a list of the thirteen vessels.

"Do you know where they've gone?" Sciarra asked.

The dockmaster stated he didn't, as the twelve fishing vessels each had their preferred areas in the Mediterranean Sea that they didn't share, while the commercial transport vessel could go anywhere the client for whom it was transporting goods wanted.

"If I understand correctly, the twelve fishing vessels will be returning, but the one with cargo will not."

"The transport vessel might return if it is delivering or picking up cargo at a nearby port," the dockmaster explained, specifying that "nearby" referred to the southwest coast of Sicily. "However, this captain occasionally takes foreign transport contracts to pick up and deliver cargo in Tunisia, northeast Algeria, Malta, and sometimes Tripoli, although he mentioned he was discontinuing this route because it had become too dangerous."

"What's the name of the captain and his boat?"

"Salvatore Costa sails the merchant vessel Sogno d'Oro," the dockmaster answered. Upon hearing this, Sciarra left and called the captains of his cigarette boats.

Getting Maria to the church was both time-consuming and arduous. As they navigated the streets, the pair concealed themselves in entryways, alleys, and any other recessed spots they could find to avoid Sciarra's men, who were driving around looking for them. As the church came into view, and directly in front of it, Bruno saw a thug leaning against a rusted pickup truck and smoking a cigarette. Gently lowering Maria from his arms, he set her down behind a stone column wide enough to shield them from anyone looking their way.

"It won't be much longer, I promise," he said, brushing the hair away from her face so she could see him.

Twenty minutes later, the two men who'd searched the church and the priest's residence returned to their vehicle and left with the third man. Bruno gave them a minute to get out of sight before lifting Maria into his arms and continuing toward the church, ringing the bell to the residence when he got there.

No words were exchanged as the priest, who appeared to be in his sixties, recognized Maria and ushered them inside.

"Sciarra is looking for both of you and is offering ten thousand dollars to whoever tells him where you're hiding. In this town, that much money is a fortune," the priest said as he guided Bruno to his bedroom and told him to lay Maria on the bed.

Although she was conscious, the decrease in oxygen to her body because of her respiratory issues, and the exhaustion from being pursued, drained her energy to the point where so was no longer able to walk. Seeing her fatigue, the priest took a bottle of water from the nightstand and offered her several sips.

"We were in the prickly pear field when Sciarra set it on fire. The dense smoke made it hard for her to breathe due to her asthma," Bruno explained.

"I may be able to help," the priest said. He left them for ten minutes and returned with a portable oxygen tank, putting the mask connected to it on her and starting the flow.

"Do you require oxygen?" Bruno asked, wondering if he had a lung condition.

"No, but many of our parishioners are elderly, and during the summer, the heat can sometimes be overwhelming for them during services. I keep two oxygen tanks in the back of the church for those occasions. Perhaps this would be a good time for you to explain why the Mafia is after both of you, as the soldiers who left just before your arrival didn't share any information with me. They only said that they were going to search the church and my home, whether I liked it or not."

"This will take some time," Bruno said as he started to sit in a wooden chair. However, the priest grabbed his arm and led him to a more comfortable club chair a few feet away, while he sat in the wooden chair instead. Bruno then began to recount the events from the time of Lamberti's kidnapping up to the present. His narrative lasted over an hour, during which the priest barely moved as he intently listened.

"It was providence that led you to me," he said once Bruno finished speaking.

"I have to agree with you."

"How are your friends doing? Have they reached Malta yet?" The priest asked.

"I don't know, my cellphone went dead and Maria doesn't have hers."

"I can recharge your phone," the priest offered, going to his nightstand and removing a cable from the drawer.

Bruno took his phone out of his pocket and examined the connector before shaking his head. "It seems the Italian government doesn't contract with Apple," he said, noticing the connector was for an Apple device.

"Can you call them on my phone?"

"I don't see why not," Bruno replied, accepting the priest's phone from his outstretched hand. He dialed Donati and Donais' non-ghost-chipped phones, but both calls went to voicemail.

"No answer?"

"They may have their phones on silent or turned off until they approach Malta which, as best I can estimate, won't be for another five or six hours. Whatever the reason, they'll eventually receive my voicemails," Bruno said as he glanced at his watch, unaware that his team had turned off their personal devices and were now exclusively using the ghost-chipped phones for added security.

"Until then, let me get you both something to eat. Nothing makes someone feel better than a bowl of minestrina," the priest said, which was chicken soup with pasta and the Italian equivalent of chicken noodle soup.

He returned thirty minutes later with two steaming bowls of the Italian elixir, finding Bruno watching Maria, who'd fallen asleep. "Her breathing isn't as labored. The oxygen helped."

"Wake her up and give her this soup. It'll make her stronger," the priest instructed before leaving.

Bruno woke Maria who, although weak from her ordeal, managed to sit up and eat. Sometime later, after they'd finished their soups, the priest returned and took the bowls to the kitchen, only to come back less than a minute later telling him to pick up Maria and follow him. Because of the look of fear and urgency on his face, Bruno lifted Maria off the bed, the priest afterward straightening it so it looked unslept in. Following the priest, who'd grabbed the oxygen bottle and mask, they rushed from the room.

"Where are we going?" Bruno asked, keeping pace while carrying Maria in his arms.

"To a hiding place in the church," he said, turning his head and speaking over his shoulder. "From the kitchen, I could see that Sciarra's men were once again working their way up the street and searching every residence."

"I thought they had already done that," Bruno replied, keeping up with the fleet-footed priest.

"Sciarra's men are a disorganized group of thieves and scoundrels. Even though one group checked the church and my home, another is doing the same. I'm moving you to a hidden room, similar to a priest hole, which were used to safeguard Catholic clergy from priest hunters in Protestant England. It was built during World War II to hide the town's Allied sympathizers from the Germans," he said as they entered the church and he pressed a wooden panel behind the confessional, which opened into a large room with a bed, armoire, and bathroom.

Bruno laid Maria, who was still extremely weak but conscious and aware of what was happening, on the bed.

"You'll be able to hear anyone who approaches. If you do, don't move or speak until at least a minute or two after their footsteps have faded away." With that admonition, the priest left and closed the panel behind him, Bruno hearing the sound of his shoes echoing throughout the church.

The priest returned to his kitchen and quickly washed and put away the two empty soup bowls, leaving only his on the table. His timing was perfect, because less than a minute later another pair of Sciarra's soldiers knocked on the door.

The priest was cooperative during their search, telling the men they could go anywhere, which was their intent with or without approval. Twenty minutes later, they left and radioed someone to report that they'd finished their search and found nothing out of the ordinary.

Once they were gone, the priest returned to the secret room with a stack of towels and bedding. "Sciarra's men have left. As I said, they're a disorganized group of thieves and scoundrels and no one person seems to be coordinating a systematic search of the town. Therefore, the men who were just here may not be the last who want to search this Church."

"Thank you, father," Bruno replied.

"I'll bring your food a little later. Until then, I'll be praying for you both," he said before leaving.

"You look tired," Maria said, that she spoke surprising Bruno so that he turned around—seeing that she'd removed her oxygen mask and was sitting up in bed.

"And you look much better," he replied. "How's your breathing?"

"Good enough so that I no longer need this mask."

Bruno shut off the oxygen and placed the mask on top of the cylinder.

"It looks like we'll be here for a while," she said.

"I know. I could be hours or days. There's no way of knowing."

"It occurs to me that I know very little about you. Could you tell me about yourself?" Maria asked as Bruno picked up a couple of bottles of water from the case against the wall and handed one to her.

"Alright, but only if you share something about yourself in return," he replied.

She nodded in agreement.

"My two partners and I have an investigative agency in Milan," Bruno began, only to be stopped by Maria, who raised her hand.

"I'm not interested in you as a businessperson, Mauro. Tell me about the brave person who saved my life and carried me here. I want to know about you," she said.

Bruno, like most men, was uncomfortable discussing the details of his personal life and would rather talk about business, sports, or another topic rather than rip away the layers of armor he'd used to hide his personal side.

Maria, noticing his hesitation, gave him an encouraging look that conveyed he could feel safe opening up to her.

"I'm fifty-three years old, and I was born and raised in Milan, where my father served as an attorney and the city's chief prosecutor," he began. "I loved and admired him, and I intended to follow in his footsteps. After graduating from college, I was set to start law school in twelve weeks. I felt burnt out from my final exams and wanted some time away from Milan before diving into what I knew would be years of relentless study to gain the knowledge necessary to become a lawyer. My parents supported this idea, and as a graduation gift, they sent me to Venice, a city I have always loved for its beauty and history. While I was there, I met my future wife, Katarina. She was enjoying a drink with two friends at a bar, and there was an instant chemistry between us. Later that night, I went home with her, and from that moment on, we became inseparable."

"That must have surprised your parents."

"Not as much as my decision to forsake law school and move to Venice to be with her."

"Ouch."

"Their reactions were much stronger than just a simple 'ouch' because it meant that I was moving away from home to a city where I had no job. I had a business degree, but without any marketable skills, it only qualified me to wait tables or work at a car rental agency."

"You're exaggerating."

"Not by much; better-paying white-collar jobs are typically reserved for those with advanced degrees and specialized skills."

"You're in Venice, unemployed but in love. What's next?"

"Figuring out what I wanted to do for the rest of my life and acquiring the necessary skills was crucial, as we both agreed that our relationship would suffer and possibly not survive if I couldn't find a career that made me happy, or at least provided a sense of satisfaction."

"That makes sense."

"Katarina was an administrative officer with the local police, the vigili urbani. She understood me well enough to realize that being a local law enforcement officer wouldn't be challenging enough to satisfy me, but that national police work might. Therefore, she suggested that I consider becoming an officer in the Polizia di Stato. I explored this option, liked what I discovered, and graduated after completing a one-year training program. Afterward, we got married but," Bruno said, his voice reflecting the intense pain of his loss, "ten months later, she and our unborn child were killed by a home intruder while I was on night duty."

"That's horrific," Maria said, her eyes welling with tears as she reached out to touch his hand. "Did you ever find the intruder?"

"I learned his identity many years later and killed him," Bruno answered without a hint of remorse. "Tell me about yourself," he said, quickly changing the subject because discussing his wife's death made him uncomfortable.

Maria understood his state of mind and redirected the conversation to herself. "I'm forty-five years old, an only child, and as I mentioned earlier, my husband and his family were from Canicatti and we were married in this church by the priest who's hiding us."

"How long were you married?"

"Twenty-one years."

"Do you have any children?"

"We had one child. He and my husband were killed in an automobile accident not far from Favara."

"My sorry," Bruno said. "I don't think there are words that express the trauma you must have felt."

"As you well know, there aren't."

"Your farm is in Favara, while your husband is from Canicatti. How did you meet and decide to live in your town and not his?"

"My husband's family weren't farmers; they owned a small printing shop. We met when he came to my farm to buy walnuts, which for decades my family has sold by the bag to anyone who knocked on our door. His mother needed them to make crostata di noci and taleggio tarts," she explained. "We developed a fondness for each other, and after that, he found any excuse to come and buy walnuts, even if it was only a small bag, just to see me. One thing led to another, and we fell in love and married."

"Isn't it a Sicilian tradition for the wife to move to the groom's town."

"It is, but just like you, my late husband didn't want to go into the family business saying, in his words, the work was repetitive and unfulfilling. Instead, he preferred being outdoors and enjoyed the variety that comes with farming. My parents were alive at that time and lived with us until their deaths, after which I inherited the farm."

"How do you manage a farm of that size by yourself? You must harvest thousands of pounds of walnuts."

"Each acre produces approximately three to four thousand pounds per season, depending on the weather. I hire contractors for fertilizing, tree trimming, harvesting, and transportation for sale, as these tasks require a significant investment in equipment and ongoing maintenance. I only have a few permanent workers who come to the farm three days a week outside of the harvest season."

"You're smart, resourceful, self-reliant and, as you must know, very attractive," the last remark causing her to blush. "I can't believe someone hasn't already proposed to you."

"Several have, but the chemistry just wasn't there. I could say the same about you. Perhaps we're both content with the memories of our past because we believe we had spouses who only come along once in a lifetime."

"Perhaps," Bruno agreed.

They continued to talk throughout the day, only interrupted by the priest bringing them dinner.

Chapter Fifteen

It was dark when the four investigators spotted lights on the horizon, indicating they were approaching the port city of Marsa in Malta. Lamberti had awakened and was rapidly regaining her faculties, able to recall most of her ordeal. To help fill in the gaps about what had happened while she was held captive by Sciarra, everyone contributed to updating her. They explained how she was rescued and cared for until she was brought onboard the vessel. They also shared Maria's involvement in getting her to Malta, Bruno's decision to stay behind and help her escape from Sciarra and his men, and that her plane was waiting at the airport to transport them to Rome.

"Have you heard from Bruno?" she asked, her voice filled with concern.

"No," Donais replied.

"When was the last time you spoke with him?"

"At the farm, before we went our separate ways," Donati volunteered. "We kept our personal cellphones turned off to avoid being tracked by anyone who knew those numbers. Instead, we used the ghost-chipped phones we were given."

"That was a smart decision regarding your personal devices," Lamberti noted. "However, I was informed that it was impossible to track you or intercept your conversations on the government phones you were issued."

ALAN REFKIN

"Unless someone has access to the algorithms or the decrypted data," Donais responded. She went on to explain the situation regarding the mole and their reluctance to use the ghost-chipped phones while at sea, fearing that this individual might be linked to the upper echelons of the government's intelligence apparatus and could potentially possess this information.

"Make no mistake, I'll find and deal with them when I return," she said, no one doubting her ability to do that given their past experience in working with her. "What are you plans for getting us ashore and to the airport, considering I don't have a passport or other form of ID?" Lamberti asked Costa.

"I have a connection with two customs agents who aren't sticklers for details such as manifests and passports; they only care about the fat envelope of cash I hand each when I arrive."

"The airport is a different story. They will require passports for us to board my plane. By the way, how did you manage to get access to it?"

"Acardi allowed us use it to expedite our investigation into your kidnapping without having to rely on public transport," Donati replied.

"How did you get involved?" She asked, looking at Hunkler.

"The Director believed that, given the Mafia's involvement, the team could benefit from my skills."

"He was correct. The decisions made and the timing of my rescue saved my life, as I don't think my body could have endured much more chemical abuse. Let's get back to how I leave Malta on my aircraft when I don't have a passport."

"We talked about that," Donati said. "A passport is only necessary if you're entering or leaving the country. Unfortunately, since Malta has only one airport, every flight is international. Therefore, the plan is to have the pilot request permission from the control tower to take the plane up and check whether the instrument landing system is functioning properly, as there was an issue when they arrived from Catania. Testing equipment while airborne is a common practice in aviation.

The plane will take off with us on board and perform an instrument approach to make it look good. After the plane exercises a missed approach and gains altitude, the pilot will inform the tower that their system is still malfunctioning and, since they're already in the air, will say that they're returning to Italy for repairs."

"And you believe that will work?" Lamberti asked.

"Based on my limited aviation experience, I think it will. What can they do? The plane is owned by the Italian government, it's approaching the jurisdictional limits of Maltese air traffic control, and soon it will be in Italian airspace. Then we will fly to Rome."

"That's very clever," Lamberti admitted. "That takes care of us, but how is Bruno going to get out of Sicily alive without resources and Sciarra after him?"

"None of us know, especially since he gave me this, which would have been invaluable in his escape," Hunkler said, showing Lamberti the government credit card.

"Does anyone have the number for Bruno's ghost-chipped phone?" Lamberti asked.

Hunkler did and, after switching on the power to his phone and dialing Bruno's number, handed it to Lamberti. The call went unanswered.

"That's troubling," she remarked. "When do you think we'll arrive at the airport?" Lamberti asked Costa, who provided an estimate but warned her that this was Malta, where things often don't go as planned.

Unfortunately, that statement turned out to be accurate. When Lamberti called the pilot of her aircraft—whose number she had memorized long ago—he responded with a statement that conveyed a different meaning to those around him than it did to her. "I'm not interested in your sales talk, and neither are the men I'm with. Sell insurance to someone else," the pilot firmly stated, ending the call with Lamberti, the statement meant to warn her that he had unexpected guests on the plane.

She told the others what he said.

"It seems that boarding your aircraft won't be as easy as we anticipated," Labriola remarked, causing Lamberti to question who he was for the first time, previously assuming he was Costa's father or another relative.

"And you are?" She asked.

"I'm a member of this team," Labriola replied.

"His full-time job is Rome's chief coroner," Donais volunteered.

"That makes me even more curious about why you were included on my rescue team."

"Would you prefer the short version or the long version?" Labriola asked.

"For now, let's set aside that explanation because I don't have time for either. I assume that if I call President Orsini or Director D'Angelo, the informant will learn of our whereabouts and thwart our rescue."

"I believe they already know our location without that call," Donati stated. "Sciarra concluded that we escaped by sea, making Malta our logical destination. He confirmed this upon learning that your plane arrived here and sent a reception committee to wait for us on board the aircraft."

"Since my plane is compromised, is there another way to get me back to Rome?" She asked Costa.

"Not on this boat. I don't have enough fuel. Let me make a call and see if I can make other arrangements."

"Do it," she said.

Costa stepped away from the group and made the call. Three minutes later, still holding the phone to his ear, he approached Lamberti, saying, "My friend can fly all of you out of here on his seaplane, but he's asking for a lot of cash—much more than what the customs officials."

"Why?" Labriola asked Costa.

"Because he understands the risks," Lamberti answered for him.

"Precisely. He's aware that the lady doesn't have a passport and that Sciarra's men are pursuing all of you. The passport isn't a concern, as my cousin mentioned she has connections to the Italian government. Sciarra, however, is a different issue because he has a vindictive nature."

"Why wouldn't this seaplane pilot hand us over to Sciarra? I'm sure he'd receive a handsome reward," Donais said.

"He wants to retire from the smuggling business. The money he's asking will give him that ability."

"Then it must be a substantial amount. How much does he want?" Lamberti asked.

Costa told her the figure, causing the investigator's eyes to widen in surprise, even though they had expected a large sum.

Lamberti grabbed the phone from his hands. "The amount you're requesting is acceptable, but I'll be paying by credit card. You'll receive your money when we arrive at the Port of Civitavecchia, just outside Rome."

"Credit card payments can be traced," the pilot countered. "If the government finds out, I'll have to pay back taxes on this money, and I could face fines or jail time for not claiming this income. I require cash."

"It would take hours to visit the numerous banks required to gather that much currency. Those withdrawals won't go unnoticed and will likely prompt one of the banks to alert the authorities, leading to questions we'd rather avoid. Hence, the credit card. Those are my terms. You're not my only option. Although it'll take longer, I could call a seaplane charter service in Italy to pick us up in international waters. They'll accept my credit card, and since we're Italian citizens returning home, there's no need for passports. So, your choice is simple: accept the credit card payment and retire, or go back to smuggling for Sciarra and risk being caught and sent to jail," Lamberti concluded, handing the phone back to Costa, who again left the group and went to a spot where he couldn't be heard.

He returned several minutes later, nodding to Lamberti that her terms were acceptable.

"He'll arrive in an hour and a half, but it will only take us thirty minutes to reach the location he provided."

"It's going to take much longer than that," Lamberti said, "because we have to make a stop beforehand. What's the range of the Zodiac on the stern of your boat?"

"Approximately two hundred and ninety miles in calm seas and fair winds. But why take the Zodiac into port, or anywhere else, when we can sail on my vessel? Unlike the inflatable, you'll be dry when you step off my ship," Costa replied.

"We're not going into port. We're not taking the Zodiac either—you are. That means we'll be dry, but you won't be," Lamberti said, drawing a questioning look from him.

An hour and thirty-five minutes later, the seaplane circled the Sogno d'Oro, its landing light raking the fully illuminated vessel as it passed over before making a two hundred and seventy-degree turn to starboard and aligning itself so the nose of the plane was into the wind. As the aircraft's powerful landing light illuminated the area ahead, it smoothly touched down. Using the water rudders, which were connected to the aircraft's rudder pedals, the pilot steered the plane as it taxied toward the boat. Since a seaplane cannot brake on water, it coasted toward the vessel. When it got close, the rear hatch opened, and an oar was extended into the water, creating drag and slowing the aircraft until it came to a stop.

Noticing no movement on the boat and believing it was impossible for the passengers to ignore the seaplane's arrival—given that it flew over the vessel at less than a hundred feet—the pilot called Costa to ask why his passengers weren't on deck and ready to board his plane.

"They've changed their minds," Costa replied, following his scripted response.

"This trip isn't inexpensive. I took this assignment based on your word," the pilot insisted.

"I understand, but I have no control over these people. The lady said you would be compensated for your time and the use of the aircraft. We're going to stay here until morning and then go ashore."

"Hold on," the pilot said, Costa hearing someone in the background speaking to him. Moments later, Sciarra came on the phone.

"Do you know who I am?" Sciarra asked.

Costa immediately identified the voice, responding that he knew.

"Put your passengers into a raft or whatever else floats and send them to the seaplane. If you don't, I'll kill you and your family."

The pilot's betrayal didn't surprise Costa. Lamberti had warned that he'd reach out to Sciarra because he feared the money would be useless if the Mafioso found out and that his terror of him would ultimately outweigh his greed. Consequently, by arranging the rendezvous, the pilot intended to keep them in one place long enough to be captured and demonstrate his loyalty to the mobster. Neither Costa nor Lamberti expected Sciarra to be on the aircraft, believing instead that he'd send his men or, at the very least, be waiting at their destination, which wouldn't have been the Port of Civitavecchia, as they planned.

"My passengers are expecting you," Costa replied in response to Sciarra's threat. "They told me to tell you—or your men, if you sent them instead—to come and get them because they won't surrender." The line went dead.

This challenge, along with the abrupt termination of the call, sent Sciarra into a fit of rage, just as Lamberti had predicted.

Moments later, a raft was pushed from the aircraft and inflated. Sciarra and four of his soldiers, armed with automatic weapons, climbed aboard it and approached Costa's boat. Using the steel ladder on the port side that extended from the deck to the waterline, they boarded the vessel unopposed.

Although the ship appeared abandoned, Sciarra knew that it couldn't be because he'd just spoken to Costa. That meant that he and the others were hiding in concealed areas of the vessel where contraband was stored. These hidden spaces, which had previously eluded detection during customs searches, would make them extremely challenging to locate.

"Tear this ship apart until you have them," the Mafioso ordered, watching as his men scattered throughout the vessel.

Sciarra joined the search, deciding to begin at the bottom of the ship. He descended the midship ladder that was in front of him and continued to the central cargo hold, the space empty except for three wooden crates that were evenly spaced within the it. Curious as to what was within, as they were too small to hide someone, he removed the lid from the first. Struggling to see inside, he turned on the light from his cellphone to get a better look.

"What the …?" The Mafioso exclaimed upon discovering two bars of plastic explosive with detonator caps inserted into them.

Costa watched the scene unfold through his binoculars from the Zodiac, which was a short distance away. Immersed in complete darkness, he was invisible to both the ship and the seaplane. In stark contrast, the powerful deck lights illuminating the Sogno d'Oro made it easily visible. He watched as five men boarded his ship and descended below deck, unsurprised that Sciarra was one of them given the taunt he had made. Not that a search would matter as they weren't going to find anything except for his insurance policy.

Years ago, he'd placed the detonators in six bars of plastic explosives, put them inside three wooden boxes, and placed them on the bottom deck of his ship as an insurance policy in the event he was going to be stopped and boarded at sea and needed to get rid of his contraband cargo in a hurry, detonating the explosives while he escaped in his Zodiac, the loss of his ship and cargo preferable to spending a decade or more in prison.

It didn't take much for Lamberti to convince him to destroy his ship, as he had long wanted to leave the business but found it impossible to do so because Sciarra wouldn't allow him. The Mafioso made it clear that not only did Costa know too much about his smuggling operations, but his reliability in delivering his goods made him an invaluable asset. The message he took away from their meeting was clear: if you quit, you know too much to remain alive.

Lamberti solved this dilemma by offering to purchase his boat at an inflated price, ensuring that he would have enough money to retire. She also promised to place him and his cousin—assuming she was still alive in a protective program that would provide them with new identities and homes. As a result, thirty seconds after Sciarra and his soldiers went below deck, Costa lifted the clear plastic safety cover off the detonation switch and pushed the toggle upward, implementing the Mafia's version of early retirement for Sciarra.

In empty space, an electromagnetic signal travels at the speed of light, which is 983,571,056 feet per second. However, the permeability and permittivity of air significantly slow down an electrical impulse. Consequently, the signal from the Zodiac to the ship only traveled at fifty percent the speed of light which, for practical purposes, was instantaneous with the push of the toggle. The ensuing explosions tore out the bottom of the Sogno d'Oro, sending it to the sea floor within seconds, along with Sciarra and the four soldiers who accompanied him.

Before Costa boarded his Zodiac, he used the inflatable boat to transport Lamberti and four investigators to a small town of three hundred people, located about forty minutes north of Marsa. He and other smugglers used this town to negotiate the purchase and sale of contraband for their employers and occasionally for their own gain, deliveries typically occurring in Marsa or at another port where officials were willing to look the other way for a price by stamping any presented manifest. For acting as an intermediary and ensuring noninterference by authorities, the town attached a small service charge to each transaction. The mayor used a portion of those proceeds to pay the head of the district police force to stay away from the town, a bounty that was shared with his officers.

Upon arriving in town, Costa showed the mayor the two fat envelopes of money that would have gone to the customs officials in Marsa and said he wanted his help: "I need you to arrange for a seaplane to be here early tomorrow morning to fly the six of us to Rome."

"Landing someplace where you could unobtrusively disembark without being seen or raising any questions," the mayor extrapolated.

"That's right," Costa confirmed.

"Of course, that can be arranged. But Salvatore, we've known each other for years and profited from that association. While I'm not opposed to making money, why don't you contact your friend who owns a seaplane? It would likely cost you much less than hiring the pilot I'm about to call."

"Because he has a conflict of interest. Maybe he ignores that and maybe he doesn't. If he doesn't, we're all dead."

"Sciarra," the mayor said, taking the envelopes. "Fair enough. As I said, he'll be expensive, but he's reliable and discreet."

"One more thing: he'll need to take a government credit card because that's all the cash we have," Costa added, gesturing toward the envelopes.

"For a ten percent service charge, the town will charge the credit card and give him the cash."

"Agreed. When can the pilot be here?" Costa asked.

"I'll check, but the last I heard, he was in Tunisia. If he's still there, it will be early morning. If he's somewhere else, I'll let you know."

"I have something to take care of before then. Please coordinate with that lady," he said as he pointed.

Lamberti, noticing the gesture, approached their table and took a seat. Costa then explained the arrangements that had been made.

"I have one more request," Lamberti said, addressing the mayor. "I believe the cellphone of a person I need to contact may be monitored. I would like someone to deliver a message to them, providing the approximate time and place where we will be landing, information you'll need to obtain from the seaplane pilot. Is that possible?"

"Is the person in Rome?"

Lamberti confirmed that they were.

"I can call a friend in the city to see if they'll deliver the message," the mayor said. He stepped away for a moment, then returned with a pen and a pad of paper he had taken from behind the bar. He asked Lamberti to write down her message, along with the name and address of the recipient.

After the deal was finalized, Costa departed in the Zodiac to position himself off the Sogno d'Oro and wait for the arrival of his friend's seaplane.

The twin-engine Grumman HU-16 Albatross landed in the small cove north of Marsa at three in the morning, and six people stepped onto the plane. The pilot and copilot, professional smugglers for two decades, knew what they were doing and, keeping below Malta and Italy's coastal radar, and with their transponder switched off, were electronically invisible as the aircraft crossed the Mediterranean and Tyrrhenian Seas and touched down outside the port of Civitavecchia two hours and forty minutes later.

The pilots, who'd flown into the port numerous times, taxied the aircraft with its lights off so they'd be difficult to see on their way to an abandoned area of the port with half-century old docks and antiquated facilities. Designed for marine cargo and passenger boats commissioned in the 1970s, the substantially larger vessels of the twenty-first century could no longer fit into their narrower and shorter slips. Scheduled for demolition to make way for the construction of state-of-the-art facilities capable of handling modern ships, the area was unlit and neglected by the port authorities while awaiting the beginning of dredging—the first phase of redevelopment.

As the plane edged to the dock to tie up, two sets of headlights illuminated. Zunino and Villa had elected to not drive onto the dock to meet the aircraft, unsure whether it could support the weight of their vehicles. Both of Lamberti's Range Rovers were bulletproofed, making their weight seventy-five hundred and seventy-two hundred pounds respectively.

Although there were no hugs or embraces, the expressions on the bodyguards' faces showed their relief and happiness at seeing Lamberti unharmed. Zunino escorted her to the SUV, while the others followed Villa to the Defender.

The ride from the port to Lamberti's estate, which should have taken an hour and four minutes in the light traffic at 5:40 am. Instead, it took forty-five minutes because Zunino and Villa had a heavy foot on their accelerator pedals and wanted to get their boss to the safety of the estate as quickly as possible. Their vehicle's license plates exempted them from being stopped by law enforcement, allowing them to speed past two police cars on their way into the city.

Before leaving to pick up Lamberti and the others, Zunino and Villa informed the estate staff about her imminent return and instructed them not to disclose this information to anyone. Zunino then contacted President Orsini using the encrypted landline set up between the estate and the Quirinal Palace, an installation arranged by Lamberti without the knowledge of any government agency.

Lamberti arrived at the mansion at 6:45 a.m. and went straight to her office on the second floor, where she called the president. The conversation lasted fifty minutes, during which the intelligence czar relayed what she remembered from the moment she entered the cemetery until her arrival at the estate. The president then briefed her on the situation regarding Acardi being the leading suspect in the killing of the Minister of Foreign Affairs and others in Paris, also informing her that Bence was covertly assisting him.

"How will we handle this? The French government suspects that Italy, or at least one of our senior intelligence officials, is behind the killings," the president stated.

"They won't have that belief for long. I'll take care of it," Lamberti replied.

"It's great to have you back," the president replied, not asking if she needed time to recover nor if she could deliver on what she promised. He realized that she was very angry about what had happened to her and the others and felt a strong desire to ensure it never occurred again. In her view, he believed that meant killing everyone involved in what happened. He wasn't about to stand in her way.

After the call with President Orsini, Zunino updated her on how they discovered that Baudo was the informant responsible for leaking information to Sciarra and Bernardi, and that he decided to ask Montanari for help. He went on to say that the Savant discovered a text exchange between Bernardi and an individual he referred to as Opus, eventually learning that was a codename for Qasim Fakhouri, the Saudi Minister of Economy and Planning.

"The minister might have delayed your meeting in order to gather information on him," Zunino speculated. "But why would the person you codenamed the puppeteer be speaking with a Saudi minister?" He asked.

Lamberti was impressed with what Zunino had pieced together from the snippets of her conversations that he had overheard. If he hadn't, she might still be in Sciarra's custody or dead, believing it would probably be the latter.

"The late minister and I had already agreed that Corrado Bernardi wasn't the puppeteer. His scope of performance was too defined," Lamberti stated. "Instead, he's an intermediary."

"Did you suspect Fakhouri?" Zunino asked.

"We suspected someone in the Saudi government. Thanks to you and Villa, I'm now certain of his identity."

"What will you do next?"

"Deal with Baudo and help Mauro and Dante," Lamberti replied, referring to Bruno and Acardi by their first names as she abruptly left her office and, walking down the stairs, entered the kitchen and opened up her refrigerator.

"Where's are my cannoli?" She asked, clearly irritated that they were gone.

"About that," Zunino replied.

Chapter Sixteen

Qasim Fakhouri listened in stoic silence as Corrado Bernardi described a series of disastrous events, his incompetent employee admitting to a grave error in judgment for not killing the French minister and Lamberti as soon as he learned about their investigations into his activities. Although their deaths wouldn't have permanently concealed their activities, they would have allowed more time to achieve their objectives.

Bernardi further demonstrated his poor judgment by orchestrating a kidnapping utilizing the services of Dante Sciarra. Fakhouri considered him to be a person of limited intelligence who relied on violence because he lacked the mental capacity to devise more sophisticated plans. Therefore, despite his employee viewing Sciarra's departure as the tragic loss of a valuable asset, he had the opposite point of view—supported by the reality that the Mafioso hadn't extracted a scintilla of information from Lamberti, even though they'd taken an enormous risk in kidnapping her. As a result, following Sciarra's unsuccessful efforts to interrogate the Italian intelligence czar, he concluded that the Sicilian had outlived his usefulness. Consequently, he'd already planned to eliminate this unreliable and incompetent loose end who knew too much when fate intervened.

"Why did you send me a text in the clear?" Fakhouri asked.

Bernardi cleared his throat before responding. "That was

a careless mistake," he admitted. "However, I only used your moniker. 'Opus' could refer to anyone."

"Let me explain the situation. First, replacing my name with a pseudonym in a message is irrelevant because the Italian government has the resources to link the number you texted to my cell phone's French billing address, whether through legal or illegal methods. As the owner of the residence at that address, my name will be on record. France, unlike Italy, won't allow cellular devices to be billed to an offshore corporation, an attorney, or other intermediary because this disassociation could shield terrorists. Consequently, the Italian government is now aware that Opus refers to me and will link your business activities to those of the Saudi government, something they would never have otherwise suspected."

"I'll straighten it out," Bernardi responded.

"You can't undo what's already been done. From this moment on, you will no longer have autonomy in any aspect of our business dealings. Every decision now requires my approval, and you will follow my directions without exception."

"Understood," Bernardi meekly replied.

It was clear to Fakhouri that Bernardi had outlived his usefulness and he needed to get rid of his judgmentally-challenged employee, having his replacement already in mind. The good news was that Bernardi sent him an executed copy of every contract and agreement he'd negotiated, and his computer system was mirrored to a server at Fakhouri's estate. The bad news, at least for his soon-to-be ex-employee and his staff, was that they'd all need to die, and the company's computer system and records destroyed, to eliminate documentation of their activities and those who could testify to them.

Refocusing, he shifted the conversation to the AISI director. "Brief me on Acardi," he stated.

"Baudo told me that no one has heard from him since the

explosion. Therefore, I presume his body was blown apart and vaporized in the explosion."

"A fragment of clothing, his watch, wallet, or a trace of something that was on his person should have survived and been discovered in the rubble."

"Something should have survived," Bernardi admitted.

"Until I have proof to the contrary, assume that he's alive and, when he reappears, kill him. The time for subtlety has passed. Is that understood?"

"Yes."

"That leaves us with Lamberti. What's that latest?"

"I suspect," he began, "that because the seaplane captain didn't see her or the investigators on the smuggler's ship before it exploded, that they're in Malta and trying to arrange their return to Italy," Bernardi stated.

"She's not in Malta. The witch is back in Rome," Fakhouri stated, selecting the term he'd learned was the nickname used by her adversaries, and deciding it was appropriate given the circumstances.

"I respectfully disagree. Baudo would have told me. He'd know if government assets were deployed to bring her back, or if she returned by some other means," Bernardi insisted.

"She didn't rely on the resources of the Italian government and didn't tell anyone of her return because she knows there's an informant within the government who's reporting on her."

Bernardi still disagreed but wasn't going to argue the point.

"You previously said that Sciarra told you she sailed from Sicily to Malta with the assistance of a local," Fakhouri continued. "With that ingenuity, let's assume she could also effectuate her return to Rome. You don't have the position of intelligence czar unless you're smart and creative. If we assume she's back in Italy and has had time to reflect on the events that transpired, she likely concludes that only an informant within the government could have provided the necessary details for her kidnapping. Also, I'm confident she will have narrowed her list of suspects down to Baudo. Given these assumptions, we need to focus more than ever on protecting our operations because my plan hasn't yet taken root. It would be extremely disruptive, if not catastrophic, for her to discover, or even suspect, our endgame."

"I don't believe she has the necessary data to reach that conclusion. No one else has either," Bernardi stated.

"Don't underestimate Lamberti. My dossier on her indicates that she's analytical, resourceful, and unemotionally merciless in her decision-making. This implies that she is a street fighter wearing designer clothing."

"What should we do?"

"What you'll do," Fakhouri corrected, "is get rid of Baudo before he's confronted with treason and makes a deal to save himself in exchange for revealing what he knows about me and our endeavors. He's outlived his usefulness and is now a liability."

"It'll be done today," Bernardi confirmed, after which Fakhouri ended the call without further comment.

Bernardi's plan to eliminate Baudo began with an invitation to meet at their usual spot: a restaurant in Tor Bella Monaca. Government officials or those higher than the bottom rung on the social ladder were unlikely to go to that section of the city because it was a notoriously dangerous with its inhabitants suspicious of outsiders, viewing them as intruders. However, Bernardi and Baudo felt safe because Dante Sciarra had accompanied them on their first visit and, even though he was a Sicilian Mafioso, word had spread that they were to be left alone or face severe consequences. As a result, no one in the area wanted to risk incurring the wrath of a Mafia don by harming either of them.

After his call to Baudo, Bernardi contracted for the hit with a killer Sciarra had previously used to eliminate a person hiding from him in Rome, believing that being in another Mafia don's territory would protect them. It didn't. Therefore, while Bernardi remained in his penthouse, Baudo took the metro to their dinner meeting, walking the last two blocks to the restaurant with an air of invincibility. Along the way, he passed several rough-looking groups of men, each of whom gave him passage because of his association with Sciarra. However, as he walked down the narrow one-way street next to the restaurant, a round from a silenced rifle impacted his chest, causing his lifeless body to collapse onto the asphalt road. The person who'd taken the shot from the recessed alley across the street then ran to the body, removed a silenced handgun from his shoulder holster, and put two into Baudo's head for good measure before leaving unseen.

D'Angelo was deep in thought on how to resolve Acardi's situation without alienating the French when his cellphone vibrated. Seeing that it was Pia Lamberti's office number, he expected to be speaking with Zunino when he answered the call. Instead, he was surprised to hear the unmistakable voice of Italy's intelligence czar greeting him.

"How did you escape your kidnappers and return home without anyone knowing?" He asked, knowing the call could only have originated from there and getting straight to the point.

"I'll explain when you come here."

"That's not a good idea. I heard that Baudo left the building for a meeting, but no one seems to know where he went or who he is meeting with. This could mean that, knowing you escaped, he's monitoring your home to see if someone like me shows up, which would confirm your presence there. That makes those who visit you targets."

"Baudo's dead. I'll see you shortly," Lamberti stated, concluding their call and leaving the speechless AISE director staring at his phone.

The security at Lamberti's estate returned to normal with her arrival. When D'Angelo arrived, he was buzzed into the compound by Villa, the director knowing where to park because he'd previously had meetings at the residence and was familiar with the visitor parking area. As he stepped out of his vehicle, Villa was there waiting with a wand in his hand and, as with every visitor, the director was scanned and patted down. He was then escorted past the two front door guards, each armed with an AR-15 assault rifle, and up the staircase where he saw Zunino standing outside the double doors which led to Lamberti's office. After receiving a nod from Villa, he opened the doors.

The director considered Lamberti's thirteen thousand square feet residence the most beautiful home he'd ever seen, both inside and out, believing it could have easily graced the cover of *Architectural Digest* if it belonged to someone other than Italy's privacy-obsessed intelligence czar.

Externally, the three-story mansion combined elements of nineteenth-century classical architecture with stylistic features from the sixteenth-century Renaissance. It boasted prominently bracketed cornices, a campanile (bell tower) at one end, and a belvedere (a structure designed to take advantage of the view) at the other, along with adjoining arched windows.

Internally, the most striking feature was Lamberti's office, which featured a white coffered ceiling made up of a series of sunken octagonal panels bordered by twenty-inch-wide triple-crown molding, which matched the twelve-inch-tall baseboard trim that surrounded the room. The floor was polished Brazilian cherry hardwood, adorned with black and gold patterned Persian rugs.

In the center of the room, on one of the rugs, was a seating area dominated by two plush white sofas facing each other, with an elegant low-rise antique table between them. At both ends of the table were equally plush club chairs upholstered in the same white fabric. Lamberti sat in the club chair at one end and waved for the director to join her, extending an arm toward the couch on her right.

One look at her frail body and gaunt face revealed the hardships she must have endured during her brief time in captivity. That she asked for this meeting within hours of arriving in Rome demonstrated the iron-willed nature of the person before him. Since neither of them excelled at social niceties or small talk—viewing them as a waste of time—Lamberti began by summarizing what had happened to her.

"It's remarkable that you managed to escape," D'Angelo acknowledged.

"Now that I'm back," she replied, dismissing any further discussion about her escape, "we have urgent matters to address. First, we need to persuade the French to end their manhunt for Acardi by clearing the director—and, by extension, the Italian government—of the accusations against him."

"I believe he is innocent, but the process of exonerating him will not be easy or quick," replied the career government employee. "Just like Italian politicians, those in France will also be sensitive to public opinion. Neither President Orsini nor I will be able to convince them of Acardi's innocence unless we identify those responsible for the minister's death and the hotel explosion, and provide proof to support our claims. If the French president or anyone in his government agrees to clear Acardi without proof of his innocence, for the sake of political expediency, they will face severe criticism from the media and their party members."

Lamberti agreed.

"By the way, I'm interested to know how you found out about Baudo's death, as I take pride in always knowing more than the person I am meeting with."

"Baudo's body was found on a street in Tor Bella Monaca and reported to the police. When the officers searched the body for identification, they discovered his government ID, which indicated that he worked for the AISI. They then notified the duty officer, who followed procedures for the death of a senior staff member and sent an email to those on his checklist. I was one of the recipients. You weren't notified because the AISI is a domestic agency."

"Question answered," D'Angelo stated.

"Staying focused, how do we identify the guilty party for the French? Zunino informed me about Baudo's surveillance recordings and mentioned that you had seen them. This is evidence which clearly indicates that Baudo is the informant supplying information to Dante Sciarra and Corrado Bernardi. I'm sure you learned of their involvement when you decrypted Baudo's previous conversations."

The AISE director confirmed that he had analyzed the recordings stored in the government's database and had taken an in-depth look at both men.

"You can ignore Sciarra; he died in a ship explosion," Lamberti stated matter-of-factly. "Bernardi is intriguing, but he's not a decision-maker. He's just a functionary of Qasim Fakhouri."

"The Saudi Minister of Economy and Planning is involved in this?" D'Angelo asked in a shocked voice. He was familiar with the MEP by name, although they had never met.

"He's the person directly responsible for everything that's happened to me, Acardi, Bruno, and others. If you were to metaphorically compare him to someone, it'd be Oz, the person orchestrating others behind the curtain in the Wizard of Oz."

"It seems implausible that he or the Saudi government is involved in any of this. They export a billion plus dollars of oil each day. Why would they be concerned with anything beyond adjusting their oil production, which influences global prices and helps maintain their profitability?"

"I found myself asking that very question and came up with two plausible explanations that I intended to discuss with the French minister. The first is that Fakhouri recognizes that Saudi Arabia's oil is a dwindling resource, with most of it expected to be depleted in the next decade. Like anything extracted from the earth, the supply is finite. As the Minister of Economy and Planning, he's likely orchestrating the next source of revenue for the Kingdom's as oil exports decrease."

"Why wouldn't that revenue source be Saudi Arabia's sovereign fund and the royal family's outside investments? I've been told their combined value is around two trillion dollars and that they generate sizable profits and revenue."

"I believe that Fakhouri has done the math and found that the cost of maintaining his country's infrastructure and continuing to subsidize approximately fifteen thousand members of the royal family, along with their palaces, aircraft, luxury goods, staff, and so forth would be impossible if he had to rely solely on investment profits and cash flow. His research would have shown that the average annual return on investment globally is 6.4 percent, with some years yielding higher returns and others lower. Therefore, the $1.6 trillion in foreign investment made by the Saudi government would, on average, generate just over a $102 billion a year, which is significantly less than the current annual revenue of over $365 billion," Lamberti said, D'Angelo not disputing the figures, knowing that Lamberti had a photographic memory and was renowned for her accuracy with statistics. "As a result, in the not-too-distant future, Fakhouri would find himself in the unenviable position of either significantly tightening the royal family's belts as to what they can spend, or cannibalize the principal of the sovereign fund to make ends meet. Consequently, he must find a way to replace the country's oil revenue with another ubiquitous commodity."

"What could be more ubiquitous than oil in Saudi Arabia?"

"Technological oil—a metaphor I use for rare earth metals, which don't have to be found within its geographic boundaries."

"I don't know anything about these metals," D'Angelo admitted.

"I was in the same position, but now I can give you their positions on the periodic table," Lamberti said. "There are seventeen rare earth metals, also known as rare earth elements (REE). The term 'rare' is misleading because these elements are found globally in the earth's crust. However, they typically exist in tiny quantities attached to other minerals, which makes the process of producing a pure oxide of these elements both time-consuming and expensive. On average, a pound of shale, or whatever material a REE is embedded in, yields only 0.005 ounces of oxide."

"Which seems to make them no different from gold, silver, and platinum, begging the question as to why Fakhouri is betting his country's future on them," the director stated.

"Unlike precious metals, rare earth elements are incorporated into hundreds of thousands of consumer and high-tech products, making them essential for maintaining our way of life. Furthermore, demand for these elements is expected to increase sevenfold over the next fifteen years as new uses for their unique properties are discovered."

"Making the scarcity and demand for your technological oil a suitable replacement for traditional oil."

"Exactly. The minister and I discovered that for years Fakhouri has been acquiring the rights to mine and process known concentrations of specific rare earth elements, believing his goal was to achieve the same global dominance in them that Saudi Arabia currently holds in oil. However, acquiring these rights must be done slowly because he doesn't want to tip his hand by revealing that his government is trying to corner the REE market. Therefore, he uses Corrado Bernardi as his front man, equipping him with the nearly limitless financial resources of the Saudis."

"You mentioned mining rights. Why doesn't Bernardi purchase the land? Presumably, the Saudis have the money."

"I'd speculate that there would be considerable resistance to a country selling its land to a foreign government instead of leasing it, and the approval process would likely take much longer, if they ever received final authorization," Lamberti stated. "However, since typical mining contracts last for ninety-nine years and include the rights to process and export the oxide, the Saudis essentially gain de facto ownership."

"And the leases are owned by offshore corporations to conceal Saudi involvement," D'Angelo speculated.

"Which makes it nearly impossible to identify the true beneficiaries of the leases," Lamberti concurred.

"Therefore, Fakhouri is your puppeteer as he manipulates,

through Bernardi, officials, politicians, law enforcement, and anyone else necessary to secure the desired leases, processing facility contracts, and export licenses," D'Angelo stated, afterward adding that Zunino mentioned the puppeteer when he and Villa came to his office, although not the person she associated with it.

Lamberti agreed with the assessment as to the identity of the puppeteer.

"How did you become involved?" The director asked.

"By chance. As the country's intelligence czar, I'm notified of all contracts that domestic companies are considering with foreign entities. Bernardi's requests on behalf of his offshore clients to mine, process, and export rare earth elements in Sardinia and Sicily came to my attention. From what I can gather, Sicily was the first mining contract for rare earth that Fakhouri obtained. Since there was no evidence that this would impact national security, there were no objections."

"It's a mystery to me why the Saudis chose Bernardi's company as their intermediary when they could afford the best law and consulting firms in the world to represent them."

"My theory is that the first rare earth mining property that the Saudis' wanted was located in Agrigento province and, being savvy businesspeople, they realized that nothing significant occurs in Sicily without the Mafia's approval. Therefore, after discovering that Sciarra was the head of that family, and knowing they needed him on their side for the contract to be signed and for the mine and processing plant to operate smoothly without labor issues or outside interference, Fakhouri's staff would have researched the most effective way to win Sciarra's approval while avoiding a direct link between Saudi Arabia and the Mafia—as such a connection would cause a diplomatic nightmare if discovered."

"Which is why they needed an intermediary who had a connection to Sciarra," D'Angelo stated.

"They would have conducted a thorough background check on Sciarra, which would have led them to his childhood friend and classmate, Corrado Bernardi, who owned an unremarkable consulting practice in Rome. Continuing with my theory, the Saudis likely hired Bernardi with the understanding that he would enlist his classmate's help in securing the mining lease and processing plant licenses for this initial property, going on to help them obtain other rare earth mining leases in his province for a piece of the action."

"Bernardi must have thought he'd won the lottery when the Saudis approached him. And once he secured Sciarra's agreement to assist him, local mine owners and government officials had no option but to accept the terms that Bernardi proposed," D'Angelo stated.

"Those contracts paved the way for further operations in Sicily, Sardinia, and mainland Italy, with Sciarra likely referring his classmate to Mafia leaders in those regions for a fee. These initial successes would have prompted Fakhouri to engage Bernardi's firm for transactions outside of Italy, as he understood the Saudis' requirements and knew how to structure deals with their offshore entities. Moreover, since it was vitally important for them to keep their activities secret, having Bernardi as their sole intermediary would have helped achieve this."

"Excluding Italy and the mob, why wouldn't government officials or local mobsters in other countries, noticing the substantial profits being made, want to participate for their cooperation and to not interfere with production?"

"A French informant told the Minister of Foreign Affairs that many of the local and government officials, whose approvals were essential for permitting and licensing their operations, granted their endorsements only after receiving a piece of paper containing the access code to an offshore bank account. Afterward, quarterly deposits were made into these accounts, provided there were no labor disputes or government demands that could disrupt their mining, processing, or export activities. A further condition, he was told, was that all requests for mining permits from other entities were to be denied. As a result, these officials had a vested interest in fiercely protecting Bernardi from competitors and ensuring that there were no obstacles to his operations."

"Fakhouri has mining operations on French soil?" D'Angelo asked.

"His extraction and processing operations are mainly conducted in the Massif Central, a highland region in south-central France where mining has been practiced since Gallo-Roman times."

"The startup capital required for these operations must be staggering."

"It is a daunting challenge and a double-edged sword," Lamberti said. "Most rare earth elements are found in remote areas, which often lack utilities, infrastructure, and adequate roads and rail services. This means that the local and national governments must provide this necessary support if they want to attract companies interested in leasing and exporting these elements. Unfortunately, they typically do not have the available funds to do so. Therefore, whether by loans or grants, a Saudis offshore corporation likely covers all the expenses associated with getting the technological oil to market. When you factor in the startup costs for the mine, the extraction of the elements, and the construction of the processing plant, you're looking at an investment of around half a billion dollars per site."

"Given that huge expenditure, the other edge of the sword must be very sharp," D'Angelo stated.

"When the mine and processing plant are fully operational, the profits are enormous. Europium, for example, sells for $712,000 per metric ton, while the same weight in copper brings in $8,800."

"And that differentiation is only going to grow because, as you stated, the demand for rare earth metals is projected to increase sevenfold over the next fifteen years. Given the growth of Fakhouri's mining empire, how is he managing to keep his operations a secret?" D'Angelo asked.

One reason is that Bernardi is the only person, at least to our knowledge, who is negotiating contracts. Additionally, it seems that each mine is associated with a different offshore corporation, which doesn't raise any red flags since it is common practice in the mining industry to separate liabilities by site. Another possibility is that Bernardi might be using fictitious names in some or all of his negotiations.

"Fakhouri can't keep pulling these strings and maintaining this secret forever. If you and the minister have figured this out, others will too," the director said.

"That's a foregone conclusion, which I don't believe has escaped his notice. If the Saudis aren't already close to dominating the global market for rare earth elements, they are certainly on the verge of it, after which discovery of their ownership positions may become irrelevant. They'll likely use this technological oil as a geopolitical weapon to give them exponentially more control over world politics than they ever had with oil.

The allocation of rare earth products can profoundly impact not only a nation's economy but also the financial stability of businesses within that nation. It's not unlikely that, if their sovereign wealth fund has invested in a company and wants to increase its stock value, they'd reduce the price of an element to that company or increase it for their competitors. Geopolitics is an unethical arena, and the Saudis are particularly skilled at exploiting it."

"It seems we're too late to change the outcome, since we can't undo what they have already achieved."

"There is a way," she replied.

"How?"

She explained it to him.

"Can you do that?"

"I can't, but I know someone who can."

Indro Montanari sat down to enjoy the meatball sandwich he'd just prepared. He had spent six hours cooking the meatballs in his homemade tomato sauce before selecting several to place inside a baguette. After covering them with sauce and shredded mozzarella cheese, he put his creation in the oven until the cheese melted into a gooey consistency. He was a third of the way through devouring his sandwich when there was a knock at the door. Ignoring it, he put on the headphones that were within arm's reach, determined not to give up the pleasure of savoring one of his favorite comfort food meals. Consequently, he didn't hear the second knock and a voice asking him to open the door. There was no third knock, even though he wouldn't have heard it. Instead, the door was swung open by Zunino, with Lamberti entering ahead of her bodyguard who was returning the lock picks to their carrying case. As they walked in, the startled Savant set down his sandwich, removed his headphones, and stared at the witch.

"Zunino informed me that you successfully hacked into the French national database, which allowed us to recover the minister's files. That was impressive," Lamberti said, speaking as if everything was business as usual and the kidnapping never occurred.

"Bence made that possible by giving me his login information," Montanari responded, wanting to lower Lamberti's expectations because he knew she wasn't there on a social call, but to ask him to do something that would be extraordinarily difficult and probably illegal.

"Nevertheless, you made it happen."

Here it comes, Montanari thought.

"I have an equally challenging task," she continued without pause and getting directly to the point without bothering to ask if he was willing to help again. "I'm going to give you a list of offshore banks and the names of specific depositors. I need a copy of their financial statements as evidence of their corruption."

"The security of offshore financial institutions is comparable to, and in some cases even surpasses, that of nation-states. The reason they're so security-obsessed," the Savant explained, his hands becoming animated as he did, an imbued habit of many Italians, "is that the bank's existence, and a major portion of their sovereign state's economy, depends on keeping someone like me out of their systems. Coupled with the fact that they guarantee anonymity and disregard court orders from other countries to release bank records, and you can understand why people choose to hide money there. How many names are we talking about?"

"The late minister and I gathered the names of hundreds of government officials involved in the leases negotiated by Bernardi's company. I suspect most of them have offshore accounts," Lamberti stated, handing him a printed list.

"Every government is concerned about corruption, and individuals and domestic corporations hiding money offshore to avoid paying taxes. Without exception, each wants to access these offshore banks and employs skilled hackers tasked with this objective. To my knowledge, however, no one has successfully breached all of their firewalls."

"Have you tried?"

"No."

"Why not? If anyone can accomplish this impossibility, I would be you."

"I have a great deal of common sense. Also, given that I'm now a law-abiding citizen, except when you force me to cross to the other side, it's illegal," Montanari replied.

"Do you know why we both excel in our careers?" Lamberti asked as she walked to the stove and, taking the wooden spoon resting on the counter, tasted the tomato sauce, afterward nodding in approval. "It's because, while we understand and respect the challenges we face, we don't dwell on the obstacles. Instead, we search for the hidden path to success. You've explained the obstacles; now let's focus on finding that path. Start by explaining how someone accesses their offshore account."

"Every financial institution is slightly different. However, generally speaking, they provide depositors with a login process, a username, and an access code linked to that username. To start, the depositor enters this information to get past the first firewall, after which they'll need to input their account number and a personalized passcode, which usually consists of a ten-key alphanumeric-character string that's associated with their username, although the length of this key varies by institution.

It's important to complete each step of this process within a specific time frame; otherwise, the system will reset and require the user to start over. If the user fails to log in after three attempts, they will be locked out and must initiate a video call with the bank to reset their username, passcode, and alphanumeric string."

"How would you short-circuit the process?" Lamberti asked, knowing the Savant enjoyed demonstrating his talents at overcoming obstacles that everyone believed were impossible to surmount.

Montanari tilted his head slightly to the right and was motionless as he stared straight ahead in a Zen-like state, decoupling from external stimuli as he contemplated Lamberti's question. Two minutes later, he turned towards her and asked, "Do you have the ability to obtain the cellular numbers of those on your list and intercept their communications and data?"

"Yes, if they're within Italy. Outside the country, we would need the cooperation of that nation. Countries with which we have a good relationship usually provide us with the necessary data without requiring a court order, but others may not be as cooperative. In those cases, I'll need to ask the Americans for help, as they seem to record and store voice and data communications for everyone on the planet and know their cellular numbers. Obviously, what I told you is sensitive and should be kept to yourself."

"Obviously," Montanari replied without thinking, his mind somewhere else.

"Why did you ask that question?" Lamberti pressed on.

"To accomplish the impossible, I need the cellphone numbers of everyone on the list you gave me, and to arrange for each to receive a large cash payment."

"That's very generous of you. Why?"

"You won't be handing them a stack of cash. The money will be in a legitimate bank account to which they'll have access via a link. There will be no red flags because everyone will receive the cash on request, as represented in the message we'll send. However, the link will have embedded in it a keylogger trojan virus, which even the most sophisticated antivirus programs used by financial institutions won't detect. This is because the virus won't be transmitted to either the bank holding the money or the offshore institution. Instead, it'll be downloaded into their device."

"I don't understand the process, or what we gain from it."

"I'll explain latter."

"Now," Lamberti insisted.

"Once the person activates the link to receive the money, a keylogger virus installs itself on their communication software, masquerading as an authorized update. Since it does not alter the existing software, it will not be flagged or rejected. The virus then records every keystroke and stores the information until it receives a command to transmit the data, at which point the information will be intercepted by us."

"This means the virus doesn't need to insert itself into the system software," Lamberti said.

"That would be very complicated. Instead, it operates on top of it, recording all keyboard communications as they enter and pass through the virus," the Savant replied.

"Will the user be aware of an update to their cellphone?"

"It's doubtful. The system won't send them an update message, and inserting the virus only takes a few seconds. If they try to make a call or access an app during that time, they will likely attribute any delay to a slow connection."

"That seems reasonable."

"No one will suspect that the message isn't genuine since they will receive the promised money. Afterward, they will likely transfer part or all of it to their offshore account since they want to avoid having a large sum appear on their local bank statement, as it would be difficult to explain.

As the transfer takes place, we'll record their institutional login information—which will include their account number, username, personalized access code, and any other entry required to access their account. However, to incentivize them to transfer this money offshore instead of withdrawing it, we're not talking about $5,000. It needs to be a large sum of money."

"I understand," Lamberti replied. "While they might be able to explain the receipt and withdrawal of $5,000, they couldn't explain $50,000."

"Is that how much you're thinking of depositing into each account?" Montanari asked, surprised at the dollar amount because he was going to recommend half that number.

"As you said, it needs to be a large sum to ensure that it's transferred offshore instead of merely pocketing it. Considering the number of names involved, I will need to transfer about $25 million," she stated matter-of-factly. "Once I've set up the bank account and transferred the funds, I'll provide you with the link and instructions to access it."

"Is there anything specific you would like me to include in my message about their recent good fortune and the receipt of $50,000?"

"Keep it simple. It's a bonus to thank them for their past help, and it should remain confidential because not everyone received a bonus," Lamberti said.

"Do you want the text to come from Calvario or Bernardi? I planned to send it from Calvario in case Bernardi used an alias with some people on the list."

"Use Calvario," Lamberti agreed. "The biggest risk I see is that one of the recipients may thank Bernardi for the bonus, who then asks to see the message they received. He'll call Fakhouri to verify whether he sent the message on behalf of Calvario. If Fakhouri confirms he didn't, they'll realize that someone has discovered what they're doing and has the names of those involved in assisting them."

"That seems to be an unavoidable risk. However, if this works as planned, we'll have what we want before then."

"How long will it take to create the virus?"

"Since I only need to modify an existing one, about an hour."

"You'll have the bank information and my login procedures for the account containing the $25 million by then. However, getting you the cellular numbers for devices obtained or used outside of Italy will depend on what the NSA wants in return."

"Do you have any idea what that might be?"

"No, but I can assure you it'll be painful," Lamberti replied.

Chapter Seventeen

Acardi and Bence continued to discuss how Qasim Fakhouri's involvement tacitly meant that the senior members of the royal family of Saudi Arabia must also be involved. Both men felt that making decisions with national implications without their approval would have dire consequences for Fakhouri and could create a vacancy at the top of the Ministry of Economy and Planning. They also revisited Zunino's conversation with D'Angelo and considered how, with Montanari's assistance, they might further investigate the relationship between Bernardi and Fakhouri. While they were discussing this topic, Bence's phone chimed. Answering it, a suppressed smile came across his face as he listened to the voice on the other end.

"This is for you," he said, handing the phone to Acardi.

"I hear you've set back French-Italian relations by a century," Lamberti remarked.

Acardi, unaware of the rescue or that she was back in Italy, grinned when he heard her voice. "It was difficult, but the BD&D investigators showed me how it could be done," he replied, knowing it would bring a smile to Lamberti's face.

"I'm bringing you back to Italy," she said firmly, making it clear that there would be no discussion about it. "In forty-five minutes, someone from the embassy will pick you up in a private vehicle and drive you to an aircraft that is waiting at the private air terminal in Le Havre, which is two and a half hours away. Departing from Paris is too risky due to your notoriety. You'll be flown to Ciampino Airport, where Villa will be waiting to take you to the estate."

"I assume the French authorities at Le Havre won't ask for my identification since the flight is a charter with a flight plan to a domestic location. However, en route the pilot will change the destination to Rome. The French won't be concerned because the crew and I will be the Italians' problem, having to adhere to their customs and immigration laws upon arrival as we're an international flight."

"Precisely. I will arrange for someone to contact the tower as well as airport customs and immigration. Your aircraft will be directed to a hangar where, once the doors are closed, you can disembark without anyone outside the crew—who are on my payroll—and Villa noticing. As a result, your return to Italy will remain a secret, and you will stay with me until this situation is resolved."

"Bence saved my life, and I can't abandon him. The French government will eventually find out that the breach of the minister's servers originated from his login. They will also discover that he and I had dinner together and that he was seen with me at the hotel before the explosion. Once these facts come to light, they will realize he was assisting me, and they'll imprison him."

"I have other plans for Bence. Until then, he can stay in Donais' apartment. I'll see you in a little over six hours," she said, ending the call.

"I heard your side of the conversation. What did she say?" Bence asked.

Acardi told him.

"What does she mean by *other plans*?" Bence inquired.

"It's hard to say with Lamberti. However, based on my experience, I can confidently say that you're not going to like it."

After the call with Acardi and having already arranged for

his return to Italy, Lamberti reached out to President Orsini. This was necessary because the request for assistance from the NSA needed to be made between heads of state rather than government officials. Lamberti was asking the Americans to acknowledge that the Agency collected communications from citizens of other nations—something that wouldn't surprise anyone. However, the issue was that these nonexistent communications had to be given to the Italian government. While in-house use by the NSA was one thing, providing documented evidence of their signal intelligence (SIGINT) capabilities to another government was quite different.

Orsini listened patiently to Lamberti's request, knowing the potential consequences of what she was asking. The responsibility for issuing the licenses to mine, and the permits to process, rare earth oxides lies with the host nation. These countries would be furious with Italy if they discovered that Orsini had received intercepted conversations of their government officials from the NSA, regardless of the illegal activities being discussed, perceiving it as a flagrant disregard for their sovereignty. They would also be equally outraged by the repatriation of funds from the accounts of these officials, even if the money had been acquired through bribery. At a minimum, they would insist on having it returned.

The United States would share some of the blame, although these governments would likely be less angry with them because there was a general belief that the NSA indiscriminately spied on everyone and served as a central repository for global communications. As a result, governments had long accepted this reality and didn't take it personally, recognizing that there was nothing they could do about it. Moreover, the NSA showed no concern for what anyone, including members of Congress, thought about their global monitoring practices.

"If you add the receipt of this information from the NSA to the French already believing that Acardi killed their minister and committed other violent acts in their country, and the potential discovery that an Italian hacker extracted information from their government's servers, this could sever the already thin and frayed thread of diplomatic relations between our countries."

"I know, and it's not only the French who could sever their ties to us; it's also the Saudis. And they won't just be angry; they'll be vindictive," Lamberti stated.

"Especially considering that we've interfered with something that's vital to their future prosperity. If they discover our involvement, I can confidently say that the four and a half million tons of oil we import from them annually will never reach our shores. Additionally, trust in us by other nations will be severely damaged."

"I understand the significant political and economic risks you and our country are facing," Lamberti said. "However, the potential for the Saudis to gain a virtual monopoly on rare earth elements poses a threat not just to us, but to the entire world. While there are alternative energy sources besides oil, there is no viable substitute for rare earth metals in the foreseeable future."

"That alone would induce me to call President Ballinger and seek his help. However, let's not forget that the Saudis orchestrated your kidnapping on our soil. That makes me just as vindictive, if not more so, than them. For this reason, and considering that the world could become economic hostages of the Kingdom for generations, we need to ensure they don't get away with this. Since you are more knowledgeable about this situation than I am, I'll include you in the conversation with the American president."

"When will that happen?"

"There's no time like the present," Orsini said, using his intercom to ask Palmieri to put President Ballinger on the phone.

The call with President Ballinger exceeded Orsini's expectations. The president appreciated the intelligence Orsini provided and was adamant about not allowing the Saudis to gain significantly more economic power than they currently held, potentially for generations to come. During their conversation, the president connected General Parker McInnes, the director of the NSA, to the call. He then brought Libby Parra, the Chief of the Global Issues Analysis Office, into the discussion.

Parra paid close attention to what Lamberti needed and asked for the list of government officials, which she was told included the countries and cities in which they resided. During their conversation, Lamberti promptly sent it to the email address that she was given, the email appearing on Parra's desktop less than a minute later.

Parra reviewed the list. "I'll begin this right away," she told President Ballinger, and by extension Orsini and Lamberti.

"How long will it take to find the data?" Ballinger inquired.

"There are several hundred names on this list, representing individuals located across the globe. Writing the algorithm, scanning the names, and incorporating search parameters to include their government positions will take time," Parra said. "Contrary to popular belief, we don't electronically monitor every inch of our planet, and some of these officials reside in those blind spots. However, since there aren't many of them, I can deploy electronic intelligence-gathering drones and aircraft to monitor those areas, assuming they're in their search zones when your person sends the money to their financial institution."

"Can you tell me when those assets will be in place and the database search can occur?" The president asked.

"Six hours from now," Parra replied without hesitation.

"I'll ensure the link is transmitted in exactly six hours," Lamberti stated. Then she added, "I have one more request," surprising Orsini, who had no idea what she was about to say.

"Now is the time to lay everything on the table," President Ballinger remarked.

"To neutralize what the Saudis have already been able to accomplish, I need you to deploy a special operations team."

"Where and for what objective?"

She explained her plan. "I know that may pose a problem," Lamberti admitted, with Orsini agreeing.

"Only if you're on the other side," Ballinger responded, agreeing to her request.

Following the call, Lamberti walked downstairs to the kitchen, where she found Hunkler, Donati, Donais, and Labriola having a bite to eat.

"I know that I've already thanked you for saving my life, but I also want to express my gratitude for your perseverance and an admiration for your investigative skills in finding me so quickly."

The four investigators seemed embarrassed by the praise and remained silent.

"I also want you to know that I'll do whatever it takes to find Mauro and ensure his safe return. Therefore, while I'm working on that, I have something that will keep the three of you very busy," she said, pointing to Donati, Donais, and Hunkler.

"The four of us," Labriola interjected.

"What I have in mind will be very dangerous, even for trained professionals."

"I may not be as skilled with a weapon or in a fight, but don't underestimate my analytical abilities. Sometimes it's better to think your way out of a situation than to shoot your way out."

"I have no disagreement on that point. What do you think?" Lamberti asked while looking at Donais, wanting her opinion on whether Labriola should stay with the group or return to the morgue.

"He was a big help in Sicily, and he's much more analytical than the three of us, or even Bruno. His skills are accretive to ours. It wouldn't hurt to have someone with his talents on the team."

"I agree," Hunkler stated. Following his comment, Donati also expressed his support for Labriola.

"Alright, doctor. Let's hope you don't end up on one of your tables," Lamberti remarked after hearing the unanimous support for the city's senior coroner, confirming that he would stay on the team with that comforting comment.

"What would you like us to do?" Donati asked, wanting to understand their assignment.

"Go to the penthouse in the Eurosky Tower where Corrado Bernardi lives and bring him to me. It's time we had a talk. Since he won't come voluntarily, and I understand this goes against your usual methods, I want to emphasize the importance of being discreet," Lamberti instructed.

"We're kidnapping him," Hunkler pointed out. "As you said, he's not going to come willingly."

"I have confidence you'll find a way that avoids involving security or becoming a trending topic on social media."

"No one will know what we've done," Donati assured her, even though he had no idea how they would keep that promise.

Donais, Donati, and Hunkler knew from experience that when Lamberti said that she would have a talk with Bernardi, she didn't mean that he would be coming to her office for a casual conversation over coffee. Instead, he was headed for a steel chair in the concrete-floored basement, where she would interrogate him about matters he would rather avoid. Depending on his level of cooperation, she would employ whatever methods were necessary to extract the answers she needed, using techniques similar to those found in rendition and black operations sites.

"Is he there now?" Hunkler asked.

"Yes," Lamberti confirmed, explaining that she had asked D'Angelo to have his agents surveil Bernardi. "Villa will take you to the armory to get your weapons, identifications, and anything else you'll need."

"Identifications?" Donati questioned.

The Eurosky Tower has stringent security measures in place. To enter the building, guests are required to obtain authorization from a company employee or tenant to access their office or residence. Since you cannot allow the security desk to contact Bernardi, you will present them with law enforcement credentials—identifications that I can create—and inform them that you need to go to the penthouse without alerting Bernardi to your presence.

None of the elevators have buttons for selecting floors. Access to each floor is controlled by front desk security or requires an RFID card. Therefore, they must grant you access to the penthouse. Additionally, be aware that the elevators are equipped with cameras that are viewed by front desk security.

"This is not unlike breaking someone out of prison, except the person doesn't want to leave voluntarily," Hunkler stated.

"What if security wants to call and verify our identifications? With the current state of technology, we've all seen fake IDs that are nearly impossible to detect," Donais said.

"Your IDs will have holograms embedded in them, which are extremely difficult to replicate. However, you raise a valid point," she replied. She accessed the contact list on her cellphone, then walked to the kitchen counter where she wrote down a name and phone number on a slip of paper. Afterward, she handed it to Donais.

"Have them call this person. He's a captain with the Polizio di Stato and will verify your identities and authority. I'll contact him once I return to my office. I don't know what difficulties you'll face in bringing Bernardi to me, but whatever they are, ensure you do so discreetly. Anything less will forewarn the Saudis, putting us at a significant disadvantage."

"In deference to what you told Labriola, capturing Bernardi seems like a difficult assignment, given the need to ensure no one knows he'd been kidnapped, but it's hardly a dangerous one," Donati said.

"Capturing Bernardi isn't; it's what comes after."

"What can you tell us about that?"

"Nothing until you complete this task. Focus on one thing at a time. Looking ahead will just distract you. That said, you should get moving because I don't know how long Bernardi will stay in the building," Lamberti said, as she turned to leave the kitchen with Zunino following.

Villa escorted the four to the armory and, familiar with using the system for creating Polizio di Stato identification cards, he entered their names and took digitized photographs of each person, the program embedding a hologram of their face on each card. Afterward, he handed each a police badge and issued them weapons along with a spare magazine of ammunition. Hunkler also took several flex cuffs from the shelf and placed them into his jacket pocket. Villa then escorted them to the Range Rover Defender and handed Hunkler the fob.

The traffic was surprisingly light, and they arrived at the Eurosky Tower in just under thirty minutes. When they reached the reception desk, they presented their police IDs and badges, which were accepted without issue, after which Hunkler said they needed to go to the penthouse to question Corrado Bernardi, cautioning the two security personnel behind the counter not to alert him. The guards had no objections and directed Hunkler to elevator number one. As Lamberti noted, there were no buttons inside, and once the doors closed, the elevator took them directly to the penthouse on the thirty-first floor of the building.

As they stepped off the elevator, they entered an atrium that was adorned with black Calacatta marble, with a massive Murano blown glass chandelier hanging from the fifteen-foot ceiling. The walls, which extended from floor to ceiling, were crafted from African Blackwood. The entrance to the residence was through a set of double brass doors, with no doorbell or brass knocker to announce one's presence, probably because no one came here unless they were announced.

Hunkler pounded on one of the doors, the four able to hear the echo permeate the residence. After nearly fifteen seconds, he stopped.

"Since he hasn't left the building, and he doesn't appear to be in the residence, he's probably downstairs in his company office,"

Donati speculated, the four having seen Calvario listed in the lobby directory at the security counter, noting that it was on the thirtieth floor.

"We can use the stairway to get there," Labriola suggested, pointing to a door twenty feet to the right of the elevator that had a sign above it indicating that it was an emergency exit.

"Assuming he is on the floor below, we can't force him to leave because, if we put on the cuffs or drag him to the elevator, one or more of those in the office may record us on their phones and we could be on social media within seconds," Donais stated.

"One way to get him out of Calvario without making a scene is to ask for his assistance by saying we have a case involving a dozen victims of a precious metal mining scam, and that his company's name came up as a reputable mining consulting firm. We ask him to come to our office to review videos of the suspects and see if he recognizes anyone, helping us put names to the faces. We then drive him to Lamberti's estate," Labriola said.

"That's quick thinking, but how did we determine he was a reputable mining consultant?" Donati asked. "It's unlikely he advertises or that his clients, who probably want to avoid publicity, would be singing his praises."

"Because our database has Calvario associated with Italian mining contracts and it's never, to our knowledge, had a complaint lodged against it."

"That's weak."

"Unless someone has a better story, we have to stick with it because it will only take us thirty seconds to go between floors," Labriola concluded.

"He's right, and time isn't on our side. Even though the guards say they won't warn Bernardi, if we lose the element of surprise, our story won't matter if he has time to think about it and calls his attorney, or flees the building," Hunkler said, leading the way to the emergency exit.

Entering the stairway, they made their way to the floor below.

However, what they hadn't foreseen was that, as an emergency exit in a highly secure building, the design dictated that all doors in the stairwell only opened into it, leading everyone to the safety of the ground floor and the lobby where they could escape the building. As a result, they found themselves stuck in the stairwell, with no choice but to walk down the remaining thirty floors to the lobby where they would need to request access to the thirtieth floor from security.

One of the security guards, knowing what must have happened as the four emerged from the stairwell, smiled as they approached. "He wasn't in the penthouse and you want to try the thirtieth floor," he stated.

"Please," Donais replied.

As she said this, a man of Middle Eastern descent in his early thirties, who was pushing a heavy-duty folding dolly, thanked the guard as he passed the desk and returned to the van."

"If you'd come a few minutes earlier, you could have taken the elevator to the thirtieth floor with him," the guard stated.

"Who is he?" Hunkler asked.

"Someone delivering for Amazon, FedEx, or another major firm. They're increasingly turning to private companies to assist with their deliveries."

"You don't ask for an ID or call for authorization for their deliveries?" Labriola asked.

"With this many offices and residences, deliveries are constant. In every residential and office building where I've worked, standard procedure has been to allow FedEx, Amazon, DHS, and other delivery services to enter without interference.

I've been in some which required me to call and get permission for each delivery, which creates chaos and simply doesn't work. In a business setting, the receptionist doesn't know what's been ordered, leading to automatic approval for entry. Residential customers are frequently not home, meaning their packages aren't delivered because the delivery person is turned away. They blame security.

The procedures here are like those in every other security conscious building. We can't sign for the deliveries because management doesn't want the responsibility or liability. Meds and perishables, such as groceries, require refrigeration. Every package needs to be secured, and then there's a risk of the recipient saying that we damaged their delivery. As I said, chaos. Consequently, because of these issues, the policy is eventually revised, just as it has been in this building, to allow delivery services to operate smoothly and without obstruction."

"Good to know," Hunkler said, glancing at his watch.

The guard took the hint. "Take elevator two, officers," he said after a few taps on his keyboard.

As they crossed the lobby heading toward the elevator, a tremendous explosion shook the building, triggering alarms and causing red flashing lights to illuminate throughout the ground floor lobby. In response, the security guard quickly grabbed the red phone to his right, which was connected to the building's public address system, and told everyone to calmly evacuate.

"Are you thinking what I'm thinking?" Hunkler asked as Donati and Donais nodded in agreement, while Labriola tried to understand his meaning.

The colonel led the way outside, Hunkler explaining to Labriola what he believed had happened. As the four moved away from the building, they could see thick black smoke billowing into the sky from what had once been the upper floors. Disturbingly, there was no distinction between the top three floors. The bomb, which they suspected had been delivered by the Middle Eastern person who had just left the building, not only destroyed the thirtieth floor but also took out the floors above and below it.

"If Bernardi was in either his office or penthouse, he didn't survive," Donais said, a sentiment echoed by the others.

"For all we know, he may not have been in the building at all," Donati replied. "The only way to be certain is to see him in a body bag, assuming there's anything left. We need to stay here until the bodies are recovered and somehow get a look inside those bags."

"Depending on if the building is stable enough for a rescue team to search for them," Donais interjected. "Otherwise, we could be in for quite a wait. In the worst-case scenario, they might bring the building down and then search for bodies afterward, once it's safe and recovery won't put anyone at risk."

"The problem is that the police will arrive soon, and they will establish a security perimeter to keep people away. We can show them our IDs and give them the name of the person Lamberti gave us to verify our identities. However, since they know most of their fellow officers, they may run our names through their system anyway. When they do this, they won't find any records of us, which could lead to our arrest and questioning, along with the person who vouched for us—if they are contacted, all of the above decidedly the opposite of our mission mandate of being discreet."

"Maybe we can approach this from a different angle," Labriola suggested, pulling out his coroner's ID from his wallet just as the first police vehicle came to a screeching halt in front of the building, closely followed by the fire department.

Labriola approached the police when they arrived and showed them his credentials. However, this proved unnecessary since several officers already recognized him from their visits to the morgue. The coroner then introduced the three with him as his assistants, no one having a reason to question that statement.

"If you find any bodies, please let me know," he said to the officers, who were more than willing to comply with the request as it shifted the responsibility of notifying the medical examiner, the coroner, and the removal of bodies to Labriola.

As it turned out, Bernardi was standing near the windows with a half dozen Calvario employees when the explosion occurred, the force of the blast propelling them through the glass and onto the ground below. Because of the physics of such a fall, accelerating toward the ground at over one hundred twenty-five mph where the body weights seventy-five hundred times what it did before it fell, and then instantaneously decelerating to a speed of zero on impact, results in the body's cells and blood vessels, including the aorta, being torn open and ripped from their organs. Consequently, the only way Bernardi and four of the six surrounding him were identified by the police was through the contents of their wallets. The other two victims were women who had no identification on them.

The police were good to their word and notified Labriola when the bodies were found and ID'd. Bernardi and his assistants were identified using their driver's licenses, as the condition of their bodies made visual identification impossible. After the police photographer, forensic team, detectives, medical examiner, and coroner's office personnel arrived to carry out their duties, Labriola and his assistants quietly left the scene and returned to the estate, where they reported Bernardi's death to Lamberti.

"With Baudo, Bernardi, and the Calvario employees dead, it appears that Fakhouri is cleaning house to eliminate any potential evidence against himself and the royal family," Lamberti stated. "This means that your next assignment is even more crucial and remains very dangerous because you'll be confronting Fakhouri at his chateau in Louveciennes, which is twenty minutes outside of Paris."

"Can you define 'confront'?" Donati asked.

"You're going to present him with my non-negotiable terms for the future sales of rare earth elements."

"That should start the meeting on the wrong foot, and why would he agree to meet with us?" Hunkler asked.

"Because our Minister of Foreign Affairs will request it, explaining that he has only been informed that the subject to be discussed is highly sensitive and restricted to the involved parties, which is true."

"Will the Saudis accept such a vague explanation?" Hunkler asked.

"Vagueness is an inherent part of diplomacy. The fact that someone of the minister's stature called will pique his curiosity. He'll meet."

"Does he know you've returned to Rome?" Donais inquired.

"I believe he does, and that will be confirmed when you mention me and present my terms," Lamberti replied.

"That raises two questions," Donais said. "First, why don't you just call him and tell him what you want directly? And second, why would he listen to you?" She asked, echoing her team's concerns.

"To answer your first question, he won't have a choice. As for your second question, he will listen because you're going to give him this," Lamberti said, handing her a flash drive.

"What's on this?" Donais asked.

Lamberti told her.

"What if he still says no?"

"He can't. He understands the consequences this could have on his mining leases and the royal family if it becomes public," Lamberti assured her. "Fakhouri is smart enough to realize this and knows a mutual agreement can be reached which, while it doesn't give the Saudis entirely what they want, gives them enough."

"So far, I don't see the very dangerous part of your plan," Labriola stated.

"The minister becomes angry, kills all of you, seizes the drive, and launches a multi-billion dollar campaign to counter its contents, believing the world values a stable supply of rare earth elements over who provides them."

"That's a good argument," the coroner agreed.

"It's probably the option I'd choose in his position."

"That's reassuring," Donati stated.

"My plane is waiting at the Ciampino Airport to fly you to Paris, after which a car service will take you to a farmhouse that I've rented. You'll wait there for Bence's arrival."

"Bence?"

"He's bringing someone with him," she said, going on to

explain the significance of the visitor that Bence was taking to the farmhouse.

As the four were flying to Paris, Acardi's plane landed at the Ciampino Airport and taxied to a hangar where Villa was waiting. Prior to his arrival, Lamberti called President Orsini's assistant to request that Palmieri speak to the airport's customs and immigration office to ensure that Acardi's plane would be treated as a domestic flight and the arrival document would list only the crew as being onboard. After consulting with the president, she received his approval for these arrangements.

Once the aircraft arrived at the hangar and came to a stop, Villa parked beside it and waited for Acardi to disembark. As the AISI director approached the vehicle, Villa called Lamberti to inform her of Acardi's safe arrival and the lack of a customs and immigration official.

The drive to the estate was quick. Upon arrival, Acardi was taken to the kitchen where Lamberti greeted him with a warm embrace before directing him to the kitchen table.

"You look almost as gaunt as I do," she stated.

"Stress," he replied, needing no further explanation.

"That's understandable, but we'll both need our energy for what lies ahead. Zunino told me that you enjoy chardonnay shrimp and scallops in a creamy butter and Parmesan sauce. It's being prepared as we speak," she said, pointing to a chef who was cooking. "While we're waiting, tell me what happened in France."

As she was speaking, Villa brought them two cups of espresso and a bottle of Sambuca, an Italian anise-flavored liquor. He poured a shot into Acardi's cup, having heard from his partners that he sometimes enjoyed a splash of it in his espresso.

Acardi briefed Lamberti, during which their meal arrived and both began to eat as they continued their conversation, Lamberti occasionally interrupting to ask questions and add what she knew.

"So far, the Saudis have done an excellent job of keeping their involvement in rare earth elements a secret," she said after he finished speaking.

"By all accounts, they've done an outstanding job," Acardi agreed.

"I don't doubt that they conducted extensive research before concluding that the rare earth market was the most feasible— and possibly the only—way to replace the revenue from their rapidly depleting oil reserves. I also think it was critical to keep their mining leases confidential. If it became known that they were acquiring rare earth leases, the costs of future contracts would skyrocket. Additionally, other governments would likely intervene to prevent them from monopolizing the global supply, as access to these elements is essential for both the economy and the national security of most countries."

"The Saudi government has, in the opinion of intelligence professionals, a reputation for exceptional planning and a long-term approach to economic situations. Their decisions are seldom incorrect, as their adept management of oil reserves and strategic geopolitical tactics serve as prime examples," stated the AISI director.

"Their reliance on rare earth elements as a future revenue source will mark the country's second economic transition," Lamberti stated. "The first occurred in the 1930s when the economy shifted from an agricultural-based society to one focused on petroleum."

"The costs associated with this transition must be enormous."

"Establishing a rare earth mine, building the processing plant, and developing the necessary infrastructure typically requires an investment of around half a billion dollars. Normally, a country or corporate entity would aim to quickly extract these elements, convert them into oxides, and sell them to achieve a satisfactory return on their investment and justify the expenditure. However, it seems that Saudi Arabia has taken a different and more patient approach. If they had followed the usual method, the laws of supply and demand would have come into play, leading to an increased supply and lower prices. The fact that prices and availability of these metal oxides have remained relatively stable suggests that Saudi Arabia is pursuing an alternative strategy."

"They're stockpiling whatever is being produced."

"Follow that statement to its logical conclusion," Lamberti said.

"They plan to flood the market with their stockpiled products, severely depressing the prices of these oxides. This strategy will likely force many producers—who are understandably burdened by the costs of constructing, operating, and maintaining their facilities—out of business. After that, they intend to acquire these companies through one of their offshore corporations, further consolidating their position and creating a virtual monopoly," Acardi concluded.

"A monopoly that will remain unnoticed until it's too late, because the numerous offshore corporations create the illusion of a fragmented market."

"If rare earth elements are being stockpiled, the amount of warehouse space needed would be significant. They couldn't be stored at the processing plant, as this would raise too many questions about why they're producing oxides that aren't being sold. Therefore, it's likely that these elements are being sent to a centralized location, creating the appearance of distribution and sale," Acardi speculated.

"According to intelligence reports compiled by the late French minister's contacts, the Saudis built a large climate-controlled warehouse in Jeddah, Saudi Arabia. It's believed that this is where the oxides are stored."

"A sizeable climate-controlled warehouse in a port city, especially given the extreme temperatures in Saudi Arabia, should be quite common. So, why this particular warehouse?" Acardi countered.

"As you said, a sizeable climate-controlled warehouse in a port city is common, which is why it's gone unnoticed for so long. What makes this warehouse unusual is its interior, which is sectioned into low-pressure environmental zones in which vacuum-sealed containers are purportedly stored. These rooms are airlocked and filled with argon, an inert gas that displaces oxygen," Lamberti explained.

"The vacuum sealing and the use of argon preventing oxidation, which occurs when a rare earth element is exposed to air," Acardi said.

"While the size and environmentally controlled interior of this warehouse aren't unique within a Saudi port, the added feature of being designed to also be oxidation-free is. If we did the math, it could potentially hold nearly a decade's worth of production from every processing plant that we suspect is secretly owned by the Saudis," Lamberti stated.

"Meaning they're hiding their rare earth storage facility in plain sight. However, if I take the position of the devil's advocate—since someone will likely question this in the future—do we have the right to stop the Saudi government? We aren't the ethics police, and it was Bernardi, not Fakhouri, who is responsible for your kidnapping and the murders."

"From all indications, Fakhouri is our puppeteer, pulling the strings on everything that's occurred to you, me, the minister, and everyone else related to the Saudi government's initiative to execute their long-term plan of shifting their revenue sources from oil to rare earth elements, by any means necessary. The Saudi government is complicit, and their actions can't go unchallenged; otherwise, life as we know it will change, and it won't be for the better."

"The Saudis will play hardball. If you accuse them of any wrongdoing, they will expose your position in the government and manipulate the situation to turn global opinion against Italy, and especially you. Given their wealth and geopolitical influence, especially in manipulating oil prices, they are the stereotypical eight-hundred-pound gorilla. What can we do to prevent them from continuing to acquire the mining rights to areas containing rare earth elements, which will eventually lead to their domination of the economies of the world's largest countries?"

"We take away Fakhouri's bargaining position."

"The bargaining position of someone representing one of the wealthiest nations on the planet, which has likely accumulated enough rare earth oxides to monopolize global markets and plummet current pricing, potentially driving most of their competitors out of business?"

"Yes."

"How?" Acardi asked.

"By halting production and compromising his supply of oxides," Lamberti stated, explaining what she had in mind, and what the four investigators were about to tell Fakhouri.

Chapter Eighteen

The priest's knock on the wooden panel outside their hiding place startled Bruno and Maria, so engrossed in their conversation that they hadn't heard the approaching footsteps. Alarmed that something might be wrong, their fears vanished when the panel opened to reveal the smiling face of the priest.

"I've been informed that Sciarra had his meeting with God sooner than expected," he said.

"He was killed?"

"I only know that he died in a boat explosion."

Maria's mind immediately jumped to her cousin, wondering if he might also have been a casualty of the explosion. In a moment of panic, she texted his cellphone. To her relief, she received a response shortly thereafter, confirming that her cousin was fine and that the four investigators had safely made it to Rome with the woman Sciarra had been pursuing.

"That's great news," Bruno replied.

"It is for them, but it still means you need to leave Canicatti and this province. Sciarra's men will have gone back to their towns, waiting to see who the Commission will appoint as his successor. There will be a long list of those posturing to be awarded some or all of his territory," the priest said.

"Didn't Sciarra have an heir?"

"His wife and two sons were killed over twenty years ago in

a car bomb explosion that was meant for him. Afterward, it's said that he was prepared to marry a distant relative with whom he had an ongoing affair and a son, but that she reportedly died suddenly from an illness before they could hold the wedding."

"An illness like a heart attack or cancer?"

"More like a bullet to the head. At least that's the rumor. It appears that she was a closet alcoholic and had kept this a secret from him. When she was with her friends, she would share details about what her fiancé was doing. One day, a notice appeared in the obituary section of the newspaper stating that she had died of a brain aneurysm and was cremated the same day, obviously before anyone could examine her body. Several of her friends and her son left the area afterward, with no one knowing where they went. It's rumored that Sciarra intended to marry another distant relative, with whom he also had an affair, this one resulting in two sons. I guess he thought he had more time."

"I have no doubt the Commission will appoint someone else in his place to continue his illegal activities and the flow of money to them," Bruno said.

"Nothing will change," the priest acknowledged with a note of disappointment.

"This might be our only chance to leave the province without being noticed," Maria stated.

"Just because you're leaving the province doesn't mean you're out of danger," the priest warned. "I've heard that your photos have been circulated throughout Sicily. If anyone who received them recognizes you, you'll be taken prisoner to gain favor, and possibly a reward, from the Commission or whoever they decide to place in charge of this province. The only way you're going to stay alive is to leave Sicily."

"Any idea how we get out of Canicatti?" Bruno asked the priest.

"The best way is for you to take my car. It's parked behind the church," he replied, pulling the key from his pocket and handing it to Bruno along with his cellphone.

"Somehow, I'll get the car and cellphone back to you," Bruno assured him.

"They're not my priority. God be with you," the priest said as he turned to go back to the rectory.

"It seems like it's time we leave Sicily," Bruno said.

"We could take the ferry from Messina to Reggio Calabria," Maria suggested. "It would be risky because we'd need to travel across the island and then be on a ferry from which, if we're recognized, we have no way of escaping until it docks. However, the greatest danger we'd face would be after we land in Calabria, as it is home to the most powerful Mafia organization in the country and they routinely have men stationed at transportation hubs because it's a major source of income. They might have our photos."

"I believe there's a better way for us to leave Sicily. Now that Lamberti's back in Rome, I'll leave that problem to her," Bruno said.

Using the priest's cellphone, he called her private number, aware that her system only accepted calls from contacts in her database. As a result, he went straight to voicemail, where he left a message. Less than a minute later, she returned his call. Knowing she became impatient if someone didn't get to the heart of the matter quickly, he briefly explained their situation and the need to leave Sicily as quickly as possible to avoid capture by Sciarra's men who, despite his death, would still be looking for them.

"Do you have a car?"

"Yes."

"They'd probably expect you to drive to Catania. How far are you from Palermo?"

Bruno asked Maria, who replied it was less than a hundred miles, the drive taking about an hour and forty-five minutes. He repeated this to Lamberti.

"My plane is en route to Paris. After it drops off your partners, Hunkler, and Labriola, I'll send it to the private air terminal in Palermo. If you get there before it arrives, wait in your car and don't enter the terminal until you see it on the tarmac."

ALAN REFKIN

Bruno wanted to ask why his partners were going to Paris but decided to hold off on that question until he met Lamberti, knowing that now wasn't the time for an explanation just to satisfy his curiosity. "We'll be there," he said instead.

"We'll?"

"Maria Bianco and I. She arranged for her cousin to take you to Malta."

"I'll look forward to personally thanking this lady for her quick thinking. She saved my life. Villa will pick you both up at Ciampino Airport and take you to the estate," Lamberti said, ending the call without further comment.

"Lamberti is sending her plane to Palermo to pick us up," Bruno said with an apprehensive look on his face. "That means we need to drive across Agrigento province. How many miles is until we reach the province of Palermo?" He asked.

"Agrigento province ends just outside the village of Santo Stefano Quisquina, which is approximately fifty miles away. Once we reach it, we'll enter Palermo province. However, getting there will take about an hour and fifteen minutes."

"That seems disproportionately long, considering it's half the distance to Palermo airport, which is an hour and forty-five minutes away."

"There are no roads or highways leading north from this area. This means we need to retrace our steps on the same routes we took to get here. We'll be going through Castrofilippo, Agrigento, and Siculiana before heading up the coast to Ribera. From there, we'll turn northeast toward Santo Stefano Quisquina."

"This means that the last fifty miles and thirty minutes of our drive to the airport must be on a modern highway."

"That's right."

"You're the navigator," Bruno said, as they left the priest hole and went to their vehicle which, in retrospect, made Maria's Fiat look like a Rolls Royce. The Zastava Koral, sometimes referred to as a Yugo, was a subcompact hatchback that had been marketed from

1980 until 2008. Judging by the faded and peeling blue paint, Bruno guessed this was one of the earlier models. The car was unlocked and they got into the relic. Surprisingly, it started right up.

With Maria giving directions, they left Canicatti knowing they only had to travel about fifty miles to exit Agrigento province. Although the Yugo wasn't much on acceleration, going at a paraplegic-like speed of from zero to sixty mph in seventeen seconds when it came off the factory floor, Bruno found that it handled well on the twisting and undulating roads they were navigating. Everything was going smoothly as they passed the turnoff for Ribera, both feeling confident that they would remain unnoticed on their way to the airport. However, that expectation disintegrated when the Yugo began to shudder, jerked several times, and lost power, Bruno managing to pull off the road before the car rolled to a stop.

"I know a little about vehicles, but my mechanical knowledge of a Yugo is nonexistent," he told Maria, who was looking at the instrument panel.

"You won't need those skills because we're out of gas," she replied.

Bruno glanced at the gas gauge and saw that the indicator needle was pointing well past empty. "I forgot to check the gas before we left," he admitted. "Do you have any idea how far we are from the airport?"

"Ribera is twenty miles from Santo Stefano Quisquina, which is at the edge of Agrigento province—the halfway point to the airport. Therefore, about seventy miles."

"Have you been to Ribera before?"

"I've only driven by it on my way to Palermo, which is why I'm familiar with the distances."

"I'll see if there's a farm, residence, or gas station near this off-ramp where I can get a can of fuel to at least get us off this road. Until I return, it might be a good idea for you to hide in that cluster of rocks and bushes over there," Bruno said, pointing twenty yards off the road.

"That's a good place to hide," she agreed. "It'll be very difficult to see me from the road."

"Let me see if there's a gas can in the trunk," he said as he got out of the car, only to return a few seconds later empty-handed.

"There's no gas can," Maria remarked.

"And no spare tire either. I'll make do. Stay hidden because, no matter what, I'll come back for you. No matter what," he emphasized, giving her a reassuring smile before heading back toward the Ribera off-ramp.

Ribera, which is half the size of Canicatti, was an agricultural community often referred to by Sicilians as the "City of Oranges" due to its numerous groves of Washington navel oranges, a variety introduced by immigrants from the United States. As it turned out, the village wasn't remotely close to the state highway. After spending thirty minutes walking down the feeder road to the commune, Bruno believed he would be wasting his time going any further. Instead, he decided to call Doctor Albani, asking him either to bring gas or to drive them the rest of the way to Palermo. Although he'd thought about this earlier, he hesitated because he didn't want to involve the doctor any further, fearing that he might be caught and harmed if seen with them. However, with no other way to reach the Palermo airport, he had no choice.

Pulling his phone from his pocket, he was pleasantly surprised to see that there was reception in the area, with two bars appearing at the top of his screen. However, just as he was about to make the call, he realized that he didn't have Albani's number—Maria did. If he wanted the doctor's help, which seemed to be their only option, he needed to get the number from her. Phoning wasn't an option because nothing revealed the location of someone who was hiding more than the chime or vibration of a cellphone.

Turning around, he quickened his pace back toward the highway, hating the idea of leaving Maria to fend for herself.

However, when he got close enough to see his vehicle, he noticed four men, two of whom were on cellphones, loitering around the Yugo. Behind it were two pickup trucks. Deciding to get off the feeder road before he was seen, Bruno entered the orange grove to his right and worked his way toward the dense shrubbery where Maria was hiding, approaching from the rear. She heard his approach and looked over her shoulder.

"We won't be needing gas after all," Bruno whispered. "I was about to call Doctor Albani to see if he could bring us gas or pick us up, but I didn't have his number," he confessed, holding up his phone for emphasis. "Now, even though he'd want to drive us to the Palermo airport, I'm thinking it's better if he stays away as I suspect the men on the highway will stop and search every car traveling into or out of the area, being especially suspicious of those passing through at night."

"They seem to be hunting for us with the same fervor as Sciarra, and his death doesn't seem to have stopped the search," Maria said, keeping her voice low as she saw several more vehicles arrive.

"We can effectively hide here until daylight. After that, this area will be teeming with people, and they'll find us."

"How can we escape?"

"Lamberti is our only option."

"But her plane will be in Palermo. How does that help us?"

"She has other resources—lots of other resources. Do you know why some of those she associates with, in addition to her enemies, nicknamed her 'the witch'?"

"No."

"You're about to find out." He made the call and explained their situation.

"I'll handle it," she said, ending the call with that three word response.

It was 7:30 pm, two minutes past sunset, and the surrounding area was rapidly shifting from semi-darkness to pitch black.

The only sources of light came from the thug's vehicles, and the numerous others who'd joined the search after hearing that Bruno was in the area. Everyone knew he was the driver of the Yugo because he'd left his inoperative phone, which had his business card taped to the back, in the cigarette tray.

The reason Bruno's rumored presence attracted a crowd was that local Mafiosos had learned he, and possibly the woman accompanying him, whose pictures had been distributed throughout the province with a ten-thousand-dollar bounty on each, were believed to be in or around Ribera. Moreover, Arturo Salucci, the new provincial leader appointed by the Commission to maintain order and ensure a steady cash flow into their coffers, kept the ten-thousand-dollar bounty. However, no one knew the reason for this was that he wanted to know what information they possessed that justified such a significant reward. He also wanted to demonstrate to the rank-and-file Mafioso that nothing had changed from his predecessor—the consequences to anyone who challenged the authority of that position remaining unchanged.

Eventually, the line of cars extended a quarter mile on each side of the Yugo, their headlights illuminating the area so heavily that neither Maria nor Bruno could move from their hiding place without being seen. Given this, their only hope of survival was to bury themselves deep in the shrubbery, hoping that the thugs—many of whom were staggering around with bottles of alcohol or beer in their hands—would soon become too drunk or oblivious to notice them. However, the law of unintended consequences took effect as the alcohol consumption increased, and their situation became more significantly perilous when one of the drunkards started a rumor that Salucci would pay the bounty whether Bruno was dead or alive. Without any oversight among the group, this rumor quickly took on a life of its own, and soon the drunkards began shooting at anything that moved, with some bullets coming within inches of Maria and Bruno.

As the indiscriminate shooting continued, the drunken thugs

heard the sound of approaching helicopters. Although no one could see them, they could hear the direction from which they were approaching and began firing their weapons indiscriminately at them believing, again by rumor which spread throughout the area, that they were sent to rescue Bruno. Too intoxicated to consider who might be sending these aircraft or the potential consequences of initiating an armed conflict with them, they continued their barrage of bullets unabated.

The four helicopters approaching the area had been dispatched from the Naval Air Station (NAS) Sigonella, a joint Italian Air Force Base and U.S. Naval installation in Lentini, Sicily, ninety-four miles east of Ribera. The three lead aircraft were A129 Mangusta attack helicopters, followed by an Italian Navy EH101 medium-lift transport.

Each aircraft was equipped with advanced night vision and infrared capabilities. Using the coordinates provided by Lamberti, they identified the huddled pair hiding in a large bush. The aircraft then established a protective electronic ring around them to ensure that the three-barreled 20mm cannons positioned in the nose of each aircraft—capable of firing six thousand rounds per minute—would not inadvertently target them if the aircraft had to open fire.

"There's a lot of people below, and they all seem to be shooting at us," the gunner of one attack helicopter told the mission commander, who also heard the multiple rounds ricocheting off the Mangusta's armored fuselage.

"With the caliber of bullets they're firing, they might as well be throwing spit wads at this beast. I'm more concerned about the safety of Mauro Bruno and Maria Bianco," the pilot replied into his headset mic, recalling their names from the mission brief. "The infrared images on my screen show there are three tangos standing five feet behind them and another five a dozen feet to their right. If any shoot into the bush where they're hiding, it'll be all over," the commander remarked.

Realizing they needed to act immediately or they'd be returning with corpses, the commander alerted the other aircraft to Bruno and Maria's location, although they too had detected them, the Mangusta pilots also placing a protective electronic ring around them.

"Keep casualties to a minimum and fire in front of this group, sweeping them back toward the highway," the mission commander ordered. "We'll keep them contained while the transport lands and brings Bruno and Bianco onboard. If anyone points a weapon toward the them, or fires in their direction, take them out," he mandated, providing his group with their rules of engagement.

Once the team received their orders, the three attack helicopters opened fire. The shock and awe of them collectively spitting out almost eighteen thousand rounds a minute into the ground surrounding Bruno and Bianco was beyond what the Mafiosos could comprehend, most of whom believed an AR-15 was the ultimate game changer in an armed conflict. Subsequently, the pilots didn't have to worry about getting them to run toward the highway because they were already scrambling in that direction.

As the drunken group rushed toward their vehicles, the EH101 aircraft quickly landed. Two crew members emerged from the craft, ran to where Bruno and Maria were hiding, and escorted them to the aircraft while the Mangusta attack helicopters hovered nearby. After they boarded, the transport lifted off and, flanked by its escorts, landed at Sigonella thirty-five minutes later.

On the way back, the pilot asked Bruno to come to the cockpit and informed him that a Gulfstream was waiting to take them to Rome. "I don't know who you both are or why those people were trying to kill you, but you must be very important for the president to bypass the Minister of Defence and the chain of command below him to personally order our squadron commander to rescue you at all costs."

"Thank you for saving our lives. I don't think we would have lasted another minute if you hadn't opened fire on that group,"

Bruno responded without explaining why the president was concerned with their safety, although he had no doubt it was because he received a call from Lamberti.

"What were you doing in Ribera? That village is the very definition of being in the middle of nowhere," the pilot remarked.

"That's something that will have to remain a mystery," he replied with a smile, which the pilot acknowledged with a nod.

"You seem unfazed for someone in the predicament you were in. I assume that being in that type of situation isn't unusual."

"Surprisingly, it isn't," Bruno said, prompting a laugh from the pilot. "Which makes me think it would be a good idea for you to share your phone number with me. That way, the next time I need your help, we can bypass those in the middle."

"Judging from Ribera and what you just mentioned, I expect I'll be hearing from you in the near future," the pilot said with a grin as he took a pen and a piece of paper from his flight suit to write down his cell phone number.

It wasn't long after Acardi left Donais's apartment that Bence received a call from Lamberti, and as the director confidently predicted, he didn't like what he was told.

"You need me to find the mole in my government who's feeding information to the person you call the puppeteer?" Bence asked, wanting to ensure he didn't misunderstand what Lamberti was asking.

"I can't move forward with my plan to neutralize the situation until they're out of the equation. If they inform the Saudis about my actions, it will negatively impact the outcome, and the game will be over. Also, the Italian government does not have the authority to arrest or question anyone on French soil. You do."

"Only in the broadest and most liberal interpretation of my authority. Although the government has never rescinded my appointment as a border security officer with the French National Police, I'm now the head of the Mission for Research and Restitution of Spoliated Cultural Property, a nonsensical title that essentially means I'm tasked with searching for artwork looted during World War II. Law enforcement outside of that confine isn't part of my job description."

"But you're still a police officer. You have your badge and, I assume, access to a police vehicle if necessary," Lamberti persisted.

"I've retained my badge and technically have access to a vehicle. However, that's not the main issue. The government has 5.3 million civil service employees, thirty-five percent of whom work for various ministries. I'm not sure where to start in narrowing down my search."

"You'd begin by identifying someone who's in a position to know what the late Minister of Foreign Affairs was investigating, his schedule, the procedures of his security detail, and my involvement. Their position would also allow them access to government data on where the highest concentrations of specific rare earth elements in the country are located. Check off the boxes. There can't be many in your government who have that confluence of information," Lamberti stated.

Bence was impressed with Lamberti's analysis. "Given what you said, and putting myself in the position of your puppeteer, I'd recruit my mole from the Ministry of the Interior."

"That's interesting. Can you explain why?"

"Because they oversee the national police and have responsibility for providing security for government officials, which includes arranging safe transport for visiting government officials. Therefore, they would have been informed about Acardi's upcoming visit to France to meet with the late minister, and given his arrival and departure schedules.

They'd also know where he was staying in Paris because he, like all foreign visitors, would need to present their passport to the hotel. This information is then entered into the ministry's computer system. Additionally, the Ministry of the Interior serves as the link between local and national governments when it comes to natural resources, maintaining records of the types and concentrations of minerals, metals, and other earth deposits found within France. As you asked, they check off the necessary boxes."

"Who in the ministry, excluding the minister, would have this information?" Lamberti asked.

"Let me pull up the org chart," Bence responded, afterward accessing his government account and viewing the organization chart for the Ministry of the Interior. "If we exclude the minister and his deputy, and departments such as training, human resources, and asylum and immigration—none of which would provide the mole with the necessary access—we can narrow down which department they might be a part of, assuming they even work in this ministry."

"Let's go with that assumption. Where would you hide them?" Lamberti asked.

"They would be the most inconspicuous in the Department of Information Technology, the Department of Administrative and Financial Affairs, or the Department of Legal Consultancy. These are common functions within all agencies, including mine. All would have the ability to access files within the Ministry of Foreign Affairs, revealing what he was investigating and denoting your involvement. This access would also give someone the opportunity to look at the minister's schedule and provide details about Acardi's visit. The procedures for protecting the minister could be obtained from the national police database, as it's part of the Ministry of the Interior and tasked with the protection of government officials.

"What about access to mining deposits?"

"Mining oversight and governance is a core focus of this ministry. Its legal function, just as with my legal section, has access to mining contracts, amendments to agreements, reports on the discovery of new deposits, and so forth. Essentially, everything related to mines or potential mining opportunities within France will be stored in their database."

"If you were the puppeteer, in which of these three ministry functions would you place an informant?"

"I've already discussed legal," Bence answered. "The Administrative and Financials' audit function would also have access to ministry files. They conduct unannounced audits of the various ministry functions as well as the office of the minister to ensure funds have been properly disbursed, which is government parlance for determining if someone is embezzling money. This gives them access to the minister's database and his schedule.

However, both the Department of Administrative and Financial Affairs and the Department of Legal Consultancy have the same inherent issue: their access generates a digital record that only someone of Montanari's expertise can effectively erase," Bence said, having interacted with the Savant in the past. "That leaves the Department of Information Technology as the informant's most likely workplace. Within that environment, they could easily access every file within the Ministry of the Interior and Ministry of Foreign Affairs, including the ministers' calendars, and erase any record of their activity."

"Does everyone in the IT department have that authority?" Lamberti asked.

"Not if their IT hierarchical access mirrors that within my agency, which may or may not be true. However, if we assume the government has standardized the setup of their IT functions, which seems reasonable, only the Chief Information Officer (CIO) and the Information Systems Manager (ISM) have the authority to erase a digital record, with the CIO being the more senior of the two."

"And of those two, which is more likely to remain undiscovered?"

"There's no way to know for sure."

Lamberti paused to think. "I might have a solution," she said.

"Which is?" Bence asked.

"I'll going to text the CIO and ISM a message from Fakhouri saying that he wants to meet with them immediately at his chateau in Louveciennes, and that they're to only respond to this number as his other phone has been compromised. Since Donati and his team are already on their way to the town, they'll let us know which one of them shows up."

"Don't you think that text might seem suspicious? It would to me."

"I'm hoping the mention of Louveciennes will be all the credibility that we'll need, and they'll go there after receiving it. If not, you'll need to return to Paris and kidnap both individuals, keeping them incommunicado while my plan is being executed."

"That means one of the people that I'm kidnapping, and possibly both, may be innocent. If either goes to the police, I'll end up in jail since I have no intention of harming them. Given that police officers don't fare well in prison, I prefer living with the consequences of the text," Bence stated.

"We'll see where that gets us."

Bence was surprised at Lamberti's lack of emotion or empathy. "Out of curiosity, is this way of thinking the reason for your nickname?" He asked, intentionally avoiding mentioning what it was.

"You mean, the witch? I was given that stigma for many of the idiosyncrasies and tendencies ingrained in my personality, some of which you might not want to uncover. Trust me on that."

Bence remained silent, but based on what he already knew about Lamberti, he agreed with her last statement.

"I'll call Donati and tell him that you'll intercept the appropriate party on their way to the chateau. Under no circumstances must they reach it," Lamberti emphasized.

"I'll intercept them before they get in sight of the chateau," Bence confirmed. "What's our next step once they're detained?"

"That depends on what I learn from the NSA," Lamberti replied.

"The NSA?"

Six hours after Parra received a list of over three hundred government officials worldwide who were involved with Saudi mine leases, the NSA created its algorithm, retrieved their cellphone numbers from its vast database, and coordinated its air and satellite assets to intercept their communications, even in areas that had previously been of no strategic importance and where coverage had been nonexistent.

When Montanari received the phone numbers, he sent a text message to each device stating that the person was receiving a $50,000 bonus, and provided a link to access the money. Seventy percent of the recipients suspected the link was fraudulent and thought it was a clever tactic to install a virus on their phones, believing the message came from someone other than Calvario. As a result, they forwarded the text to their computers and ran it through their antivirus programs—most of which were standard, off-the-shelf versions, none being able to detect the sophisticated keylogger trojan virus. The fifteen percent of recipients who didn't use antivirus software, aligning with the global average for laptop and desktop users, believed that since the message was on their cellphone and not their computer, their data wouldn't be at risk. Enticed by the promise of money, they clicked on the link after reading the message.

Once the link was accessed, each official logged into their offshore bank account and transferred the money, afterward receiving confirmation from the financial institution as to the receipt of funds. Almost to the person, they rechecked their account a short time later, wanting to dwell on their good fortune. This time, they were startled to see their account balance was zero. Montanari's virus had emptied their accounts by exploiting their login information and passwords, directing the institution to wire all the funds to an offshore account accessible only to him and Lamberti. Afterward, the Savant transferred these funds to Italy's treasury.

As soon as the government officials realized they had been deceived and found themselves poor once again, they directed their anger at Calvario. They attempted to contact the numbers that

Bernardi, or the alias he had used, had provided them. However, since Bernardi was dead, those calls went unanswered. This only served to further infuriate the dishonest officials. Unable to lodge a complaint with their government or the police, and unable to sue Calvario, Bernardi, or anyone else involved, they resorted to the only option available to them: seeking revenge.

They began searching for any pretext—no matter how flimsy or illegal—to revoke the mine leases, the permits for the processing plants, and the shipments of the oxides. Within the next six hours, all of Saudi Arabia's rare earth element mining and processing operations were brought to a halt.

The Saudis problems weren't over. Before the dishonest government officials were in full panic mode, President Orsini and Lamberti had spoken with President Ballinger and Vice-President Houck, the latter becoming increasingly involved with the country's sanctioned and off-the-books clandestine activities. In line with their agreement, President Ballinger approved the deployment of a special operations team tasked with destroying the massive, rare earth storage facility in Jeddah.

Because the attack would take place in a country that was technically an ally—and that currently hosted five U.S. military bases—the president mandated that the facility's destruction must appear to be an accident. This meant that the special operations team assigned to this mission had to carry it out without being detected.

To keep the incursion confidential within the United States government, where leaks were as frequent as finding sand on a beach—particularly regarding Congress—the president summoned his Secretary of Defense, Jim Rosen, to the White House. Ballinger then briefed him on the situation, emphasizing the need to limit knowledge of the off-the-books operation to a minimal number of individuals.

"I'll keep a tight lid on the operation. Except for those directly involved, no one else will know about this mission," Rosen promised.

"Won't that be difficult for those in the team's chain of command? They'll ask where you're sending them and what they're doing?"

"No, they won't, because it's not uncommon for those outside the team to not be read-in on the operation. Access to a mission brief is on a need-to-know basis, regardless of rank or position. Since the team's orders originated from my office, the assumption will be I, the CIA, or someone else above their pay grade requested a team for a highly classified operation. End of story. That's life in the special ops community. When do you need this to happen?" Rosen asked.

"Yesterday. Once the Saudis find out that we're on to them and responsible for the mini-insurrection of government officials— which will inevitably happen—they'll remove their inventory from Jeddah and disperse it globally, possibly to their embassies, which is what I'd do to protect it. This can't be allowed."

"Can you help me understand why destroying their inventory is so crucial?" Rosen asked. "The Saudis should be out of the rare earth business because, as you explained, numerous government officials will believe they've been cheated and have turned against them."

"The money from the sale of these oxides in the open market is estimated to be tens of billions of dollars, even after the anticipated steep decline in prices. This will force many producers, particularly those who are heavily leveraged or lack the financial resources to endure a prolonged downturn, out of business. Afterward, the Saudis will buy their mining and processing companies for pennies on the dollar, further consolidating their grip on the market.

Destroying their inventory prevents them from eliminating many of their competitors. The mini-insurrection will eventually end, the Saudis' blaming whoever they must for what happened and buying their way back into the good graces of officials, no matter the cost," the president stated.

"What does deploying the special ops team and destroying the storage facility achieve if they're back in business?" Rosen asked.

"It prevents them from significantly lowering market prices to harm their competitors. It also allows us time to implement a plan to ensure they won't dominate rare earth elements in the same way they've controlled oil."

Rosen said that he now understood the dynamics of the situation. "Returning to our discussion of the special ops team, we have a logistical challenge. In a standard deployment, a team would fly from the United States in the rear of a C-17 aircraft and parachute into the target area, with the flight to Jeddah taking approximately thirteen hours. However, since the operation needs to take place at night for obvious reasons, if the aircraft were to depart the U.S. right now, nighttime wouldn't occur in Jeddah for another eight hours. Therefore, at the earliest, the accidental destruction of the facility couldn't occur for over twenty-one hours from this moment."

"That's way too long. Given what else is happening, the Saudis could move the oxides before we get there. There must be a faster way," Vice President Houck interjected.

"The only way I know is to pull a team that's in the vicinity from their current assignment. However, the extraction won't be instantaneous and comes with its own set of problems, as most teams are embedded in areas which are decidedly unfriendly and getting them to safely exfiltrate from their present location may be dangerous. That said, there is a team that's just completed a mission in the Wakhan Corridor, but they're on the far side of ragged."

"Ragged meaning they've completed an especially tough mission and their gas tanks are empty?" The president asked.

"Meaning getting into position was grueling and the situation that they faced was not what anyone anticipated and they should be dead, but aren't. taking everything into account, and when you're in a firefight of that magnitude, it takes time to de-stress."

"Was anyone injured in the firefight?" Vice President Houck asked.

"None of the team, but the terrorists won't be collecting a pension," Rosen answered.

"Ragged or not, they're what I need for this mission," the president said.

Rosen said he'd issue their orders. "Because time is short, mission planning will be a problem. Given the flying time between their current location and Jeddah, they'll have approximately four and a half hours to devise a plan to make the destruction of the warehouse appear to be accidental. Also, since we lack a schematic of the storage facility's interior and cannot deploy one of our stealth drones overhead to watch over the team, this further complicates the situation."

"And we need a stealth drone because the Saudis are technologically sophisticated enough to detect one which isn't?" The vice president asked.

"The electronic equipment they've acquired from us and the Russians enables them to detect and destroy non-stealthy UAVs," Rosen explained. "If that happens, the markings and equipment found in the wreckage will clearly identify the aircraft as belonging to the United States. The Saudis will realize that we've violated their sovereign airspace and are engaging in espionage, which undermines our efforts to make the destruction of the warehouse appear like an accident."

"And we have no stealth drones which can be reassigned? The vice president asked.

"None that can be re-tasked in time."

"Which means the team is left to their own devices to achieve the mission objective, with failure not being an option. What do you think about our chances for success?" Ballinger asked Rosen.

"I expect the team to arrive at the target without being detected.

Tactical surprise is a fundamental part of their training, as is the ability to navigate unexpected situations despite any mission-related fears. In my opinion, the warehouse will likely be destroyed, but the survival of the team is a toss-up given we don't want our fingerprints on the operation."

"Get them moving," the president ordered.

Chapter Nineteen

Fakhouri began his day on a positive note, receiving news that Bernardi and everyone at his company were killed in an explosion, which also destroyed the company's files and data. However, the satisfaction and confidence he felt in tying up loose ends quickly faded when he learned that the government officials who'd been bribed to protect his interests were shutting down his mines and processing plants around the world.

Convinced there must be a commonality to what caused their sudden change in attitude, and needing to find it quickly so he could resolve the situation, he contacted the Saudi ambassadors in countries where Bernardi had signed contracts on behalf of an offshore entity. His request was straightforward: determine why the government officials, whose names he would provide along with the contracts they signed, had revoked or altered their agreements with the corporations named in those contracts. Afterward, the ambassadors were instructed to call him with what they'd discovered and ensure the destruction of what he'd sent them, along with all notes, calendar entries, or other documentation relating to the non-existent meetings with these government officials.

The ambassadors, having no knowledge of the offshore companies referenced in the contracts or the individual signing on behalf of those corporations, would typically seek clarification before committing to the requested actions, wanting to avoid becoming embroiled in a complicated diplomatic situation with their host country. However, as all were hesitant to challenge the respected minister, they agreed to assist without raising any objections.

The information Fakhouri received was consistent, indicating that every government official now suspected the Saudi Arabian government actually owned these offshore corporations and had sent the individual with whom they negotiated the contracts. Therefore, they felt deceived at not being told of the Saudi's involvement and believed his government was behind the bonus payment, viewing it as a clever tactic to obtain their financial institution login credentials and drain their accounts of all the money they had given each official. Consequently, they blamed the Saudi government for this treachery.

Fakhouri realized that Bernardi could not have carried out these actions, as he was already dead when they occurred. Instead, he suspected that a sophisticated nation-state was behind this scheme, not only because of the large sum of capital involved in the up-front bonus money but also because they'd somehow obtained the list of government officials and their offshore bank account numbers—information that he believed only he and Bernardi had access to.

He wasn't sure how this situation had come about, although it didn't matter because he had to quickly rebuild trust with these officials; otherwise, his project would fail. The only strategy he could think of restoring for that trust was to offer them significantly more money than they had lost, planning to make the payment in cash rather than through a wire transfer.

However, a major obstacle to implementing this plan was the loss of his intermediary with Bernardi's death. Although, even if he were alive, the government officials would never trust him again. Given the current circumstances, he needed a replacement who could re-establish the trust necessary for the continuity of his operations. Due to the sensitivity of his undertaking, he felt uneasy bringing in someone new to oversee this critical aspect of his plan. However, this impasse seemed to vanish when he thought of his French informant, who'd provided him with critical information and, at least so far, had proven to be trustworthy and dependable. Subsequently, at least for the time being, he could serve as Bernardi's replacement and become the new face of his offshore empire.

Onfroi Lapierre had been a civil servant for twenty years and served as the Chief Information Officer for the Ministry of the Interior. After graduating from college with an advanced degree in computer science, he envisioned a career at a technology company that would eventually become a publicly traded entity with an exorbitant valuation, leading to him becoming a very wealthy person. However, it soon became clear to those in the tech industry who recognized talent that he was a mediocre programmer, whose skills were better suited to being a technocrat or customer support representative than writing code. Therefore, after having been shown the door at several tech companies, he decided to apply for a position with the French government.

The short-sightedness of government hiring played to his advantage, as they only considered his degrees when bringing him on board. However, as his job performance was far from impressive, Lapierre's rise through the ranks to become the CIO took eighteen years, promoted to that position based solely on his seniority, the criteria for advancement within his department based on the assumption that the person with the longest tenure was the most knowledgeable and capable.

His involvement with Fakhouri stemmed from a chance encounter. The Saudi minister had bought a large property just outside of Paris, but he was struggling with an inconsistent internet signal on the estate. He wanted to enhance the signal so that he could have a strong connection not only within his chateau but also throughout the expansive grounds of the estate. He briefly considered flying someone from Saudi to perform the work, but ultimately decided against it because, in addition to wanting to improve his internet signal, he also sought to enhance the quality of his voice communications, which often broke up during conversations. Therefore, he felt that a local technician who was familiar with the data and voice services in and around Paris would be better suited for these tasks.

Since his residence underwent daily electronic checks for devices, and technology experts in Riyadh, with the same regularity, used advanced programs to remotely scan his system for malware, he felt secure that software or a hardware device couldn't be covertly placed within his system. As a result, hiring a local technician didn't seem risky to him. Unsure where to find such a person, he asked a minister within the French government and was given Lapierre's name.

Before his promotion to CIO, Lapierre struggled to make ends meet on his government salary. To supplement his income, he installed and maintained personal media and internet devices for government officials and their friends. The scope of work required by Fakhouri was extensive and took several months to complete, Lapierre working on the project after work and on weekends. The minister was pleased with the results, as he now had a uniform internet signal and uninterrupted cellular voice and data throughout the estate.

Converting Lapierre into an informant took time, and first occurred to Fakhouri once the future CIO began working on his system and started discussing the government officials with whom he had performed a similar service. Recognizing that his country had a chance to gather valuable intelligence from this individual, Fakhouri slowly began the civil servant's transition into an informant. He started by requesting trivial information from his ministry—data that he could have easily found through a Google search—but for which he deliberately overpaid the civil servant. Over time, his inquiries shifted from publicly available information to classified state secrets. This change also meant that the monetary compensation to Lapierre increased significantly, with the public servant receiving quarterly tax-free payments that were several times higher than his government salary.

Since the two couldn't meet frequently at Fakhouri's chateau without raising suspicions, as Lapierre couldn't use the excuse of enhancing the chateau's telecommunications and internet systems forever, they decided to communicate through burner phones and exchange written communications and classified documents using drop locations. Subsequently, when Lapierre received a text from Fakhouri to meet at his chateau, he didn't think much of it or the new number that appeared on his phone, assuming the Saudi had simply acquired a new burner phone, as he had often done in the past. Subsequently, fifteen minutes after receiving the text, Lapierre got into his vehicle and headed to Louveciennes.

The team which drew the short straw for the Jeddah mission was Squadron Three, sometimes referred to as the Gold Squadron, which was part of Seal Team Six—officially known as the United States Naval Special Warfare Development Group, or DEVGRU. Each squadron within DEVGRU had a color that identified its operational function: Squadrons One through Four being the assault squadrons, with Red, Blue, Gold, and Silver as their designators. Squadron Five was the intelligence or Black Squadron. Operational support focused on maritime operations was the purview of Squadron Six, or the Gray Squadron, with Squadron Seven, or the Green Squadron, responsible for training.

Master Chief Petty Officer Peter Hasen was a team leader in the Gold Squadron, which had just come out on the winning side of a firefight that followed two days of reconnaissance from a jagged crevice in the earth at the base of the Pamir mountains outside Dasht-e Mula—a tiny village in the Wakhan Corridor, which was a narrow strip of land that stretched between Afghanistan and China, also touching the borders of Tajikistan and Pakistan. Hasen stood five feet eleven inches tall with short black hair and a scraggly beard. The thirty-one year old, who'd enlisted thirteen years ago in his hometown of Bozeman, Montana, had broad shoulders, a narrow waist, and piercing brown eyes.

The reason that he and his team had traveled fourteen and a half hours from their home base in Virginia Beach, Virginia, before stepping off a C-17 and parachuting into the rugged mountains behind them, was that U.S. intelligence had intercepted a transmission from a terrorist group that was planning to bring a kidnapped Pakistani nuclear physicist to Dasht-e Mula, where he would be handed over to Iranian officials for a pile of weapons and cash. Since the exact time of the exchange was unknown, it was decided to position the team within a jagged tear in the earth until the bad guys showed up with the scientist, which didn't happen for forty-eight hours after they'd wedged themselves into the earth under the cover of darkness.

The CIA pitched the operation to the Pentagon as a simple snatch-and-grab, claiming their analysts determined there would only be a few terrorists accompanying the scientist because they would want to avoid surrounding him with a large protective group that would draw the attention of surveillances drones. They further justified this belief by stating that, since they were exchanging the scientist with the Iranians, there was no need for a large security detail because they were meeting with their allies. The Agency went on to tell the Pentagon officials at the briefing that once the exchange was made and the weapon-laden trucks left the area, it would deploy a drone to target them with Hellfire missiles.

Most of the military's hierarchy distrusted the Central Intelligence Agency, often viewing its name as an oxymoron because the information it provided was frequently inaccurate and seemed to serve an agenda known only to the Agency. Therefore, when they claimed the mission was a simple snatch-and-grab operation that didn't require the extensive planning typical of most covert operations on foreign soil, Pentagon officials expressed skepticism. However, lacking concrete evidence to disprove the Agency's assertions, and given that the scientist was allegedly heading to Iran, they approved the operation.

In retrospect, the only thing that the Agency was correct about was that the terrorists wanted to avoid their surveillance capabilities. However, what they didn't foresee was the route they'd take to get the scientist to the meeting site, having assumed they would use trucks on dirt roads that were carved into the mountain. Instead, using ancient animal paths known only to locals, they approached the site from an entirely different direction with a team of more than two dozen pack mules to transport the arms and suitcases of cash they were to receive, accompanied by a corresponding number of terrorists to guide them.

Therefore, as Hasen and his team scanned the area through their night vision scopes, they saw the Pakistani scientist dismounting one of these mules, after which he was brought into a nearby rectangular clay and brick hut. Doing a quick count, the squadron commander saw there were thirty heavily armed men instead of the *few* terrorists the Agency had predicted. This meant they were outnumbered by more than four to one.

"Let's get moving," Hasen said into his headset mic.

The team stealthily left the crevice and made their way toward the small compound, one member splitting off toward the two trucks driven to the site by the Iranians while the rest took up positions near the hut in which the scientist was taken.

As the diverting member approached the trucks, he observed the Iranians unloading a box of weapons for inspection by the terrorists who, holding flashlights and lanterns in the unlit area, removed several arms from the box to verify they were functional. With everyone at the rear of the vehicles absorbed with the verification of the weapons, and hidden by the darkness, the SEAL planted an explosive device under the center of each vehicle, flipping the activation switch on each before he left.

"We're good to go," he said into his mic before leaving to join the rest of the team. Once there, Hasen told him to detonate the devices.

Although the initial blasts were loud, the secondary explosions were enormous, with four-foot-deep craters replacing the trucks and shaking the ground so violently that the team had trouble staying on their feet. Around them, several of the older clay and brick huts had collapsed.

"Those explosions didn't come from rifle rounds or gas in the vehicles," the member who set the charges remarked.

"I'm guessing there were IEDs in those vehicles," Hasen said, referring to improvised explosive devices, which were essentially homemade bombs. "From the size of the explosions, they were probably 155mm artillery shells. With each weighing around a hundred pounds, it wouldn't take many to replicate those explosions."

Following the detonations, the mules scattered while the terrorists unslung their rifles and spread out in search of the perpetrators. However, because the SEALs had night vision goggles, scopes, and silencers on their weapons, they rapidly began dwindling the number of terrorists.

To those within the clay and brick building, the explosions indicated that an attempt was underway to rescue the scientist, and they needed to leave as quickly as possible. One of the Iranian militants gripped the scientist tightly by the arm and dragged him toward the exit, only to be stopped by the terrorist in charge who wasn't going to let him leave until he received the promised payment. The Iranian, who didn't know that he was the only surviving member of the escort team, didn't hold that distinction for long as the terrorist, believing the explosion destroyed his weapons and cash, and needing the scientist to negotiate another deal, bullet in the Iranian militant's head to settle the matter.

The confrontation lasted thirty minutes, with the SEALs eventually whittling away the number of terrorists to one, the last being the person in charge who was holding the scientist with his left hand while spraying a volley of bullets in every direction with the automatic weapon he held in the other. He took a bullet to the head.

Once the engagement ended and they'd captured the scientist, Hasen called for the extraction helicopter, which had been on standby in a barren area of the Wakhan Corridor. It took ten minutes for the aircraft to get airborne and fly to Dasht-e Mula, and thirty seconds for everyone to board. An hour later, it landed in Gilgit, a city of approximately a quarter of a million people, well-known among those aspiring to scale K2, the second-highest peak in the world.

The team was gathering their gear from the helicopter and looking forward to the two days of R&R that DEVGRU had arranged when two athletic-looking men stepped onto the aircraft, showed their creds, and asked for the team leader. Hasen, seeing their CIA IDs, handed over the scientist as they requested. He then followed the men off the aircraft along with the rest of his team.

As he watched the scientist being escorted to an unmarked private jet, Hasen felt a sinking feeling in the pit of his stomach when he saw the C-17 parked beside it. At that moment, he knew the team's plans for enjoying a cold beer and taking a hot shower were about to vanish. His suspicions were confirmed when he saw the C-17's loadmaster striding toward them.

"Where are we going?" Hasen asked before the Air Force master sergeant could tell them there'd been a change in orders.

"The pilot said he'd provide you with the details once you're onboard," he said, his gloomy expression suggesting that their destination wouldn't be any better than Dasht-e Mula. "Before arriving here, we made a stop at Al Udeid Air Base in Qatar," the loadmaster added, not needing to tell Hasen that it was the largest U.S. air base in the Middle East and its supply depot was a special ops superstore. "DEVGRU sent the base a list of what you'll need for this mission, and I ensured every item was loaded onto the aircraft," he continued as they walked up the boarding ramp.

"I hope there's a lot of ammunition," one of the team members said, aware that they had nearly depleted their supply.

"You'll see when you get onboard," the loadmaster again deflected as he turned to lead them to the aircraft.

As they entered the Globemaster III, Hasen saw the Rigid Hull Inflatable Boat (RHIB), which had a speed in excess of forty mph and a range of over two hundred miles, secured to a pallet with a DragonFly GPS-guided parachute delivery system, which would ensure it landed within one hundred fifty yards of the designated drop zone. Beside it was a row of rebreathing diving tanks, commonly referred to as rebreathers.

"I take it the pilot will let us know where he's going to shove us off the plane," Hasen said, drawing a nod from the loadmaster.

"Where are the RHIB's machine guns and ammunition?" Hasen asked, referring to the M2 and M60 weapons that were standard on the craft. "This is the civilian version."

"I asked myself the same question before confirming that this was the configuration DEVGRU designated for your mission," he remarked, shaking his head. "However, it fits with the clothing I was instructed to bring onboard for you to change into," the loadmaster said, pointing to the items he'd placed on some of the webbed seats along the fuselage.

"Should I ask if you brought weapons and ammunition?"

"That's not going to improve your day. You need to read your orders."

"You've been around for a while, and my guess is that you know what we're getting into. What do you think about this mission?" Hasen asked as they continued toward the cockpit.

"I believe your team must be the best in DEVGRU."

"Why?"

"Because if you weren't, they'd call this a suicide mission," the loadmaster replied without a smile as they entered the cockpit and he turned and left.

"I hear you have some good news for us," Hasen said to the

pilot who, along with the copilot, saw the Master Chief's rugged condition, indicating that his team had come straight from the field.

The pilot remained silent as he handed over the communication he'd received, which was marked Top Secret/SCI—indicating that it contained sensitive compartmented information. There were two sets of orders in the communication, one pertaining to his team and the other to the crew of the C-17. Additionally, the pilot handed him pertinent satellite imagery for the mission, which shared the same classification, along with a list of supplies the loadmaster had brought on board. Hasen looked at what he'd been handed.

"As you can see, I've been instructed to destroy all documentation before your team leaves the aircraft," the pilot explained.

"How are you going to do that?" Hasen asked.

"My loadmaster has a battery-operated shredder that he picked up at the Al Udeid Air Base. After he shreds the documents, he'll put the pieces into a burn bag and hand it over to the security officer when we return," the pilot replied.

"You've read that my orders require me to plan this operation while we're en route to the target area," Hasen said with a condescending voice. "Can you tell me how long we have until we parachute from this plane?"

The pilot told him.

"Also, if I understand your orders correctly, you're not filing a flight plan to Jeddah or anywhere near it because, reading between the lines, the brass doesn't want anyone to associate what's about to happen with this aircraft having been overhead. Instead, you're filing a flight plan to a Saudi air base near Riyadh that the U.S. Air Force uses. Along the way, you'll develop a serious problem with the aircraft that requires you to divert to the Jeddah Airport, which is how you're going to get us close to our target area."

"That's the plan, and I'll do my best to get you and your team as close as possible to that warehouse without tipping our hand," the pilot confirmed."

"Have to thought about the maintenance problem that requires you to make an emergency landing in Jeddah? It's going to need to be plausible."

"Just like you, I'll have a good four hours to come up with something," the pilot replied.

Both Hasen and the pilot shook their heads, aware that those orchestrating the mission wanted as few of their fingerprints on it as possible, which meant that the crew and team would be blamed if anything went wrong, but that they'd take credit if the mission succeeded.

"You understand that, as part of that narrative, you're going into this unarmed because the bureaucrats want to make sure that you and your team are not seen as part of a military operation. If something goes wrong, wearing civilian clothing will provide the government with plausible deniability from a diplomatic perspective regarding your actions. The other part of the official narrative will be that you and your team acted independently," the pilot stated. "However, I'm not sure that story will hold up; after all, why would you and your team be destroying a warehouse in Jeddah unless it was done at the government's direction?"

"I know, but as you mentioned, even if everyone realizes the story isn't credible, it allows the government plausible deniability and a diplomatic way to move past this incident."

"My guess is that if your mission goes wrong, neither side will want you around to share your opinions," the pilot said.

"Then we need to succeed and make the destruction of the warehouse look like an accident."

"Your orders specify that exfiltration will be made by submarine, which is currently waiting at the coordinates you were instructed to memorize. However, it's unclear what you're to do if you're unable to escape by sea and need to use a land route instead."

"I assume you're asking for a reason."

"As I received these orders well before you boarded my aircraft, it gave me an opportunity to study a map of the area. The challenge for you is that, since Jeddah is on the coast, all the roads leading away from it go inland, which is open desert until you reach Mecca, about fifty miles away."

"What you're saying is that a land exfiltration from Mecca, a holy city that non-Muslims are prohibited from entering, and consequently where there's nowhere for us to hide, is impossible. Sending a helicopter into the desert to rescue us also wouldn't work, as it'll be detected on radar and expose our mission. Beyond that, given Saudi air defenses, it probably wouldn't make in or out of the area without being shot down. Therefore, an extraction by land is highly improbable and unsurvivable."

"That's exactly what I'm saying. So, make sure you get to that submarine."

"I appreciate your advice," the Master Chief said. "How we exfiltrate isn't our only challenge. We also need to decide our method of infiltration. Based on the equipment in the back, we have two options: we can either parachute onto the warehouse or sail through the Red Sea and enter the port using the RHIB.

Parachuting onto the target offers a stealthier and safer approach, as it allows us to avoid sailing through the port and bypass the area's security. However, there is a downside: once the warehouse is destroyed, we won't have the RHIB. This means we need to steal some type of motorized vessel, if one is even in the area, and get past port security which, given that a warehouse is ablaze, will be on high alert. If we somehow manage to overcome these obstacles, we still need to sail in open water until we reach the submarine."

"The warehouse you're supposed to destroy must be very important to risk a team and potentially create an international incident."

Hasen shrugged. "I don't know what's inside any more than you do."

"If you need longer than four and a half hours to mission plan, I can document in my flight log that we encountered severe turbulence en route that necessitated cutting power until we passed through the undocumented weather cell."

"Thanks for the offer, but I don't think that extending our planning time will make a difference. Since we can't use weapons, explosives, or flammables, I don't know how I'm going to completely destroy what appears to be a hundred-thousand-square-foot warehouse and make it look like what happened was no one's fault. We may have to figure that out once we get there."

"Then I'll put the pedal to the metal and get you to Jeddah a bit sooner than the four and a half hours it would normally take. That'll give you more time to get the job done and escape before sunrise."

"That would be appreciated," Hasen replied before leaving the cockpit.

Once the aircraft took off from Gilgit, Hasen gathered his team and read the orders he'd been handed, giving them the same summary of problems he'd discussed with the pilot.

"What time will we get to Jeddah?" Hasen's number two asked, each member of the team having a number corresponding to where they were in the pecking order of command.

"The pilot said it's a four-and-a-half-hour flight, but he'll try to get us there sooner. Gilgit is at Zulu plus five, and Jeddah is at plus three," the Master Chief stated.

Zulu was the military equivalent of Universal Time Coordinated (UTC), which disregarded time zones and daylight saving time to establish a global standard based on the prime meridian, or zero degrees longitude, located in Greenwich, England. As a result, 2am in Greenwich was referenced as zero two hundred hours Zulu (0200Z) in military terminology.

"For once something is working in our favor because it'll still be dark when we arrive," Number Two replied.

"These are exterior shots of the warehouse we're going to destroy," Hasen continued, passing around the satellite imagery he'd received. "Because there are no interior photos, we can't assess the structural integrity of the building, which makes determining what it will take to bring it down a judgment call. Consequently, let's assume it's an exceptionally strong structure and proceed from there."

Everyone agreed to go with that assumption.

"As you can see, the warehouse is in a fenced enclosure in an isolated area at the western edge of the port, with the nearest building situated some distance away. Getting inside appears to require recognition and approval at the guardhouse, which looks to be the only way in short of breaching or scaling the fence. There's a side gate near the warehouse," he said, pointing to it, "which we'll assume it's locked, alarmed, or both. This road connects the compound to a nearby dock," the Master Chief explained, moving his finger to it, "suggesting that whatever is stored inside arrives by ship. The challenge we face is that, without an intelligence brief, we don't know how many personnel are involved in port and warehouse security, where they're stationed, and other critical details.

That leads to the question of how we arrive at the target. Do we attempt taking the RHIB across a short stretch of the Red Sea and through the Port of Jeddah, afterward docking outside the facility and penetrating the warehouse's security perimeter without being seen? That's option one. Or do we parachute onto the warehouse roof, knowing this infiltration method means we would later need to steal a motorized vessel, which may or may not be available. And, if we find one, we'd have to evade port security long enough to reach the Red Sea and catch our ride home? That's option two."

"Definitely, option two," one of the team members volunteered. "Crossing even a short stretch of the Red Sea into Saudi Arabia's territorial waters and what looks to be a mile of the Port of Jeddah at night in a RHIB without being detected will be difficult. Additionally, entering a fenced and guarded compound without knowing anything about its security measures would be even more challenging, especially since we aren't carrying weapons or even a pair of wire cutters to get through the fence."

"Using wire cutters would defeat the illusion that the warehouse destruction is accidental," another team member reminded him.

"Good point. If we parachute in, we'll land on the warehouse with the only additional challenge to option one being that we need to find a vessel for our escape. I think we need to go with option two," the team member concluded.

"I agree," the Master Chief confirmed, ending the discussion on how they'd infiltrate.

During this time, Number Seven, the junior member of the team, was examining the photos of the warehouse. "I see several large air conditioning units on the roof," he interjected, capturing the attention of the other team members. "If we loosen a couple of wires within one of the units and touch them together, they'll spark. Holding those wires against something flammable will start a fire."

The team liked what they'd heard and took a closer look at the warehouse photos.

"That might give us a flame, and set on fire something flammable like a shirt. However, I'm not convinced that it would start a large enough fire to destroy the warehouse, especially since its exterior appears to be made of aluminum," another team member stated. "I like the idea of how to create a fire, but we need to find a way for it to spread inside the structure which, for all we know, may have fire suppression sprinklers."

"I might have a way where the size of the fire and the existence of a fire suppression system won't matter," Hasen said, pointing to a barbecue grill located near the stairway leading to the roof.

"The barbecue?" Number Two questioned.

"If you look at the side view of the building, you'll notice that a propane line runs from the barbecue and down the side of the building to a large fuel tank on the ground," the Master Chief explained, pointing to the gas line that extended to one of the two ten thousand-gallon fuel tanks next to the warehouse, each measuring twenty-seven feet long and eight feet in diameter, meaning each held enough vapor to fill 560,000 propane grill cylinders.

The tanks were primarily used to ensure uninterrupted power to the warehouse for an extended period through a microgrid, and to refuel the building's forklifts and the compound's propane-powered vehicles. Later, the warehouse manager connected a propane line to the barbecue, as he wanted to cook Dajaj Mashwi, a popular dish made of marinated chicken breasts.

"If one of those tanks were to explode, the resulting blast and fire would completely demolish the warehouse and then some," Hasen remarked.

"I've worked around industrial propane tanks as large as the ones below. They require a combination of extremely high heat and pressure to ignite, especially this size because of the thickness of the casing. It won't be easy. Propane tanks are exposed to the intense Saudi Arabian sun all day, where temperatures must reach 110 degrees or more," Number Two stated. "If you set a shirt or other fabric on fire and place it on top of the tank, it wouldn't explode."

"Let's forget about the shirt. Here's how I see this going down: We'll loosen a couple of wires in one of the units and bend them together so that they continually spark. Next, we'll open the gas flow valve on the barbecue, allowing the propane gas to escape into the surrounding air and drift toward the unit. When the gas reaches the sparking wires, it will ignite, causing a fire that travels down the connecting line to the propane storage tank. The resulting explosion will destroy the warehouse," Hasen explained.

"That'll work," Number Two agreed. "When investigators look into the cause of the explosion, they'll find that the valve wasn't closed properly, allowing gas to escape and ignite due to a short circuit in the wiring of an air conditioning unit."

Another ten minutes of discussion followed, with each team member giving their input. With no other feasible option that would guarantee the destruction of the warehouse and make it appear like an accident, they went with Hasen's plan.

"That leaves us with how to escape to the submarine, which will be waiting for us twelve miles off the coast," Hasen said.

"If I was the head of security and the only fenced and guarded warehouse in the port suddenly exploded, I'd believe it was from a terrorist attack and shut down the harbor, stopping all vessels from leaving. I'd then search the surrounding area, sweep the harbor, and examine the vessels within it. It won't take them long to locate us," one team member remarked. "In my opinion, the only difference between the first and second options is the certainty of reaching our objective if we parachute onto the warehouse. Both options ultimately lead to the same outcome: free room and board in Saudi Arabia for quite some time."

"Who says we're sailing out of here?" Hasen asked. "Consider this. These scaled images indicate that it's about a mile from the harbor entrance to the warehouse dock, and we know it's twelve miles from there to our rendezvous point. Our rebreathers can handle that swim."

The Master Chief was referring to a closed-circuit diving system that removes carbon dioxide from exhaled breath and adds oxygen, creating the correct air mixture for rebreathed air. One advantage of these systems is that they don't reveal a diver's position by releasing exhaled carbon dioxide into the water, which would rise to the surface as bubbles. Another benefit is that they extend dive times by recycling the air the diver breathes, significantly reducing the consumption of breathable gas. Because this consumption is determined by metabolism rather than water depth, the average oxygen delivered to someone using this system is around a liter per minute. In contrast, scuba divers consume up to ten liters per minute depending on the situation, while a person at rest uses approximately half a liter per minute.

"We parachute in and swim out. It should take us about eight hours to cover the thirteen miles to the submarine, which is about the maximum time we can expect from the rebreathers," Hasen concluded.

With everyone on the team liking this plan, they headed to the back of the aircraft to inspect their gear.

The pilot decided that the C-17's malfunction that necessitated it to deviate from its flight plan and request an emergency landing at the Jeddah Airport would be a non-functional pitot-static system.

The pitot-static system consists of a small metal tube that extends into the airstream from the side of the aircraft and a tiny hole in the fuselage, both providing variations in the outside air pressure to instruments that calculate the aircraft's forward and vertical speeds, as well as its altitude. Although the pitot tube is heated, if the heater fails and the tube's opening becomes blocked with ice, both the pilot and autopilot receive inaccurate readings for airspeed and changes in altitude. This could lead to inadvertently stalling the aircraft and crashing due to a loss of lift, or flying into a mountain or other obstacles due to incorrect altitude data being fed to the crew and autopilot. Therefore, when this situation arises, pilots and air traffic controllers are hellbent to get the aircraft on the ground as quickly as possible.

Consequently, when the pilot communicated his situation to the Jeddah Airport control tower, he was cleared for a straight-in approach to runway 34R, a 13,000-foot asphalt strip that was one of three parallel runways at the airport.

"Thirty seconds," the loadmaster said as the C-17 began its descent toward Jeddah Airport, with was thirty-eight miles from the port.

Waiting for the signal to jump, the SEALs stood several feet from the open cargo door. Dressed in civilian clothes featuring European brand names, they wore night vision goggles and used steerable parachutes, both made in Great Britain, going with the Pentagon's desire to not tether the United States to their actions. However, as Hasen pointed out to the loadmaster, who was as much a pawn as they were in this situation, that made no sense as they were clearly American, and even a cursory check of the internet would reveal that they were in the United States military. However, as Hasen and his team were accustomed to bureaucrats living in denial, he and the team went with the flow and put on their civilian clothing and foreign gear. Besides what they wore, each had attached to them by a long lanyard an equipment bag containing a rebreather, dive gear manufactured in Germany, and a few other useful items.

One by one, they left the aircraft. The night was still, with no wind and a dark moon hanging just before its waxing crescent phase. The pilot aligned them with the warehouse, and the team had no trouble silently landing on the roof. Afterward, they quickly changed into their diving gear, attaching their fins to clips on their weight belts, knowing they needed to get into the water as swiftly as possible after the explosion. In preparation for their quick departure, they put their civilian clothing, which they would have worn had they exfiltrated by the RHIB, on top of the parachute they'd stuffed into their equipment bag, which they'd dispose of at sea.

"Did anyone see security patrols or guards near this building?" Hasen asked his team, expecting the outside of the warehouse to be guarded, but unable to notice an enhanced security presence as Squadron Three descended from the plane onto the rooftop.

"Only at the entrance," one team member replied, the others adding their agreement.

"They must believe that port security and this compound are sufficient to protect whatever is stored in the warehouse," Hasen remarked.

"That, and being in Saudi Arabia," Number Three added.

"At least something is working in our favor. Let's get started,' Hasen stated.

While Number Seven worked to remove the cover of the rooftop air conditioner closest to the barbecue, the rest of the team fanned out, feeling vulnerable without their weapons. Equipped with night vision goggles, they kept watch as Seven loosened two of the wires, causing the air conditioning unit to shut down. Although he brought paper with him to start a fire he'd create by crossing the wires on top of it, he noticed that those using the barbecue didn't seem to care what the top of the roof looked like, probably because no one saw it. Therefore, they discarded everything from greasy rags to food wrappers into nearby trash cans, which clearly weren't emptied often as they overflowed with rubbish.

Faced with an opportunity, Number Seven took one of the greasy rags and, placing it on the uninsulated wires, touched them together creating the spark that ignited the rag. He then replaced the cover on the unit, making it seem as though the wind had blown the rag into the open underside, where it came into contact with the wires and loosened them, this chain of events ultimately causing the wires to spark and initiate the fire.

That theory, although it appeared plausible, would have its doubters because there was a high acrylic windscreen surrounding the top of the building. This helped block the wind and keep the blowing sand away from the air conditioning intakes, with a side benefit of keeping it off the food on the barbecue, which explained why it was located on the roof instead of beside the building.

However, while there would be skeptics that doubted a fire could have started in this manner, Hasen believed this theory would ultimately prevail. The only other possible scenario was that outsiders had infiltrated the fenced enclosure and caused the warehouse's destruction—something that no one associated with the warehouse wanted anyone to believe, and would to great lengths to refute because the consequences to them for lax security would be disastrous.

As Number Seven worked on creating the fire, Hasen took an adjustable wrench from his equipment bag and loosened the connecting nut between the propane line and the barbecue until they separated. He then opened the flow valve to allow the gas to escape.

"Let's get out of here," he said, grabbing his bag and following his team, who were waiting at the stairway that descended from the roof to ground level, ironically put there by the building's architects as a fire escape to prevent anyone from getting trapped on the roof, with a side gate nearby that allowed for a faster evacuation of the premises than going the greater distance to the entry gate. Although the side gate was locked, with a sign and symbol affixed to it indicating that it was also alarmed, the team had no trouble scaling the fence to escape the compound.

Since propane is colorless and odorless, Hasen had no idea as to the intensity of the gas that would flow from the line after he loosened the connection nut. Additionally, as propane is heavier than air, it sinks and collects in low-lying areas which, as the burning rag was lying beneath the air conditioning unit, was precisely where it was heading. Because propane gas had an ignition point of 157 degrees Fahrenheit once it left the storage tank, an explosion was inevitable when the gas traveled along the roof and came into contact with the 495 degrees Fahrenheit flame from the oil rag, which occurred just as the team arrived at the dock.

The explosion disintegrated the warehouse, replacing it with flames that reached temperatures between 3,600 and 3,800 degrees Fahrenheit— more than twice the intensity of a gasoline or natural gas fire. Although the team was at the dock and wearing their diving gear, and despite being a considerable distance from the warehouse when it disappeared, the high-energy forces generated by the compressed air of the blast wave, along with the spherical propagation of the blast wind, hit them like a punch. Gold Squadron was thrown along the ground, afterward experiencing dizziness and disorientation due to the explosion's impact on their inner ears.

Hasen didn't need to give the order to keep moving. The bright light from the explosion illuminated the area around the dock making them visible, and the people at the port would soon be converging on the area. If they didn't get into the water quickly, they'd be seen and their mission would fail, as the Saudis would realize the explosion wasn't an accident. Subsequently, with their equipment bags in hand, they crawled and stumbled the last twenty yards, leaping into the water by one of the dock pilings just before emergency vehicles rushed up the road leading to the compound.

Once in the water, Gold Squadron put on the fins that had been clipped to their weight belts. Afterward, the Master Chief secured an underwater communication device to the same clip, which allowed him to send text messages to the submarine as they approached. He then strapped onto his wrist a navigation board, both items having been included in the team's equipment bag as ordered by DEVGRU.

The navigational device integrated a depth gauge, dive chronometer, underwater compass, and path-to-target. This last function gave the direction the user needed to swim to reach the source of the transmission, with that frequency pre-set in the device. This directional tool was crucial for the team's survival. Given a distance of thirteen miles and the changing speed and direction of the ocean's currents during the expected eight-hour dive, it was the only automated means they had to locate the submarine. If it failed, they could use a traditional compass, although that would necessitate making constant and time-consuming adjustments to keep them on course. Given the operational limitations of the rebreathers, extending their time underwater wasn't an option.

The team discarded their equipment bags in the deeper water, away from the dock. The swim was grueling, especially since they'd been continually operational for nearly four days—having spent fourteen and a half hours reaching the Pamir mountain range, afterward trekking through the steep and rocky terrain to hide in a crevice outside of Dasht-e Mula, where they waited with little sleep for two days for the scientist to arrive. This was followed by a shootout with terrorists before being given this mission without any rest, their four-day ordeal culminating with an eight-hour underwater swim.

As a result, Gold Squadron was utterly exhausted when they finally came within range of the submarine, Hasen texting the submarine commander when they saw the vessel. The team entered through a small compartment known as the lockout trunk. When they stepped out, the captain was there to greet them.

"Well done, gentlemen. Secretary Rosen wanted me to tell you as soon as you stepped onboard that satellite imagery of your objective indicates your mission was successful. We're on underway to the Israeli Port of Eilat in the Gulf of Aqaba, where an Air Force plane will take you back to the States.

Hasen said that was welcome news, as he slumped against the traverse bulkhead, the wall that spanned the vessel.

The captain, seeing that the team barely had enough energy to stand, said food was waiting for them in the crew mess and racks, the term for a bed on board a naval ship or submarine, had been prepared so they could get some sleep.

Twenty-one hours later, Gold Squadron was back on board a C-17 Globemaster III heading to Virginia Beach.

Chapter Twenty

Onfroi Lapierre never made it to the chateau for his meeting with Fakhouri. Instead, his vehicle was intercepted three miles before reaching his destination by Bence, who'd signed out a police car and was waiting at a road crossing just outside Louveciennes where vehicles coming from Paris had to pass to enter the town. Armed with the license plate numbers of the ministry's CIO and its operations officer, he was looking for those numbers when Lapierre's car stopped at the crossing. Turning on his flashing lights, he pulled the car to the side of the road and, although dressed in civilian clothes, approached the CIO's vehicle and asked him to step out.

Because Bence wasn't wearing a uniform, Lapierre was suspicious about the situation and, not rolling down his window, instead stared at Bence while deciding what to do. However, that decision was made when Bence opened his credentials case, revealing his government ID and badge, the CIO unable to distinguish the badge of a senior government official from that of a law enforcement officer.

Upon seeing the badge, Lapierre rolled down his window and asked what he'd done wrong. Bence didn't answer. Instead, he asked to see his driver's license and, after verifying his identity, told the CIO to step out of the car and put his hands on the roof of the vehicle so he could be frisked.

Lapierre, angry at being subject to this indignation despite not having committed any crime, asked the officer to explain why he was being treated like a criminal. Bence, who didn't respond, instead patted him down, intensifying Lapierre's anger, which quickly turned into rage when he noticed the disdainful looks from passing drivers. He considered taking a swing at Bence for what he believed to be an unwarranted search, but knew that being charged with assaulting a police officer *was* a serious crime. Also, since Bence looked to be in excellent shape, while his only exercise involved lifting a bottle of wine and pouring it into his glass, he didn't think he'd be conscious after taking the first swing. Thus, the CIO gritted his teeth and submitted to the frisk.

"You're under arrest," Bence stated authoritatively once he verified that Lapierre wasn't carrying a weapon, then proceeded to handcuff him.

"For what?"

Bence didn't respond. Instead, he placed the CIO in the back of the police car before returning to Lapierre's vehicle, where he grabbed the computer bag that he'd seen on the passenger seat and brought it to the police vehicle. After that, he called Donati to inform him that he had their houseguest and was on his way to the farmhouse for which he'd received directions. During the five-minute drive the CIO lost it, yelling at Bence and protesting his innocence.

"I'll have your badge for this. Do you have any idea who I am?" The CIO shouted.

"I know exactly who you are, which is why you're handcuffed and sitting in the back of my car."

"When we get to the police station, I'll call the Minister of the Interior, and you'll be fired on the spot. Guaranteed."

"We're not going to the station, and you're not calling anyone," Bence replied in a calm and unhurried tone, demonstrating his control over a situation that Lapierre did not understand.

The fact that the officer in front of him didn't feel threatened, which in his way of thinking meant that he believed the CIO to be a lightweight on the scale of importance, again sent Lapierre over the top. Going into a profanity-laced tirade, he demanded to know the name of the officer's superior while reiterating that he was an important government official who was not to be trifled with and could crush his career with a call to his influential friends."

Bence, who'd had enough of this tirade and was getting a headache, pulled over to the side of the road and stopped the car. "This is getting tiring. Here's the deal," he said as he turned to face Lapierre, who was in the back seat. "We should arrive at our destination in less than five minutes. During that time, you're not going to say a single word. If you do, I'm going to shoot you with this," he said, holding up the taser that was on the passenger seat.

Lapierre's eyes widened at the sight of the weapon, the CIO remaining silent for the remainder of the ride.

Louveciennes is known for its picturesque hills, vibrant flower-filled landscapes, vineyards, and farms, all of which have inspired over one hundred twenty paintings by nineteenth-century impressionists, including Renoir, Pissarro, Sisley, and Monet.

The farmhouse that Lamberti rented was a gentrified three-thousand-square-foot property typically used by wealthy Parisians to escape the city during the summer, when Paris' streets were flooded with tourists and the traffic worse than usual. Surrounded by fruit groves and vineyards, the nearest neighbor lived a mile away, giving those who rented the property a great deal of privacy. That the farmhouse could only be rented for a minimum of one month didn't bother Lamberti, who had stayed there on several occasions with her late husband. After signing the contract and wiring the money, she instructed the property agent to leave the front door unlocked and place the key on the kitchen table inside, as she preferred not to be disturbed. This request was unusual for the agent, who'd rented the farmhouse to celebrities and others whose fame often necessitated wanting to get away from the scrutiny of others and escaping the pressures of their professions by living anonymously for a short period.

As Bence turned onto the gravel driveway leading to the property and brought his vehicle to a stop in front of the garage, he was met by Donati, Donais, Hunkler, and Labriola, who'd heard it approaching the farmhouse.

"Did you have any problems?" Donati asked Bence as he stepped out of the vehicle.

"None," he replied as he opened the rear door and removed Lapierre from the back of the vehicle, keeping him in restraints as he brought him into the farmhouse and pushed him onto a kitchen chair.

"Who are you and why have I been kidnapped?" Lapierre asked, swiveling his head in a semi-circle to look at the five people in front of him.

Since no one knew whether Lapierre spoke any language other than French, Donati initially considered Bence, an experienced law enforcement officer, to interrogate the CIO—the French-speaking and listening skills of the Italian members of the team leaving something to be desired. However, he ultimately chose Donais for the task, not only because she was French, but also because she was well-acquainted with the entire investigation and understood the specific information they needed to extract from Lapierre. Therefore, while Donais was interrogating the CIO, Bence would interpret for Donati, Hunkler, and Labriola.

"You're here because we know you're Minister Fakhouri's informant within the French government and that you've been providing him sensitive information, which resulted in the death of the Minister of Foreign Affairs and the kidnapping and attempted murder of a senior Italian official. Take a look at this," Donais said, placing a laptop in front of the CIO with the flash drive that Lamberti had given them. She then began scrolling through its files. "The sensitive information and assistance you've provided the Saudis will be considered treason."

Lapierre's eyes widened as he stared at the computer screen. Taking a deep breath to compose himself, he vented his anger at Donais by asserting that what he saw had clearly been obtained illegally and was therefore inadmissible in court. Consequently, he claimed that he had done nothing wrong as a matter of law, unlike them—who had kidnapped him and would face imprisonment for their actions.

"Forget the legal jargon and threats; they don't apply to us. The only thing you should worry about is honestly answering my questions, because your responses will determine your fate," Donais stated.

Lapierre was on the verge of launching into another tirade when Donais, sensing his intention, raised her hand to signal him to be quiet, after which the rest of the team nodded or smiled, liking how she'd taken control of the interrogation.

"Under normal circumstances, you would have three choices. The first is to refuse to tell us what we want to know. The second is to hire the best attorney in Paris to find technicalities that could dismiss all charges against you, such as claims of being kidnapped or asserting that the evidence on the computer, which would be presented at trial, was obtained illegally. However, both of those choices are off the table because you won't have an attorney or your day in court. As far as anyone knows, you left your office and disappeared without a trace. Your car will be found at the airport and they'll be irrefutable documentation that you purchased a ticket to Riyadh and boarded that flight. Therefore, whatever we decide to do to you will be off-the-books because anyone investigating your whereabouts will believe you went to Saudi Arabia."

"You can't do that."

"It's done. You've already boarded that flight. Let me be clear. We can do whatever we want to you with impunity because no one knows you're here," Donais stated. "Therefore, if you choose not to cooperate with us, choices one and two will be replaced with an alternative choice: The CIA picking you up at this farmhouse and, by means which they won't share, transporting you to one of their rendition sites in Africa, where you'll be questioned unrelentingly until you tell your interrogators everything you know, which you eventually will. All the CIA wants in return is a small diplomatic favor from our governments, which has already been accepted.

You should understand that once your usefulness in providing information has ended, you'll be killed and buried in the desert because neither the CIA, those at the rendition site, nor us can have you telling anyone where you've been or what happened."

"And my third choice?" Lapierre asked, his voice conveying fear.

"Tell us everything you know about Minister Fakhouri and those associated with him, what they've done, and what they plan to do. In exchange for your cooperation, you'll be tried in private and sentenced to prison, serving your term under an alias in one of the thirteen French territories outside Europe. After completing your sentence, you'll enter a witness protection program, where you will live out the rest of your life in one of these territories. However, if we discover you've lied to us, there will be no second chances. You're on your way to Africa."

"Are you willing to reduce that prison sentence if I provide you with documented evidence regarding Fakhouri and the Saudis' illegalities?"

"You don't have a strong negotiating position. What we have on the flash drive links Bernardi and Calvario's global illegalities to Fakhouri and, by extension, the Saudi government," Bence replied after Donais gave him a look indicating that he should respond to the question.

"What you have is minimal. While it may cause some diplomatic embarrassment, it can be presented in a way that allows the Saudi government to blame an intermediary for these issues, ultimately leaving them with only a few cuts and bruises. The documentary evidence I possess will, in comparison, put them in intensive care."

"What do you have?" Bence asked.

"I recorded every email, text, and phone call that was sent or received by Fakhouri, and have it stored on my computer," Lapierre replied.

"That's hard to believe, considering the security awareness of a nation-state operating on foreign soil. What am I missing?"

"That I'm the person who upgraded their systems."

"Even so, considering that the Saudis have the financial resources to purchase the most advanced spyware detection equipment available, and that they would be watching you closely the entire time you were in the chateau, how could you possibly install recording devices in their system?" Donais asked.

"Because Minister Fakhouri has a highly competent, although not flawless security team."

"And you exploited these weaknesses."

"Shamelessly. Although security conducts daily sweeps of the chateau for bugs—an ongoing process given the size of the residence and its grounds—and the tech team in Riyadh checks the minister's computer for malware every six hours, these security protocols didn't impact my devices; in fact, they worked to my advantage."

"That's difficult to believe."

"Not once you understand that they'd let the fox into the henhouse, as I provided the Saudi minister with upgraded equipment to enhance his internet and voice signals throughout the chateau and its grounds, including within them some discreet modifications. After this equipment was installed, his security team placed tamper-proof security strips on the cases to ensure they couldn't be opened and something placed within. However, they were unaware that my recording devices were already inside."

"They could have opened the cases and looked inside before affixing the security strips," Donais remarked.

"They're not computer engineers who could detect an extra circuit card, antenna, or another piece of hardware."

"And these devices periodically transmitted data to your server or other device," she stated.

"Precisely."

"But how would that transmission go unnoticed?" Donais asked. "They must have detection equipment to pick up unauthorized transmissions from the chateau and grounds."

"It didn't need to go unnoticed. My standard service contract includes daily checks of all systems and recalibrations as necessary to ensure optimal performance. During these system checks, the data from the recording devices I installed is compressed and transmitted to me along with the performance parameters of the equipment. This transmission isn't considered unusual, as it's part of my maintenance contract. Riyadh doesn't detect the malware in the minister's computer because it's hardware based. Get my computer bag; I'll show you what I have."

"It's in my car," Bence said, going to his vehicle and returning several minutes later with the computer bag. After searching the bag for weapons, he uncuffed the CIO and handed him the bag.

The CIO logged into his computer and opened the folder labeled with Fakhouri's name, revealing two hundred fifty-six subfolders. "Here are my intercepts from the chateau," Lapierre stated, opening a subfolder and clicking on a file to reveal its contents.

"Is all this data in French?" Donais asked.

"All of it. I used various translation programs to convert the emails, texts, and voice communications from Arabic and Italian into a language I could understand."

"May I?" She asked, taking the laptop from him. Donais, who was tech-savvy, navigated to the properties section on the laptop and discovered that the size of the main folder was 50-gigabytes, containing a total of 52,170 files within its subfolders.

"I didn't expect to see this many files," she remarked.

"Fakhouri regularly communicates with officials from foreign governments, senior members of his ministry, the royal family, and individuals in other ministries. He's also kept in the loop on matters that don't directly involve his ministry but where it's essential for him to be informed," Lapierre replied. "He's a crucial part of the machinery of the Saudi government."

"Given the enormity of this data, how were you able to organize and direct it to specific subfolders," Donais inquired, seeing one labeled *Corrado Bernardi* and another *Dante Sciarra*."

"I am a programmer," the CIO admonished, stating the obvious. "The folders are organized by sender and people. If someone's name appears in a written or verbal communication, that communication will show up in more than one subfolder."

"Let's see what you have," Donais said, opening files in Bernardi and Sciarra's subfolders, which she read along with Bence. Thirty minutes later, they both felt they had seen enough.

"What did you find?" Donati said, asking what Hunkler and Labriola also wanted to know.

"It appears to be a record of Fakhouri's communications with others, just as he said," Donais stated, nodding toward Lapierre.

The CIO smiled upon hearing this. "About that prison sentence. I was thinking of Martinique," Lapierre stated.

"I wouldn't be opposed to a tropical incarceration," Donati agreed.

"As an aside, what's to stop me from telling the world what you've done once I'm in prison or after I'm released?" LaPierre asked. "You and your associates aren't exactly free from sin."

"If you did, you'd be dead within days," Bence said. "Do you really think the Saudis will let you live after giving us these files? Revenge is deeply rooted in their culture. Moreover, I would take the betrayal personally and would gladly inform them where you're hiding and share your alias. A deal is only a deal if both sides keep their word," he emphasized.

"How can I be sure they won't find me in prison? Given what I've done, the Saudis will never stop searching for me, and they have the resources to eventually track me down, alias or not."

"They won't be searching for you because, figuratively

speaking, you'll be dead. Before your sentence begins, there will be numerous newspaper articles detailing of how you died in a car accident, with comments from the police, the coroner, and the French government confirming your demise. We'll also create a file on the accident and put it in both the police and coroner's databases, in case those systems are hacked. I previously worked for an attorney who cooperated with the police to make this happen," Donais explained.

Lapierre appeared to be satisfied with her response.

"You should call Lamberti and tell her what we have. She'll be waiting for our call," Donati told Donais, who agreed and stepped out of earshot of the CIO.

The call lasted just over fifteen minutes, after which Donais was instructed to send the file containing the subfolders to an internet address provided by Lamberti.

"It's a 50-gigabyte file. I'm not sure if this internet connection can handle a file that size or how long it will take if it can," Donais said.

"The farmhouse has fiber-optic internet to accommodate the important business dealings of the guests who stay there. It won't take long to transmit the files," Lamberti assured her.

"What do you want us to do with Lapierre?"

"Keep him there until after I've spoken with Minister Fakhouri. I may need more information from him. Afterward, I'll arrange for his transport."

"You're speaking with the minister?" Donais asked reflexively, surprising her teammates with her boldness, as none of them had ever heard anyone question Lamberti about her plans. What astonished them even more was that she actually answered Donais's question.

"I'm going to give him my terms for his country's future sales of rare earth elements."

"Why would the Saudis listen to us?" Donais persisted. "Given what's happened, legally and politically speaking, everyone's covered in so much mud that we all need a shower."

"They'll listen because they won't have a choice," Lamberti replied cryptically.

Fakhouri, having decided that Lapierre would replace Bernardi as his intermediary, picked up his phone to invite him to the chateau for an urgent discussion, but wouldn't mention the topic of their talk would be to persuade the CIO to leave his job at the ministry for a new career. Although he didn't believe that would be a difficult choice for the civil servant given the generous salary he intended to offer, he wanted to have that discussion face-to-face to better assess Lapierre's reaction and gauge his long-term commitment.

However, before he could make that call, he received one from a member of the Consultative Assembly of Saudi Arabia, the country's formal advisory body to which he provided frequent updates on his progress in establishing their nation's dominion over rare earth elements. The advisor who called was the most important person on that body, being a member of the royal family of Saudi Arabia and a trusted confidant of the king.

He quickly sensed something was amiss when he heard the tension in the member's voice. This was confirmed when he was told that the centralized rare earth storage facility in Jeddah had been demolished and set ablaze when the two propane tanks next to the warehouse exploded. Although the investigation was still in its early stages, the initial theory was that a rooftop air conditioning unit had caught fire and ignited gas in a nearby line, which spread to one of two propane tanks on the ground. That conclusion was reached because those units had the only electrical connections on the roof, where a gas line led to one of two propane tanks on the ground. There was no evidence that the fire or explosion was caused by an outside influence, as he phrased it, or an explosive device.

Feeling as though he had taken a gut punch and struggling to suppress the urge to vomit, he realized that the supply of oxides he had relied upon to establish Saudi Arabia as the dominant global power in rare earth elements—an ambition that could have spanned generations—had instead gone up in flames, quite literally.

Collapsing into his chair as he absorbed the enormity of the situation, and knowing that he still needed to re-establish a relationship with numerous officials if he was to mine and process the rare earth elements, his meeting with the CIO became even more important. As he again prepared to phone Lapierre, he received a text from a phone number that wasn't on his contact list, the sender identifying herself as Pia Lamberti—a name he recognized given the circumstances. Not believing in coincidences, he now understood that what happened in Jeddah wasn't an accident and that he would soon speak with the person who orchestrated it to appear as such. The text indicated she would call within a few seconds. He answered the phone.

"I assume you're calling about the incident that occurred in Jeddah," Fakhouri said, opting not to call it an accident.

"I could pretend that I don't know what happened in Jeddah, or that I'm unaware of the massive closures of your rare earth mines and processing plants, which you attempted to conceal behind offshore corporations," but I won't waste our time," Lamberti said, not disclosing that she had obtained this information from D'Angelo, who linked the offshore entities to Bernardi and the Saudi government, giving Lamberti the leverage she needed to dictate her terms.

"What's the purpose of this call? What do you want?" Fakhouri demanded.

"You're going to realign your country's global ambitions for rare earth elements; otherwise, you'll end up with nothing."

"Threatening me is equivalent to threatening my government. You'd better have a good reason for dictating policy to a sovereign nation. If not, this conversation is over, and there will be consequences for your indiscretion," he responded with arrogance.

"You wouldn't have answered this call if you didn't know who I am. If you need a reminder: I'm the person you had kidnapped, interrogated, and ordered killed. And, you're not going to end this discussion until you gather more information about what I know regarding your country's involvement in rare earth elements, so that you can relay that to Riyadh."

"Your accusations are absurd and not worthy of serious consideration. Tell those in your government with whom you work, that Italy should refrain from making unfounded accusations and interfering in our affairs, or face diplomatic and economic repercussions."

"You and I both know there won't be repercussions because you're afraid other nations might investigate my accusations."

"Accusation is an appropriate word choice because you have yet to provide any evidence of wrongdoing," Fakhouri replied, puzzled as to why she seemed supremely confident and didn't back down in the face of threats that would have made seasoned diplomats walk away. "What evidence do you have?"

"Tell your government that I have the name and position of every individual that was bribed to secure your mining contracts, including the initial amounts they were paid and the ongoing monies they received. I also have the records of their offshore bank accounts to which your surrogate, Corrado Bernardi, wired the money. Furthermore, I can directly link you, and by extension your country, to these transactions. I can also tie you, Mr. Minister, to the assassination of the French Minister of Foreign Affairs, the bombmaker involved in his death, the attempted murder of the head of my domestic intelligence service, and to my kidnapping. "Consequently, I believe I have a substantial amount of evidence to support my accusations."

"None of which I've seen. Subsequently, your accusations lack any substance. I should also point out that investigating me for alleged wrongdoings is pointless, as I am entitled to diplomatic immunity," Fakhouri replied smugly. "I believe you're bluffing in an attempt to extract information from me."

"Here's an insight into my personality: I deal with facts. I never bluff or make accusations without solid evidence, as doing so is ultimately a waste of time. Therefore, I'm sending you a link to a site that contains several files from 50-gigabytes of data that detail your nefarious activities. Review them and call me back at the phone number displayed on your screen. Don't take too long, or you may find this on the evening news. Diplomatic immunity or not, you and your country aren't immune from being taken to court, the seizure of assets, or having permits and licenses revoked. I'm not a patient person, don't keep me waiting."

Shortly thereafter, the link appeared on Fakhouri's phone. When he read the files, which displayed word for word his conversations with Bernardi and Sciarra, his involvement in the minister's assassination, Lamberti's kidnapping, the attempted murder of Acardi, and the contract to kill Bernardi, he realized that all of his communications had somehow been intercepted, something that Riyadh had assured him could never happen.

He also recognized that releasing these conversations, along with other communications he believed to be equally damaging, which he assumed she had, could severely damage Saudi Arabia's relationships with France and Italy and result in the king being compared to Putin on the global stage. Furthermore, as these dominos began to fall, he anticipated that the canceled mining contracts would be offered to other countries, which would be eager to accept them once they understood that his nation intended to control the global pricing of these critical elements and exert this control for geopolitical purposes.

After pulling himself together, Fakhouri contacted the member of the Consultative Assembly who was the king's confidant, explained the situation, and requested guidance from the king on how to proceed. Fifteen agonizing minutes after their conversation ended, the member called back to convey the king's decision.

"What do you want in return for not releasing this information?" Fakhouri reluctantly asked Lamberti when he called, shrewd enough to realize that asking her to destroy the information she had would be pointless, as she would want to keep her leverage over his country.

"I've already told you: You're going get rid of all but fifteen percent of your offshore corporations."

"Meaning that, because the host government won't reimburse my country for their $500 million investment per site, we'll be effectively transferring ownership to the governing authority."

"If they haven't already seized your assets when they canceled your lease, that's precisely what I mean. This will fragment the market enough that no single entity will have control or the ability to manipulate the prices of these commodities."

"I may not be able to reach fifteen percent because I don't know how many of these leases are recoverable once it becomes known that my country owns these offshore corporations and is transferring ownership of most to host nations. As a result, every mine could be nationalized, seized, or caught up in litigation. We might end up with virtually nothing."

"Which is essentially what you have right now. However, I believe deals can be made to help you reach fifteen percent, since it requires a significant amount of capital to operate a mining and processing complex."

"Possibly. It's still a bitter pill to swallow, which is why I'm not sure I can sell this to the king. Getting his approval will take time, as acting quickly is not in the royal's genome," he said, attempting to buy himself some time to negotiate the terms he'd received, even though he was instructed to resolve this matter immediately, regardless of the cost.

"You acted decisively when it came to my kidnapping, the assassination of a French official, and the attempted murderer of someone in our government. To be clear, you have sixty days to reduce your offshore ownership to fifteen percent. This can be achieved either by reassigning the contracts or by closing the offshore corporation following the repatriation of the mine and processing plant. If, for any reason, you hold a greater percentage on the sixty-first day, I'll release my documentation. After that point, the loss of your mining operations will be the least of your nation's concerns."

Fakhouri was recalled to Saudi Arabia the following day and suffered a heart attack that night, according to the housekeeper who found him unresponsive at home the next morning. While the death certificate officially attributed the cause to a heart attack, it was only partially accurate since his heart had indeed stopped, but failed to mention the knife wound which caused the organ failure. The government official who accompanied the body to the morgue held a completed death certificate, which he handed to the medical examiner for his signature—a procedure that both men had performed numerous times before.

Following Islamic tradition, Fakhouri's body was taken into the desert for burial within twenty-four hours of death. He was positioned on his right side and laid to rest perpendicular to the direction of Mecca.

A majority of Saudi Arabia's offshore corporations for rare earth elements were closed after the host government took control of the mines due to the emptying of the government officials' accounts. Ultimately, the Kingdom managed to retain ten percent of its mining contracts by offering the host government cash and promising to provide capital for the expansion of their operations.

Due to his cooperation, Lapierre was able to avoid prison and was granted a new identity, along with the opportunity to choose which Italian island he wanted to live on. He decided against moving to Martinique after Lamberti explained that, under French law, if it were discovered that he was a Saudi informant and his actions indirectly led to the death of their minister, the French government would classify him as a terrorist, imprisoning him there without trial and throwing away the key. As a result, he chose Sardinia, the second largest island in Italy and the Mediterranean Sea.

After spending months in a safe house learning to read and write in Italian, he was flown to the island, where he received a car and a small house in the mountains. The following week, he began working for Sardinia's largest internet service provider where, because of his technological expertise, he quickly advanced and became the company's Chief Technology Officer (CTO).

Before her call with Fakhouri, Lamberti spoke with Bruno and Maria, who expressed their concerns that those in Favara and Canicatti who assisted in their escape might face severe consequences from Arturo Salucci, the Mafioso who replaced Sciarra. They also worried that both towns could be punished as a warning to others.

"I'll handle the situation," was all that Lamberti said, not providing details.

Although Maria didn't know her well, from what Bruno had said about the person he sometimes referred to as the witch, she felt certain that the villagers would somehow be shielded from the Mafia's retribution.

"Could you please go downstairs and get me a cup of espresso?" Bruno asked Maria who, seeing that both Zunino and Villa were at the back of the room and could have gone instead, understood that this was a polite way of asking her to leave while he discussed something confidential with Lamberti.

"I'd like one as well," the witch said, shaking off Villa, who made a gesture that he would go.

"It would be my pleasure," Maria said, everyone remaining silent until she left the room.

"I'd like you to meet with Donati and Donais in Bergamo," Bruno began, referring to the picturesque town twenty-five miles northeast of Milan. "They're involved in a situation that requires your immediate attention."

"A situation resulting from an assignment that I obviously didn't give to BD&D investigations, as I'm only learning about it now."

"It's in response to what occurred in Sicily."

"Could you be a little vaguer?" Lamberti said, indicating he should get to the point.

Bruno told her what Donati and Donais were doing in Bergamo and why they required Lamberti.

"That law of unexpected consequences," Lamberti remarked. "You were right to send Maria out of the room; she would want to get involved. I admire her tenacity, but in this situation, it's better if Donati, Donais, and I handle this while you stay here with her. If she found out why we were in Bergamo, I'm not sure you could keep her away."

"That was my feeling."

"Hopefully, this will go smoother than my extraction from Malta," Lamberti remarked.

"That sets the bar pretty low," Bruno replied as Maria entered the room carrying a tray with two cups of espresso.

Once Bruno and Maria left her office, Lamberti spoke with President Orsini and received his approval to protect the residents of Favara and Canicatti, as well as to assist Donati and Donais. Afterward, she spoke with the commander of Naval Air Station Sigonella and, upon the conclusion of that call, instructed Zunino to get her pilots to the Gulfstream and have them file a flight plan there.

One hour and fifteen minutes after that call was made, her plane landed at the Naval Air Station. Stepping off the aircraft, she walked a short distance across the tarmac and boarded the same EH101 transport which rescued Bruno and Maria, the three A129 Mangusta attack helicopters which previously escorted it parked nearby. Thirty-seven minutes later, the transport touched down in the courtyard of Sciarra's former residence. As Lamberti stepped off, the three attack helicopters conspicuously hovered nearby, their powerful miniguns conspicuously sweeping the area.

There was no ignoring the noise made by the four helicopters. Upon hearing their approach, numerous thugs rushed out the front door of the residence, convinced that their boss was under attack by someone reckless enough to land helicopters on his property and deploy their men. However, each immediately dropped their weapon and raised their hands in surrender when they saw the twenty heavily-armed troops who were on Lamberti's aircraft pointing automatic weapons at them, and that the miniguns on the three Mangusta aircraft hovering above were also aimed in their direction.

Following the commands they were given, the thugs knelt and interlocked their fingers on top of their heads while their weapons were confiscated and placed in the transport. Afterwards, they were secured with flex cuffs, with five men staying outside to guard them while the remaining fifteen accompanied Lamberti into the mansion.

As the heavily armed soldiers entered, Salucci's five bodyguards, who'd remained behind to protect their boss, dropped their weapons as if they were on fire upon seeing the soldiers aiming their guns at them. They were quickly placed in flex cuffs. Watching the situation unfold and his bodyguards surrender, Arturo Salucci's face displayed a terrified expression, believing that they were there to take him away in a body bag. He raised his hands and began begging for his life.

"Sit down," Lamberti said, ignoring Salucci's pleas and instead gesturing toward a couch. The Mafioso did as he was told while Lamberti stood several feet away, casting a scrutinizing gaze down at him.

"Do you know who I am?" Lamberti asked.

"No," Salucci replied.

"It's better that you don't."

"Here's the situation: The military is currently establishing a base between Favara and Canicatti, where army personnel and helicopters will be stationed. This base will employ civilians from those towns as well as other areas within the Agrigento province. I am holding you personally responsible for the safety of these employees. Consider this to be a public service. If anything happens to these towns or their residents—whether it be an accidental fire, a highway accident, or any other unfortunate incident—an unfortunate military training accident will occur wherever you are. You won't survive," Lamberti stated before pulling out her cellphone and making a FaceTime call.

"Commander, proceed," she ordered.

A few moments later, two attack helicopters opened fire with their miniguns, obliterating the back third of the mansion's second floor, which contained the master bedroom and the adjoining study. This produced an earthquake-like vibration throughout the residence, causing pictures to fall off the walls, dishes to crash to the floor, and generally leaving the interior of the mansion in disarray.

When the gunfire erupted, Salucci quickly dropped to the floor, curling into a fetal position and covering his head as the back of his house was being destroyed. Once the shooting stopped, Lamberti knelt and handed him her phone so he could see the aftermath of the helicopter's assault on his home in real-time.

"One final reminder: If any harm comes to these towns or their people, I'll send these helicopters to find and kill you, whether you're in Sicily or anywhere else," she said, turning to leave without waiting for a response. As she headed for the front door, she ordered that Salucci's men be cut free of their cuffs, and that their weapons were to be confiscated and brought to the aircraft.

Once Lamberti and the soldiers boarded the transport helicopter, it lifted off and, along with the other three aircraft, departed from Agrigento and flew to the coordinates that she'd previously given the pilot. As the aircraft circled the area, she looked closely at the barren hilltop situated between Favara and Canicatti, having tentatively selected this location for the base after the military sent aerial photos of government-owned land in the area to her phone while she was en route from Rome to NAS Sigonella.

The large hilltop was relatively flat, which meant that construction would be shorter and cost less compared to removing thousands of tons of dirt to level the land. Additionally, being the highest point in the area was beneficial during bad weather, as aircraft could operate without the risk of striking a higher hill during takeoff or landing. Overall, Lamberti believed it was an excellent location for a minibase that would protect the locals from the Agrigento Mafia, enhance domestic security for western Sicily, and serve as a refueling depot for that end of the island, thereby extending the range of military helicopters into the Mediterranean Sea. She was confident that President Orsini would approve its construction for these reasons and that it would hinder the Mafia's exploitation of the local economy by providing employment opportunities for the job-starved province, offering residents a better choice than joining the Mafia.

After surveying the area, Lamberti returned to the naval air station and boarded her aircraft, instructing the pilot to take her to Bergamo to meet with Donati and Donais.

As Lamberti was instilling a change in attitude into Arturo Salucci, Hunkler stepped off a helicopter alongside Salvatore Costa in Cortina D'Ampezzo. This picturesque town, nestled in the heart of the Dolomitic Alps in northern Italy, was chosen by the former captain of the Sogno d'Oro as his new home—Lamberti keeping her promise to Maria's cousin to give him a new domicile and identity, and enough money to retire in compensation for the loss of his fishing/smuggling vessel. Hunkler was there to ensure everything went smoothly, after which he'd return to the Vatican to resume his duties.

"I'm curious why you chose Cortina as the place you want to retire," Hunkler said as they entered the hamlet of Alverà and he parked the rental car in front of the sixteen hundred square feet villa, which featured floor-to-ceiling windows that offered magnificent views of the surrounding Dolomites.

"I came here many years ago with a group of friends. We didn't have much money, so we stayed in a hostel and taught ourselves how to ski. I instantly fell in love with this town and would have moved here had it not been for the reality that I'd not only be leaving my family, but had no way of making a living. Fishing and smuggling were, and still are, my only skills, which seem incompatible with earning a living in this area. However, now that my circumstances have changed, I have the perfect opportunity to pursue my dream. Also, there's the reality that I had to leave Agrigento province before Sciarra's replacement finds and kills me which, given enough time, would surely happen."

"You know how to get ahold of me or Lamberti if there's a problem."

"I memorized the procedures," Costa confirmed.

"Signora Lamberti asked me to show you the garage before I leave," Hunkler said, opening the door from a short hallway off the kitchen. Inside, there was a white Range Rover Sport. "This is a personal thank you for saving her life. She had the dealer bring it here, and I was told the keys are in the cup holder."

Costa was speechless as he gazed at the elegant vehicle, finding the key fobs in the cup holders.

"She also requested that I give you this," he said, handing the former ship's captain a thin envelope.

As Costa opened it, his eyes widened in surprise, and he turned to Hunkler with a questioning look.

"Until then," the colonel said, returning to his rental without commenting on the contents of the envelope.

Chapter Twenty-one

Four months later

The Dassault Falcon jet landed smoothly at the Milan Bergamo airport and taxied to the VIP terminal. Onboard was France's newly appointed head of the Directorate-General for External Affairs (DGSE), which was comparable to the CIA or MI6. The previous director had been dismissed due to several significant failures, including his inability to identity the global accumulation of rare earth mining contracts by the Saudis, one of which was located in the Massif Central region. Additionally, the directorate failed to detect a mole within the government and uncover a plot to assassinate both the Minister of Foreign Affairs and a foreign dignitary. In light of these shortcomings, the French president decided that a change was necessary. Edgard Bence was selected to head the foreign intelligence service due to his pivotal role in revealing these intelligence failures and his prior success in recovering art looted by the Nazis—an effort that had eluded government agencies for over seventy-five years.

After discovering the truth as to who was behind these atrocities, the French president called Orsini to apologize for mistakenly believing that the Italian government had been involved in any wrongdoing.

Villa greeted Bence as he stepped off the aircraft and, after putting his bags in the back of the vehicle, they left the airport. Their destination was a one-hundred-acre walnut farm, on which a luxurious six-thousand-square-foot farmhouse was built. Located just outside the city of Bergamo, this property had been purchased by Donati's trust fund and now served as the new headquarters for BD&D Investigations.

The partners unanimously chose the site for its serene country environment and its proximity to Milan, allowing them to enjoy the city's amenities, such as its restaurants and social activities. The location had no effect on their business, as a majority of their clients were referred by Acardi and Lamberti or they acted on behalf of the government, with most of their investigative work taking place outside of Milan. However, they all felt that having Milan and Paris listed on their business cards enhanced their professional stature. Therefore, reasoning that Bergamo, although not technically a suburb, was close enough to Milan to be perceived as one, they modified their business cards to list both cities in the upper right corner without providing the company's actual business addresses, since both were residential locations. Instead, only their names and phone numbers appeared in the center of the cards.

When Bence arrived at the farm, Villa led him onto the patio, which presented a magnificent view of the walnut grove. As he looked around, he noticed approximately twenty people mingling on the spacious patio, most of whom he recognized. Acardi hadn't mentioned that this was a social gathering, although it was evident because there were servers circulating with glasses of wine, champagne, and platters of hors d'oeuvres. This led him to believe that the event was a surprise celebration for his promotion, which explained why he was there without being informed as to the purpose of the gathering.

"I'm glad you're here," Acardi said, finding Bence at the edge of the patio.

"You shouldn't have gone to all this trouble for me," he said, raising his glass toward him.

"That's good to know because this isn't in your honor, although congratulations on your promotion; it's well deserved," Acardi stated. "You're here because Mauro wanted you to ensure your attendance."

"What am I attending?"

"You'll find out," Acardi deflected. "Until then, enjoy the wine and food. In our business, relaxation is rare."

Looking over Bence's right shoulder, Acardi saw D'Angelo and waved him over, making the introduction between foreign counterparts.

"Lamberti has told me good things about you, and as you likely know, she doesn't give praise lightly. I look forward to working with you," D'Angelo said before excusing himself, as his assistant, Bianca Ferrara, was holding up her cellphone to indicate he had a call.

As he walked away, Donati and Donais stepped forward to greet Bence.

"I envy your new office," the new director said, giving Donais a hug. "Mine doesn't even have a window. By the way, can you tell me what's happening here? Villa picked me up at the airport, and I noticed Zunino standing near the door leading into the building. I heard that Lamberti never goes anywhere without one or both of them. I also see presidential-level security around the perimeter."

"The president and Lamberti are inside."

"Does everyone but me know why we're here? With all this secrecy and their presence, it must be important. Until I find out, what would it take to get a tour of your residence and offices?" He asked.

"Only the pleasure of your company," Donais replied, leading the way inside with Donati following.

Labriola arrived next and was greeted by Hunkler on the patio, who handed him a glass of champagne.

"Am I speaking to a retiree or a newly-minted investigator?" The colonel asked.

"Neither. I don't play tennis, my golf game is poor, and I have no desire to travel. In a group, I'm the most boring person there because other retirees have no interest in hearing what exciting forensic evidence I discovered during my career. As a result, I'd find myself at home, staring at the walls."

"What's left? You've already retired from the coroner's office."

"I'm going to be the assistant coroner and the associate medical examiner in another city," Labriola replied.

"In Favara?" Hunkler guessed.

"Doctor Albani and I quickly became like brothers during our brief time together. Since we're both unattached and I'm retired, at least from my coroner's position in Milan, he asked me to work with him."

"Good for you," Hunkler said. "Will you live at his home office or have your own place?"

"We'll perform our medical duties at his office. However, since Maria has moved here, we'll be living on her farm and managing it for her. We'll be busy."

"Go back. Maria has moved here?" Hunkler asked.

"With Mauro. I believe they live in that corner of the house," Labriola remarked, pointing to a set of windows. "We'll speak later," he said upon seeing Albani walk onto the patio and heading in that direction.

As Hunkler watched Labriola leave, he noticed Acosta walking onto the patio. His plane had arrived at Milan's Malpensa Airport an hour late due to delays in Venice, making him the last guest to arrive. Upon seeing him, Patrizia Palmieri marked the last check on her list of invitees and went inside to inform Lamberti, who was in charge of the arrangements. A few minutes later, Palmieri stepped out of the residence and nodded to the six-member musical ensemble, who had had been playing soft classical music and now transitioned to Pachelbel's Canon in D.

President Orsini and Bruno, both dressed in black tuxedos, and the priest from Canicatti, walked out of the residence in single file, stopping at center of the large patio and facing the doorway through which they had just exited. Shortly after, Lamberti appeared with Maria Bianco a dozen steps behind. The soon-to-be bride looked radiant in a white, floor-length sheath dress, holding a small bouquet of white roses. After taking their positions to the right of the priest, Maria handed her bouquet to Lamberti. She and Mauro then held hands, facing each other as they exchanged their vows.

"Both of us have known the pain of prematurely losing the spouse with whom we intended to spend our entire life, growing old and creating a library of memories together. When I became a widower, I thought that library would be all I'd have to look back on for the rest of my life, intending to remain single until my last breath because I believed that my happiness was forever behind me. I was wrong.

As I look at the beautiful woman before me, I am filled with joy once again. You bring out the best in me, surrounding me with your love, warmth, and understanding. You are my partner and the greatest adventure of my life. I promise to support and cherish you on this journey, hand in hand as we build our life together."

Maria, unable to hold back her tears, tightened her grip on her fiancé's hands. "I love you more than life itself. Through the hardship we've experienced, I've come to know the noble and honest person I'll soon call my husband. Your presence brightens even my darkest days, your kindness inspires me to be a better person, and the love you show me fills me with joy. I want to embark on this journey hand in hand with you, promising to stand by your side and support your dreams through both joy and hardship. I will cherish the life we build together and the library of memories we create."

Bruno placed the wedding ring on Maria's finger, and after she did the same, the priest pronounced them husband and wife, introducing *Mr. and Mrs. Mauro Bruno.*

Author's Notes

This is a work of fiction. The characters, government agencies, and corporate entities depicted are not intended to represent or implicate any real individuals, organizations, or entities. Any portrayals of corruption, illegal activities, or actions taken by governments, agencies, corporations, individuals, or institutions, along with their officials, are included solely to advance the storyline. These depictions do not suggest or imply any wrongdoing or illicit behavior by those who currently or previously held positions within these entities. However, as written below, substantial portions of *The Puppeteer* are factual.

Saudi Arabia exports approximately one billion dollars' worth of oil every day, which amounted to 13.39 million barrels in 2023. However, just as there is a finite quantity of any resource taken from the Earth, there is a limited supply of oil. Eventually, this supply will be depleted. *Experts* estimate that Saudi Arabia could run out of oil as early as the next decade, a revelation that surprised me during my research. Reading about this at ten in the evening, and afterward going to bed, I couldn't get to sleep pondering the implications and the geopolitical and economic changes that would follow. What would the Saudi's do before their wells ran dry? I knew they had invested around $1.6 trillion in diversifying their surplus earnings outside their country. Given their immense wealth and financial savvy, I believed they had the resources and intelligence to establish another area of dominance. But where? It was then, around midnight, that I asked myself: if I had the power to create a cartel similar to the one that exists for oil, which indispensable asset would I want to control? For some inexplicable reason, I found myself thinking about rare earth elements, probably because I'd researched the topic a month or two earlier, as I intended to include them in one of my upcoming manuscripts. Yes, I do a lot of research, much of which is interesting but not always significant enough to be woven into the storyline. However, this time was different. Therefore, in the very early morning, I began typing the outline for *The Puppeteer*, finishing around 6:00 am in an over-caffeinated state due to the large amount of Nespresso Intenso I consumed. The most challenging part of creating this outline was figuring out how to explain the significance of rare earth elements and incorporate them into the narrative without destroying the novel's momentum. In concept it's easy, but in practice it's more difficult—unless you're Michael Connelly or David Baldacci. If you're interested in learning more about the depleting oil supply and Saudi profits and foreign investments, you can explore the following links: (https://www. worldoil.com/news/2022/5/26/saudi-arabia-s-making-1-billion-from-oil-exports-every-day/#:~:text=%28Bloomberg%29%20 %E2%80%94%20Saudi%20Arabia%E2%80%99s%20oil%20 exports%20reached%20%2430,year%20on%20year%2C%20 the%20kingdom%E2%80%99s%20statistics%20office%20said.), (https://www.statista.com/statistics/265190/oil-production-in-saudi-arabia-in-barrels-per-day/), (https://www.bbc.com/news/ blogs-trending-30047096#:~:text=Saudis%20are%20feeling%20 insecure%20because%20oil%20prices%20recently,run%20 out%20of%20oil%20to%20export%20by%202030.), and (https:// mep.gov.sa/files/en/KnowledgeBase/EconomicReports/ Documents/Ministry%20of%20Economy%20&%20Planning%20 -%20Investment%20Report.pdf#:~:text=The%202022%20 UNCTAD%20World%20Investment%20Report%20indicates%20

that,%241.6%20Tn%20in%202021%2C%20growing%2064%25%20
from%202020.).

In an effort to find a more creative way to transport the kidnapped Pia Lamberti, I decided against using flex ties, which would allow her to continually attempt to free herself during the journey and distract from the story. Instead, I opted to sedate her with Propofol, the same drug commonly administered during colonoscopies. Any inaccuracies in explaining how an IV is inserted, the sedation process, and related details should be attributed to the author, who relied on various articles for this information and the descriptions used in this story (https://www.mdanderson. org/cancerwise/colonoscopy-anesthesia--7-things-to-know. h00-159618645.html#How%20Do%20Patients%20Benefit%20 from%20Deep%20Sedation%20For%20A%20Colonoscopy?) and (https://www.healthline.com/health/intravenous-medication- administration-what-to-know#introduction).

In Hollywood, the truth serum of choice is Sodium Pentothal, where all the interrogator has to do is ask a question, and the truth effortlessly emerges. However, in reality, this drug is an anesthetic that reduces the brain's metabolic activity, making it more difficult to think and consequently more challenging to lie. Understanding this, intelligence agencies train their spies to resist the effects of this drug. Additionally, one of the side effects of Sodium Pentothal is that, since the brain doesn't want to think, a person may end up saying whatever they believe the interrogator wants to hear. More information on the use of Sodium Pentothal can be found in an October 19, 2023 article in *ScienceABC* by Armaan Gvalani at (https://www.scienceabc.com/eyeopeners/are-truth-serums-real. html).

The CIA has conducted experiments involving various psychoactive drugs to extract information during interrogations. One notable program, codenamed Project Medication, involved the use of a benzodiazepine drug known as midazolam, or Versed, which is commonly used by doctors for procedural sedation. While decreasing the anxiety of the patient and inducing sleepiness, it also produces anterograde amnesia, making it unlikely that the detainee would remember being interrogated or what they disclosed to their captor. The CIA primarily administers this drug to individuals they believe would be more willing to talk if they were in a relaxed state and felt less intimidated by their surroundings. You can read more about the CIA's use of this psychoactive drug at (https://www.theguardian.com/us-news/2018/nov/13/cia-doctors-truth-serum-terror-suspects), (https://bigthink.com/the-present/cia-truth-serum-9-11/), and (https://www.cnn.com/2018/11/13/politics/cia-documents-truth-serum-drug-interrogations/index.html).

The description of Mafia tattoos is accurate and taken from a March 24, 2023 article by Jack in *TattooQuestions.com* (https://tattooquestions.com/sicilian-tattoos/), and a September 5, 2023 article by Gidian in *Inked Euphoria* (https://inkedeuphoria.com/omerta-tattoo-meaning/). The symbolism of Mafia tattoos is quite complex and goes far beyond my description, which I kept brief to maintain the flow of the story. For example, a tattoo depicting a dagger piercing a skull symbolizes death, danger, and the willingness to resort to violence in order to protect one's loyalty and honor, with the skull representing mortality and the transient nature of life. An omerta tattoo may feature a pair of sealed lips, which signifies silence, secrecy, and solidarity. You can find more on this symbology by going to the links above.

Maurizio Di Gati and Giuseppe Falsone were Sicilian Mafia leaders in the Agrigento province (https://www.famousfix.com/list/gangsters-from-the-province-of-agrigento#:~:text=Maurizio%20Di%20Gati%20%28Racalmuto%2C%20July%2010%2C%201966%29%20is,Agrigento%20province%20before%20his%20arrest%20in%20November%202006.). Although members of the Italian Mafia are known for their numerous tattoos—some even featuring the faces of former family leaders as a sign of respect—it is unclear whether any Agrigento family members, past or present, had the images of Di Gati and Falsone tattooed on them. However, for the sake of the story, and as a way to verify they were from Agrigento and not Rome, I ensured these faces appeared on the bodies of the corpses.

The information on bulletproof vests is taken from a March 21, 2024 article by Aaron Davila in *Atomic Defense*, which is referenced below. Bulletproof vests fall into two categories: concealable and tactical. Additionally, they can be classified as either soft or hard body armor.

Soft armor vests, as explained in the novel, are composed of multiple layers of Kevlar. In contrast, hard armor vests are constructed from materials such as ceramic or polyethylene. Concealable vests are specifically designed to be worn underneath clothing, providing protection against small arms fire, including rounds from 9mm, .44 Magnum, and .357 SIG firearms. I was impressed to learn that a concealable vest, which weighs just under six pounds, can stop a powerful round like the .44 Magnum. Additionally, according to *Atomic Defense*, these vests are made with moisture-wicking fabrics that keep the wearer cool and dry, even in hot climates and during extended use.

Tactical vests, in contrast, are worn over regular clothing and are generally heavier because they include extra protective features. A standard military tactical vest typically weighs between eleven and seventeen pounds, while vests designed to stop armor-piercing rounds—projectiles that can travel at nearly three thousand feet per second—can weigh between eighteen and twenty-two pounds. You can read more on bulletproof vests at (https://www.atomicdefense.com/blogs/news/the-ultimate-guide-to-choosing-the-best-bulletproof-vest).

The effects of being shot while wearing a bulletproof vest can vary significantly depending on several factors, including the type of vest, the caliber of the weapon, the type of ammunition used, and the distance from which the shot is fired. Ultimately, the primary function of the vest is to prevent bullets from penetrating the material and to distribute the impact energy over a larger area. Since the energy transferred to an individual can vary, this leads to a wide range of experiences. Some may suffer broken ribs, have the wind knocked out of them, feel as though they've been hit with a baseball bat, experience a stinging sensation, or in some cases, feel almost nothing at all. In researching this area, I gathered information from the following: (https://sciencing.com/effects-after-being-shot-in-a-bullet-proof-vest-13583728.html), (https://bac-tactical.com/what-does-it-feel-like-to-get-shot-wearing-a-bulletproof-vest/), and (https://www.ponderweasel.com/shot-wearing-a-bulletproof-vest/).

In the story, I noted that the developer may have received variances to install the natural gas pipeline under the street instead of routing it through the large backyards of residential properties, thereby meeting the required distance specifications outlined by code. I did this to give a plausible explanation as to why the bombmaker was unaware of the pipeline location before situating the explosive devices. While I prefer using actual numbers and statistics in my narrative, I was unable to find the setback requirements for utilities in this specific area of France and, believe me, I tried. Therefore, I modified information taken from the article below to fit the situation (https://www.utilitysmarts.com/gas/natural-gas/how-close-can-you-build-to-a-natural-gas-pipeline/).

In researching the science of how a vehicle tumbles when it goes off a mountainside road, I read a number of articles about the physics of such mishaps, finding out that vehicles typically land on their roof or strike the ground nose-first when the fall isn't from a considerable height.

When a vehicle drops off the edge, the front tends to go over first, producing an upward force on the back axle which causes it to lift, as the front is already descending. When this happens, physics dictates there's a corresponding torque, meaning the vehicle tumbles. If the fall isn't significant, the car usually rotates only a quarter to half turn, resulting in it landing on either its front or its roof, with gravity pulling down on the engine. However, if the height is significant, as with the Touran, the vehicle might come to rest in any position, the author abstractly choosing the roof. The best information describing the science of a car tumble came from the following article: (https://physics.stackexchange.com/questions/147622/car-driving-falling-off-of-a-cliff-will-it-land-upright).

A concussion occurs when a sudden movement of the head causes the brain to strike the interior of the skull or twist within it. Although symptoms can vary widely from person to person and may take hours or even days to appear, I opted for Donati's symptoms to become immediately noticeable. The symptoms of a concussion were taken from an April 3, 2024 article by Angelica Bottaro in *Verywell Health* (https://www.verywellhealth.com/how-to-tell-if-you-have-a-concussion-5188754). I also chose only a couple of the many possible symptoms of a concussion because I didn't want Donati to be sidelined in the story for too long; I needed him back in action. Furthermore, it goes without saying that you should absolutely ignore the medical treatments and advice rendered by the author, which were done solely for the sake of the narrative, as my medical expertise is limited to applying Band-Aids.

Favara has a population of approximately 32,000 and is located five miles northeast of Agrigento. The area that is now Favara was first settled during the Copper Age, around 2400-1900 BC, the name derived from the Arab word "fawwāra," which means "spring water." To learn more about the Greek, Muslim, Roman, Norman, and other settlers who have occupied the region around Favara, you can visit (https://sicilyenjoy.com/en/favara-the-charm-of-a-thousand-year-history/). I took some liberties in describing the town and its distance from the highway because I wanted to prevent the sound of the crash from attracting a crowd. I also transformed a gentle hilly slope into a gray rock embankment to create a crash that would utterly demolish the Touran to such an extent that those in the Hummer would believe the occupants of the VW had perished.

Many small towns in Sicily have experienced depopulation as

younger generations move to larger cities like Milan and Rome in search of excitement and better job opportunities. As a result, these small communes have experienced an unemployment rate averaging fourteen percent, compared to just over eight percent on the Italian mainland.

To address this issue, Favara took action in 2010 by converting several semi-abandoned buildings into what is now known as the Farm Cultural Park. This hub hosts exhibitions and showcases local and international artists, as well as an international short film festival during the summer. The transformation has attracted shops, wine bars, and various retail establishments, revitalizing the town and drawing in tourists from around the world. Additionally, it has encouraged some younger people to return to Favara.

I drove through this revitalized area on the day I explored Siculiana and Agrigento, hoping to find a small town within a reasonable distance of both places, of which there were several, where I could set the crash and build a story that focused on two residents who were pivotal to the evolution of the story. That search came to an end upon entering Favara, where I quickly fell in love with its friendly locals, thereby making it impossible to consider another commune for Dr. Albani and Maria to reside in, or for Labriola to retire. You can read more about Favara and the transformation of this community at (https://www.sicilianpost.it/en/a-dreamers-utopia-the-small-miracle-of-favara-cultural-park/), and (https://www.sicily.co.uk/nearby_town/favara/#:~:text=The%20first%20settlement%20of%20Favara%20was%20founded%20in,the%20construction%20of%20the%20current%20old%20town%20centre.).

As most of the action in the novel takes place in Sicily, I researched the historical, cultural, gastronomical, and other differences between Italians residing on what I'll refer to as the mainland, and those in Sicily. I began by examining the island's history. Due to its strategic location, Sicily has been conquered numerous times over the past two millennia. It has been invaded by the Arabs, Byzantines, Phoenicians, Greeks, Moors, Normans, and Romans, among others. Each of these groups contributed to a unique genetic pool and cultural identity that distinguishes Sicilians from other Italians.

For example, notable differences exist between northern and southern Italians in terms of physical appearance and attitudes, which can be found in an October 18, 2023 article in *Curiosify* (https://curiosify.net/northern-italian-vs-southern-italian-appearance/) and a June 30, 2014 article by M.E. Evans (https://survivinginitaly.com/2014/07/30/northern-italians-versus-southern-italians-are-they-really-that-different/). Sicilians and people from the southern parts of the Italian mainland typically share similarities with surrounding populations, influenced by the region's proximity to Mediterranean countries and historical ties to North Africa. This gene pool reflects attributes from Greek, Roman, and Arab ancestry, resulting in Sicilians generally having olive skin, brown eyes, and dark hair. In contrast, those living in northern Italy, which borders Switzerland, France, Austria, and Slovenia, tend to be taller, and often have fair skin, lighter hair, and lighter eye colors.

Location has significantly influenced the attitudes and behaviors associated with different regions in Italy. Northern Italy is highly industrialized, while the south relies on an agriculture-based economy. As a result, cities in the north tend to be more prosperous. This divide has led to distinct socio-economic perspectives between the two regions. People from the south often view those from the north as the "New Yorkers" of Italy, perceiving them as capitalists who prioritize wealth over relationships. Conversely, people from the north sometimes regard southerners as uneducated, narrow-minded, and overly focused on family and religion. Subsequently, there's not a great deal of warmth between these groups.

Having spent significant time in both regions, I can confirm that there is some truth to the stereotypes. However, I also believe that Italians share commonalities, one of which is a unique zest for life that they seem to embrace more fully than people in many other countries where I've spent a similar amount of time. That said, my perspective may be influenced by my family's history—my grandparents immigrating from Siculiana, Italy, when they were eighteen, their ancestors having been fishermen in southeastern Sicily for generations. I felt very fortunate to have my grandparents living with us as I grew up. However, if I ever referred to them as being of Italian ancestry instead of Sicilian heritage, I was immediately corrected. This distinction may seem unusual, given that Sicily is part of Italy, but Sicilians take great pride in their unique identity. As a result, Sicilian and not Italian is the recognized language of the island, with villages and towns having a variant dialect that's specific to it.

Due to its strategic location, Sicily has been invaded numerous times over the past two millennia. The island has seen invasions by the Arabs, Byzantines, Phoenicians, Greeks, Moors, Normans, and Romans, among others. Each of these groups has contributed to a unique genetic mix and cultural identity that distinguishes Sicilians from other Italians. These historical influences are also reflected in Sicilian cuisine (https://www.ncesc.com/geographic-faq/how-are-sicilians-different-from-italians/#:~:text=Sicilians%20can%20have%20a%20wide%20range%20of%20physical,These%20characteristics%20are%20typically%20seen%20in%20Mediterranean%20populations.) and (https://curiosify.net/northern-italian-vs-southern-italian-appearance/).

Pasta alla Norma is one of my two Kryptonites, and during my research in Sicily, I enjoyed it daily for lunch or dinner. For the sake of the storyline, I mentioned that most Sicilian restaurants in Rome don't carry it on their menus. However, that's not accurate, as I've had the pleasure of savoring this wonderful dish at Sicilian restaurants in the Eternal City. Miriana, from the Four Seasons' Anciovi restaurant, shared her recipe with me, and my wife has successfully prepared it for us on numerous occasions after my less-than-stellar attempt at replicating the dish.

My other Kryptonite, as noted in previous Mauro Bruno novels, is cannoli—crispy pastry shells filled with a sweet, slightly tangy ricotta-based cream that has hints of vanilla, cinnamon, and citrus. Sara, a friend of ours in Taormina whom you may have seen in one of my blogs, knew where the locals went to get these delightful desserts and kept me well-supplied while I conducted research for this novel.

Like Montanari, I too enjoy a great pasta sauce. While I prefer the Bolognese style, which is a meat-based sauce, you may have noticed that I didn't include any meat in the sauce preparation mentioned in this novel, nor in those of previous Mauro Bruno books. The reason for this is that the Savant wanted to keep the preparation simple. He made sauce not only for his consumption but also as a form of therapy—an escape from the intensity of his work or a way to clear his mind while reflecting on a problem. Montanari's recipe was taken, at least in part, from a February 25, 2024 article by Gianna Ferrini in *Mortadella Head*, which you can find at (https://mortadellahead. com/italian-tomato-sauce-recipe-homemade-authentic/).

Information about the history of the Mafia was sourced from Adam Volle's writings in *Britannica* (https://www.britannica.com/ topic/Sicilian-Mafia), while statistics regarding the number of Mafia families in Sicily were derived from (https://en.wikipedia.org/ wiki/List_of_Sicilian_Mafia_clans#:~:text=In%20Sicily%2C%20 there%20are%2094,Mafia%20families%20subject%20to%2029%20 mandamenti.). Although I associated the term *black hand* with the Mafia, it was actually a popular name for secret societies in the nineteenth century, particularly among Spanish anarchists. It was also associated with a secret society of Italians in the 1880s—which was the precursor for the Mafia, the term denoting a method of extortion where individuals could be injured or killed if they failed to comply with the Mafia's demands. For more information about this and other terms related to organized crime, you can refer to an article by Angela Tung in *Mental Floss,* which you can find at (https://www. mentalfloss.com/article/68509/10-gangster-pieces-mob-lingo).

Although the terms "Mafia" and "Camorra" are sometimes

used interchangeably, they refer to different criminal organizations that operate in distinct regions of Italy. The Camorra is a loose network of independent criminal groups connected by a common culture, primarily based in the Campania region, which includes Naples. The name "Camorra" comes from the Neapolitan dialect and translates to "group" or "gang."

In contrast, the term "Mafia," which originates from the Sicilian dialect, means "boldness" or "bravado." Unlike the Camorra, the Mafia is a highly structured organization with a hierarchical system and clearly established rules. My explanation on these differences was taken from an article by Shawn Manaher in *The Content Authority*, which you can find at (https://thecontentauthority. com/blog/camorra-vs-mafia#:~:text=The%20answer%20is%20 both.%20Camorra%20and%20Mafia%20are,have%20a%20 long%20history%20of%20operating%20in%20Italy.).

During my research I found it fascinating that the Catholic church had a relationship with the Mafia, relying on them in the late nineteenth century to monitor its extensive property holdings in Sicily and keep its tenant farmers in line (https://www.history.com/ topics/crime/origins-of-the-mafia). That association endured and led to a tolerance of the Mafia. This association persisted and resulted in a degree of tolerance towards the Mafia. A clear example of this was in 1964, when the Cardinal Archbishop of Palermo, Ernesto Ruffini, publicly stated that the Mafia was merely an insignificant minority of criminals and that the negative portrayal of them was a slander spread by communists to dishonor Sicily. (https://www.dw.com/ en/catholic-church-was-inconsistent-with-mafia/a-36366247).

The Mafia initially began as an informal alliance of individuals known as mafie, who protected landowners and towns from foreign invaders and oppressors. Over time, it evolved into an organized criminal society that broadened its activities to extortion, crimes aimed at landowners, gaining control over Sicily's construction sector, and smuggling goods onto the island. In the 1960s, competition among families for these lucrative opportunities led to violent confrontations, including shootouts and car bombings, which resulted in the deaths of police officers and innocent bystanders. As these killings continued and attracted public outrage, Italian law enforcement intensified efforts to arrest Mafia leaders on the island. Subsequently, they began focusing resources on combating criminal activities within Sicily, rather than directing their attention solely to the Italian mainland or maritime operations.

Today, the most profitable crime family in Italy is not located in Sicily, but in Calabria, where the 'Ndrangheta family is based. A significant player in the global drug trade, their apparatus extends to countries such as Germany, Switzerland, Australia, Canada, and the United States, as well as maintaining extensive ties throughout Latin America (https://theconversation.com/meet-the-ndrangheta-and-why-its-time-to-bust-some-myths-about-the-calabrian-mafia-54075). In addition to drug trafficking, the 'Ndrangheta engages in money laundering, extortion, and various other criminal enterprises for profit. According to a December 10, 2018 CNN article by Tim Lister titled *Inside Europe's most powerful mafia – the 'Ndrangheta*, it's estimated that they generate $60 billion in revenue annually and may control as much as eighty percent of the cocaine entering Europe (https://www.cnn.com/2018/12/08/europe/ndrangheta-mafia-raids-analysis-intl/index.html).

Due to the extraordinary profits generated by organized crime, its members receive substantial compensation. Similar to the corporate world, higher positions come with greater salaries. Members are given a monthly stipend, a term preferred over "salary." After reading an October 16, 2014 article in *FYI* by Roberto Saviano, I learned that the newest member of a Mafia family, known as a picciotto d'onore (translated as "boy of honor" or informally as a "soldier"), receives a monthly stipend ranging from $2,500 to $4,000. With experience and increased responsibilities, this can rise to between $6,500 and $13,000 per month.

As one climbs the hierarchical ladder—such as becoming one of the boss's right-hand men—the monthly stipend increases to between $32,000 and $38,000. If a member ascends to the position of vicecapo or capodecina, which is second-in-command to the boss (similar to Caruso in my novel), they can expect a stipend of approximately $130,000 a month. Given these figures, one can only speculate about the earnings of the capomandamento, Godfather, or capo dei capi, the leader at the top of the organization (https://www.vice. com/en/article/av4m78/organized-crime-pays-0000477-v21n10).

According to a November 12, 2008 article by *ABC News*, citing numbers which are exceedingly low compared to today's dollars, Italy's four largest crime syndicates—the Sicilian Cosa Nostra, the Camorra from Naples, the Calabrian 'Ndrangheta, and the Sacra Corona Unita in Puglia—generate approximately $165 billion in revenue each year, with net profits around $90 billion. The primary sources of income for these crime families, in order of profitability, are drug trafficking, illegal waste disposal, loan sharking, and extortion (also known as the protection racket). (https://abcnews.go.com/International/ story?id=6238022&page=1#:~:text=Italy%27s%20four%20 organized-crime%20syndicates%20--%20Sicily%27s%20Cosa%20 Nostra%2C,after%20investments%20and%20expenses%2C%20 according%20to%20the%20study.).

While I mentioned that Sciarra had numerous police officers, judges, and government officials on his payroll throughout the Agrigento province, including towns like Castrofilippo and Canicatti, this was a fictional element created to heighten the story's tension suggesting that this Mafioso could call on his 'soldiers' to search for Maria and Bruno, with the local police and government officials, allegedly on his payroll, aiding in the effort.

In contrast to this fictional portrayal, I have spent many hours in small towns and villages across Sicily, including those mentioned, and I felt completely safe. I found the people of Sicily to be incredibly friendly and generous. Therefore, if you're considering a trip to the island—perhaps to see the filming locations of "The White

Lotus" and "The Godfather"—I encourage you to go. You will undoubtedly fall in love with this part of Italy.

As written, the French Ministry of Foreign Affairs is located at 37 Quai d'Orsay in Paris. This three-story building was constructed between 1844 and 1855, although construction was interrupted by the French Revolution of 1848. It boasts one of the most beautiful interiors of any building in Paris, which you can view through the link provided below. Most of the ministry faces the Seine River, offering magnificent views from the reception rooms. Since the majority of the building is aligned parallel to the riverbank, the architect placed the entrance points at either end of the structure, with the main entrance located to the west (the right side).

That said, I committed several transgressions and changed things a bit for the sake of the story. My first transgression was necessary to ensure the sniper had an unobstructed view of the ministry courtyard without being detected. Therefore, I positioned him at the top of a ten-story building located three-quarters of a mile away. To my knowledge, no such building exists, nor is there a gravel driveway for VIP arrivals where the minister greets dignitaries. However, both alterations were necessary for the story as it provided the sniper a clear shot to kill the minister and Acardi. The addition of the portico was my third transgression, as it was necessary to obstruct the sniper's view of his targets. You can learn more about the Ministry of Foreign Affairs and the building it occupies at (https://www.diplomatie.gouv.fr/en/the-ministry-and-its-network/the-work-of-the-ministry-for-europe-and-foreign-affairs/discover-the-ministry-history-virtual-tour-etc/our-buildings/the-quai-d-orsay/).

The information on Claymore mines is accurate, as is the reference to the mathematics that are utilized in the construction of sophisticated explosive devices. The motivation for writing this part of my story arose after reading an article by David C. Viano about the injuries and fatalities experienced by individuals in armored vehicles exposed to explosive shock waves. This article was published in the February 13, 2023 edition of *Scientific Reports* (https://www.nature.com/articles/s41598-023-29686-7) and includes a detailed explanation of the science behind explosions, such as how to calculate peak overpressure and other blast parameters. The article is quite technical, and clearly explains that achieving a specific outcome, and not a large explosion producing an unknown amount of damage over an indeterminate area, requires precise calculations when designing the bomb—the mathematics dictating the size and shape of the device, the amount and type of explosive to be used, and the composition, arrangement, and shape of ancillary destructive materials, such as steel balls, that are to be incorporated into it. The discussion about the Kingery-Bulmash blast perimeter calculator, which provides data on shock wave arrival times, shock front velocities, and other parameters, is accurate. You can find this information in the article I referenced regarding shock waves. For those of you who are shock wave or physics addicts, you can read more about this calculator at (https://unsaferguard.org/unsaferguard/kingery-bulmash). Likewise, if you'd like to learn more about the Friedlander waveform equation, please go to (https://www.ncbi.nlm.nih.gov/pmc/articles/PMC4841653/).

The specifics of a C-4 explosion were taken from a February 27, 2024 article by Tom Harris in *HowStuffWorks* (https://science.howstuffworks.com/c-4.htm), (https://www.digitaltrends.com/news/how-does-a-blast-wave-work/), and (https://everything.explained.today/C-4_(explosive)/). As I mentioned in previous novels, C-4 is a highly stable explosive that requires both extreme heat and a shockwave from a detonator or blasting cap to set it off. A gunshot, fire, microwaves, or dropping it won't do the job. When it does explode, it rapidly decomposes into nitrogen, carbon oxide, and water.

In movies, we often see someone removing the blasting cap or detonator to prevent C-4 from exploding. However, this technique may not always be effective. For example, a blasting cap could be designed so that so long as it receives a clock pulse, there's no detonation. However, if the blasting cap is removed and the clock pulse is interrupted, the C-4 ignites. Similarly, there's a booby trap device known as a comb switch that can detect pull or push pressure and contains its own detonator. Therefore, in contrast to Hollywood scriptwriters, removing the detonator or blasting cap from the C-4 can unintentionally trigger an explosion. Bence and Acardi knew this, which is why they jumped out the hotel window, leaving the bomb inside the room instead of throwing it outside where it could potentially harm bystanders. For more information on C-4 detonation and anti-tampering devices please go to (https://electronics.stackexchange.com/questions/438440/detecting-blast-cap-removal-from-c4).

It's interesting that, while I've watched many action movies where characters escape explosions by diving to the ground, allowing the blast to pass over them, or hiding behind an obstruction until the fire or shockwave subsides, those actions are not feasible in real life. This is because an explosive shock wave travels at a speed of over twenty-six thousand five hundred feet per second, resulting in an almost instantaneous impact. Consequently, before you can react to the explosion, the shock wave will have already reached you. Additionally, the speed and inertial energy of the shock wave is especially damaging to air-filled organs such as the lungs and ears, damage and mortality being a function of the power of the wave and distance from the device. You can read more about the composition and operational characteristics of a Claymore mine at (https://man.fas.org/dod-101/sys/land/m18-claymore.htm) and (https://www.globalsecurity.org/military/library/policy/army/fm/23-23/CH2.htm).

If you're a programmer, hacker, or computer geek, my explanation of how Montanari accessed the French Minister of Foreign Affairs' computer will seem overly simplistic and on the fuzzy edge of realistic. However, in researching how someone might hack a computer and transfer data from a robustly protected system without being discovered, I learned there are numerous methods to do this, including the use of malware as discussed in the novel. I tried to avoid making the story overly scientific, as I didn't want the technical aspects of the crime to overshadow the narrative, although I sometimes have a tendency to do that because I'm fascinated by how someone can achieve the seemingly impossible. Therefore, I went with the simpler approach, which was to disable the EDR software, although the brevity of my explanation of EDR, or selection of this method, might send a tech-savvy reader to their local bar. In describing Montanari's hack, I relied on the following articles and discussion boards, whose links are below, and incorporated their wisdom into my story.

(https://www.reddit.com/r/blackhat/comments/u8e67y/ how_to_transfer_files_from_a_company_computer/?rdt=63787), (https://massive.io/content-security/data-theft-hackers-steal-files-remotely/), (https://www.crowdstrike.com/cybersecurity-101/ endpoint-security/endpoint-detection-and-response-edr/), and (https://whatismyipaddress.com/ip-address-spoofing).

In researching how hackers penetrate sophisticated firewalls, such as those used by nation-states, I found some surprising information, even though I don't fully grasp all the complexities. I learned that a smartphone can record the acoustic signals or sound waves produced when someone types on a computer keyboard, and by using a program that employs AI, these sounds can be deciphered with up to ninety-five percent accuracy.

Although I used this technique in my story to have Montanari obtain login and password information, in real life, someone could activate the recording feature on their phone and capture what is being typed, even during a Zoom call. For more information on this method of gathering data, go to (https://neurosciencenews. com/smartphone-typing-attack-14881/), (https://www.reddit. com/r/MechanicalKeyboards/comments/bx9ev1/is_it_normal_ for_keys_to_sound_different_when/?rdt=50855), (https://www. reddit.com/r/technology/comments/15n0r2i/ai_can_identify_ keystrokes_by_just_the_sound_of/), (https://www.9news.

com.au/technology/mobile-phone-hack-how-smartphones-can-listen-to-your-keyboard-technology-news/b446c4da-3763-427c-810e-1838848a5008#:~:text=Researchers%20from%20 SMU%27s%20Darwin%20Deason%20Institute%20for%20 Cybersecurity,keys%20were%20struck%20and%20what%20 they%20were%20typing.).

The name "rare earth" originated from an unusual black rock discovered by a miner in Ytterby, Sweden, in 1788. This ore was termed "rare" because it had not been encountered before, and "earth" was a common 18th-century geological term for minerals that could be dissolved in acid. (https://www.sciencehistory.org/ education/classroom-activities/role-playing-games/case-of-rare-earth-elements/history-future/). Therefore, the term "rare" in "rare earth elements" (REE) does not necessarily indicate that they exist in very small quantities or are difficult to find, as they're scattered in trace amounts throughout the earth's crust. In fact, some of these elements are quite abundant. The only rarity is finding them in mineable quantities that can be concentrated and purified on a significant scale.

REE mining operations typically require extracting vast quantities of raw ore to obtain even a small amount of a specific element. For instance, cerium has a concentration of about 60 parts per million, while thulium and lutetium are present at only 0.5 parts per million (https://www.usgs.gov/centers/ national-minerals-information-center/rare-earths-statistics-and-information). As a result, the cost of establishing an operation to extract rare earth elements (REE) from the ground and process them into oxides is about $500 million. (https://www.clearias.com/ rare-earth-elements-ree/).

Rare earth elements are often described as the vitamins of industrial society in the twenty-first century, with demand projected to increase as much as sixfold by 2040 (https://hir.harvard.edu/ not-so-green-technology-the-complicated-legacy-of-rare-earth-mining/). For instance, Terbium is used to create phosphors for televisions, computers, and smartphone screens. Yttrium emits invisible light and is utilized in the construction of lasers. Erbium is vital for fiber optic cables, particularly those that stretch thousands of kilometers on the seafloor, as it enhances signal strength.

Neodymium plays a significant role in ninety-five percent of the world's permanent magnets; it helps generate vibrations in smartphones, produces sound in earbuds and headphones, facilitates data reading and writing in hard disk drives, and creates the magnetic fields used in MRI machines. Samarium is versatile; it enhances signals from radar and satellites and is used in high-speed motors, generators, speed sensors in cars and airplanes, and some moving parts of heat-seeking missiles, because of its resistance to heat and corrosion. You get the point. Most people wouldn't recognize the name of most of these elements and yet, without them, some of the things we take for granted in our life wouldn't exist. (https://www.sciencenews.org/article/rare-earth-elements-properties-technology). Additional information on the use of REE can be found by going to (https://www.ispionline.it/en/publication/scramble-africas-rare-earths-china-not-alone-30725), (https://geology.com/articles/rare-earth-elements/), and (https://www.bing.com/search?q=what+technologies+use+rare+earth+metals&pc=GD08&form=GDCCSB&ptag=18303&ntref=1).

No one has a monopoly on REE mining in Africa, and there's no evidence of corruption in the leases, production, and ownership obtained by nations from the governments on that continent. Besides enviable deposits of rare earth elements, Africa holds thirty percent of the world's mineral reserves (https://www.unep.org/regions/africa/our-work-africa), forty percent of its gold, ninety percent of its platinum and chromium, eight percent of its natural gas, and the largest global reserves of cobalt and diamonds. Countries like China, Russia, and the United States, among others, compete for the rights to extract these elements, minerals, and precious metals in Africa.

Pollution is a significant concern in rare earth mining. According to the *Harvard International* Review article by Jaya Nayar, whose link appears above, there are two main methods for extracting rare earth elements, both of which release toxic chemicals. The first method involves removing topsoil to create leach ponds. Chemicals are then added to dissolve the rare earth elements, allowing them to concentrate in the pond for extraction and refinement. This process raises the risk of toxic chemicals leaking into groundwater.

The second method involves drilling of holes in the ground, after which PVC pipes and rubber hoses are inserted, and chemicals pumped through them. This also creates a leaching pond and an enormous amount of toxic waste. For every ton of rare earth extracted, 2,000 tons of toxic waste are produced, including one ton of radioactive residue. Subsequently, the cost to obtain REEs in a purified form is extremely high, as noted above, making these elements more expensive than gold, silver, or platinum (https://www.workandmoney.com/s/most-valuable-metals-couldnt-live-without-1456f8f367af404d).

The REE market is projected to grow 10.8 percent annually (https://www.gminsights.com/industry-analysis/rare-earth-metals-market#:~:text=Rare%20Earth%20Metals%20Market%20size%20was%20valued%20at,propelling%20use%20in%20magnet%20and%20optical%20instrument%20application.). According to a December 29, 2022 article in *Brookings* by Gracelin Baskaran, China currently controls sixty percent of global REE production and eighty-five percent of its processing. However, African countries are well-positioned to leverage their rare earth resources to capitalize on the rapidly increasing demand. Some experts believe these countries could eventually rival or complement China's dominance in this sector. (https://www.brookings.edu/articles/could-africa-replace-china-as-the-worlds-source-of-rare-earth-elements/). Half of REE deposits in Africa reside in Mozambique, South Africa, Namibia, Tanzania, Malawi, Burundi, Kenya, Zambia, and the Democratic Republic of the Congo, (https://www.bing.com/search?q=rare+earth+deposits+from+africa&FORM=QSRE5)

(https://www.bing.com/search?q=could+africa+produce+more+rare+earth+metals+than+china&pc=GD08&form=GDCCSB&ptag=18303&ntref=1), these countries projected to provide ten percent of global demand by 2029, up from almost zero percent today (https://www.bing.com/search?q=does%20africa%20have%20vast%20rare%20earth%20metal%20supplies&qs=n&form=QBRE&sp=-1&ghc=1&lq=0&pq=does%20africa%20have%20vast%20rare%20earth%20metal%20supplies&sc=0-47&sk=&cvid=105134ADC7B24F33BB2923B75712005E&ghsh=0&ghacc=0&ghpl=). Information on countries having REE deposits can be found at (https://investingnews.com/daily/resource-investing/critical-metals-investing/rare-earth-investing/rare-earth-reserves-country/), (https://www.bing.com/search?q=locations+of+rare+earth+metas+in+the+world&pc=GD08&form=GDCCSB&ptag=18303). You can read more about the Minerals Security Partnership at (https://thediplomat.com/2023/05/latin-and-south-america-are-a-key-to-the-united-states-critical-minerals-puzzle/).

Interestingly, according to a January 20, 2023 article in *ScienceNews* by Erin Wayman, only one percent of rare earth elements are currently recycled because the process requires hazardous chemicals, such as hydrochloric acid, and substantial heat requirements, which demands a considerable amount of energy. As a result, recovering these elements can be economically unfeasible given their small yields. For instance, a hard disk drive may contain only a few grams of a rare earth element, while many other products might include just milligrams. In contrast, between fifteen and seventy percent of metals like copper, iron, aluminum, nickel, and tin can be recycled efficiently. (https://www.sciencenews.org/article/recycling-rare-earth-elements-hard-new-methods). Subsequently, the limited recycling of REEs has contributed to a continuous increase in their market prices.

The details regarding countries that offer tax exemptions for corporate, personal, and capital gains taxes are accurate and sourced from a May 29, 2023 article in *International Wealth* (https://internationalwealth.info/en/offshore-taxes/which-country-is-tax-free-for-business/). I found it interesting that, depending on the country where your company is registered, it may be possible to avoid paying corporate, personal, or capital gains taxes, depending on your business activity and assuming the money is brought into the country and not generated by activities within it. For instance the Cayman Islands, the UAE, and Bahrain have was no personal, corporate, or capital gains taxes, assuming for the latter two that the money does not come from oil or gas companies. Additionally, Bermuda, the Turks and Caicos Islands, and the British Virgin Islands impose no corporate or capital gains taxes. Moreover, income generated outside of Saint Kitts and Nevis and Panama is tax-exempt.

A list of benefits offered by these tax havens and others can be found in the link above. However, you might want to think twice about putting your money in some of these countries, such as East Sahara and Somalia. East Sahara is a disputed territory with official relations with only thirty-five countries, and Somalia is, well, Somalia.

My apologies to the Le Basile Hotel in Paris for the havoc I inflicted in my novel when I destroyed part of the second floor of your hotel. I chose this lovely establishment as the location for Mattei's attempted murder of Acardi because it was within walking distance of the Chez Monsieur restaurant and located on a quiet side street with almost no traffic, which is how I discovered it while exploring the area in preparation for this novel.

Some hotels have a way of making you feel good just by seeing them, and Le Basile, with its twenty-seven rooms and the ambiance of a large, splendid home, was one of those places. When I entered the hotel and asked if they would mind me looking around, the staff graciously allowed me to explore the lobby and other areas that didn't intrude on the privacy of their guests. After touring a bit of the interior and walking around outside, I realized that it was perfect for my storyline, although I took some liberties in describing the interior for the sake of the narrative. You can read more about this hotel at (https://www.hotelbasile.com/).

One of the interesting things you'll notice when visiting Sicily is the abundance of prickly pear cacti. These plants were something that I previously, and inaccurately, assumed were only prevalent throughout Mexico. That's where it originated, the prickly pear even appearing on the Mexican flag under the eagle. However, it turns out that although Christopher Columbus brought it to Europe, the Saracens imported it to Sicily in 827, where it literally took root and became part of the island's landscape, Sicily eventually becoming the second largest producer of prickly pears in the world next to Mexico. (https://www.sicilyactive.com/en/prickly-pear-sicily).

There are over two thousand species of prickly pear cacti (https://succulentadvisor.com/195-opuntia-varieties-types-of-prickly-pear/) and (https://housegrail.com/types-of-prickly-pear-cactus/). However, the Opuntia ficus-indica mentioned in the story is native to the United States and Mexico, not Sicily, the author needing the height of that particular variety of prickly pear to conceal Maria and Bruno. If you visit my website (alanrefkin.com), you'll see Sicily's deep connection with these plants, as they're often found in pots on patios, in front of buildings, and along the streets. Here are photos of these plants taken in the small town of Siculiana (https://i0.wp.com/alanrefkin.com/wp-content/uploads/2024/04/IMG_0797-1.jpeg?ssl=1) (https://i0.wp.com/alanrefkin.com/wp-content/uploads/2024/04/IMG_0791-rotated.jpeg?ssl=1), and (https://i0.wp.com/alanrefkin.com/wp-content/uploads/2024/04/IMG_0820.jpeg?ssl=1).

I took some creative liberties when describing the port of Civitavecchia for the sake of the story as I needed Lamberti and her entourage to arrive in Rome unnoticed and it was the perfect seaport to make that happen. Although over 3.3 million cruise passengers pass through Civitavecchia each year—making it the second busiest cruise ship port in Europe after Barcelona—I made it appear much larger than it actually is. Additionally, I invented an obsolete section of the port that does not exist, allowing the seaplane to dock and disembark its passengers without being seen.

Interestingly, Civitavecchia was not my first choice for where I intended Lamberti's seaplane to land in Rome. Initially, I'd chosen the Marina of Rome, which has a seaplane base and is just ten minutes by car from the main airport, Fiumicino. So, why didn't I opt for that location instead of Civitavecchia?

The decision ultimately came down to my belief that when the seaplane from Malta arrived—shortly before six in the morning—the seaplane base at the marina would either have staff getting ready for the day's flights or passengers waiting to board. This would make it difficult to conceal the plane's arrival, and conceal Lamberti and the others disembarking. Additionally, the marina has 833 berths, and I didn't believe the sound of the plane's propellers would go unnoticed. In both scenarios, it was likely that someone would snap a photo with their cellphone. Consequently, I chose Civitavecchia and added the obsolete area to ensure the secrecy of Lamberti's arrival.

In researching what to expect when Bernardi was ejected from the building and hit the ground from the thirtieth floor, I learned more than I really cared to know about the effects of such an impact on the body. As mentioned, traveling at speeds of about one hundred twenty-five mph, and in some cases up to one hundred sixty mph, and coming to a stop within an inch after impact, completely obliterates the body. Forget about the broken bones and crushed skull, the sudden stop bursts cells, including those which form the body's organs, and tears apart blood vessels, including the aorta, which is the main artery coming from the heart. In other words, your chances of winning the lottery are better than your chances of surviving an impact with the ground at those speeds. That said, there have been instances of individuals surviving falls from great heights, one involving a parachutist whose chute failed to open, and whose only injuries were broken limbs. However, they only lived because the ground they impacted was very soft and the twelve-inch crater they made in the earth helped absorb most of the force of the fall. You can read more on this subject at (https://www. abc.net.au/science/articles/2005/09/13/1459026.htm) and (https:// www.answers.com/physics/If_you_jump_off_a_building_what_ happens).

In studying the history of SEAL teams, I was fascinated to learn that the designation SEAL Team Six was originally created to mislead Russian intelligence regarding the actual number of operational SEAL teams, which was only three at the time. Officially, SEAL Team Six is referred to as the United States Naval Special Warfare Development Group, or DEVGRU. This group consists of four assault squadrons known as the Red, Blue, Gold, and Silver squadrons. Additionally, there is the intelligence or Black Squadron, the Gray Squadron—which provides operational support and primarily focuses on maritime operations—and the Green Training Squadron, designated as Squadron Seven. You can read more about the structure of Seal Team Six at

(https://www.armyprt.com/military-special-operations-forces/ seal-team-6-devgru-navy/devgru-squadrons/#:~:text=The%20 Gold%20Squadron,%20like%20the%20Blue%20Squadron,%20 is%20part%20of) and (https://en.wikipedia.org/wiki/United_ States_Navy_SEALs#Navy_SEAL_teams_and_structures). You can learn more about the composition of SEAL teams, including their Special Delivery Vehicle teams, at (https://science. howstuffworks.com/navy-seal17.htm).

I believed the only viable option to get Squadron Three out of Jeddah and to the submarine was to have the team swim to the rendezvous site. Since this distance was thirteen miles, using conventional scuba gear wouldn't work because they'd need too many oxygen tanks to stay submerged for the entire duration. Moreover, the bubbles produced by scuba gear could compromise their location as they moved through the harbor. Fortunately, that constraint doesn't apply to rebreathers, which are closed-circuit systems that recirculate exhaled air and, during the process, remove carbon dioxide and add oxygen, creating the correct air mixture to be rebreathed. This allows for longer dive times and reduced gas consumption, making it possible for Squadron Three to reach the submarine and escape undetected. You can read more about rebreathers at (https://divedeepscuba.com/rebreather-systems/) and (https://www.scubaforge.com/rebreathers/understanding-rebreather-functionality/).

While researching how long it takes for someone to swim a mile, I discovered that across all age groups, males take approximately thirty-seven minutes. Taking into account that SEALs are in incredible physical shape, I indicated in the story that Squadron Three would take average thirty-five to forty minutes per mile while swimming with a rebreather. Why so slow? Under normal circumstances, I'd have their time per mile be substantially lower. However, taking into account the physical exertion the team had just gone through after jumping out of an aircraft and trekking through the mountain, after which they spent two days in a crevice in the earth while performing reconnaissance, followed by a firefight in the Wakhan Corridor and then, without rest parachuting into Saudi Arabia and destroying the warehouse, swimming thirteen miles to the sub at an average pace of average thirty-five to forty minutes per mile seemed reasonable. You can read more on swimming times at (https://swimcompetitive.com/swimming/mile-swim-time/#:~:text=On%20average%2C%20across%20all%20age%20groups%20and%20abilities%2C,of%20gender%2C%20is%20 37%20minutes%20and%2039.38%20seconds.).

During the team's swim to the submarine, I mentioned their use of an underwater navigation board, a handheld device that integrates a depth gauge, dive chronometer, and underwater compass, which you can read more about, in addition to other diving equipment used by SEAL teams, at (https://www.livestrong.com/article/13727731-exercise-benefits/).

Italy's Department of Information Security (DIS) is responsible for overseeing the activities of the AISI (Agenzia Informazioni e Sicurezza Interna) and the AISE (Agenzia Informazioni e Sicurezza Esterna). Its mandate also includes ensuring the effective exchange of information between these agencies and the police forces. (https://inteltoday.org/european-agencies/italy/). As written, the AISI primarily focuses on internal security, while the AISE is dedicated to foreign intelligence, primarily utilizing human resources to gather information. Both agencies are headquartered at Piazza Dante 25, located on the Esquiline Hill, which is the largest of the Seven Hills of Rome.

The establishment of the AISI and AISE dates back to 2007, following a series of scandals that prompted a reorganization of Italian intelligence to provide enhanced civilian oversight. One such scandal involved passing forged documents to the CIA, which falsely claimed that Saddam Hussein was secretly acquiring yellowcake uranium in Africa to develop a nuclear weapon. These documents, since discredited by the International Atomic Energy Agency, were cited by President George W. Bush in his State of the Union address.

Another significant scandal involved the extraordinary rendition of Muslim cleric Abu Omar, who was kidnapped by the CIA and the SISMI (the predecessor to the aforementioned agencies) and taken to Egypt, where he was tortured for information he reportedly possessed. However, it was later discovered that he was not involved in any terrorist activities. You can read more about these scandals in a *Deep States* article at (https://www.deepstateblog.org/deep-states-guide-to-the-worlds-largest-intelligence-agencies/aise-italy/).

In the story, Franco Zunino and Silvio Villa both left the military and worked as Security Information Officers (SIOs) for the Department of Information Security. I took some creative liberties as SIOs only operated from 1949 to 1997, and were later replaced by the Centro Intelligence Interforze (CII), which serves a similar purpose: to safeguard the internal security of military bases and personnel, as well as to conduct military intelligence activities against enemy and foreign forces, particularly through signals intelligence (SIGINT) operations.

To enhance the story, I created the positions of Administrative Assistant to the Chairman of the AISI, as well as a similar role within the AISE. This was necessary because I needed an informant (or mole) in a position of authority who would be aware of Lamberti's annual visit to Carolina Biagi's grave and Acardi's activities. As previously mentioned, any reference to wrongdoing by individuals within either agency is purely fictional, crafted because the author needed a way to funnel confidential information to the antagonists.

According to an October 23, 2018 article in *How-to Geek* by Chris Hoffman, ghost chips exist in various forms, and are essentially small computers embedded within a phone that run their own operating system. The article explains that a cellphone's main operating system and its applications cannot detect these chips because they operate in a secure area that's inaccessible to them. Although Chris Hoffman goes into extensive detail, I tried to keep the description and concept of ghost chips simple to maintain the flow of the story. You can find this article at (https://www.howtogeek.com/387934/your-smartphone-has-a-special-security-chip.-heres-how-it-works/). Additional information on ghost chips can also be found at (https://gcelt.org/what-is-a-ghost-chip-for-a-phone-everything-you-should-know-in-2023/).

About the Author

Alan Refkin has written sixteen previous works of fiction and is the co-author of four business books on China, for which he received Editor's Choice Awards for *The Wild Wild East* and *Piercing the Great Wall of Corporate China*. In addition to the Mauro Bruno detective series, he's written the Matt Moretti-Han Li action-adventure thrillers and Gunter Wayan private investigator novels. He and his wife Kerry live in southwest Florida, where he's working on his next Mauro Bruno novel. You can find more information on the author, the locations used in his books, and information on future novels at alanrefkin.com.

Printed in the United States
by Baker & Taylor Publisher Services